Heat Wave

BOOK 3 OF THE AGENT MELANIE WARD NOVELS

Kate Mathis

POWWOW
PUBLISHING

PowWow Publishing
P.O. 31855
Tucson, AZ 85751-1855 U.S.A.

Printed in the United States of America
First Printing October 2012

Library of Congress Control Number: 2012913347
Mathis, Kate.

Heat Wave - Book Three: An Agent Melanie Ward Novel / Kate Mathis - 1st ed.

1. Female Spy – Fiction. 2. Mystery – Fiction. 3. Thriller Romance – Fiction.
4. Romance Suspense – Fiction. 5. Humor – Fiction. 6. Action & Adventure – Fiction.
7. Melanie Ward – Fiction. 8. Suspense – Fiction. 9. Living Lies – Fiction
10. An Agent Melanie Ward Novel – Fiction 11. Sequel to Second Chance – Fiction.
12. Espionage – Fiction

ISBN-13: 978-0-9859577-1-1
ISBN-10:   0-9859577-1-9

Book design and composition by PowWow Inc.
www.powwowpublishing.com

for my Five Star Readers

CHAPTER ONE

The clear water felt like warm fingers massaging her skin. Melanie had let the current tug her gently away from the surf, giving Agent De La Croix time to set the bait. It was the group of nurse sharks beneath her feet that finally gave her incentive to ride a swell closer to shore. Waist deep and still yards from the resort's private beach, she arranged her bikini top, plumped her meager cleavage and set her mind on sexy.

Her target this time was Peter Nichols, a 42-year-old man who had recently become involved with Germany's chancellor, a powerful woman 25 years his senior. Nichols was a political serial husband, three times self-institutionalized by a clergyman and one time forced-incarcerated by the girl's father.

His usual scores were mid-level bureaucrats. The leader of a free country was by far his highest achievement.

Melanie's cliché James-Bond-rising-from-the-sea stunt wasn't her idea. Agent De La Croix thought it would be 'hot' and had insisted it would get Nichols' attention. She shook the excess water from her short hair that had grown to a 50's-style, boyish crop.

Just as well, she thought setting her sights on the man tanning on a chaise. Long hair had a tendency to get matted with sand and salt, making her exit from the sea much less enticing.

"You're on my lounge chair," Melanie said, blocking Nichols' sun and tapping the wooden recliner with her foot.

He stared up at her from behind a pair of designer sunglasses. "Do you speak English?" she asked, with her fists pressed against her hips.

"I didn't see your name on it. All these," he made a broad, left and right gesture with extended arms, "are labeled."

"You didn't look." She reached over and peeled off the tag De La Croix had left with her pseudo name on it and held it to Nichols' face.

"Amanda Stark," he read, one brow peeking over the top of his glasses. "I'm guessing that's you?"

"Brilliant."

"What about that chaise, does it belong to your husband?" he asked, nodding to the empty one.

"No husband, no boyfriend, only an occasional lover. But right now it's me, the sea and this lounge."

Nichols tilted down his shades to expose a set of dark brown eyes before flashing a molar-bearing grin. "I apologize, Ms. Stark." He stood, kicked his feet into a pair of leather sandals and lifted his towel off the cushion.

"Thank you," Melanie said, reaching beneath the seat for a bag that contained her necessities, a towel, sandals, sunscreen and a syringe of thiopental. She didn't have to look over to feel him nearby, setting up shop on the chaise beside hers.

"You don't mind if I sit here, do you, Amanda?"

She flashed a flirty smile. "Not if you get my back," she said, handing him her tube of 50 SPF.

Peter Nichols had wandering hands as the lotion was rubbed over her shoulders and the sides of her breasts.

"Hey, stop that." She pulled away. "Not in public."

"Well," Nichols said, running his index finger under the strings of her swimsuit. "I've got a room just steps away."

Melanie looked over her shoulder as if considering his offer. "I don't usually do things like that."

"I won't tell." He lifted his brows, cocked his head and reached for her hand.

"Why the hell not? I'm on vacation," Melanie swung her bag over her shoulder took his hand and allowed him to lead her to his room.

Peter Nichols was aggressive. Before they reached the sliding glass door of his beachfront room, he had her against the stucco wall, shoving his tongue down her throat while his hands worked on the knot that kept her top tied. He was rough and Melanie returned his violent kiss.

Peter gasped out a chuckle as she slipped her hand into his trunks, groping around in his pockets for the key card that was hidden in a Velcro pouch inside the drawstring. Nichols interest was diverted with her earlobe as she lifted the key, slid it into the slot and pushed their bodies through the door.

His tongue was in her ear as she uncapped the syringe with her teeth. Setting her mouth on his, she bit down hard on his lip and inserted the thiopental into his neck.

A second later Nichols buckled to the tiled flooring. Taking hold of his ankles, Melanie dragged and heaved him onto the bed. Then went to search the closet safe. Without trouble she popped the cap off the digital keypad, plugged her phone into the system and unscrambled the code.

The locked clicked and inside on the velvet base was a penguin-shaped flash drive. She yanked the head off the flightless bird, inserted the connection into the USB port of her phone and downloaded the information. Nichols snored as Melanie hunted through the rest of his things. Other than the handcuffs in the drawers beside the bed, the room was clean of information.

Corrupting the penguin's files she replaced the drive in the exact location she'd found it. She wiped down the perfectly restored safe, went to the divine Peter Nichols, stripped him of clothing and handcuffed him to the bed. Admiring her handiwork for a moment, she noticed that Guinness World's Records wasn't going to be handing him any awards.

With her lipstick she used his waxed chest as a canvas. She drew hearts and a note that thanked him with *XOXO, A.S.*

Keeping her head down, Melanie slipped out of his room and walked casually to the resort lobby. De La Croix was waiting in the parked car.

"Got it?" he asked.

"Yup." She grinned, pulling the pile of clothes onto her lap.

"That was one sweet assignment," De La Croix said, gunning the little tourist vehicle to the private airfield.

"For *you*." Melanie glared, "You weren't pawed by a horny, warmed-tongued bastard with a 24-hour erection." She wiggled a pair of jeans over her swimsuit.

Melanie Ward had been an agent for over ten years working for a secret branch of the U.S. Government, known to very few as The Covert Defense Division. Those on the inside simply call it The Agency. Climbing to the top hadn't been easy, and she'd come out with a tough exterior and a reputation to match.

She was stationed out of the D.C. office and the summer sun was still in charge of the sweltering blue sky as the jet landed. Marcos was waiting for them with the company car.

"Good evening, Ms. Ward." Marcos greeted as he took the bag off her shoulder and placed it in the trunk. "Mr. De La Croix."

"It's Max, Marcos. Max."

"Yes." Marcos grinned, taking Max's suitcase.

"He knows your name," Melanie said, stooping into the back seat.

"I know, but where I grew up the titles Mr. and Sir were reserved for grandfathers or drug dealers."

Melanie shrugged. "I guess that's a problem you're going to have to get over."

De La Croix was a five-year veteran in the Agency. He had the quality of being perfectly average, not handsome but attractive. And like 99.9% of the agents he was too lazy and complacent to put more effort into the job and under the false notion that he was already giving it 120.

"So, what are you going to do now?" Max asked, leaning back in the seat. "Celebrate a job well done?"

"I'm going to my office, check messages and then I'll pay Mike in the control room a visit to find out if he's deciphered Nichols' information. After that I might head to the gym before bed."

"Are you serious?" Max asked, looking exhausted. "I'm meeting a few other agents at a bar where I plan on drinking a beer and finding a single lady."

"Well, you have a good time." Melanie said, confirming her 99.9% diagnosis.

⟡

The Agency operated out of a refurbished building in D.C. that was lovingly referred to as The Manor. Originally it had been designed to house agents who were between assignments. Five floors and a basement, The Manor was completely autonomous, outfitted with apartments, a kitchen, gym, medical lab, offices, a communication center and conference rooms.

Marcos delivered them to the underground garage as Max continued his argument regarding the use of his first name. Marcos nodded politely.

"See you around, De La Croix," Melanie said, waving and giving Marcos a smile. She'd tried for years to have him call her Melanie.

Passing through the levels of security, she climbed the stairs to her office. Jane, her assistant, was gone for the day and her small workplace with plain walls and a single window looking out over the parking lot was quiet and peaceful. Melanie sat in her squeaky office chair, and breathed.

Going through messages and email was habit, Jane had already forwarded everything to her cell and there was nothing pending. Except phone calls. Conversations she'd been avoiding. Melanie looked at her contact list and debated. Not who to call first, but whether she really needed to call any of them.

"Knock, knock."

Melanie looked up from her phone to Ben standing in her doorway. She answered his verbalized entrance with a smile. "Hi boss," she said, to the man that was her mentor as well as a father figure.

"How was the Caribbean?"

"Tropical."

"I was actually asking about Nichols. Was he transferring information?"

Melanie nodded. "He was. We don't have the details yet, his drive was encrypted. Mike's working on it. Nichols' buyer is going to be pissed when he gets a corrupted file."

"Good. Do we know who was buying?"

"There was an Italian ambassador in the room that backed into Nichols', they had a few sneaky conversations at the bar and in the men's room. But what he wanted specifically with German intelligence, I don't know. He could be climbing the cabinet ladder. Any word on the chancellor?"

"She's in Argentina."

"Don't you wonder why a smart woman like that would let a worm like Nichols' into her house?" Melanie leaned back in her seat and shook her head in disgust.

Ben looked torn for a moment before answering. "Loneliness is a strong motivator."

"She's got a country to run." She said, "You'd think a busy woman like her would have something more pressing than Peter Nichols to occupy her time."

"Well, whatever her reasoning, at least we're keeping her misstep quiet." He smiled. "We'll be able to win a favor or two with this one."

"I love the benevolence. Her poor judgment puts leverage in our pocket."

Ben shrugged. "Mind if I have a seat?" he asked, his pale blue eyes turning somber and she noticed he was carrying a manila file.

"I'd offer you a scotch but I seem to be completely out," she teased, uncomfortably. Her office didn't come with decanters of alcohol, like his did.

"I know you're joking but," he reached into the breast pocket of his suit jacket, "I thought the situation called for it."

"You realize you're not helping my blood pressure." Melanie watched as he pulled out a flask along with two small glasses and poured. "Since when did you start traveling with a personal supply?" She reached for a glass.

"Since today," he said, sliding the file onto the mostly empty spot beside her computer. "Before you open that," he lifted his brows toward the file, blew out a deep breath and caught her eye. He didn't speak again until she was at the point of jumping across the desk to wring the information out of him. "Local PD is interrogating a man in connection with Agent Parker's assassination." Ben let the words hang.

Melanie's chest constricted. Her jaw opened and then closed as her forehead beaded with sweat. Finn's killer. Finn, her rival and the person who'd made life as difficult as possible. But it was his murder that woke her up at night dripping with terror. She blew out a sigh and took a moment to remember how to speak. "Who?"

"An American. Military background."

Melanie slowly raised the cover of the file to stare at an 8x10 glossy of a white male. Whatever her expectations had been, it wasn't this man. This man had a bloated, acne-inflamed face and cheeks that encroached on his puckered mouth. The whites of his dark eyes were yellowed and he looked like he'd been living under a bridge.

"Christopher Aaron Bell. He was court marshaled a couple of years back. Battery. Nearly beat a fellow soldier to death with a folding chair and released from the disciplinary barracks last June." Ben spoke as Melanie examined the man from his kinky black curls to his third chin. It was difficult to tell what he looked like beneath the layers.

A queasy sickness wormed its way into her abdomen. Last fall Finn was in the market for an assassin, and he'd ended up with this man. She glared at the photo. *Finn hired this pig to kill me, and if he wasn't such a fuck-up his plan might have worked.*

She hadn't dodged the bullet, it had been redirected – Melanie pushed the thoughts out of her mind before another could take its place. She felt cold and hot all at once.

"How sure are we that this is the guy?" Melanie asked, jabbing her index finger on the forehead as she flipped the file around for Ben to see. "This guy?"

"Beneath his soft exterior he's got skills, and a possible mental illness."

"No doubt," she said, reading the briefing upside down. "This doesn't say how he was caught."

"Three weeks ago he was arrested for domestic violence. He was loud and disruptive and once on the inside repeatedly used his calls to contact Senator Parker's private line. He told the officers he and the senator were business partners."

Her fists were clenched in tight, painful balls and she felt her shoulders rubbing the bottom of her earlobes. She took a deep breath and tried to relax.

"Then the other night he boasted about Finn Parker and, well, these inmates aren't new to the system. The D.A.'s phone was ringing off the hook the next morning. Three different men were begging to make deals."

"Ben." She shook her head, the likelihood that he was blowing smoke rising exponentially. "How can this be?"

Ben stopped her. "He knew about the type of weapon. Though he was incorrect about the accuracy of both shots, claimed both hit Finn's heart. But," he held her gaze, "he knew about a female agent."

"Me?"

"I'm assuming."

"What did he say about … her? Did he say agent?"

"The details were sketchy."

Melanie rolled her eyes. "What's Hugh saying?"

The slow shake of his head revealed the gravity of Hugh's situation. "They're keeping his condition very private, but the stroke was severe. I'm told he's unable to communicate, spending his days in a wheelchair getting transported to and from therapy."

She couldn't even begin to imagine the larger than life, super-villain senator confined to a chair. Finn's father had a powerful presence that wasn't limited by physical restrictions.

"How are his cognitive skills?" she asked. "Because I bet he's still able to pull strings, no matter what his condition is reported to be. Ben, we're not talking about just anyone, we're talking Hugh Parker!"

Ben's watery blue eyes glazed. The distant focal point seemed to pass through her, then clear. "You know, I didn't think to ask about his mental state. I'm sure he's grieving over the loss of Finn as well as his physical ailments." He scratched the back of his head. "I heard about his challenges and assumed." He nodded. "You're thinking he's still working his plans from a wheelchair?" Melanie said, and looked away before giving up too many of her thoughts about Hugh Parker. *If he's working his plan behind a veil of illness, he's that much more dangerous.*

She tugged the glossy photo of Bell from the paperclip. A second picture was beneath, of Bell in uniform. "Whoa. It's like two different people." She leaned in close to get a better look. A hundred pounds lighter, shaved head with an emblematic beret set askew, a buttoned-up collared shirt … medals on his chest. "What happened?"

"Back story is in there but," he shook his head, "the short version is that he went to bed one night and woke up the next morning a lunatic. Assaulted his commanding officer and," Melanie slid the pages over her desk, "five years later, he's sitting in D.C. lockup."

"Can I get to him?" she asked, the nausea inching up her throat. "To interrogate."

Ben shook his head. "Afraid not. It's in local hands. And we don't exist, remember?"

"You would think someone in Hugh's inner circle would have moved on Bell." She couldn't stop trying to unwind the thread – lead it back to Parker. "And you don't know if they've been to see him?"

"I got word on Bell an hour ago. I came over here as soon as I heard you were back. I didn't want you to hear it from someone else."

She heard the words but her mind was elsewhere.

"Melanie, stop. Perhaps Hugh's people have spoken with him," Ben said in his diplomatic tone.

Almost ignoring him completely, Melanie continued to think out loud. "Why wouldn't he send someone to investigate? Hugh snubs local PD. Doesn't he want to punish the guy who killed his son?"

Ben looked directly into her eyes. "Before his stroke, Hugh was firmly convinced that you're that *guy*."

"He's got a *guy* in lock-up that says otherwise." Melanie retorted, her fuse short. *If I were responsible, then so was Hugh*, she thought. *Hugh had a chance to stop the assassination and didn't. He slipped up, Finn fucked up and I'm still standing.* "Well, whatever he wants to think doesn't change the fact that there's a man in prison taking credit for the hit."

"He didn't think you actually pulled the trigger," Ben offered, casually.

"Really? What did he think, then?"

Ben fidgeted uncomfortably in his seat. "The official statement he gave to the Board of Executives the day before his stroke was that you lured Finn out to the park to put him in direct line of fire. Don't." He put his hands up to stop her from protesting. "I already know what you think."

"It's not what I THINK. It's what happened." This conversation always caused her blood to boil. It'd been months and in that time she'd been through psych evaluations, released back to work and sent on a three-month assignment in Africa. But in an instant it was as if that time had vanished and she was standing in the morgue with Finn's purple body stretched out on the stainless steel table. She was quaking and it was all she could do to keep her teeth from chattering.

"Well," he swallowed the last quarter inch of scotch and stood, "I thought you should hear it from me. You finished with your glass?" He smiled as she coughed down the burning liquid. "And Ward, I don't want to find out you've gone and done something foolish."

"Me?" she asked innocently, gaining control of her emotion, at least until he was gone. "No, you don't have to worry. I'm not interested in Bell. In fact, I'm trying to get as far away as possible from that day."

"How ready are you for another assignment?"

"Do you want me to stay involved with the Nichols case? I could find out what the Italians want or wait for confirmation on the contents of the flash drive?"

"I've got something else for you. Get some sleep, we're meeting in the morning."

As he left, her need for pretense went with him. She shivered at the memory of that cold December day. The events had replayed in her mind hundreds of times and it wasn't any easier or any more distant. No matter what she tried, she couldn't force the thoughts away. She'd struggled through all the tricks. But she found that if she simply let them wash over her, it was less torturous. So she sat, closed her eyes and consented to the pain.

It always started the same, as if it were happening to another person. The door between the inner Manor and the lobby is pushed open. There's a flood of emotion as she sees Danny. Danny Ashe, her heart thumps out of rhythm every time he's near. He was her college-crush, her first love and his boyish charm was heart stopping. Danny Ashe with his back toward her and now, months later, she knows that her happiness is going to be short lived. Danny. Her lungs expand and she can still feel the weight of the ring on her left hand. Knowing the outcome twists the knife that's already lodged in her gut.

"Stupid girl." Melanie softly scolds, absently rubbing where the ring had been and swiveling her chair to face the window. Having someone walk in while she's reliving the past would only add to her misery.

Her thoughts take liberty with time and she finds herself on the snow-covered park bench. Her knee touches Danny's as he wrings his hands. His distraught face, even in her memory, still causes her pulse to race.

"You know how much I love you," he looks down at his empty hands as he tells her how he meant every word he'd ever said. But his ex-wife's marriage to the Italian racecar driver isn't working out and she'd changed. She regrets. They have a child who needs both a mother and a father. "I still love Lauren." It was those four words that made it all perfectly clear – she was being dumped for his cheating ex-wife.

He'd effectively drained the fight out of her. Slipping the ring off her left finger was the first time she noticed the numbness beneath her rib cage.

What would've happened if Bell hadn't chosen that moment to fire his first shot? Sucking in oxygen, she knew, *the pain of losing Danny would have been unbearable.* She would have dwelled on the loss, tortured herself with the details. But the events that followed the breakup surpassed her selfish existence. Her chest tightened. Being with Danny had been so easy that she'd almost convinced herself that they could have a normal life together.

Since that day, she's felt the pain of losing him, every time she ran into someone who has his traits: his huge smile and naïve view of the world.

But Christopher Aaron Bell changed her future. Finn's blood draining from the gaping hole in his neck, life leaving his body, was the memory that haunted her from that fateful night.

If there was one thing to be grateful for, besides the fact that Bell hadn't focused his sight on her was that she hadn't gone public about the engagement. Her mom's disappointment and criticism would have been overwhelming. The situation was already bad enough.

The soft spot behind her eyes throbbed and she took deep breaths to lower her pulse. She needed a distraction.

"Hey, Mom."

"Hi, Honey. Is everything all right?"

Melanie swallowed and nodded, blocking the moisture from her eyes. "Yeah, I'm calling to see what's up with you."

"Oh." Rita Ward sounded relieved. "I'm going over your cousin's registry. I don't know if I should go for the crystal vase or something practical like a waffle iron."

Melanie's forehead tightened as she did her best to decipher what her mom was saying. "Nope, I've got nothing."

"What, Dear?"

"I have no idea what you're talking about. Registry?"

On the other end of the receiver her mother sighed. "Rachel is getting married." Melanie stalled, trying to remember if she had a cousin Rachel. "You know, Peggy."

"If Peggy were marrying Rachel I think I'd remember that invite."

"No, Silly." Rita huffed. "Peggy is Rachel. A few years back she changed her name and now goes by Rachel. Said Peggy didn't stand for anything and was tired of the jokes. What's the matter with you? Are you eating your vegetables?"

"Obviously not enough." That did ring a bell. "But isn't Peggy already married?"

"Two years ago. But she met this new man and – wham-o – decided he was her soul mate. So out with the old and in with the new. Do you want to hear something funny?" Rita didn't pause for an answer. "Not funny ha-ha but funny strange? This one is named Ron, too. Rachel believes she was destined to marry this Ron but fate put the other one in her way first and it confused her. Sort of kooky, but romantic, don't you think?"

"Um," she wasn't sure. "I'll get back to you on that. Anyway," she tried to shake the thoughts out before an opinion set. "When's the wedding?"

"In a few weeks, mid-June in Montana. Seems like the world is moving to Montana these days. That's where the new Ron works as a ranch hand. It's a shame, really, because the old Ron is a wealthy banker."

"I guess it's true that money can't buy happiness."

"Well, it sure does help."

"How's Penny?" Peggy's older sister was the one Melanie had played with as a child.

"Still not married. I don't know what it is about the pair of you…" Rita's words cut off sharply. "Probably cursed by that duck."

"We did not kill the duck!" Melanie growled, irritated at having to defend herself for twenty years. "Peggy and Bruce were the ones who thought a duck couldn't drown … Penny and I were giving it CPR! She compressed its chest while I gave it mouth-to-beak resuscitation."

"That's ridiculous."

"I know, but we were kids and we were trying to save its life."

"If Peggy and Bruce killed the duck, then why are they both married and you and Penny aren't?"

"Because," she said, slowly, "there isn't any correlation between the two."

"You don't have to get huffy. I'm sorry I mentioned the marriage thing. I know you're still sad about Dan. What happened with that, again?"

"He liked his ex-wife better," Melanie said, feeling like she wanted to puke.

"You'll find the right man soon. I'm sure of it."

"If you say so."

"At least pretend, for my sake. I'm still your mother. I worry."

"I'm fine, Mom. Would you believe me if I told you I've been busy at work?" Her mother's tsking was thunderous. "I really have been busy."

"You always are. Make time for us and I promise I won't trick you into any blind dates." Melanie could hear the humor in her mom's voice. "Just come before August, that's when your father and I are going on the vacation you gave us for Christmas. We had to postpone it because of your father's convention."

"Greece is going to be warm in August."

"My friend Mary has already told me." Rita launched into her many complaints about Mary. Melanie sat back, listening contently for half an hour. It was just what she needed to calm her nerves.

"I'll see when I can get home."

"Soon. We miss you."

"Okay. I love you. Bye"

"I love you, too."

Melanie ended the call ready to get online and book a flight. Hesitation was the great equalizer, between rash impulses and common sense. Instead she decided to lace up her running shoes and hit the gym.

CHAPTER TWO

"Yeah?" Melanie answered with her best attempt of sounding awake. She squinted at the clock on her phone. Ten minutes to seven.

"Good morning, Ms. Ward. Mr. Jackson called. There's a meeting in ten minutes and he asked that you be in attendance."

"Okay. Jane, I left some files…" Melanie said, rubbing the back of her head. She didn't miss her long hair often but it still surprised her that it was gone.

"I already sent them up to Mr. Jackson's assistant."

"Great. Thanks." She hung up. Her tongue felt thick and her eyes were coated with a film. They were the symptoms of the morning after a wild party. *Figures,* Melanie thought, having missed the party entirely. She groaned and reached for the discarded jeans at the foot of her bed.

In January she'd moved into the Manor full time, abandoning her apartment without a second thought. She hadn't been back to her tiny place since Danny, since Finn. Since life had changed completely. But living at the Manor had its perks and rolling out of bed into yesterday's pants was just the tip of the iceberg.

With thirty seconds to spare Melanie entered the conference room with coffee in hand and was greeted by the two internal agents and Jack. Landing in her spot beside Agent Jack Scott, who skillfully articulated his hello with a sharp nod, she rolled her seat up to the table and selected a chocolate-iced donut from the large pink bakery box.

"What's this about?" she asked, licking her fingertips.

"Thought you'd know," he said, looking at her sideways. "You really should eat better."

"You mean cleaner?" she asked, looking around for a napkin.

"Healthier."

"Please, I already have to suffer through tofu salads thanks to you. I really wish you'd leave my assistant's dietary habits alone. It's great that you two lovebirds decided to go vegan. But, seriously, I don't push sirloin at you."

Jack laughed. Whatever his comment would have been, it was interrupted.

"Good morning," Ben said from the doorway as a tall man in a cheap suit trailed behind him. He was clearly a civilian with baby white skin and soft fat tucked under his jowls. His flittering eyes seemed to be looking for a place to hide.

"Who is that?" Jack whispered.

"Why do you think I know?"

"Over the last two days," Ben started, "there have been cyber attacks on our financial system. Hackers have systematically been testing its security, searching for weaknesses and areas of vulnerability. They've aimed their focus on the credit card processes." Ben spoke from the head of the table, a remote in his hand. "Which brings me to our guest, an expert in the field of … well…" Ben's-salt-and-pepper brows pulled in tightly above his glasses. "Anyway, let me introduce Bob Karwoski."

"Hi," Bob said with a sideways grin and an awkward, girly wave.

"Bob is a special consultant and new to the Agency. I think his unique talents will be of great benefit to our organization." Ben smiled and did his best to appear confident. "He's top-notch on the computer and this security issue is right up his alley."

As Ben spoke Melanie studied Bob, who fidgeted noticeably under the scrutiny. Whoever he was, he wasn't trained, he was young-ish – twenty-something – and his black hair sat like a lid on the top of his round head. His blue dress shirt still had the crease marks from the packaging and his sloped shoulders didn't fill out the yoke, which caused the cuffs to extend past his knuckles. The guy was a visual train wreck.

"Bob, why don't you tell us about yourself?" Ben said, taking a couple of steps back.

"Hi, again." He grinned nervously. "I'm Bob Karwoski – I know, it's a long name, I used to go by BK. But I'm trying to shed my old image and in lieu of the nature of this work, I thought Special K would be fitting, if that's easier for any of you to remember," he said, his nervousness increasing. "I, um, um…" he stumbled. "I ah, didn't go to college but am pretty good with programming and," he tipped his head, "basically just about anything that has to do with a computer. I worked for AIG before it went belly-up and I couldn't find another job. There were so many of us looking and I had a lot of time on my hands." As he spoke he stared directly into the box of donuts. "I think that if I'd been diagnosed they'd have told me I was clinically depressed."

Melanie looked over to Ben, silently urging him to stop this guy.

"I was watching about twenty hours of TV a day and one thing led to another – it felt like my two worlds collided. Like I had reached my destiny. Well, before I knew what I was doing I'd hacked into email and Twitter accounts and…"

"Whose accounts?" Jack asked, interrupting.

His gaze zeroed in on Jack as he answered. "Celebrities mostly, but anyone in the media. It's way easier than you might imagine." His grin broadened. "Took three years to get caught and that was only because the heat was turned on when that newspaper scandal broke. Those assholes put all hackers at risk, even us clean ones." He shrugged. "Spent the last few months in the pen. And, well, that's about it."

Ben put his hand on Bob's shoulder. "Though we don't condone his illegal behavior, we do recognize the skill it took to break into so many private accounts and to hide the trail for years. At a time like this we're lucky to have a man like Bob on our side. Someone who thinks like a hacker, knows the ins and outs, and can lead us to our target."

"I'm sure going to try."

"Bob, you can meet the agents later, but for now let's get started," Ben said, clicking on the projection screen and turning off the lights.

Ben began with the credit card basics. Projecting simplistic drawings of buildings, arrows and dollar signs as he described the process of a credit transaction. Tracking the steps from the initial point of purchase when a customer swipes a credit card to the holding bank that sends out the digital information of the account to charge. "Security measures are in place but recently the network has experienced blips."

"And by blip you mean?"

"A noticeable attempt of entry into the code. Breaking into the credit system isn't a new idea but the methodical way in which it's being done is," Bob said.

"Do we have any idea who is doing this?" one of the other agents asked.

"Basically, it could be anyone. Kids trying to prove themselves, which I doubt, or it could be someone with a sinister agenda."

"Could attacking the technology break down the entire financial sector?"

"That's what you four are here to find out," Ben said. "Bob is going to give us the run down on how the intrusion is being carried out."

"What we have is a stream of information traveling to the points of destination, right? Those points being the retail stores, the holding banks, credit companies, private accounts and to the retail accounts." Bob's confidence emerged as he spoke. In the dark, with only the light from the screen, Melanie could almost believe it was a different person presenting the information. "These guys are hitting the information stream. The attempts are sophisticated, that's why I don't think it's a college or high school student playing a prank. Feels like hackers with a definite motive."

"So, they could be idiots or geniuses?"

"I've got friends that are both," Bob snorted. "Sometimes it's hard to tell the difference."

"We're taking the threat seriously," Ben added.

"Billions of dollars could be rerouted to off-shore accounts. Or the wider, scarier prospect is that they could seriously fuck up ... excuse me, seriously damage the economy. Imagine if even one day's total credit receipts vanished." Bob stood in silent awe, letting his words sink in.

The light flicked on and Bob blinked rapidly, as if blinded by the 60-watt bulb.

"Here are your files," Ben said, handing out the familiar dossier folders. "Ward and Scott, I'd like you to team up with Bob in stopping these terrorists." He turned to the other two agents. "You two, contact the credit networks and prepare for the worse-case scenario. Agent Scott will head up this assignment. Keep him in the loop so he can communicate and strategize as necessary."

The two other agents filed out of the room.

"I'm going to leave you three to figure things out," Ben said, squinting a behave glare to Melanie.

She caught Bob's eye and he turned two shades of red.

"Don't worry, Agent Ward hasn't bitten anyone in years," Jack said, standing as he leaned to offer a handshake. "I'm Jack Scott. Nice to meet you."

Bob giggled slightly and extended his pudgy hand.

Melanie sighed. "Why don't you pull up a seat?"

"Over here, Special K. Take the chair next to me." Jack laughed, patting the arm of the seat opposite Melanie. "I suppose you're never too old to get tongue tied around a beautiful woman. She's not as scary as she looks."

"Jack," Melanie warned.

"Usually." Jack grinned at Melanie, tilted his head toward Bob and shrugged.

"Have you had a chance to look over the data?" Melanie asked, ignoring the conversation as Bob plopped down.

"Yeah." Melanie waited for him to continue, trying not to look scary. "Oh, okay. Um, what we need to do is narrow our search and figure out who is behind the keyboard."

Melanie felt her efforts lag as her brows pulled in.

"How do we do that, Special K?" Jack asked gently as he opened the file Ben had distributed.

"I've already been working on this for 24 hours and haven't gotten anywhere," Bob said, sliding a quick glimpse at Melanie. "I was told you guys were the creative thinkers."

"What have you been trying? Special K?" Jack snapped his fingers, breaking Bob's stare.

"I'm sorry, it's just that you remind me so much of my mom," Bob said apologetically.

Jack reacted faster than she did. Barking out a laugh that he tried to disguise as a cough. Melanie gasped.

"Your mom?" she asked, horrified.

"That was the wrong thing to say, wasn't it?" Bob cringed, rolling his chair back and forth. "I only said it because I was embarrassed, you know, because you're so pretty."

Melanie's forehead crinkled.

"I'm really bad with girls."

"It's fine." Melanie breathed. His mom? "How about we forget the last few minutes ever happened?"

"Can't do that," Jack said, still grinning ear-to-ear. "It's just too perfect."

Bob's tendency to blush was irritating.

"Karwoski, right?" Melanie asked.

"It's Special K. And no worries, Ward, I'll have the chat with him … Look," Jack said swiveling his seat to face Bob, "Ward is off limits. Sure, she's pretty when you first meet her but after a while…"

Melanie waited in dread for the second part of his statement. "You realize you haven't got a shot and she becomes completely asexual."

"Hey, I'm right here."

"I don't believe it," Bob said, glancing over at her with new eyes.

"It's true." Jack nodded sadly. "Tell her you're sorry about the mom comment and let's get back to work."

"I meant that you looked like her in pictures when she was young. I'm sorry." Bob smiled bashfully and then did something unexpected. He leaned across Jack and offered her an arrangement. "I won't believe everything I hear about you, if you promise not to believe everything you hear about me. Deal?"

Jack looked up, surprised.

Melanie smiled back at Special K. "Deal."

"Okay." Jack elbowed Bob out of his space. "How do we fend off a cyber attack?"

"I haven't been able to catch them. He knows what he's doing – or they do. They're online for a split second at a time, testing different areas. There isn't any pattern I can make out. To trace their activity I'll need to get lucky and be at the right spot at the exact right moment." He puckered his lips. "I'm not a mathematician, but what are the chances of that?"

Melanie and Jack threw out suggestions that Bob quickly dismissed. He drew diagrams explaining of the processing networks, how transactions were batched and paid out from one financial institution to another.

"The entire process is electronic. No actual money changes hands, only information. If that flow is interrupted or diverted commerce would stop."

"There has to be back-up security to prevent that from happening,"

Melanie stated, pacing the room. "This is hardly the first time someone's tried to break the system."

"There are levels to the security. But technology is only as good as the software updates and it is way more difficult to build a secure system than it is to sneak in through a crack. We're lucky they aren't going after Wall Street."

Time ticked painstakingly slow as they each constructed their own disaster.

"Do we know if other countries are having similar situations?" Melanie asked. Bob shrugged. "If this is global? No."

"What if we … you … put up a fence around the entire system? To push the hackers further from their goal," Jack suggested.

"I don't know." That was the most positive Bob had been about any suggestion. "It would have to be huge," he said, his mind in obvious calculation. "I could probably do it."

"Could you trace an intruder to their IP address?" Melanie asked.

Bob pursed his lips until they disappeared into a thin line. He blew out a breath. "I don't think so."

"A line of text that captured the IP address when an unauthorized hit took place?" Melanie tried again. While Bob was still thinking she picked up on a very fine train of thought. "What if … wouldn't their computer be more vulnerable to a virus at the moment they're attacking the system?"

Bob's entire face pinched and he groaned. "Hold on, let me think." Apparently he thought on his feet, following Melanie's tracks in the carpeting around the table, mumbling to himself.

Bob was somewhere deep inside his digital brain. Melanie and Jack shared a grin as they watched him. He was over six feet tall with a face so tight-in-thought that he looked like he was about to throw a tantrum.

"Even if I could, what would it do, planting a virus?"

"Spread to all the contacts on that computer, email, social media and then we work backwards for the common link. And if there's more than one hacker we'd bring down the pack." She answered thinking off the cuff.

"As well as corrupting files of innocent people," Bob noted. "But I guess we could produce an anti-virus for those guiltless ones." He nodded approvingly. "I like it. I'll set up a website for anyone affected by the virus … then…" Bob was talking at a slower pace, hatching a plan as the words escaped. "We could follow the virus back to its origin and," he looked up smiling, "nab the sucker!"

"Okay then," Jack said, standing.

"It's never been done before."

"Yeah, but there's only one Special K, right?" Jack added the push Bob needed.

"I'll need a quiet space to work. Preferably someplace dark without windows. And I'll need the fastest computer you've got."

"Come on, Karwoski, I'll take you to the War Room," Melanie said.

"Special K, how old are you?" Jack asked as they walked.

"Twenty-seven."

"What did you do for AIG?" Melanie asked, unable to stay out of the conversation.

"Sold online insurance. I used to think my dream job was creating video games. But no matter how many interviews I went on … I was always passed over."

Melanie nodded. "Interview with women?" She asked leading him down the corridor.

Bob smiled. "Sometimes. I get nervous. I think that's why I'm so good on the computer. I'm a lot of fun once I know you, but to interact with strangers, I crash and burn."

"What was with the celebrities?"

"Curiosity. I mean they're on magazine covers, tweeting about their lives … it felt like they were begging for me to know more. I knew it was wrong. But I never sold anything or put out nude photos. I was depressed and I invaded their privacy. I learned my lesson." His voice cracked and Melanie looked away while he wiped his eyes.

"You were given a huge break," she said, wondering how good this guy had to be to get a ticket out of prison and land a high-security clearance. "And, Karwoski, just so you know, this job is way better than video games."

She held the door open for Bob and Jack. Mike's chair was empty and Ed was busy tapping away on his keyboard.

"Ed," Melanie called, waving her hand between his face and the screen.

"Hey, Agent Ward," he said without looking up.

"Where's Mike?"

Ed shrugged. "Agent Jackson came in about an hour ago and they left together."

"I need a computer for Mr. Karwoski."

The color from Ed's monitor gave his complexion a bluish tint as he lifted his gaze to give Bob the once over.

"Okay," he said with the 'that's weird' tone. "Um, we have an open computer in the corner." When Ed stood he was only a few inches taller than when he was sitting. "I can get it set up if you'd like."

"Please. Okay," she turned to Bob, "explain to me exactly what you are going to do."

Bob went through the plan, going too far in depth and losing Melanie before the halfway point.

"Dude," Ed said, having forgotten his job, "that is so cool. Can you really manage that?"

"Think so." Bob grinned.

Ed stuck his hand into Bob's. "If I can help in any way ... just holler."

"There you go." Melanie nodded, happy for the camaraderie – could've gone either way. "You're in good hands and Mike will be back soon." She felt comfortable leaving him but she took a look back before stepping into the hall. Bob was already wheeled up to the keyboard and entering his password.

"What do you think of him?" Jack asked, materializing at her shoulder.

"I think he's going to be sort of awesome." She laughed and Jack winced at her faulty impersonation of Bob.

"I like him, too."

"Then what's with the teasing?" she asked, shutting the door.

Jack didn't shift his gaze, as if he had X-ray vision and was still watching Bob through the door. "Special K reminds me of my little brother."

"Oh," she nodded. "I didn't know you had a brother."

"Yeah, he's a total screw up, but you should see his artwork – the guy can paint. He just needs direction."

"You think Bob is a screw up?"

"I think he's a wiz who's made bad choices. I wonder if we get to keep him."

Melanie shook her head. "Like a mascot?"

Jack changed course, looking at her. "Want to grab some lunch while we wait?"

"I'm going to pass."

"Well, I'm going for a cheese steak." Jack smiled and winked.

"You can't. You and Jane are vegans."

"I'm only telling you this because I know you can keep a secret. I need meat. I tried to tell Jane, but she's so into this lifestyle … I can't let her down."

Melanie bit her tongue. "You two should talk." Last week she'd caught Jane with a grilled chicken salad. "I'll see you later. Reports to file."

Late nights with Jack normally involved pizza and a six-pack. This time it was cheese balls and coffee.

"Think it's going to work?" Jack asked, stretching in his chair while checking his watch.

"It's the only plan we came up with," Melanie said, squinting at the clock. Midnight. "All those hours of plotting and this was our only bet. Jack, I'm starting to think that we may be becoming dinosaurs."

"What makes you say that?" His face squashed.

"Look." She opened her empty hands. "We're not doing anything. Bob's over there, neck deep in megabytes, or whatever the hell it is, and you and me? We're sitting around shooting the shit."

"We're there for the dangerous element," Jack offered. "The take down."

"I'm just suggesting that we might want to start broadening our horizons."

"Can you picture the Mike's and Bob's of the world overseeing the safety of the planet?"

"It'd be like giving a monkey a gun." She laughed.

"Holy shit! That's it!" Bob yelped as he leaped out of his chair, knocking it over and tripping on a cord.

Melanie and Jack rushed over as the flashing alert on Bob's screen faded and computer script raced across the monitor.

"Watch," Bob breathed. "Here it comes."

The gibberish ended and was replaced by the picture of a man with a receding hairline and a cigarette dangling from his pale lips.

"Yes!" Bob said, jumping up and down. "It worked. That's him! That's our hacker. I didn't want to say anything in case it didn't work but that's a live shot direct from the asshole's web cam."

Melanie looked at the face of an asshole. "Incredible. Can we pull facial recognition?"

"What's his location?" Jack asked at the same moment.

Minutes later, with the IP address and digital recognition they had his name and a lengthy rap sheet.

"Great work! Let's go bring him in." Jack straightened, slapped Bob on the back and invited him along, "You coming, Special K?"

"Really? Hell, yeah!"

"You're a damn genius," Jack said, putting his arm around Bob.

"I know."

CHAPTER THREE

"Thought you might like some iced tea." Becca said, handing him a tall glass. "Mind if I have a seat?"

Adam stopped the swinging bench, knowing his aunt was only asking to be polite. Nothing but an act of God would prevent her from doing what she wanted.

The old wood and hinges creaked under her weight. "I hear you're thinking of leaving us soon."

"Four months is a long time to hide out." He said, setting his tea on the side table.

"You don't have to go, you know you're always welcome. You could get a house in town, start a life."

"You know I love it here. It's home. But I have a life and I've got to start facing reality."

Becca couldn't leave the silence unfilled. "But, Honey, you're doing so well and I worry about you. Stay until you figure out what it is you want."

He knew what he wanted. His heart ached with the slightest

mention of her.

"Tempting," Adam said looking out over the green expanse of peacefulness. "I wish I could."

"Why don't you call her?"

"Bec," Adam sighed.

"What? Why not?"

"Because..." Becca's scolding clung to the breeze. "Because she's not ready for me."

"You don't know that, maybe she's waiting for you to make the first move."

"No." Thinking of all the mistakes he'd made was painful. "I blew it." His whisper was low and raw as the ache of missing her took hold.

"I don't think so. That girl who came to see us last fall, she loved you."

"Past tense." He put his hand over Becca's to soothe her worries. "I need to get back. And," he smiled, "Uncle Rob's new barn is finished, the old one has a new roof, the well's cleared and the fences are up. It's all done. He's having trouble thinking of new things for me to do. And has taken off more fishing days in the last month than he has in years."

"There are restaurants you could work at," she suggested. "Nearby."

"Bec, stop hounding the boy!" Rob said, climbing the porch steps with Adam's oldest cousin Robin at his heels.

"I'm not hounding."

"She means well," Adam defended.

"Thank you, Sweetie."

"Well, if it's a wife you're looking for..." Robin, the spitting image of her mother, scooped up his untouched iced tea, "you could have your pick of any of my friends. Married or not." She said, with the glass to her lips ready to take a swig.

"Robin," Bec shook her head. "That's awful."

"But guilt tripping him into staying on your farm, isn't?" Robin asked, leaning on the porch railing.

"Stop." Adam broke into the discussion. "Uncle Rob, Aunt Becky, thank you for your generosity. Robin, no offense, but I'm not interested in marrying anyone, not even one of your friends. I can't stay. Though it is heaven, I've got to get back on my feet."

"And you can't do that with us?" Becca asked, hurt.

"Bec," Rob admonished. "The boy needs his space."

"I've been toying with the idea of opening a restaurant again."

"I think that's a good plan," Rob said. "Very solid, reasonable goal. Lord knows you can cook."

"Where would you open the restaurant?" Becca wanted to know.

"There were a few possibilities the last time I researched, maybe San Francisco, Dallas, Seattle." He made sure not to mention D.C.

"Those are all so far, and you don't have any family there," Becca said before getting 'the look' from Rob. "But," she shifted her gaze, "all beautiful cities."

Adam smiled. "Nothing is set. I haven't even started checking out places. Florida's an option, too. You could retire from the farm."

"Ha!" Rob barked, "How about we go for a visit?"

"I'm going to miss you," Becca said, the corners of her mouth tilting down. "The house will be so empty."

Ah, his heart squeezed.

"Mom, you'll have me. And you know Cody loves baking with his grandma." Robin went to give the older woman a hug.

"I know, Sweetie." She puffed out her bottom lip. "I'm sorry,

Honey." She attempted to smile at him. "Promise to stay in touch."

"I promise."

CHAPTER FOUR

"Karwoski did well," Ben said.

"He did," she answered, holding back.

"What do you think? Keep him or let him finish off his sentence behind bars?"

"Will he be Agency property?" She smiled, Ben didn't. "Not in a humorous mood, I see. Okay then, I think Bob's a keeper."

"I'm glad you said that." Ben's sour expression melted into a dangerous grin. She'd fallen into a trap. "I want you to guide Karwoski, take him under your wing. He's cleared a background check," Ben said tilting his head, "with the exception of his current troubles. I've been holding back but I'm going to grant him consultant status. Obviously, he can never be a full agent."

"Me?" Melanie sighed, not wanting a pet. "Why not let Jack have him? They seem to have bonded."

"I want to test Karwoski a bit and I'm afraid Jack's already grown too fond to be neutral."

"So what you're saying is that I get to baby-sit," she said, annoyed.

"I don't want to be leashed to the Manor or to Bob. I'm an agent. I've been cleared; I've done my time behind a desk. I thought you realized I was ready, unchanged and … I want excitement, danger … I want the tough cases. You sent me to Africa, I want another long assignment."

"Take it easy, I'm not holding out." The corners of his mouth twitched slightly. "I've got big plans for you, Ward."

"Really?" she asked, reading the truth in his eyes.

"Big plans," he repeated with a grin. "But it takes finesse and subtlety."

"Two traits I could work on."

"I've been thinking about taking your talents in a new direction. Are you up for it?" he asked, knowing her.

She glared at him. "What do you have in mind?"

"The Intelligence Training Challenge."

"I thought you were being serious."

"I am." Ben widened his heavy lidded eyes.

"You hate the ITC."

"That's not entirely accurate."

"Your loathing of the games is legendary," Melanie reminded him.

"I've been rethinking my qualms." They studied each other for a moment.

"Qualms? I once compared the ITC to the Olympics and you said – and I quote – 'that would be true only if the Olympics was a complete farce and unilaterally rigged.' And then you compared it to Hitler's regime."

"That might have been a bit harsh," Ben said with a grimace. "I wish I had your knack for recall."

"Why me? Why the games?"

"I've experienced an awakening and you told me you were interested in working with the recruits."

"Not the ITC. I believe you're on the radical side, but I agree that it's a worthless, unfairly judged sham," Melanie said, knowing that if Ben had already made up his mind … she would be participating in the Intelligence Training Challenge.

The ITC was an Agency-wide competition that pitted one- and two-year recruits against each other in physical and psychological competitions. Four teams from four satellite branches with one agent who had the specific job of being ITC authoritarian. Originally there were five teams but Agent Jackson barred headquarters from participating and now it was down to four.

The Executive Board placed bets and high-stakes rode on the outcomes. Rigged or not, there clearly was favoritism and like it or not … "I'm not a favorite."

"You're a wild card." Ben smiled.

"I'm doing this, aren't I?" He nodded and she sighed. "Just a reminder, Ben, I have no experience training. And I'm clueless to the rules or regulations." She threw up her hands in early defeat.

"True, and the June event starts next week, so you're behind there, too."

"Nice. I hope you're not thinking about putting any money on me. I won't pay you back."

"I don't think you'll lose, but that's not my main goal."

"Which is?"

"In a word?" he grinned. "Change. That's the goal. Shake things up. And you're the best at that."

That's not a compliment, she grasped. "Can't I do that without the ITC? I've never paid attention to the games. I have no one in my corner. I haven't met the recruits and according to you everyone is already ahead of me. Then to top it off, you expect me to win."

"You're competitive. You excel under pressure. However, I do suggest you get started immediately."

"Who are my recruits?"

"I believe you get to choose." He looked at his watch, "they're having lab work done downstairs. Oh, and FYI…"

"Yeah?" she asked, standing.

"You get three. No substitutions or alternates. So choose wisely – and don't forget you're taking Bob on this journey." Ben's laughter followed her down the hall to the stairwell.

In the waiting room outside the small in-house clinic, three seats were filled and the chatting was just above a whisper.

"Agent Ward!"

The voice belonged to Logan Holland. Logan was actually the reason Melanie had told Ben she wanted to become involved with the recruits. The young agent had impressed her. She had shown potential in a case they'd worked together.

"Hi, Logan. Where's your trainer?"

"Agent Williams is in with the lab technician."

"Hey, aren't there supposed to be more of you?"

"Not anymore, the other recruits were chosen for the ITC. We're what's left." She sounded pathetic and embarrassed.

"Really? Teams have been picked?"

"Like two weeks ago."

"Thanks," Melanie said, taking a glance at the three leftovers before pushing open the stainless steel door. "Jordan?" she called out as the chemical scent of the state-of-the-art laboratory hit her senses.

"Melanie?" Jordan Levitz asked, rolling her chair out from behind a cubicle.

"I'm looking for Williams."

"Yeah?" Roland Williams poked his head over the top of the same cubicle.

"I'm sorry," Melanie said, feeling uncomfortable. "Didn't mean to interrupt." She looked away to the silver refrigerators lined up like suspects along the wall.

"It's all right," Jordan said with a shy grin and quickly standing to put her arms through her lab coat.

Roland tucked his shirt into his belted pants. "You wanted to speak with me?"

"I need to ask about your recruits."

"What about them?"

She'd had limited dealings with Roland, he hadn't made any special impression. Except that he carried himself with an unsubstantiated arrogance and she was surprised Jordan was seeing him.

"I'm going to take them off your hands for the next couple of months." Melanie raised her brows. "I've been assigned the ITC for Headquarters."

"What!? I've been asking to … when did you get word?" His fuse was shorter than hers. Already his coloring had flamed and a nasty vein bulged above his left brow.

"Ten minutes ago," Melanie replied, on guard for violence.

"That's not right," he turned to Jordan. "Did you know about this?" He stabbed his index finger in her face.

"Hey!" Melanie spat, getting his attention, "Nobody knew until, seriously, ten minutes ago. If you've got a problem I suggest you take it up with Jackson or the Board."

"I will. This sucks! I work with those idiots everyday and they give you the games? Fuck you, Ward!" Roland shouted and stormed out the door.

Melanie looked over at Jordan.

"He's not always like that." Jordan blushed.

"They never are."

"No, really. He's super sensitive and he's been begging Agent Jackson for years to captain the D.C. team."

"Jordan, when you're finished making excuses consider that he's six feet tall and outweighs you by a hundred pounds. What happens if he turns that temper on you?"

Jordan broke their eye contact and Melanie hoped it was contemplative, and not denial. "He's had his psych evals. We all have."

"You're right," Melanie answered. *It's your life*, she thought. "If you change your mind, call me. I don't care about his size. I carry a gun."

The three recruits were huddled, buzzing with gossip. One thing she learned was that her position was titled Captain.

"Enough," Melanie said and the room hushed. "I'm Agent Melanie Ward and you are just the people I'm looking for. Have you all had you blood drawn? Are we ready to leave?"

"Agent Williams just took off without any instruction," Logan said, pointing to the door.

Jordan, her hair pinned in a bun, appeared. "We've finished," she smiled.

"Since there are only the three of you I guess it makes this simple." She looked into each face and wondered what about these recruits made them the runts. "We're going to be a team. Agent Jackson has decided to allow headquarters to participate in the ITC this year."

The small room erupted in a mass of hysteria. Melanie and Jordan enjoyed the happiness that was seldom expressed so jubilantly.

She ordered her crew to change into workout clothes and meet her in the gym. As the last disappeared out the door she turned to Jordan. "Physically, is there anything about them that I need to know?"

"It'll take a couple of days for the lab results to come in."

"I need it sooner," Melanie said, her clock counting down. "What'd you think?"

Jordan shrugged. "Fredrick Lasota is cute."

"How about any helpful thoughts?"

"Can I ask?" her voice was cautious, "how did you get this assignment?"

Melanie shrugged. "I'm assuming ten years of annoying Jackson. He called me into his office this morning and told me he had a plan."

"I thought Agent Jackson was against the ITC."

"You and me both."

"You know there're only five captains, it's an established post. Only death creates an open spot." Jordan stared quietly for a moment. "Roland is kind of a jerk, but it's so hard to meet people and I'm here all the time." She looked away bashfully.

"You can do better than Williams."

"I heard about your engagement. I'm really sorry, Melanie."

"Yeah," she cringed, "that bit of info seems to have made the rounds." She spewed out her usual response. "I dodged a bullet. Really, can you imagine me married to a civilian?" her words were detached of emotion.

"The wrong men are always more interesting." She shrugged. "I'm attracted to bastards."

"Too bad there isn't a pill for that." Melanie drew a breath so deep it hurt. "Well, I've said enough, and I've got work to do."

"It isn't you Roland should be angry with."

"Take care, Jordan."

By the time she got to the gym her recruits were on the machines. They'd obviously been whipped into shape, doing precisely as told. *Good and bad,* Melanie knew from experience, *sometimes those people can't think on their feet.*

She hopped up on the treadmill next to Logan.

"I see you've been working on your endurance," Melanie said lightly.

"I have. Those couple of days with you really opened my eyes," Logan said, not skipping a beat. "So if you're here scouting for a prodigy, I'm your agent."

"I'll keep that in mind." Melanie grinned at the girl's chutzpah.

"When Agent Williams barged out of the lab he was muttering that you could have whatever you wanted on your way to Hell."

"I guess he's not a fan." Melanie laughed. "How are you feeling about the ITC?"

"Relief. The three of us were passed over by every other team. It's humiliating."

"I'm grateful," Melanie said.

"Are you sure?" she asked, her confidence clearly depleted.

"I'm surprised you weren't snatched up on the first round. What happened?"

"They made us take tests with ambiguous questions. One of the captains was creepy." Logan said, her face contorted into a scowl. "I think he drooled on my paper. And then they interviewed each of us and I guess I just didn't cut it with any of them."

"You're the reason I asked to be more involved with the recruits.

And that the other captains weren't wise enough to realize your potential makes me realize that we're up against a bunch of idiots."

"You're not just saying that?" Logan hopped off the belt, one foot one each side of the treadmill. "You mean it?"

"I mean it. Logan, you're going to have to trust my word. I'm not here to spare your feelings so if I tell you something, good or bad, it'll be the truth."

"Yes, Ma'am. Thanks. Just so you know, Agent Ward, I'd follow you into any battle."

Melanie's smile twitched. "Okay, then. I've got to go talk with your colleagues."

She moved around the room. From her vantage point on the elliptical machine she watched their efforts in the gym.

"So, this is where you ran off to," Williams said, pushing his way into the gym and looking around the room until he found Melanie.

"I'm glad you're here," she said when none of the young agents responded. "I was just about to go over what I know about the assignment."

"I spoke with Agent Jackson and he suggested that if this year went well then perhaps I could captain in the future."

So he's expecting me to compete in all three challenges. Melanie shouldered her disappointment as Williams leaned in and lowered his voice to a nicotine-flavored whisper.

"You'd better not fuck this up for me. I want the ITC."

With his face lingering close to hers, Melanie rose to her full height and placed her lips to his ear. "I am not one of your recruits. If you ever think of speaking to me like that again, I will slice off your scrawny balls and feed them to the crocs at the zoo."

Straightening he glared down at her from his height advantage.

"You threatening me?"

Her voice was low, not to be overheard, but the intensity was clear. "Yeah, you and your balls."

⚙

"Hi," she said, falling into the chair beside Mike.

"You look awful." His look was barely a glance.

"What's wrong with you?" she asked, scrutinizing his foul mood. Mike wasn't a deep man. Sort of the food, shelter and computer type and as far as she could see he was doing fine in all three categories. Chips within arm's reach, a comfy chair and the jumbo-tron above his head.

"Nothing," he grumbled, glancing over at Ed's empty chair.

"Oh," Melanie sighed, keeping the laughter out of her voice. "It's Bob. You're still upset about him getting attention? Don't you think that's a little childish?"

"I don't trust the guy. He's a convict, a Peeping Tom, and everyone's in love with him. I don't get it."

Mike's profile frown reminded her that he'd lost some weight and had gotten a haircut but her eyes fell on the small diamond stud in his earlobe. "You know I'll always love you best."

"Hmm." He grumbled.

"It's true."

"I'm sick of him." Mike motioned to the corner. "Ed won't shut up about Bob." Somehow Mike turned Bob's name into one long open vowel sound.

"Really?" She eyed Ed's vacant space. Lately he seemed to be sinking into a silent computer generated world.

"It's annoying."

"Well, he's harmless." Melanie said, turning back to Mike. A smiled played at the corners of her lips, she couldn't think about Special K without a hint of amusement.

"Easy for you to say, he's not after your job. But me? I'm the techie here!" Mike turned to Melanie with venom. "You were assigned a case with him, weren't you?"

"Well," she hesitated at the betrayal in Mike's eyes, "it's the ITC." His reaction was the same one everyone else was having to the news.

"What?" the question came out as a whisper at her unbelievable statement. "The Intelligence Training Challenge?"

"The one."

"But that's impossible. Jackson hates the games." Melanie shrugged. "It's not fair! I'm your technical support guy, I should be the one to participate."

"Apparently, tech support travels with the agents," she said, knowing Mike's trigger. He hated every place that wasn't his chair.

"Oh, really? I thought..." his expression tightened. "I'd be no good at that."

"See, he's already doing you favors. I think if you get to know Karwoski you'll end up liking him. He's a man-child who plays video games." She stood. This was not the unwinding place she'd thought it would be. "I'll see you around."

Melanie walked the halls, troubles that weren't hers weighed heavy on her shoulders. She felt alone and the issues on her mind weren't quite enough to push away the pangs. She couldn't muster the energy to sleep, she took a detour to the file room.

"Wow, they really spared no expense down here," she said, flipping on the lights. Most of what was stored had been transferred to digital. Melanie picked open the pathetic cage that once had been manned by an agent and started going through the dusty boxes.

Mostly trash. Her last resort was the dented three-drawer file cabinet shoved against the back wall. She pulled open the lopsided top drawer and along with other non-classified information she found two folders with notes from the beginning of the ITC.

The games started in the late 60's with five senior agents peacocking about their victories. The first few years the games were based on egos and bets were kept between the five of them.

It wasn't long before their private competition expanded to include recruits but continued to be exclusive to the same five agents. This was the birth of the Intelligence Training Challenge. In keeping with their sense of humor a prize was added: the title of Agent Elite and a tiny brass trophy.

The challenge consisted of three games played over the months of June, July and August designed to test the skill and agility of each of the agent competitors. Teams included three recruits with no more than two years tenure with the Agency, a technical advisor and a team captain. On the ITC Board was one Master Liaison to head up the games and three judges to observe and award points. Each game was uniquely scored based on time, accuracy and completion of the task; Additional points were granted for finesse, creativity and sportsmanship. Each challenge was designed months in advance by the ITC Board and limited to the five original teams.

Melanie read about the previous winners, the tasks and how haphazardly the points had been divided.

"Random. Preferential treatment. Discrimination toward outsiders." She left the file room feeling nervous. She had three recruits with confidence issues, a civilian technical advisor with the maturity of a gnat and she was ITC-challenged. *I have zero experience with the games and even less experience as a trainer. I'm screwed!*

⚜

"Okay, so maybe I shouldn't have pissed off Williams," Melanie conceded to Jack after three stress-filled days of yelling at her team. "They're just so clueless. I know they aren't meaning to do everything wrong but," she felt bad, "I get mad, I yell, I feel guilty and go to apologize and then they open their mouths and I'm angry again. It's a cycle I haven't been able to break."

"What if you apologized to Williams?"

"I told him I was going to feed his balls to the crocodile at the zoo." She flinched, at the memory of his expression.

"Yeah, I guess that would make an apology difficult." He chuckled after a moment's pause. "Damn, Melanie, I'm enlisting you in an anger management class."

"I'm not angry, I'm fucked!" she snarled and exhaled.

Jack in his passive, ever-calm demeanor, squinted his blue eyes at her. "Where are they now?"

"I have them at the shooting range. I decided it wasn't safe for me to oversee that training."

"I'm here if you want help," he said. "We could trade jobs for the next couple of days. I train and you manage my live cases."

"Really? You'd do that?" She felt the weight of her solo obligation lifting with his offer.

"I'm in your corner, Mel. We help each other out," he said patronizingly.

"Is that how it works?" she grinned. "Thanks, it helps. But the recruits are my problem and it should be me teaching them. We have to figure out how to work together."

CHAPTER FIVE

"Tomorrow." Melanie sighed out all the air in her lungs looking over her crew. Logan, Anthony, Fred and Bob. *What was Ben thinking?* It'd been a long, difficult week evaluating their skills, training, learning the ITC basics and reigning in Bob's theatrics.

Her opinion of him had fluctuated throughout the week. He never walked into a room of strangers, seeing the world as his friend. He was also boisterous and easily distracted. Taming his behavior was a team effort. But any device with a computer chip fell instantly in love with his touch.

With the team members he joked and patted their backs as he reassured their every move.

"Why don't you smile more?" Bob had asked her. "And maybe not shout so much."

"Are they improving?"

"Yeah, but…"

"They're in the wrong career if coddling is what they need." She looked at him. "Besides, if they want mothering they've got you."

"What's that supposed to mean?"

She'd left him with that thought but the truth was, he wasn't bad for the team. Williams hadn't been lax with their education but the other teams had captains with years of ITC experience.

"We're at a serious disadvantage," she said, pressing the play button. "One last time." Her voice was drowned out by groans. "It's this or the gym, you pick."

"Come on, guys, let's make it a game," Bob cheered. As the first slide started he began humming the Star Spangled Banner tune and then came the words. His words.

Oh, say can you see
the agent to the right
part of the L.A. team
and her name is Keating
But those big, bright eyes and the left one is droopy...

"What are you doing?' She mouthed.

Bob shook his head with a scowl and went right on with his song. All three of the agents bobbed their heads trying to learn Bob's lyrics, which were amazingly on target.

Okay, Melanie thought, *I can lighten up and enjoy a specialized rendition of our national anthem.* The first few verses were difficult but slide after slide his observations were right on, hitting aspects of the other agent's characteristics.

Ben popped his head into the room and nodded for her to join him in the hall. "What's going on in there?"

"Honestly, I have no idea. Bob is entertaining them in verse. I think I should just be grateful he didn't pick a Lil Wayne tune." Slowly

Ben's expression took on a confused look. "He's trying a new tactic."

"Singing?"

As much as she hated to admit it, "I think it's sort of working. They're exhausted and I've crammed a month's worth of information into them, but he has them singing along."

"Well, this is your baby," Ben said. Melanie grimaced, not liking the correlation. "You leave tomorrow?"

"Yeah, we'll get our task after take off. Almost feels like a real mission."

"I came by to wish you luck."

"Thanks." She hesitated. "Ben?" About to leave, he stopped. "I'm still unclear about what *exactly* you expect from me."

"Be yourself, that's all I want." The look in his eyes as he walked away only added to the mystery.

"You know I hate surprises," she said, anticipation sending a charge through her blood stream.

⚜

The recruits were as ready as they were going to be by morning. Buzzing from the caffeine and adrenaline, they were bouncing off the garage walls.

"To the airstrip, Ms. Ward?" Marcos asked as he loaded the luggage into the trunk.

"Yes, thanks," she said, looking over her shoulder at her crew doing a personalized line dance. "Guys!" she snapped, taking the front seat. Not able to look at any of them because, *unlike any of them, I've got a reputation. I'm a respected agent,* she thought. *This gig is a career killer. Shit!* "Seriously, I need you to focus." She held her breath as the giggles faded and the back seat fell silent. "Thank you."

The excitement resurged on the tarmac, as soon as they spotted the Agency plane with the steps lowered and the oval door open.

"Hello?" She called once inside the compact jet.

"Yes, I'm here." It was one of the usual flight attendants, Valerie, the one who always reminded Melanie of a porno star. "Captain Teddy is doing his pre-flight check." She smiled as she buttoned the top button on her collar to greet the contestants. "Hello. Welcome. Take any seat you'd like, we'll be taking off soon."

Her team fidgeted in their seats until Captain Teddy entered to introduce himself. As he spoke, Valerie pulled a 5X7 screen down from a compartment in the ceiling.

"This is a live satellite feed," the captain said, taking up a spot in the back to hold up the wall.

Lights flickered and an image snapped to focus. A round, larger than life face appeared. Agent Krueger. It was impossible to tell his age without the use of carbon dating. The man had an intimate relationship with the scalpel. And though his neck drooped into his collarbone, his face had the skin of a choirboy.

"Good morning, teams. I'm Agent Krueger and it's my great pleasure to be the new Master Liaison for the Intelligence Training Challenge. I know you are all excited and I am too." Agent Krueger smiled. "I think we're all here. Let's do a quick roll call, just to be certain. First team, L.A.?"

"We're here. And I have a few questions about…"

"Yes, we'll get to those, Agent Batista. Denver?"

"We're here."

"Headquarters?"

"Here, Sir," Melanie answered.

"Good. Chicago? Houston? What?" he said, to someone off picture, "Oh, there we go." Just then, above Krueger's head, the strip was divided into five even sections. The face of each captain filled the segments.

The image of her stern face staring back from the screen was so startling she missed Krueger's next few words.

"Where's the camera?" she heard Logan ask Anthony.

"Don't know."

Without moving her lips, Melanie shushed the two.

"I want to welcome you all to the first challenge of the season. I'm proud to be here and I've got many things planned."

"Agent Krueger, I have a few questions about…" A voice Melanie didn't recognize came from the sound system.

"Let's hold questions until the end. We're doing things a little bit differently this year." As Krueger spoke Melanie checked out the other captains, all of who looked as anxious as she did. With Batista actually looking fierce. "Instead of artificial challenges, we've decided to get some actual work done. You, my dear friends, are going live! Isn't that wonderful?"

The immediate uproar was surprising and Melanie wondered what she was missing. She was fine with going live; most of the recruits had been involved, in some capacity, with an assignment last winter.

The blending of complaints made it difficult for her to sort out the issues.

"All right, calm down." Krueger held his wrinkly, liver-spotted hands up to the camera.

He's had some serious cosmetic surgery, she thought, forcing herself to listen to the rage. Melanie's gaze bounced from one captain to the next as they all expressed their opinion at once.

"Let the man speak!" Melanie finally burst into the fray.

The roar flared and went suddenly dead. Melanie felt as if she were looking into an aquarium, the mouths of the other captains moved but the sound had been cut off.

"That's better," Krueger said. "As I was saying, this year we are implementing a new strategy: a fact-finding mission of goodwill to the U.N." His smile had been vanquished by the hostility. "Each team will have a week to investigate and write a report that will be submitted to the U.N. by the CIA. The subject is human trafficking. Gather as much information as you can and at the end of the week – that's two days travel and five on the ground – I want a concise report that can be delivered as is. You'll be judged and graded on the information as well as your final paper."

It was obvious he was examining each face as his almond-shaped eyes scanned from right to left.

"Good, you're all quiet. I'm going to turn the sound back on, but I'll turn if off if you can't control yourselves." He gave a curt nod to someone off screen. "I'm going to draw the order of teams and then draw the location that you'll be heading. Questions?"

"Sir, these agents aren't necessarily ready for a covert mission. What are the parameters?" Melanie asked.

"Very good question, Agent Ward. This is more of a research assignment. But I suspect that you would treat it as you would any other assignment. Do what you normally do." Krueger gave a nod and a slight grin, deciding he'd given proper advice. "Yes. Consider this a quasi-mission. Any other questions?"

"I haven't been out in the field in five years," the captain from Denver complained.

"It's a bit like riding a bike, Agent." Krueger delivered a weary smile. "Hop on and start pedaling, you'll be fine."

Melanie smiled, thinking about these unpracticed colleagues and how cagey Ben could be.

"The information you obtain will help in the coming months when a task force is put in place. Human trafficking is a worldwide epidemic with an estimated 12.3 million people enslaved. I don't have to mention the obvious threat to national security it causes."

"I've participated in the ITC for sixteen years, this is a deviation from anything the ITC has ever required. Agent Phillips never did things this way. There are rules!"

"I realize you and Agent Phillips are friends but he is no longer Master Liaison."

"Well, I don't like it."

"Your complaint is duly noted. What else?" After that no one said anything. "Very well, the five locations are Guinea-Bissau, Lebanon, Thailand, Myanmar and Democratic Republic of the Congo. I have this little bingo cage," he lifted five slips of paper, each one with an Agency branch written on it and dropped them into the hatch. He spun the wheel and plucked out the first city. "Denver, Houston, Chicago, L.A. and finally Headquarters." Then he dropped in the tags with the locations on them and repeated the process. "First is Lebanon, that makes it Denver's assignment."

Melanie judged the countries and the captains as each of their cities were pulled. Houston was being sent to Guinea-Bissau, Chicago to Myanmar.

"Let's see, two left," Krueger said, having trouble with the sliding window of the cage.

Melanie sucked in a deep breath. It was going to be Thailand or Congo. She didn't know which to root for – neither were a picnic.

Come on, she held her expanded lungs still. "Looks like L.A. is going to Congo. And that means Headquarters, you're assigned to Thailand. These countries have all been on the U.N.'s radar and four have risen to a Tier 3 threat. While Thailand isn't a Tier 3, yet, it's in the spotlight. Whatever your opinion is of the change of the games, I expect the best from each and every one of you. What you do this week is more than an Intelligence Training Challenge. Pilots, your flight instructions are being sent as I speak." His cheeks rose up in pink little balls to make room for a creepy smile that didn't reach his nipped and tucked eyes. "Good luck. I'll speak to you one week from today in D.C. for your presentations."

The lights on the screen flickered and went dead.

"Holy all things crazy!" Bob announced, "This is far out!"

Melanie reached for her computer.

"Let's wait until we're in the air, okay?" Captain Teddy asked, passing her on his way to the cockpit.

She swiveled her seat to face her team. "Thailand." She looked at the wide-eyed faces and grinned.

"Okay, guys. We are no longer underdogs. The game has officially changed and we're in it." She laughed. "As soon as we get airborne we're going to listen to a Thai language program to get familiar with the speech patterns and learn a few basic phrases."

Her recruits nodded as the engines revved and she felt the power surge.

"Are we ready, Agent Ward?" Logan asked.

"Yes. We are. But I'm going to need you to do exactly what I ask. Bob?"

"Yeah?" With a glance she ordered him to behave. "I get it. Lives are at stake." Bob nodded.

"Yeah. Ours."

Melanie inhaled and leaned back on the leather seat to prepare for the change in altitude of take off. She didn't understand how anyone could be afraid of flying. It was peaceful, more peaceful than on the ground, where all your problems could catch you. Cutting through clouds thirty-five thousand feet from the Earth's crust, nestled inside the shelter of a cocoon, she was invincible. Though, given the choice she'd trade it in a second to control the helm.

"Hey, Agent Ward," Anthony said, leaning in close, "I might have forgotten to mention that I'm fluent in Mandarin."

"Good to know, thanks Anthony." Melanie said, "Anybody else with skills they forgot to mention?" They'd been over this, on the second day of training but she needed to explain, "Languages, boating, wire tapping, rock climbing, karaoke singer?"

"I can Dougie," Fred said.

"Who's Dougie?" If she didn't want to be laughed at, it was the wrong question to ask.

"You know," Fred stood, bent his knees and swayed while flapping his arms. It wasn't until Bob joined him that she got it was a dance. "Dougie."

Melanie shook her head. "Really? That's how you guys spend your time?"

"It's fun, Agent Ward."

"That's another thing. You can't be calling me Agent Ward."

"Yo, Melanie," Fred said, dropping to a baritone and Dougie-ing toward her.

"Nope." That wouldn't work.

"What about Boss?" Logan offered.

"I like it! Boss." Bob grinned. "Sounds tough and scary and no one will know we're agents."

"No. But they'll know to either kidnap me or take me out first."

"Agent Williams has us call him Sir. We could call you Ma'am."

I'd almost rather be kidnapped, Melanie thought. "How about you don't call me anything and if you have to I'm Ward."

"In private can we call you Boss?" Bob asked with a look of complete sincerity.

"Fine. When it's just us you can call me Boss, if you'd like." With that settled they began listing off their attributes. Fred found his high tolerance for alcohol beneficial in college, Logan had an ear for dialects and could mimic voices, Bob had battled plenty of virtual armies and Anthony, besides speaking Mandarin, was mechanical.

Initially, brainstorming seemed like a good idea. But the ideas included using hot air balloons, hiring strippers to lure would-be traffickers or using Logan as bait. The novelty wore off. "I think we can do better than that," had become Melanie's mantra.

Finally, mostly ignoring them, she set off to develop a strategy on her own as her eager team researched Thailand, the UN and human trafficking.

She only had the length of the flight to develop a strategy.

Melanie glanced out the window at the solitary light blinking at the end of the wing. The night extended beyond the dark sky and into the blackness of the ocean below. She gave her reflection a quick grin. This was a good case. Human trafficking.

It was going to take a certain amount of finesse to gather the needed information, a ruse to blend in and enough danger to keep her on her toes.

The final hour of the flight, Melanie outlined her plan. "I would really like to be able to speak to the farmers on the passage route from Laos but we don't have time for that. So, we're heading directly to Bangkok."

"What if we split up?" Anthony, who was her only second-year recruit, asked.

"No." Melanie shook her head. "We're in a foreign country and to let you stray off doesn't sound safe."

"I could do it," Logan offered, surprising Melanie. "Take a day to interview some of the locals? I could do that, if I had a partner."

"I could go with her," Fred added. "I've traveled abroad since I was a kid. We'll be safe."

Melanie decided instantly, letting her instinct rule. "Okay," she agreed, "but Anthony, I'd rather you and Logan interview the locals. You can communicate and I have plans for you, Fred. But I want us all in Bangkok 36 hours after touch down. Bob," she turned to her tech support, "they'll need badges for a fictitious organization. Something UN like, Unified Nations or whatever, just be sure it doesn't actually exist. Put a phone number on the back that flows to my cell." She could feel her energy building. "All right. Bob, update me on your whereabouts every hour until you get to a place to stay. Remember this isn't home, you can't go around drawing attention."

"Boss," Bob said, his tone deep. "I'm sorry if I've given the impression that I can't handle myself. I understand the risks here and I won't screw up."

"I'm counting on you."

"I know." He smiled and in his eyes she read the reason for the grin. *I'm reminding him of his mom again.*

"Do you want to go over your part of the mission?" she asked, not knowing how far to push the instructor aspect of the job.

"Nah, my part's easy. Been preparing my whole life," he said, his expression returning to business.

"Okay." She took him at his word. "Fred, you ready?"

"I'm excited."

She huddled her crew into a tight circle. "Let's not forget why we're here. This is espionage, even if it's a quasi-mission. Remember to double check that you aren't being compromised. The danger here will be because we screwed up and weren't being careful. Keep your eyes open and your mouth shut. There's no telling what a person will do when backed into a corner. All I'm saying is be diligent."

"Took years for anyone to catch me the first time," Bob chimed in.

"Maybe, but if you're caught this time, it won't be jail."

"Sobering thought," Bob agreed.

"Good luck, everyone," Fred said, breaking the circle and grabbing his luggage. "Coming, Boss?"

She swallowed down the lump as she watched each of them grab their gear and exit the safety of the jet. "Hey, you guys," she said, erasing the concern etched on her face. "Be careful."

"Don't get mushy on us now," Anthony grinned and bumped his fist on her shoulder. "We've got this."

The first step outside landed her in a hot soupy climate, though really no worse than a bad summer day in D.C. The group divided and she let them go, her worries suspended by faith.

"Let's see what sort of lowlifes we can drudge up," Melanie said as she and Fred took a cab into the city.

Bangkok was a sprawling, jumbled mess of a city covered by a dirty brown sky. The driver headed directly for the tourist sector, bypassing the roadside temples and mass of overhead wires. Turning one magical corner and a modern city emerged out of the cinder blocks. The road opened up to a well-maintained artery with vegetation in the median.

Fred peered out of the window angling his head to see the tops of the glass and chrome skyscrapers. They drove by parks with green grass and clean city sidewalks. It was the financial district and where they were going to find a hotel.

Melanie trained Fred on the procedures of sweeping a room.

"We're disinfecting the bugs," he said with a foreign accent and a villainous cackle while rubbing his hands together.

"Hi, Bob," Melanie said, answering the phone.

"Hi, it's Bob."

"I know."

"Oh, yeah," he snickered. "I'm at a piece of crap hotel by a shipping yard. But Christ, you should see this place, miles of containers. Not what I was expecting. I'm going to set up the equipment."

"Give me the address. I'll meet you over there and make sure your room is clean and the locks are tight."

"It is completely not clean," he said.

CHAPTER SIX

Of the three prospects on the Agency's database, one had the most potential: Kasam, an enterprising thief willing to do anything for a price.

"Kasam's a bookie at Lumpinee Stadium. I want you to take lead. You know, male-dominated society and all that. Your attitude will make the decision for him. Be confident and indifferent. You're the one with the cash and there are a hundred other Kasams in the room. Am I clear?"

"Got it. I'm a smooth operator for a wealthy American family looking for domestic help."

Melanie studied him, analyzing with her eyes rather than her ears.

Fred returned her long gaze. "I wasn't hired for my looks," he said, flashing a sideways grin, "not solely, anyway."

"If I see you getting into trouble…"

"You'll be there, I know."

"Okay. But stay close and don't ever leave my line of sight."

❦

Bangkok's main tourist and business drags were heavily monitored to protect its most valuable resource, tourism. But stray off that path and the seedy and sordid were lurking right around the corner.

If this had been her mission she'd have been on a motorcycle, cutting through the ever-snarled traffic. The city was an overpopulated metropolis with a never-ending stream of pedestrians, bicyclists and the occasional tuk tuks.

Approaching the stadium was impressive with fifteen-foot colorful posters of fighters draped from the roof along with advertisements. Muay Thai was the style of boxing. Vendors sold trinkets, souvenirs, shirts and fighting equipment, while the food carts had lines twenty people deep.

"Good thing you had me change," Fred said, looking down at his jeans and untucked collared shirt. Most of the crowd looked poor, in wife-beater tanks and jeans that barely clung to narrow hips. These were the locals coming to see their favorite boxer.

"Kasam will be on the second floor." Melanie said, lining up behind a group of Australians. It was the line for tourists brave enough to handle the city grime and rich enough to pay for the overpriced seats.

"Are we sitting ringside?" Fred asked, reading the signs and checking out the rankings.

"We are, and I think you should place a bet."

"A big bet." Fred grinned, the surrounding energy was contagious.

Inside, the air was rank. The stench of urine permeated from the corners of the stadium and the cracked wooden bleachers had protruding nails that threatened to deliver a nasty dose of tetanus.

Their seats were on the ground floor where blood stains permanently discolored the rough concrete.

"Looks like a nice place ... from the outside," Fred observed, but his attention was zeroed in across the wire fencing that kept the fans from the fighters.

Melanie scanned the small group of boys, their faces intent, throwing punches in the air as their managers tried to wrap their moving fists. None were over the age of twenty-five. They were thin with abs that got lost beneath brightly labeled silk shorts.

The crowd went wild as the first pair of fighters were led into the ring. The roar in the stadium dulled during the prayer dance. The only movement was from the bookies and waitresses. Melanie lifted her eyes to the higher seats and found their target. He was taking bets, gesturing with hand signals.

"Kasam," she said, pointing her chin. Stopping a beer girl, she ordered two and asked about speaking to Kasam, offering incentive. "Ten thousand baht if he comes down himself," she said, peeling off a sizable tip for the messenger.

"I'll see what I can do." The girl smiled and stuffed the bill in her blouse.

Melanie turned to Fred. "Ten thousand baht is about three hundred bucks. Think it'll work?"

"We're about to find out," he said, watching the girl weave in and out of view as she set a direct course for Kasam.

Melanie watched as he took bets yelling and communicating with hands. She tried to decipher how it all somehow translated into cash.

"She's in his ear." Fred's commentary was discreet. "She's pointing at us, he's looking."

Melanie shot a glance at Fred who winked at Kasam. Allowing

her gaze to shift she scrutinized the man. He was either a very poorly maintained twenty-something or in his fifties. The collar on his light blue polo shirt was frayed and his jeans sagged. His eyes were dark, the iris and pupil blending into a sharp, penetrating laser. Kasam snapped his fingers, calling for a replacement to take bids.

The bell sounded and in the ring the first round began with the two men charging each other and immediately becoming ensnarled in each other's arms. Holding close, each using his knee to ram sharp thrusts into his opponent's groin.

A spiked athletic cup would sell like gangbusters in this sport, Melanie thought. Cheers exploded as the violent embrace continued.

"He's coming," Fred said, pulling at the hem of Melanie's top.

Her eyes remained on the ref, who was peeling the fighters apart. The men appraised each other for a millisecond before rushing back together like magnets.

"You know what to do," Melanie whispered, grimacing at a blow so forceful she heard the impact. She kept Kasam in her peripheral as Fred took a deep breath.

"I was told you have a bet to make," Kasam said to Fred.

"I've got more than a bet," Fred began, "I've got a proposition."

Kasam's leather sandals pulled several inches away from Fred. "And what would that be?"

Melanie felt his gaze on her.

"I'm looking for domestic help for a family back in the States," Fred blurted.

Melanie's cringe was slight and could've been caused by the splattering of blood from the ring. *Too fast, Fred,* she thought, sending out mental guidance.

"I don't know what you're talking about," Kasam said, turning a cold shoulder toward Fred.

"That's not what I heard," Fred added. "The lawyer of the family that employs me gave me your contact information."

Melanie kept her gaze fixed on the ring, but Kasam's discomfort showed in his body language. She knew his wheels were churning as he evaluated the American.

"I want to make a wager on the fighter in blue shorts," Melanie jumped in and pulled out a thousand baht note.

Kasam took the bill between his rough fingers. "What about the larger bet?"

"That one was attached with the assumption that you could help me with my domestic service problem." Fred made solid eye contact, shrugged. "Since you can't, I have to take my business elsewhere."

Kasam looked around. Everyone in the stadium was on their feet, screaming and the difference between cheers and taunts was minimal.

"This is not how business is done," he pressed.

"This is my first time, learning curve and all that. I'll get better next time." He worked his smile well. Never too long or too wide but with a touch of arrogance and sincerity. Melanie turned her face to the ring.

"I'll have to make a call," Kasam relented. "Where can I reach you?"

Fred slipped his card from his back pocket and handed it to him. "I won't wait for a response. If I don't hear from you within the hour assume I've moved on."

The man nodded, reading the card and dipping between a pair of goons to blend in with the mob.

"Where'd he go?" Fred asked.

"Behind us." Melanie picked up her phone and called Mike. "I need you to triangulate a call. I'm at the Lumpinee Stadium and I want you to catch all calls going out from this building. Right now."

"Easy, Ward. Let me flip screens," Mike huffed, "Aren't you in the challenge?"

"Yeah," she breathed, turning back to the fight as the crowd moaned in pain.

"What's going on?"

"Boxing."

"Okay, got it. Wow, with the noise I thought there'd be way more outgoing calls but I've only got a couple of dozen."

"Narrow it down." She gave Mike the name. "I need to know who he's calling. Get back to me." Melanie hung up, her blood roiling with excitement. "Damn!" she groaned as the boy in red shorts clocked her guy and he went down. "We'd better go."

"One more match?"

Melanie was drenched in sweat from the stagnant heat; the smell of piss had burnt into her nostrils and esophagus and was no longer intrusive. She'd gotten used to the stench.

"We've got no other leads, anyway," Fred added, gazing up at the leader board.

Melanie's mind spun. Should they follow Kasam? She looked back to the second level. He was hanging behind the bleachers, phone still attached to his ear and staring straight at her.

"Let's play along," she said, slipping bills off the top and handing them to Fred.

"Who do you like?"

Melanie laughed. "Doesn't matter." Fred was debating it when her phone rang. "Hold on."

"I've got your information," Mike said. "Kasam called an import/

export mogul who owns three shipping yards in Indo China. The biggest is in Bangkok. The only name I can pinpoint is Aanon."

"Got an address?"

"You know I do."

Aanon lived north of the city on the Chao Phraya River, inside acres of untamed wilderness.

"I do love you," Melanie said to Mike.

"You're fickle."

"Bye." She grinned.

Melanie and Fred stayed through a few extra fights, without a call from Kasam or his associate. They grabbed dinner from a street vendor before heading back to the hotel.

For most of the night she lay awake, assessing the situation, pushing away her worries about leaving Logan and Anthony on their own.

Logan had been upset when they spoke. Something about the terribleness of the situation and how they had to stop whoever was behind stealing people, whether they left willingly or not. Melanie shook her head, knowing at some point Logan was going to lose her innocence.

Melanie sighed. "How am I going to wrap this up in a couple of days? All we've got is Kasam, Aanon and an emotional plea." Bob's end had turned out zip; the shipping yards were too vast to monitor cellular or online activity.

"I have found an aspect of this job that I really suck at," she mumbled into the night. "They're trusting me and I am not walking into that presentation empty-handed."

An hour later she woke with an awareness that comes from hours of pondering.

Before breakfast, Bob was dragging his equipment into Fred's room.

"This place is slick," he said, admiring the recessed lighting. "And it doesn't stink of fish."

"I want you to focus on Aanon, get me what you can about his businesses. Who he deals with and where he got his first rush of cash."

"What? Sorry. I got a little nostalgic for my old place. Who'll take care of the rats now that I'm gone?"

"The other place was a shit hole, I get it, now get to work." She turned to Fred. "As soon as Bob gets us the address, we're paying Aanon a visit."

Aanon's office wasn't anywhere near the docks. Melanie and Fred took a stroll to the business district where international companies were housed in modern, expensive high-rises.

The building that held Aanon's office was divided into hundreds of individual suites. The directory on the wall listed his trading company on the eleventh floor.

"Let's take a ride," she said, hitting the up button.

The elevator opened to a drab cement hallway with brown, hollow doors every twenty feet. Melanie walked the desolate corridor and found suite 1122. Absently, she pinched the inside of her cheek with her teeth, aching to get inside.

Her pulse rose sharply. The only surveillance were cameras at each end of the hallway and there was no way there'd be a good view of Aanon's office.

From her back pocket she slipped out the nylon case that carried her picking tools.

"Cool," Fred said, trying to act normal.

"We're here, we might as well as check it out." She looked into

Fred's eager eyes. "I'll show you how to do this later."

"How can you be sure there isn't some booby trap attached to the lock?"

"This is low-level security," Melanie said, hearing the familiar click. Soundlessly, the door swung open wide. Melanie and Fred stood peering into an empty room.

"Where is everything? Not even a chair," Fred said, taking steps into the closet-sized office.

"Or carpeting. Let's get out of here," Melanie said, locking the door behind her. "These are just high-priced mail boxes with an address to appear affluent. Meeting spots to transfer cash, who knows what else."

She was dialing Mike as the elevator doors opened to the lobby. "I need an address. An actual, physical location for Aanon's business."

"Are you sure I'm supposed to be helping you? Aren't you competing and don't you already have tech support?"

"I thought you were my guy. Besides, I asked Krueger and he said to stay within the parameters of a regular mission. You're within those guidelines.

"Doesn't he know you have no parameters?" Mike laughed. "Why aren't you laughing? I'm funny, Mel. All right, be that way. I'll get back to you."

In the hotel room, Bob was squinting at his monitor. "Hey, guys. Research isn't my thing," Bob said, apologetically opening the container of sweet and spicy shrimp. "I'm more of a technical guy." He lowered his face into the food and breathed in. "God this smells good."

"When we get back, I want you to apprentice with Mike," she said, looking over his mess. "You need organization. How'd you keep all those celebrities apart while you were figuring out their passwords?"

"That was different. I understand English. These are symbols and strange sounds. I'm completely confused."

"Okay." She could live with that explanation. "It'll come with experience. I want you to continue pressing for anything on Aanon." She walked away, lifting her cell to her ear.

"You're not going to like this," Mike started.

"Is that why you took so damn long?" Melanie asked, keeping the anxiety out of her voice.

Mike laughed. "He works out of a building in the center of a mile-long shipping yard. The security compares to a military base. I don't know how you'll ever get in there."

"What about eavesdropping? Can you do that?"

"For a few minutes at a time every couple of hours or so. I can get you heat imaging, too. But nothing on a constant basis."

"Send me the aerial photo," Melanie said, too deep in concentration to consider etiquette. Seconds later her phone buzzed and the shipping yard appeared on her small screen. Mike had drawn a circle around a speck of a building in the heart of the photo.

She sent the photo to the laptop for a larger visual inspection. *Damn it*, she thought, *Mike was right. I don't like it.*

Driving back and forth along the freeway that butted up against the huge shipping yard didn't ease her irritation.

"Thousands of containers," Fred said as they passed for the third time.

"And any one of them could be used to transport people."

He sighed. "What's our next move?"

"I'm not sure." She slowed and looked between the metal units and caught a glimpse of the little white building. "I'd really like to get in there."

"How?"

She parked off the side of the road to study the photo. Barbed wire curled at the top of the tall iron fencing; she could guarantee security cameras, along with a pack of vicious dogs. *Still*, she thought, *me, by myself, at night, while Fred causes a distraction on the north end and Bob on the south end.*

How much danger would it put them in and was it an acceptable amount? She drove back to the hotel in deep thought, running the courses of most likely outcomes.

"I'm going to take a shower," Melanie said, opening the door to her room.

The cold, cascading water felt good, washing away the sweat and city grime until she was shivering. By then, her mind was made up. She changed into dark clothes and knocked on the door that adjoined the two rooms.

"Hey, Boss."

"Have either of you secured the room?"

"I did when we got back. Nothing."

"Show me," she said, watching as he repeated the steps she'd shown him. "Good job. Have a seat. She led them to the dining table. "I'm going to run a plan by you, and if you're not comfortable with your part tell me. I can come up with something else. Understand?"

Fred scooted to the edge of his seat and Bob leaned forward, interested.

"I want to search Aanon's office."

Fred's jaw slackened for an instant.

"I'm going to need both of you to help," she said, laying out the plan and keeping a close eye on the pulse of their jugulars. Too rapid meant fear and she wasn't going to risk their safety or hers.

"You just need us to make noise and stay hidden?" Bob asked, his words were filled with disappointment.

"It sounds simple until you're at the edge of a dark shipping yard with barking dogs and flashlights surrounding you. The spooky atmosphere will affect how you respond."

"I'm in," Fred said, quickly. "I'll keep up the distraction until you're out."

"Definitely."

Melanie sucked in a deep breath and nodded. "Let's go over the plan in detail."

At night everything that made Bangkok plain during the day lit up in a brilliant display of color. It was late when Melanie drove to the shipping yard. The car was silent but for the tires passing over cracks in the road. There were no more questions. She'd beaten the plan into them.

"Look at that," Fred said, leaning close to the windshield. "It's busier now than it was during the day."

Two sets of headlights were heading away from Aanon's center building and there was movement in the distance. "Let's take a second pass," Melanie said, cutting across the lanes to make a U-turn.

Three sets of eyes watched the trail of lights until they were hidden by the maze of containers. The place was left in darkness and quiet as a graveyard. Parked at the side of the road they watched for forty minutes.

"Holy shit!" she said when two more vans arrived. "Try and keep track of where they go."

It was difficult to tell, the containers were stacked three and four high. "What time is it on the East Coast?" she asked, Mike's number ringing in her ear. "Don't you ever go home?" She asked.

"How would I be able to help you from home?"

"I need a live satellite shot of the shipping yard."

A minute later, she ended the call and looked at the blank faces of Bob and Fred. "We're going to wait for him to call us back and see when the activity stops."

The information Mike sent was clear in identifying where the vans were parked. But not what was being loaded off the vehicles.

"Wake up," she said, turning over the engine. Disappointed as she watched the vans parade out at sunrise. Time was ticking, only one day left. And the uncomfortable gnawing was grinding her stomach, she had to know what was going on in those containers.

Melanie's heart thumping in the 'that was too close' rhythm she lived for.

"If we'd gotten there ten minutes earlier," Fred whistled, "you would've been stuck in that yard for hours."

"Or caught," Bob added.

Logan and Anthony had arrived at the hotel sometime during the night and were sacked out on the couch when she, Bob and Fred ambled into the room.

At breakfast she laid it all out on the line. Sneaking into Aanon's shipping yard was too risky. "I'm sorry, I haven't done a great job as captain." She apologized for their wasted efforts. "Logan and Anthony your interviews are so personal, so heartfelt. You put a face to the problem." *I wish it were enough,* she thought. "What do you say we spend the day on a training assignment?" Melanie asked, already knowing where Kasam would likely be. "At least you'll learn something job related."

Trailing Kasam was like being on a tour of the city. He hit all of the major tourist attractions, the floating market, the Wat Pho temple of the recumbent Buddha and the Grand Palace. At each stop he connected with bright eyed and cagey local kids who handed him plastic grocery bags.

"What do you think is in the bags?" Fred asked.

"Wallets, purses, watches, passports. He's a pick-pocket ring leader."

"Like Fagan."

"His fingers are dipped into all sorts of easy commerce. Let's stay with him until we find out where he calls home."

The team was soaked in sweat as she taught them the art of invisibility and avoidance while following Kasam home. Which turned out to be in a neighborhood of rotting barges floating on the muddy river.

"If it were up to us to take action," Melanie said, as they approached the entrance to the maze of boathouses, "we could pay for information that would lead us directly to Fagan." She smiled, using code. "But we're not at that point and we don't want to tip-off a lead. So we're going to hang back and put the information in our report. Let the UN deal with him."

The possibilities of Aanon played heavily on her mind throughout the day. But she couldn't devise an acceptable plan.

"Boss, are you all right?" Anthony asked, sitting at the table and leaning in with concern.

Melanie looked at him and then at the others. "I'm torn," she started. "I really believe Aanon is involved in something. I have no proof that it's trafficking, but Kasam did call him."

"Then we should go back to the yard tonight." Fred stated, confused.

Melanie shook her head. "It's too dangerous."

"But we're here to save people." Logan's expression was full of emotion. "Boss, if you can fix this I think we should try."

"I can't fix anything. Besides, our flight takes off tonight at ten and the airstrip is an hour out of Bangkok. We have to be on that plane."

"If we don't act, who will?"

It was a good point. Melanie looked at her young, inexperienced team.

"We're going to have to learn sometime." Fred said, reading her mind. "The four of us will stay outside the fencing and keep watch. How much risk is that?"

"How about you four take the car and I'll meet you at the airstrip at ten." She offered.

"That's not a team spirit."

"We want to be involved."

"All of you?" she asked, each team member nodding their head. After the decision was made, the doubt lifted. "You have to do exactly what I tell you to do. No going rogue. Agreed?"

CHAPTER SEVEN

They got to the yard at sunset. The shadows were long and the previous night's procession of vans hadn't begun. Melanie had a wireless earpiece connected to the recruits' phones in walkie-talkie mode. They left her at the far northern corner of the extensive yard and each took their positions. Using Mike's thermal photo from the night before she knew which containers had been of interest. Melanie counted the rows as she jogged in the channel between the containers that were stacked two and three high.

"Shit," she said, running into a blocked path that wasn't on the earlier image. Deciding it would be easier to traverse, she scrambled up the hot metal sides and from that vantage point she could see her destination as the last bit of sun dipped below the horizon. She ran crouched along the top of the freight cars, leaping from one to the next, making good time.

"Melanie." Four sets of voices spoke at once.

She pulled to a hard stop and squatted.

"They're coming!" Logan's panicked voice came through her

earphone. "Can you hear me? They're at the gate, one truck with three men and a sedan. Two dudes with guns just hopped out of the truck. They're running the perimeter."

"I hear you. It's okay," Melanie said, already on her feet and racing to get to the target container before Aanon's men.

"Looks like they're stopping at the white house to pick up more people," Fred whispered.

Reaching the box, she believed housed humans, her heartbeat accelerated. Her labored breath mixed with the humid air as she leapt, her feet landing softly. The diffused sky left her in shadows. There was only seconds to spare as she examined the container's massive lock. It was more than intimidating. It was impossible.

"They're on the move."

She reached in her pocket for her picking tools. "Come on, Mel." She breathed and had the first notch in place when she heard the tires.

It took a full beat for her to force herself to give up. With her tools between her teeth she ran, jumped and pushed off the side of one container, stretching for a handhold that was almost out of reach on the neighboring freight box. The headlights swept over the spot she'd just occupied as she swung her legs up and over the side.

Panting, Melanie rolled flat on her back, giving her adrenalin a moment to even out. The hot metal burned through her clothing as the vernacular from below was rushed and harsh. On her belly she edged to the corner of the container to listen. She couldn't see how many people were at the base and they were speaking quickly – so quickly that their speech was strung together in one ridiculously incomprehensible line. Melanie picked out individual words of the conversation, deciphering what she could.

It was enough to realize they were transferring the contents of the container beneath her into another that was being shipped out.

"Ward?"

From the lighter shades of night above the outline of the horizon there was movement. The top of a slow moving crane eased toward her.

"I'm here. Hold your position and radio silence," she whispered, sliding backwards toward the center.

The hinges screeched and a low rumbling vibrated through the container below. The orders from the men were sharp and pointed as in one movement the weight from the front of the container shifted to the back. After severe words a dozen, quiet and dirty, people single filed out of the steamy metal crate and into the other. Her gut wrenched, but she held her tongue. Armed with only her phone she snapped shots of the lineup. There were no options, she was on her own against criminals with guns. Melanie kept her head down, breathing in the dust until the transfer of humans was complete; the other box was sealed and lifted. She took a picture of the white numbers painted on the side of that container.

The shouts and engines grew distant as the crew followed the crane to the dock. These people were being shipped as cargo to an unknown destination.

She rolled on her back and waited. Right above her head the first star was beginning to break through the light pollution of the city. She gave herself an extra second of hard listening before landing in a crouched position on the ground.

"I'm on my way back," she said in a low voice, the sounds of the crane only a memory. Melanie gazed down at the giant lock that had been secured but was now dangling, disengaged.

She stepped inside. It was hot and stunk of human waste but there wasn't the rush of humanity pressing to escape. She pulled the collar of her black shirt up over her mouth and nose to breathe. *If there's evidence in here, this is where it's going to stay,* she thought, taking one last glance around the dark.

"Boss, it's almost nine," Anthony's voice whispered in her ear.

"I'm..." she whispered. The rustling came from the farthest reaches, hidden in shadow and muck. Her skin crawled with the thought of living in a rat-infested trailer. "I'm coming." She squinted to see what was beyond the light.

"Hello?" She was ready to dodge a pack of rodents, but swiveled the doors all the way open. Letting in as much light as possible from the swaying dock lamps. Her pulse spiked. "Anyone in here?" She gagged, either from the stench or the muffled moan and then held her breath.

"I'm not going to hurt you," Melanie said, wondering if her ears were playing tricks. "I want to help." She repeated herself in Thai.

From the far corner, movement caused Melanie to freeze. A girl. Her grungy face peeked out from behind a cardboard box.

"I'm not going to hurt you," she repeated, slowly reaching out with her hand. "It's going to be okay."

The girl shuffled out of the bleakness, staring at Melanie with big, dark eyes.

"We have to go." Melanie didn't think anyone would be coming back ... especially for a single girl, but there was always the chance. She took slow, deliberate steps toward the girl.

And suddenly the girl rushed her, wrapping her arms around Melanie's waist and pressing her face into Melanie's chest.

"Boss!" The shouts in her ear rattled her instincts.

"Boss, it's Bob. He's in trouble!"

"I think they've got him!"

"Where?" Melanie asked, trying to maintain her cool for the girl's sake as she scooped her up in her arms, held her close and ran.

"Two soldiers. They're taking him toward the office from the southeast quadrant."

Melanie raced. "Got it."

"They have weapons."

The front gate was the closest exit to the shack. "Be ready," Melanie said, slowing to watch a pair of armed guards flanking Bob, who stood a foot taller and forty pounds heavier than his captors.

Ducking at the rear of a black sedan, she faced the girl. "Wait here," Melanie whispered, pointing to her feet and gesturing to stay before she put her finger across her lips. The girl nodded.

Melanie turned her attention back to Bob. Her senses were on full alert as she slipped around the white building, ready to come at them from behind.

The guards were yelling at him and speaking into a phone as she chose the biggest of the two and rammed her boot into the back of his knee, then using his club she knocked him out. Bob was as surprised as the guards. Melanie was swift, jabbing the end of the club into the second guard's abdomen and head, leaving him in an unconscious heap.

"Come on," she said, tugging Bob by the shirt and running toward the sedan.

"But..." He started to protest, then shut up.

Melanie slowed, not wanting to scare the girl. She checked the doors to the car. Locked. "Damn it." Too little time. "There's a chain link section of fencing ten meters north of the gate," she said, hoping Anthony understood. She lifted the girl in her arms and raced on foot.

If she hadn't been watching the red taillights, the fencing would've crushed them. Anthony backed the rental car over the demolition, paused to put the car in drive. In that second they jumped in and Anthony flew across the freeway.

Minutes lapsed in complete silence.

Melanie turned her attention to the little girl in her lap. "You're going to be okay," she exhaled.

"What happened?" Fred asked, turning to see who was in the back seat.

"Later," Melanie answered. "You know how to get to the airstrip?"

"I've got it," Anthony said, staring at her from the rear view mirror. "Are we taking her with us?"

"Where do you live?" Melanie shifted, leaning back to get a look at the kid. She tried in two other languages.

"Nowhere." The girl mumbled in English with a British accent.

"Parents?" Melanie asked.

The girl's spine sunk as she withdrew into her shoulders and merely shook her head once.

Melanie pushed the air out of her lungs. "We're taking her with us." She tightened her hold on the girl, who wasn't as young as Melanie had first thought. "How are we on time?"

"Close."

"Drive faster." Melanie sat in quiet thought, figuring out a way she was going to sneak an unauthorized person on the flight. "We're going to need a distraction. There'll be two pilots and one attendant."

"What's your name?"

"Ina."

"Ina?" Melanie asked, giving the girl another look. "Where are you from?"

"South Africa. My parents are missionaries. But there was fighting and we were separated … that was almost a year ago."

"How old are you?"

"Seventeen."

"Okay, Ina, this is going to be tricky because you have no papers and I shouldn't be transporting you. I know you've been through a lot, but I'm going to need you to do exactly as I say. Understand?"

She nodded. "Where are you taking me?"

"America. Then we'll find your family."

"Thank you."

It was ten sharp when Anthony pulled up alongside the jet and popped the trunk. The crew was waiting outside the plane. Melanie, Bob and Fred approached the three, who looked relieved to see them.

"You were almost late." The pilot, who Melanie had only flown with a few times, grouched.

"I think that's translation for on time." Bob grinned.

"I was ready to leave you," he mumbled as he passed.

Anthony was handling the luggage while Logan blocked the crew's view of the girl and then led her inside the plane beside Anthony, his arms full of bags. Ina was to hide out in the restroom and wait until Melanie went for her.

Everyone was buckled and quiet as the engines revved and the wheels broke free from the tarmac.

The flight attendant disappeared behind a curtain dividing the seating area from the kitchen and all gazes fell on Melanie.

"What are we doing?" was the question.

"Not yet," she said. "Logan, don't bring her out, but can you check on her? Get her some water."

They were two hours into the flight and the recruits had settled into their distractions.

Melanie dialed Ben. "We need to talk."

Ben never actually yelled but it was implied in the gaps between words. He was sending authorities to the shipping yard to release the people in the cargo box and arrest Aanon. Ina caused a different set of problems. The weight on Melanie's shoulders eased with her confession.

"Hi," Melanie said, opening the door to the restroom. "Are you hungry?"

Ina nodded.

"Logan," who was waiting just outside the door. "Could you find some crackers or bread?"

Ina was a waif of a girl with fair skin and eyes. It looked as if she'd tried to wash her face, leaving dirt streaks down her cheeks and neck.

As Logan got Ina comfortable in one of the big chairs, Melanie went to the cockpit. The problem was that Ina wasn't on the manifest. Pilots usually have a negative response to that kind of news.

"I've got to radio this in," he fumed, glaring at Melanie. "We're going to have to land."

"Just meet her and then make your decision. Her name is Ina, she's seventeen and was separated from her parents while living in South Africa."

"What do you want from me?"

"To fly this plane to D.C. Just like planned." Melanie said, trying to simplify the situation.

The vein on his left temple throbbed under his heated skin. But he didn't reach for his headset.

"She's just a kid and has been through a lot, too much. I promise to take whatever consequences are dished out. Come meet her." Melanie said, "Do you have kids, Captain?"

Ina was curled up under a blanket, already asleep and looking utterly vulnerable and alone.

"Okay, Ward, but this had better not come back to bite me in the ass," he said, his eyes not straying from the girl.

"How is she?" Melanie asked as the captain retreated.

"She nibbled and then passed out."

"What's going to happen to her?" Logan asked.

"We're going to find her family." Melanie said, her tone challenging anyone to disagree, then softening. "I haven't thought that far out."

"She was left in a container to die?"

"I think she hid." In a low voice she whispered the details.

"How'd you know to look?"

"I didn't."

"Will we get into trouble?" Anthony asked. "Could we lose our jobs?"

"That won't happen." Probably.

⬥

The jet landed in D.C., at the bottom of the steps a limo waited, engine running, and the driver beside the door wasn't Marcos.

Melanie glanced at the pale faces of her team. "Bob, have you got your end of the presentation ready?"

"Yeah. Do you think that's what this is about?"

"It's a limo and I don't see any handcuffs," Melanie's joke fell flat. "We're home." Smiling gently to Ina she asked, "Are you ready? There are going to be questions but no one is going to hurt you."

"I'm better."

She looked better. Wearing Logan's sundress and tennis shoes. Her hair was combed through and the dirt scraped off the top layer of skin. Melanie was glad she had taken photos of the girl in her abused state.

"Good evening," the driver said as all six exited the aircraft, bags in tow.

"Where are you taking us?" Fred asked before dropping into the back seat.

"I'm not at liberty."

"Well, wherever it is, would it be possible to make a run to a drive-thru first?"

"No."

"Boss?" Logan whispered.

"I've never participated in the ITC," Melanie intercepted the rest of the questions. "I have no idea where we're going. But I'm guessing it's to debrief the judges."

"Really?" she sounded relieved. "Do you think the other teams are here, too?"

Melanie was the last to enter the car and the buzz energized as she did. "Hey." Was all she said for the team to remember that Agency ears were everywhere.

Anxiously, they kept their eyes turned out the windows. She felt her tension notch up a level as the driver pulled into the underground parking of the headquarters building and park behind the other limos.

Melanie knew these halls. They brought out her worst fears. So many times Finn had accused her of unfounded charges and … she sucked in a quivering breath, remembering the inquiry after his death.

They were led to the auditorium, with seats that sloped down to a stage. From the higher vantage point, Melanie's eyes traveled the dozen rows to the other teams grouped behind the judges who were sitting front and center. A white projection screen had been set up for the, Melanie sighed, presentations.

In the wings was Ben Jackson.

She looked to Bob, who was reading her question and nodding that he could handle the job. They'd printed out paper reports, which Logan carried. If they weren't an extra person strong, Melanie would've felt confident.

"There they are!" Krueger's voice sounded excited. "Now that we've all arrived, we can start the presentations." His tone filled with delight.

"Since Team Headquarters is already standing, perhaps they'd like to go first?" The judge's question was clearly an order.

They don't know about Ina, she thought, looking over at Ben for affirmation. His ambiguous grin was peculiar and a bad feeling crept under her skin.

"We'd love to." Melanie smiled. "Bob, would you like to get us set up? Logan, the reports."

Bob dimmed the lights. The presentation began innocuously enough as she explained their original plan. Then the music started and the pie charts flowed across the screen. Photos flashed in procession and the video clips of the farmer interviews were more of a PSA than an Agency report.

Stopping at the point where she was going to have to admit she brought home an actual victim of human trafficking, Melanie looked at Ben. His single nod was enough.

"On our last day," *God, was that yesterday?* "We had our final chance to investigate the Aanon shipping yard."

Bob had adjusted the darkness of the photos she'd taken from on top of the freight box and they played behind her as she detailed the event.

"Inside I found, hidden in dire conditions," she swallowed and felt Krueger's anticipation, "I found a girl."

The room was silent.

"And I brought her to D.C. with us." Melanie tightened her lips and waited for the unleashing of her punishment. She looked around at the gaping faces. "Any questions?"

The eruption was instantaneous.

"Where is she now?" Ben asked, cutting through the chaos.

Melanie looked up at Fred, who opened the door for Anthony and Ina. She directed her attention from Ina's little form in the doorway to Ben, where she was glued to his response. His was the only opinion that mattered. By the expression on his face he was still formulating what that opinion would be.

The questions flew from all directions and all at once.

"You brought her here?"

"Where else was I going to take her?" she asked. Giving Anthony the look to take Ina out before reciting the girl's story.

"That wasn't part of the challenge!" Batista charged. "We can't have agents losing control!"

"I didn't lose control," she defended as Krueger's mouth began to shape into an oval, ready to speak.

"I have to admit, Agent Ward, the ITC isn't set up for this type of … what am I thinking? What is the term?" Krueger asked his neighboring judge.

"Situation."

"Yes. You put your recruits in danger that they were not prepared to handle. What if something had happened to you?"

Melanie stopped Fred from rallying to her aid with her hand.

"I took care in keeping their safety a priority. But we also had a responsibility to the lives in that box. My team had instructions on how to move forward with or without me."

"This isn't fair," the captain from Denver complained. "I didn't know we were supposed to bring sacrifices back to the judges."

"Shut up," Melanie ordered. "This isn't about the games. It's about doing our jobs. It's about teaching recruits how to become agents."

"It's not in the guidelines. Agent Krueger, I think the D.C. team should be eliminated from the competition." Batista stood and pointed at her with a manicured index finger.

"Excuse me," Melanie interrupted. "Bob, could you please replay the portion of the initial instructions when I specifically asked Master Liaison Krueger what the boundaries were and his response was I was to treat the challenge as I would any other case."

"Got it right here," Bob said, tapping on the computer.

"Our objective was to observe and report back!"

"And when was your last active assignment?" Melanie retorted. "These days we do more than simply observe. We accomplish."

Ben cleared his throat. "If I may interject," he said, clearly ending the bickering. "I have spoken with the CIA and they have forwarded the report to the UN. There is a family in D.C. willing to house the girl temporarily. She has knowledge of the inner workings of this trafficking ring. She'd be useful. In the meantime she will be placed in school until we can reunite her with her family."

"Thank you," Melanie smiled.

"This isn't about the girl." One of the captains shouted.

"Hold on," Krueger faced the mob. "Think about what you just said Agent Croft." His expression was glum as he spoke directly to Melanie. "Agent Ward, I am familiar with your record, but this seems to be taking the matter to extreme, even for you. Agent Jackson, are you supporting these antics?"

"Agent Ward is one of the Agency's best. I trust her decisions. That being said," he glanced quickly at Melanie, "my authority over the ITC is largely that of observer."

"Well, I think she should be fired – or at the very least eliminated from the games," Batista stated with pitched brows and hateful eyes. "All of us are outraged!"

"Where's the fairness if there are no rules?"

"Headquarters doesn't belong in the ITC."

"I did agree to the terms," Krueger interjected, scratching his head. "I have to admit," he looked at the other judges, "I'm impressed with the presentation, the amount of useable information the team gathered. What about the container that was placed on the barge?"

Ben gave Melanie a long glance. "It had been emptied by the time the authorities arrived. We placed Aanon on 24-hour surveillance. The local agents will inspect each container being shipped from his yard."

"Well, that is too bad." Krueger lowered his head. "Though I admire this team's efforts and accomplishments, I also believe there must be rules." He sighed. "Why don't we see what the rest of you have done and at the end I will give my decision on what or if Headquarters should received a penalty for their actions."

Melanie's body cramped. *A penalty? How about a Goddamned commendation?* Turning her clenched jaw into a taught smile she gave her team the 'everything will be fine' nod.

"Agent Ward, would you like to say goodbye to the child?" Ben asked, standing.

"I would." She was happy to leave the junior production of the Houston team. "Ben, on a scale of one to ten, how angry are you?"

"Is zero an option? I didn't put you in the challenge to mingle."

She smiled at the small sight of Ina as she introduced her to Mr. Jackson. "He's found a nice place for you to live until you're reunited with your family."

"Thank you." She said, her hug was tight, but the girl was used to goodbyes.

"Here is my phone number." Melanie handed her a card. "Memorize it and call me anytime you want."

Ina nodded and slipped into quiet step beside Ben.

Melanie watched the two for a moment before heading back into the auditorium. Fortunately the presentations were short and pointless with painfully little to report.

"Well," Krueger started as the Denver team wrapped up the final presentation. "Very good. All of you. I'm sure much good will be done because of your efforts." He glanced over his shoulder. "Points will be awarded and tallied up, and because of the unforeseen circumstances, scores will be given to each team within the week. Now about the D.C. matter. This is difficult because after all is said and done, I can see how Agent Ward might have a slight advantage," he looked over at her. "I'm forced to suspend your participation in the ITC. I'm sorry, I feel partially responsible. But it just isn't an equal match-up."

"What?" She bit down on the inside of her cheek to keep her temper in check. "I realize that I did go outside the norm, but to suspend my team because the other captains cannot keep up?"

"Now, Agent," Krueger started in a patronizing tone that hadn't been there when Ben was around. "Your experience puts you in a different mindset and though we changed up this challenge, the ITC wasn't designed to put recruits in real-time missions. It is far too advanced. You understand that. I can see how much you care about the safety of your teammates."

She listed off two of the other captains who had been agents longer than she had. "And isn't the point to train these recruits for an actual mission? They're going to be thrown out there sometime and danger is the world we live in. It's the world we've all chosen."

"By experience I didn't mean in years, I meant in depth of assignments. Agent Jackson himself said you were one of the best. If you'd be willing to step down, we can replace you with a more suitable trainer, and then the D.C. team is welcome to participate in the rest of the challenges. But that is my decision. You are overqualified."

"Wait. What?" Agent Batista asked. "Are you saying she's a better agent than I am?"

"That is exactly what he said." Melanie contained her smile. It was the spark needed to ignite these pompous and spoiled men.

"No," Krueger admonished, angling his head back as if to avoid a punch.

"Yeah. He thinks I'm so good that none of you would stand a chance," Melanie added, her mouth stretched a fraction.

"What are you doing?" Bob asked.

"Just watch," Melanie whispered back as the auditorium suddenly broke into a shouting match.

"You are a dangerous woman," Bob said, the hint of admiration reached his eyes.

The other teams still wanted her thrown out, but to be clear, not because they couldn't beat her. Joy rose from her core as she watched the battle. They were heated, impassioned and firm in their beliefs that they could defeat her in any challenge – rules or no rules – but she should be eliminated for transgressing beyond the ITC limits.

"Stop. Stop!" Agent Krueger yelled from the podium. "Enough!" he said, removing his glasses to rub his eyes. "Let me think this over. But as of now Agent Ward is not involved with the games. Not because of rule breaking … I myself gave permission … but because Agent Ward has more experience … not more talent. Are we satisfied?"

"No," Melanie said and was surprised that her voice was just one of many.

"I think all of our emotions are unbalanced. We'll regroup in a few days and I will make my final decision."

"Good work." Bob smiled.

"Can you believe them?" she glided her eyes at the small groups that had merged into one anti-Melanie unit while Krueger and his band tried to become invisible.

"All right," she said to her team that was hanging on by a thread.

"What does it all mean?"

"We didn't win, and if headquarters wants to enter any more challenges, it's without me. But there are other qualified agents who could take my place in an instant."

"No way!"

"Boss, you were awesome."

"We did the right thing," Anthony defended her. "We rescued a girl. We saved her life."

"You're sure you're okay with not winning?" Melanie asked, already knowing the answer.

"We did win!"

"We really did." Melanie watched the high-fives. "Okay, you guys go back to the Manor, get some sleep and we'll see what happens next."

CHAPTER EIGHT

"How do you find trouble so easily?" Jack asked, leaning back in Melanie's office chair.

"I have no idea. Sometimes I can't even believe it. I mean, I'm basically a good person. I have my moments, sure, but I don't go looking for problems. How come you're never in hot water?"

"Lately, it's because I'm stuck behind a computer," he groaned, bending his back to stretch and running his fingers through his hair. "I can't even get a paper cut."

"It's because you're a Boy Scout," Melanie laughed.

"I like trouble. I want to kick ass. I used to kick ass, remember?"

"Talk to Ben, he did send you to Africa."

"He sent me to watch over you."

"Bull. You're a great agent. Besides, I've been in your shoes. For years, trapped as Ben's second right hand. And I still was able to get a monthly reprimanding."

"You can thank Finn for those."

His comment wasn't meant to cause her insides to stir. She liked to keep her Finn conversations confined to her psychiatric evaluations.

"Sorry. I forget he's gone." Jack inhaled.

"Me, too." *Until I realize how nice life is*, she thought. "I hate to say it," she said, looking at her confidant, "but I don't miss him. I hate how he died but he made my life hell."

"That's the most you've said about Parker."

"Yeah, well, I'm tired. Any word on the guy they caught?"

"Nada. Odd, huh?"

"Yup."

Jack nodded, studying her face. "So, what are you going to do about the ITC?"

Melanie shrugged. "Be grateful I was given the boot. I suck as a trainer and those other captains are worthless. But what really burns is that I was fired. Keeps a flame going in the pit of my stomach."

"You know Ben wants you to captain the next game."

"I highly doubt that. I know he expects me to stray, but I think this time was too far." She smiled. "You can't have me training the newbies. Imagine a crop of lawless agents running around."

"Scary."

"Roland's been after the job for years and he fits their desired criteria." She grunted. "Lazy. Lazy bastards, all of them."

"Ever wonder why you don't have many friends?"

"Who wants a bunch of lazy bastards as friends? Not me." She sighed. "But I feel bad for my team. They worked hard and at the very least they deserved to be ranked."

"You're overambitious."

"Is that what you think my deal is? Was I supposed to let the girl die alone in that container?"

"All I'm saying is that maybe you shouldn't push so hard. It wasn't a real assignment."

"But real people are being sold as slaves."

"I'm not fighting you, Melanie. Simmer."

Melanie took in a breath. "I know. I know I should stop but I catch a scent and I can't let it go."

"Sometimes it's a good quality, just not all of the time."

He was right. "Well, I'm interested in a solo, long-term mission. A six-month assignment. Has Ben got anything like that sitting on his desk?"

Jack thought for a second. "Closest he's got is an insider job with the TSA. It's undercover, solo and long-term until you piss someone off and get your ass fired. I give you a week."

She ignored him. "TSA, with the x-ray screenings? I'll pass. But, I'm serious, what have you got for me? I want out of the country. Somalia or China, North Korea." She grinned.

"Really, Mel?"

"Gotta keep up my bad-ass agent reputation. Can't do that in a polyester TSA uniform."

"I bet you could, me, I wouldn't mind an assignment in Belize."

"I'm not against soaking up the sun, but I want a fight. A worthy fight that I can do damage, you know bruised knuckles and all that."

"Are you okay?"

"I'm anxious. Any sort of lull in work puts me too much in my head and sometimes that's not a good place to be."

"I'll go back and take another look at what's coming up. We can always hope for some hostages or a revolution."

"Don't tease," she laughed, scowled and sighed all at the same time. "I hate that I screwed up." Her smile was a thin line across her face.

"How'd Bob do?" Jack grinned obviously replaying a memory that he didn't share. "I just look at Special K and my eyes water. Did he goof off in Thailand?"

"Not even a little bit. He was focused and right on top of things. In the meeting, I asked him for something I knew we didn't have but he didn't skip a beat and went along with the bluff. I was proud of him." Jack stood to leave, "Could you do something for me?"

"What's that?" He asked suspiciously.

"Find out about Hugh. It's killing me that I'm in the dark."

"I've tried, Mel. He must be bad because it's very hush-hush from the Parker camp. No appearances, no press releases. Nothing." Jack's expression deepened, "You worried about him coming after you?"

"It's in the back of my mind. And you can never be too safe when it comes to the Senator. I think he invented the word vendetta."

"Don't lose too much sleep over it," Jack said, patting her shoulder as he turned toward the door. "I think if he were in any position to work, he'd be out campaigning."

She shrugged. "See ya, Jack."

<hr />

"What should we do, Boss?" Logan asked after a heavy-duty workout in the gym.

Melanie was waiting for Krueger's official call releasing her from her ITC obligation.

"Kind of sucks, doesn't it?" Fred asked. "I mean, we did awesome. Bob blew minds with his computer skills. Logan and Anthony were like Oprah with their interviews."

"Thanks!" Logan smiled, her brown hair up in a ponytail. "What do you think the next challenge will be?"

"Why don't you guys go get some dinner or see a movie? Just stop thinking about the games. Krueger said it'd be a couple of days." She said, exhausted from answering the same question. "Agent Williams will take over for me tomorrow and maybe he has more answers than I do."

The recruits shared a grimace before the groan.

"Whining won't help, you can still compete with a different captain. And Williams isn't doing such a bad job with you. All of you were fantastic."

"What about me?" Bob asked.

"My guess is that you'd continue too, as tech support." She grinned. "Take the rest of the night off," she ordered, climbing on the rowing machine and scrolling to the Russian segment on her iPod. Her lack of fluency in Thai had been an eye opener; she'd been lax in maintaining her skills.

When her phone rang, she was sweat caked and brain weary. Melanie looked at the photo of Trish and felt the judgment. Her eyes practically screamed at Melanie, "I told you so!" The guilt from her thumb on the end call button lasted through her shower.

Melanie had expertly dodged lengthy contact with friends. And Trish was on the top of the 'to avoid list'.

Melanie felt sick. Twelve years of knowing Trish and now all that she could think of when her name came up was last Thanksgiving. Thanksgiving with Danny, in La Jolla. That single event was riddled with strings, strings that led directly to bad memories.

She'd held out as long as possible, sitting on the corner of her bed, sucking in a huge breath and pressing speed dial.

"There you are," Carla answered on the first ring. "We've been trying to reach you."

Crap.

"Put her on speaker phone!" Trish yelped in the background.

"What's going on?" Melanie asked, confused by the happy mood on the other end of the line.

"Tell her."

"Okay, I've got news." Trish said. "You know how I've been fighting and fighting Jason about the 'M' thing?"

"Yeah?"

"Well, I've changed my mind." Trish's screaming gave Melanie time to comprehend.

"You're getting married?" Melanie asked as a strange feeling of gloom washed over her.

"I'm getting em'd! With a capital M."

"Wow! Congratulations! That's really wonderful." Her answer was an automatic, high-pitch sound that made her feel like a phony. In her heart she wanted to be happy for Trish.

"I know!"

"How did he finally change your mind?" *With a gun?* The thought rode in with the wave of emotion.

"That. Well," Trish paused. "It's not a great story. I'm going to have to rework it a bit. You know, for the grandchildren."

"Of course." Melanie smiled, happiness worming its way into her mood and she found herself wishing she was with them. "Tell me more, what does the ring look like? Have you thought about a date?"

"The ring, ugh, that's another thing I'm going to have to do something about, it's pear shaped," Trish said as if it were an embarrassment. "But he said the saleswoman helped him and I'm thinking they just wanted to get rid of the thing on a sweet, unsuspecting man."

"It's a beautiful, giant rock. Really. There is nothing wrong with that ring, Trish," Carla admonished. "Tell Melanie the zinger."

"Uh-oh." Melanie cringed. Zinger?

"Carla is just a little worked up, you know how she gets."

"I'm not worked up, I'm practical."

"I want to be a June bride," Trish said.

Melanie looked at the date on the top bar of her monitor. June 15th. "Next June?"

"Next week," Carla corrected.

"When did all this happen? How long have you been engaged?" Melanie asked, starting to feel left out of the plans.

"Last night."

"You're kidding. You mean this isn't already planned?"

"I wish," Carla replied.

"Can you arrange a wedding in a week?" She asked, knowing Trish would never consider a visit to the courthouse for her big day.

"Ask her how many people she wants to invite."

"I'm right here," Trish laughed and from Carla's squeak there was poking or shoving going on. "So what, I want to have a nice wedding, it's not like I'm throwing a weekend BBQ. At least 150 people with 12 bridesmaids and 12 groomsmen and a flower girl and a ring bearer."

"In four days," Carla snorted.

"Four days?"

"Yeah, it's Jace's schedule." Trish explained, "he's super busy in the summer and the only time is this Thursday."

"Jason has a morning game on Wednesday, he has Thursday off and an evening game on Friday. If she wants June, it really is the only date," Carla elaborated. "And we don't even have a place yet."

"I called a couple of churches and you know those stuffy zealots actually want you to belong to their organization before they'll rent the place to you."

"Preposterous!" Melanie said, with mock indignation. "Don't they know who he is?"

"I tried that. Apparently, God doesn't give favors to professional baseball players. Not even the MVP for the Padres." Trish said, truly sounding annoyed.

"Is she for real?" Melanie asked Carla.

"Sadly, yes."

"I'm still here. Look, this is my wedding. I'm only going to be a bride once or twice in my entire lifetime. I want it to be right. Special, you know?"

"Then wait a year," Carla sighed.

"Why? It's June now."

"She's got a point." Melanie sucked in a giggle, knowing that to torture Carla further was wrong. "It *is* June now."

"Don't, Mel," Carla groused. "Trish is one hundred percent serious and I'm losing my hair at an alarming rate."

"What do you have planned so far?"

"Nothing." Carla's nervous laugh was a sure sign of her stress.

"Mel, I need your can-do attitude. Carla is a grump and a dream buster."

"What about a wedding in the backyard?"

"That's a BBQ. Come on Mel I thought you'd do better than that."

"Okay." She clamped her eyelids shut, thinking. "Well, have you considered Vegas?" Melanie offered throwing out the first substantial thought.

"Las Vegas? What do you think?" Trish asked Carla in a snooty tone. "I wanted a classy wedding."

"You don't have to get married on the street. They've got resorts and I'm sure they must offer packages," Melanie added, suddenly attached to her whim.

"A resort. Maybe it is a good idea," Trish said, in a far-away voice.

"I bet they could arrange a last-minute party," Carla added, thinking out loud.

"Carla, grab my laptop. All right, now that that's fixed, when can you get here?"

"I can be there tomorrow." The timing was right. Melanie was in assignment limbo. "Just tell me if it's San Diego or Vegas."

Melanie hitched her duffle bag up on her shoulder. The Vegas heat smacked her in the lungs as she exited the air-conditioned ramp at McCarran airport.

She waited in taxi line as the soles of her shoes melted into the curb. Her cabbie drove in mindless silence as the A/C caught the five remaining hairs on his scalp in a wind tunnel. On the stark freeway to the strip, billboards shimmered in the fierce June sun advertising adult entertainment.

Trish had chosen the newest, largest, most elaborate casino in town to celebrate her nuptials. Trish, Carla and Jenny, according to the text, were already boozing it up in the hotel suite. A vacation, Melanie stared out at the wavy mirage above the blacktop.

"Jeez, look at this place," she said in a soft voice as they turned onto the strip.

"Where you from?"

Shoot! I started the talk sequence.

"Winnipeg."

The driver snickered. "You better plan on staying indoors, Chickie, but at least it's a dry heat."

"True." Melanie laughed along like it was the first time she'd heard that line. "I thought I walked into a hair dryer when I got off the plane."

"Well, you picked a top-notch place to stay."

"A friend is getting married." She divulged the information with the mixed feelings of envy, sadness and a twinge of regret.

"Ah, yeah, a wedding, they're popular here. Make sure she signs a prenup."

"She's in love," Melanie said, not realizing she sounded contemptuous.

His laugh reverberated inside his barrel chest. "I certainly hope your friend is more of a romantic than you are."

"She wasn't, until recently."

"Love will do that." His eyes peered at her from the reflection of the mirror. "I take it you were burnt."

"Scorched."

"This is the city to forget about all that."

A dozen high-towered resorts dotted the strip. In the daylight it was magnificent – the Eiffel Tower, the New York skyline, a mirrored pyramid. Tourists gleamed with sweat as they strolled the sidewalk in their short summer shorts and skin-tight tank tops.

On the cab ride, she spied Elvis, Michael Jackson and six men in boas and leotards. Her driver wasn't interested in sight seeing. He swerved around traffic and cut off a van, a Hummer and a city bus, to pull into the white marble drive of the hotel. The valet at the podium jumped to open the door for Melanie while the other went to the trunk to retrieve her luggage.

She followed the flow into the ornate building with high-powered cooling system and giant potted plants. In the center of the bustle, Melanie stood still, her gaze cast upward as she took in the incredible mixture of old world art and modern necessities. To the left was the casino but to the right the building opened up to an entire mall. Every heart's desire was packed into three floors and escalators carried the shoppers to spend their winnings or overdraw their bank accounts.

The rotunda ceiling was painted to express eternal daylight. At ground level, plump, colorful Koi swam in a lake with a seven-foot high spouting fountain.

"I love this place," she said to no one. Gazing up, she drifted between the roped barriers to the reception desk.

"May I help you?" the woman behind the counter asked with a pleasant grin.

"I'm Melanie Ward, with the Warner-Johnson wedding," she said, hoping it meant something to the woman. Carla had handled the reservations.

"Yes. I show that you are in room 518 with a Ms. Bradley and Ms. Conner until Wednesday. After that you are booked in a single room with a view of the pool. Ms. Warner is in our Bella Suite, which is on the same floor." She was efficient, speaking, typing, gathering printouts and activating a key card. Placing it all in an envelope as she slid a sheet of paper on the counter in front of Melanie. Uncapping a red Sharpie, "This is a map of the hotel. We are here." She marked their location, check. "Stairs." Check. "Elevators." Check. "And your room." Check. She looked up with a smile. "Would you like help with your luggage?"

"I'm good, thanks." Melanie said, gathering her belongings and eyeing the map.

"Have a nice stay, Ms. Ward. May I help you?" The woman called to the couple at the front of the line.

Following the map, Melanie passed a red Mercedes Roadster rotating on a car turntable surrounded by slot machines. For only five dollars she could be driving back to D.C.

Her phone ringing broke the spell. "Hi Jack," Melanie sighed into the receiver. "Tell me I don't need a car," she said, stepping away from the temptation of the machines. "Because right now I think I could win one."

"Why would you need a car?"

"What's up?" She asked, making her way through the casino floor to the bank of elevators.

"Can you talk?" He asked. "You're in Vegas, right?"

"Yeah," she answered feeling the prickles of an assignment and rushing to catch the up elevator before the doors squeezed shut. "Hold on, catching a ride."

Even in the City of Sin there was something divine about an elevator ride. The square footage was small and strangers gather in a hushed silence. Eyeing her distorted reflection in the shiny metal doors. *I look good*, she thought, *even with short hair. But Trish is going to hate it.*

"How do dirty blackjack dealers sound?"

"Like a lot of fun, if you're into that sort of stuff." She smiled, stepping off at the fifth floor.

Jack missed the humor. "There's a ring that's been doing the rounds at tribal casinos. They're Syrian and were in Atlantic City but now the word is they've just landed in Vegas. Better hone your dealer skills."

"Which casino?" Melanie asked, already knowing.

"Unconfirmed, but I'll send over the results of the initial investigation."

"I just hope it's not here," she said, sticking her phone in her pocket and reading the directory plate screwed to the wall.

She heard the party before she reached the Bella Suite. The deadbolt was engaged, propping the door open. *Not quite the intended use*, Melanie thought with a smile. Pushing the door open she took a breath.

"Rumor has it someone is getting married around here," Melanie said, dropping the bag off her shoulder.

"Melanie!" Trish yelled, bounding off the sofa to tackle her. "I am so glad you're here! Look everyone, it's Melanie!"

"Wow, the party has already started," she said, hugging Trish and looking over her shoulder – Carla, Jenny and another girl Melanie didn't recognize.

"Not really. I'm drunk with happiness, girlfriend! D.R.U.N.K." Trish laughed, stepping back without any of the telltale signs of too much alcohol. "Good Lord, what happened to your hair?"

Melanie hugged Carla, ignored Trish's comment and smiled at Jenny. "How are you?" They asked at the same time. Grinning, Melanie answered first. "I'm good."

"I've been better but I've also been worse." Jenny shrugged.

"Lori," Trish called out, "get Mel a wine cooler."

Wine cooler? She mouthed the question to Carla who only shrugged.

"Okay, but we're out of Strawberry Breeze."

Melanie tried not to laugh while recalling the last time she'd thought of a wine cooler. High school graduation. Her friend Vanessa had bribed an adult to buy a six-pack they took to Joseph Soto's party. The coolers never made it … they were mugged by masked classmates running naked down the street.

"How are you holding up?" Melanie asked, draping her arm across Carla's shoulder.

"Really happy to see you." Carla's voice dropped to a growl.

"I thought it was the bride who was supposed to be stressed." Melanie said, squeezing Carla's arm.

"She is," she lifted her brows in a conspiratorial gesture.

"Mel do you know Lori?" Trish called out from the bathroom. "She's a masseuse for the team."

"Massage therapist," Lori corrected. "I get to touch male bodies for a living." Lori grinned wickedly, handing Melanie a Fuzzy Navel wine cooler.

"Not a bad job," Melanie said, raising the bottle in thanks.

"I'd do it for free," Trish said, reentering the room and drying her hands on her white pants.

"Easy girl, you're getting hitched in a couple of days," Lori reminded Trish. "My job isn't *all* glamour. Remember I've got the coaches, too." Her expression was enough to paint the picture.

"Mel was one of my college roommates. She's the one who tricked me into dating Jace. He calls her Angel and I owe all my happiness to her."

The room filled with *awes!*

Melanie held up her cooler. "A toast to Trish and Jace, may your love last eternally."

"Thank you," Trish bowed. "Can you believe we're in Las Freakin' Vegas for my wedding?!"

"Speaking of which," Melanie asked looking from Trish to Carla. "Don't we need to prepare for the big day?"

Carla nodded with a look that was filled with frustration.

"But," Trish said, "the resort takes care of almost everything. I bought one of the packages."

"Yes, but you aren't walking down the aisle in the nude. Are you?"

Melanie looked over at Trish and had to weigh the possibility.

"No, you silly worry wart. There's a bridal boutique downstairs."

Carla gave Melanie a scrunched up, scolding glance and silently pleaded for her to do something.

"Let's go see what they've got." Melanie said, taking a pull from her super-sweet beverage. *Wow. I don't know if I'm tipsy or on the verge of a sugar high.*

"Should we go now?" Trish asked the room. "Kara doesn't get in for another hour."

"So?" Lori asked. "It's your wedding, not your sister's."

"I know, but," Trish looked around, her hyped-up manner broken, "If I buy a gown it means I'm getting married."

"You already are." Jenny giggled. "We're in friggin' Vegas."

"It's a dress," Melanie said in a calming voice. "It's a good thing, marrying Jace is a good thing."

"Yeah." Trish nodded, holding a fearful eye contact with Melanie. "You're right. You're right. Nothing to be freaked about." The swig that emptied an almost full bottle of fake wine said otherwise but Melanie wasn't about to argue.

"I'm going to drop my stuff off in the room and run a comb through my hair before we check out the gowns." She laughed and sent Trish a wink.

"It's not so bad, your hair, it's growing on me." Trish studied

Melanie's head. "Do you think you could get extensions by Thursday?"

"No," Melanie darted into the hall before Trish could talk her into anything.

"Oh, and our room…" Carla raised her thin brows. "I tried to get us into a suite but Trish said it wasn't any of our weddings so we had to stick with a standard."

"She was joking," Melanie said as Carla slipped her key card in and out of the slot then pushed open the door.

"She wasn't."

The room was small for three women, two beds, one dresser and a table. The bathroom counter was already crowded with cosmetics.

"It's nice." The view overlooked the pools. "Cozy."

"Thank God you're here." Carla groaned. Using the Lord's name in vain was as foul-mouthed as she ever ventured.

"Car's been trying for hours to get the ball rolling." Jenny added. "But you know how Trish can be."

In college Jenny had been above-average pretty. She had thick blonde hair that bounced weightlessly no matter how long she'd worn it, plus sea blue eyes and a curvy figure that made her popular with the boys. Unfortunately, time hadn't been kind. She'd married and had three kids with her high-school sweetheart, Ryan. He'd cheated, she'd forgiven … he'd cheated, she'd retaliated, and now Melanie was unsure about the current status of their relationship. Treading on eggshells, Melanie skirted any negative conversation. She'd been down that road and had no intention of a repeat journey.

"Is that all you brought?" Carla asked, giving Melanie's bag a dirty look.

Melanie looked at the giant Samsonite that bulged out of the narrow closet.

"You can have a bed to yourself, Car and I will share," Jenny offered in a way that made Melanie felt excluded.

"I don't mind sharing," Melanie said, turning her back on the tension to close the drapes.

"Who cares about that?" Carla said, exasperated. "What are we going to do about Trish and this wedding?" she paused to read Melanie's expression. "It's going to be a fiasco. Only like forty people have responded and she's booked the room for a hundred and fifty. Half the people in attendance will be in the wedding. She has no dress, we have no dresses."

"Well, we all get to make our own mistakes," Jenny said. "Let her make hers, Car."

"Easier said." Carla nodded, as Trish's bellow outside their door was too loud to ignore.

"Mel," Carla held on to Melanie's elbow, keeping her back. "I know Trish is happy right now but," she lowered her voice, "that can change in the blink of the eye. The wedding has sent her emotions to the outer edges."

"Okay," Melanie answered, not sure how to reply. "Am I supposed to do something?" Carla's stammer wasn't an answer. "You really are a silly worry wart."

They caught up with the rest of the party as the elevator opened.

"I just got a call from Kara," Trish informed them. "Her plane landed and she's on her way to the hotel. I told her to meet us at the bridal shop. Isn't this working out perfectly? Now we're just waiting for Courtney," Trish said with an odd huff. "She got a modeling job and can't be here until tomorrow."

"Six bridesmaids?" Melanie asked quietly to Carla.

"I wanted twelve. But I guess with a shotgun wedding a girl has to make sacrifices."

Shotgun? "Trish, are you pregnant?" Melanie asked stunned and doing her best not to cast a questioning glance to her abdomen but getting a mean elbow to her ribs from Carla.

"No! God no! Why would you ask that? Do I look fat?" Her wide eyes were filled with horror.

"You said shotgun and..." Melanie scrambled to retract her question. "It usually means that you *have* to get married."

"No, it doesn't," Trish snarled. The emotional build-up was almost visible beneath her creamy pale skin. "Does it?" She yelled with piercing eyes.

Whoa, Melanie thought standing her ground in front of a volatile Trish.

"Well, does it?" Trish wasn't letting this go.

"It's a shotgun because..." Melanie started.

"But not always," Jenny added quickly, at the sound of Trish sucking in all the available air.

"Oh my God, I told everyone we were having a shotgun wedding! People think I'm prego? Oh, my poor dad." Trish's hands covered her face and time stood still. Her fingers lifted, her eyes showing from the gaps between her spread out fingers. Dragging her hands down her face, she stopped and howled. "That is hysterical!" Trish was laughing and everyone breathed.

"I feel like I walked into the Twilight Zone," Melanie whispered to Carla when the elevator opened to the shopping level.

"Told you."

CHAPTER NINE

The mall was bright and shiny and held every overpriced brand a girl could dream of. As they approached the exclusive bridal boutique that was squeezed between a swimsuit shop and a store of designer bags, Trish was stalling. Staring up at the sparkling window.

"You okay?" Melanie was concerned.

"Mel?" Trish said, squeezing her bicep to hold her back from the others. "I need to talk to you. Go ahead," she called, "we'll catch up." Trish inhaled a few deep breaths. "Will you look at this place?" she asked in a hushed tone, gazing up at the wedding party poised for the big moment. "Look at them. Aren't they beautiful?"

"They're mannequins."

"I know. But they look so peaceful. I'm not that peaceful."

"They're plastic and you only have plastic boobs. Probably makes a difference," Melanie said, gazing at the contented face of the bride.

"I'm serious! Damn it!" Melanie held her breath and tightened her lips. "You're being too cavalier with my life."

"I don't know what you want from me," Melanie said, exasperated.

"I want you to tell me if I should marry Jace." Her words shot out fast, bumping into each other.

"What? Why would I do that?"

"Why not?"

Melanie examined the lines along Trish's forehead and the fear behind her blue eyes. "You're really this unsure?" she questioned.

"I don't know if it's cold feet or a sign from above. How can I tell?"

"Why don't you ask someone who's been married? Carla? Jenny? I have no idea."

"Because," she threw her arms up in the air and turned away from the display. "They'll just tell me I have cold feet so that I'll make the same miserable mistake they did. You're not married and you're totally happy."

"Well, happy is a strong word."

"I used to be totally happy. Before Jace, I was totally happy." Trish's lower lip jutted out. "Now I don't know what I am."

"Would you feel worse if you called off the wedding?" Melanie suggested.

"I can't call it off. Jace would be heartbroken. Jeez, Mel. You're supposed to tell me that I have cold feet. Do you really think I shouldn't marry Jason?"

Shit! "I," she stammered, "I only wanted you to search your heart for what you know is right."

Trish's brows separated and pulled in again. "Aw, that is so sweet and smart. I knew I could count on you. You made me see for myself!" She paused, staring up at the plastic humans. "I don't want to call off the wedding."

"Let's go try on some dresses," her face buried in Trish's embrace.

Sometimes I am really good, she thought reaching for the chrome door handles, *even if it is on accident.*

Inside the glass doors of the boutique, a faint breeze of rose scented air was welcoming. Classical music played overhead and the muted lighting made everything look better. There were hundreds of gowns and, to Melanie, they all looked alike.

One side of the store was for tuxedos, bridesmaids' dresses and an array of accessories, veils, shoes, bags, garters and toasting glasses.

"Hello," an older woman with a fresh-out-of-the-beauty-parlor up-do greeted them. Her smile friendly and her knowledgeable eyes fell squarely on Trish. "How can I help you?"

"Well, I'm looking for a dress," Trish answered, her gaze traveling over the room.

"Congratulations," she said, her smile not faltering. "You've come to the right place. My name is Yolie and if you give me some details about your wedding I can help you find your dream gown."

"Well, I'm getting married here on the terrace on Thursday," Trish answered, looking through Yolie to the wall of white.

"Thursday? Well, those gowns over there need to be ordered but the ones over here," She waved to a rounder in the back of the room, "we have in stock." Trish's gaze flickered to her options and quickly back to the wall. "Because of the timing of your wedding we are limited." Yolie, in her beige polyester pantsuit and paisley scarf, attempted to back-pedal. "There are at least seventy-five gowns to choose from so limited isn't quite the right word."

"But there's no law that says I can't look at these," she sang, already on her way, "right?"

"Of course, but..." Yolie agreed, chasing after Trish. "We don't want you falling in love with an impossibility."

Melanie went to the in-stock rounder and browsed. White dresses. She passed through the entire selection before looking up to see Trish ordering gowns pulled down from the forbidden rack. Yolie had given up. She nodded to the assistant with the grappling hook who was following Trish's directions.

"What is she doing?" Carla asked.

"Getting ready for heartache, I think. You heard Yolie, those aren't available."

Five forbidden dresses were carted behind Trish as she was led into a dressing room.

Yolie gathered the bridesmaids. "Ms. Warner will be presenting the gowns in the viewing lounge. If you wish to follow me we have snacks and champagne available. And may I suggest that you not encourage any of these gowns. I have chosen three others that resemble Ms. Warner's style and can be altered by Thursday." Yolie walked and talked, mumbling as the short corridor opened up. "Nothing less attractive than an unhappy bride."

Melanie gave Carla a smirk, which her friend returned with a raise of her brows. The viewing lounge was fitted with gray, semi-circle leather couches that faced pedestals placed in the center of an alcove of mirrors.

Lori slid onto the couch beside Melanie. "Hi Mel, Trish talks about you so much I feel as though I already know you." Her grin was bashful behind a spray-on tan that accentuated every wrinkle.

"Why does that scare me?" Melanie chuckled, knowing that Lori must know every secret.

"Because Trish blabs," Jenny snorted.

"No. It's mostly good." Lori laughed and her youth returned. "What do you think is happening back there?" She asked looking at her watch. "It's been like a half hour."

"No telling," Carla said, leaned into Melanie to whisper, "If Yolie didn't look so tough I'd think Trish had chewed her up and spit her out."

Melanie reached for her vibrating phone as a tall woman with long, slick brown hair stared from beneath the archway.

"Am I in the right place?"

"Yes. Hi, Kara. We're just waiting for Trish to come out. You probably don't remember me, I'm Carla." She stood, cartoonishly tiny, stretching out her hand to Trish's younger sister.

Melanie had seen pictures of Kara. She was pretty, not stunning. Not Trish.

From the back of the room Melanie answered her call. "Got a location?"

"They're going for broke." Jack said, Melanie growled under her breath as he informed her the blackjack ring was setting their sights on her casino.

"Jesus, Mary and Joseph. Jack, that's where I'm staying." Melanie blew out a short breath. "That's going to create the need for some finagling."

"Figure it out, because you have orientation tomorrow evening at five and you go on the floor tomorrow night."

"Not possible." She couldn't miss the party, Trish would absolutely kill her. "You'll have to fix it."

"Here she is." Yolie's tone heftier than it had been on their arrival.

"I'll see what I can do." She could tell by his tone he was concentrating. "When's the ceremony?"

"Thursday afternoon. I've got to go." She ended the call breathless and moving toward Carla. "I cannot believe I'm saying this," her eyes hadn't left Trish, "but she looks like an angel."

Trish paraded slowly into the room and up the steps of the pedestal. The gown was strapless, trumpet style – Melanie had been educated in the proper terms by the chart on the wall.

On most women the white feathers covering the bodice would've been overkill, but not on Trish. Her, they fit. The bottom of the silky gown was less avian. Crystal beading sewn into the fabric glinted casting a rainbow of color.

"What do you guys think?" Trish asked, twisting in front of the mirrors. "I can't find a thing wrong with it. Oh, I love it!" She lifted the hem and stroked the silky fabric. "Don't you? Isn't it perfect?" Her fingers stroked the feathers at her chest. "This is the one." Her gaze shot up. "Kara! You're here! What do you think?" Trish twirled. "I tried a bunch of other ones on in the dressing room. Two were terrible and the third was so hideous I didn't even bother." Trish looked out into the room from the mirror. "Okay, Yolie. This is the one I want."

"Very good." Yolie said with tight lips. "If we order today we can have it here in eight months."

"Thursday," Trish said, gazing at her reflection.

"That's impossible. I already showed you which dresses we had for immediate wear," she said, the calm exterior cracking in irritation. "There are many others just as lovely as this one, let me show you. You'll fall in love with one of them, too. I promise." Her beige Easy Spirits squeaked as she moved from the carpeting to the tile.

"Nope. I really want this one," Trish said, adjusting her breasts. "It's sexy but not in a gross way. Yolie, there has to be a way."

"No."

"Isn't the customer always right?" She tried again, this time giving the woman her full attention.

"No."

"Please." Trish put her palms together in a begging prayer stance.

"I would love to help you but I am not a miracle worker. There are plenty of other…"

Trish's ears were the first to show signs of an explosion. "I want this one."

"Wait," Melanie said, quickly raising her hand to stop Trish before the rampage. "There has to be something."

"I want *this* dress, Mel. Don't you all think I should have *this* dress?"

Kara jumped and clapped to demonstrate her support. "You look gorgeous!"

Melanie erased the glare off her face. "Stop," she scolded Kara and looked to Yolie. "Okay, as a compromise, what about *this* dress? It fits her and it only needs minor alterations."

"No way. Mel, this is a display." Trish grunted. "I am not wearing some dress that's rubbed on someone's sweaty pits. No. I want my own fresh one. Can't we call the designer?"

"In Italy?" Yolie snorted.

"I don't know if you've heard … but they've got phones there now."

"Trish. Not. Helpful," Melanie reprimanded, trying to keep control. "Yolie," Melanie said calmly. "What if we did try calling the designer? Don't shake your head so fast. Hear me out … is there somewhere we can talk?"

Yolie sighed, rolled her eyes and snapped her fingers. "Gabrielle, get her veils to try on," Yolie growled, stopping at the back wall and looked at Melanie. "What is it you want?"

"Car," Melanie said, diverting her tiny friend away from her conversation. "Could you make sure Trish doesn't go ballistic?"

"Are you sure you don't want me with you?"

"I'm more concerned about Trish. Mood swings, which is next?"

Carla looked over her shoulder toward Trish – who had finished pouting and was admiring herself. "You've got a point."

"Yolie, how about you show me those other gowns," Melanie said, leading the older woman out of the room and out of earshot.

"This way. There isn't anything I can do. It's not like I've got a magic wand."

On the showroom floor, the coast was clear and Melanie was going to seize her opportunity. "Look, I know Trish can be..." Melanie searched for the right description. "Bossy. But mostly it's the wedding."

"I see it all the time."

"Then you'll help?"

"There. Isn't. Anything. I. Can. Do," she said, snapping off each word. "She's going to have to select something else."

"You've seen this before ... Tell me, how am I supposed to change her mind?"

"It's not pretty. She'll cry to get her way, she'll storm out ... check around at all the other boutiques then tomorrow she'll come back and take a look at the available rack."

Melanie listened. That was one possibility.

"Or," Melanie said, "what if," lowering her voice. "What if you sell her that gown ... dry cleaned, altered and," she shrugged, "with a surcharge for shipping? Could something like that be arranged?"

"Lie?" Her brown eyes turned owl-like. "That would be unethical."

Melanie searched the wide gaze. "An overjoyed client with the wedding gown of her dreams. There's nothing unethical about that."

"I couldn't," she said, her mouth pulled into a ball and shifting from side to side.

"Sure you could. Listen, she wants the dress. She looks beautiful in it and she's just being stubborn about the fresh comment. This scenario is a win-win."

"Well," she pulled at a strand of hair at the back of her neck as she spoke. "We do have plenty of inventory and sales are down." Yolie yanked harder on her hair and turned a scrutinizing gaze toward Melanie. "How do I know you won't report me?"

"All I care about is Trish. Besides it was my idea and as long as the dress isn't damaged, what do I care? You have my word." She raised her three Girl Scout fingers. "Agreed?"

Yolie's darting glances were a novice mistake. "Let's do it."

"Go, make a pretend phone call to the designer in Europe and come back with the good news. But Yolie, that dress had better be like new."

"I would never jeopardize the quality of my dresses. I have a reputation to uphold." Guilt flashed in her eyes and quickly was replaced by shame. "She'll never know the difference. It'll be pristine."

"Perfect," Melanie said. "I'll go tell her you're doing your best."

Yolie went to order dinner and Melanie returned to the lounge. Trish was leaning forward for Gabrielle to balance a tiara on her head.

"I'd fly to Italy tomorrow for this dress. What do we think of this veil?" Trish asked looking in the mirror to the group behind her. When she saw Melanie, hope filled her expression. "Well?"

"I like the veil."

"You know what I mean. Am I getting the dress?"

"Yolie is making a call. That's all I can promise."

"Thank you!" she said, maneuvering down the steps without

tripping. "I'm so glad you're here. I knew if anyone could talk sense into that stubborn woman, it was you." Melanie was lost in yards of silky fabric and sucked down a feather as Trish hugged her. "You are the best! I love you so much!"

"Hey, Trish, do you think we should be looking at bridesmaids' dresses?" Lori asked.

"Ooh, we just had a shipment for a party that cancelled. Would you like to see those?" Gabrielle asked, setting a veil on the arm of a hat rack.

Everyone held their breath and looked to Trish.

"Heck, yeah, bring those babies out," Trish said before pausing. "They're new right?"

"We just got them in this morning. I'll be right back."

She was gone only minutes before returning with a rolling closet and ten canary yellow dresses.

"Those are so pretty," Trish said. "Do you guys like them?"

"The color is called Lemon Custard and it goes with practically every skin tone. They're all different styles and sizes. All the girls in this wedding got to choose which type of dress they liked best."

"And the wedding was called off?"

"Yeah, happens nearly every day."

"Do you think that's a bad sign for my wedding if we buy these? Do you think they could be jinxed?" Trish asked, her panic rising after each word.

"No, it's a good omen," Jenny piped in quickly. "We're lucky. Otherwise, what would our options be?" she asked Gabrielle.

"Other than these ... you'd have to mix and match colors and styles. We have a few sky blue, periwinkle, burgundy and some pink ones for plus-sized women."

"We'll stick with the Lemon Custard," Lori said, shuffling through the dresses.

"These are the nicest," Gabrielle smoothly placed her body between Lori's grabby fingers and the row of gowns. Gathering up the various sizes, she gave each girl an appraising look.

"Courtney's about my size," Trish said. The seamstresses had already starting pinning the gown. "When I'm done here, I could try on hers."

"These three," Gabrielle said, rolling the rack to Melanie and Carla, "are the smallest. I think they'd work for either of you. I guess you can duke it out for the better one."

Melanie liked the strapless dress, with clean lines and a pleated pencil skirt with side pockets – even the golden color wasn't too bad. The other two dresses had big bows on the back and ruffles.

"You can have it Mel. I'm going to need alterations anyway," Carla offered.

Melanie smiled. "Let's try them on and see where we're at."

"What do you think?" Jenny asked, smushing down a puffy sleeve.

"Um," Melanie looked to the more politically correct Carla to finish.

"It's," Carla started, "terrible."

Jenny looked hurt for the nanosecond before she sputtered out a giggle. "It really is. Excuse me," she called to Gabrielle. "Are the sleeves essential, or could we take them off?"

"I don't think you should be laughing," Kara whispered, leaning in her bridesmaid dress to scold. "You know how sensitive Trish has been lately."

"She's right," Melanie stifled her grin but her eyes watered.

"Good. We don't want her feeling bad about these dresses." Kara stood upright and tried to flatten down the fabric.

"Why am I suddenly craving a banana split?" Carla sputtered as they entered the dressing room.

"There are just too many ruffles," Melanie complained quietly to Gabrielle.

"We can do something about those," Gabrielle said, pulling over a woman carrying pins between tight lips. She spoke to the woman in Spanish, spun Melanie around and pointed out the excessive material.

"No, I don't want even one ruffle," Melanie said, translating when they talked about keeping the one in the back.

Trish had tried on Courtney's dress and was wearing it as she darted across the room to whisper in Melanie's ear.

"Yolie's here. Do something."

Yolie turned out to be an incredible actress, charging an additional 45% of the retail price and laughing all the way to the bank. The daggers Melanie sent were greeted with a smile and a hoist of her brows to mid-forehead.

"Thank you!" Trish leaped in the air and hugged the wedding dress bandit. "You're amazing. We're buying all our bridesmaids dresses here, shoes and everything."

"I'm just so happy and surprised I was able to make this happen for you," Yolie said. "I see Gabrielle has fitted your entire party. Very good." She nodded. "So, separate bills?"

Outside the glass walls of the bridal shop Trish stopped.

"You guys," she said getting everyone's attention with her soft voice. "I just want to thank you for being here with me. I don't know how I'd get through all of this without you." She smiled and Melanie could see the real Trish. "You guys are all my best friends and I'm sorry if I haven't … if I've," she sighed, "If I've been not nice. I really do love you."

"We know, Sweetie," Carla said and Jenny concurred.

"It's just this wedding," Trish said, wiping at the moisture under her eyes. "It's sort of making me crazy. And I know it, I just can't stop myself." Her long arms took in as many friends as she could reach for a group hug. "Please, promise me that if I do or say anything to upset you, you'll automatically forgive me."

Melanie, who was pressed into Jenny and Lori, didn't like the sound of that request.

"Absolutely!" Kara said, hopping.

Melanie wiggled out of the cluster hug just as the group began to bounce.

"Thank you." Trish gave a giant squeeze. "I just love you all so much!"

"We love you, too," Lori cried.

Melanie tugged Carla out, clutched her wrist and turned it to read her watch. "It was like a time warp in there." She said, blinking to clear her vision.

"I feel dizzy." Carla rubbed her eyes.

◦◦◦◦

The hotel/casino was completely self-contained and after a long discussion about which restaurant to hit up, they were seated in two booths, menus in hand and wine glasses filled.

"I'm going to order the biggest bowl of pasta in the place," Jenny said, putting down the menu. "I'm starving."

"I'm going to eat fast," Melanie said. "I've got my eye on a game of craps."

"Did you see the Mercedes they're giving away?"

Melanie laughed, thinking that they were hardly *giving it away* – she'd calculated the odds.

"At the slots?" Jenny gasped. "I want that car!"

"I almost think we should skip dinner," Carla suggested, biting her lip as they all looked at each other.

"Do you think we could?" Jenny asked, grinning.

Melanie swallowed down her wine, folded her napkin in a sloppy mess, set it on the table along with a twenty and scooted out of the booth.

"I'm with you," Jenny said, following. "I can get pasta anywhere."

"Hey, where are you guys going?" Kara asked, her eyes on the abandoned table.

"You're not leaving, are you?" Trish's forehead was crinkled. "Is it because I wasn't paying you enough attention?"

Carla grinned. "No, Sweetie. We're going to try our luck with the most gorgeous car God ever created."

"You aren't going to eat?"

Melanie reached for a bread stick. "Delicious."

"All right, I guess we can meet up later." Trish bowed, allowing them to leave.

"I'll even take you for a spin when I get the keys," Jenny teased.

The car was situated at the entrance, rotating on a pedestal and lighted to perfection. Surrounding the two-seater with red leather interior was a row of machines. Melanie, Carla and Jenny made a first pass around – only one was open.

"One of you had better take it," Melanie said.

"These are dollar slots." Jenny stated the obvious. "I won't be able to play for very long here. And we've still got," she counted on her fingers, "two days! Wow, that sounds expensive."

"Well, I'm going for it," Carla said, claiming the empty chair.

"You'll find me at the nickel slots."

"Good luck," Melanie said, then turned to soak up the atmosphere. She loved the feel of being lost in a crowd of strangers.

She headed toward the center of the main room where rows of tables were partitioned from the machines by ropes. It was early and the fashion hadn't moved to the outrageous. Melanie filled an empty seat at a Roulette table, traded a few bills for chips and ordered a White Russian. Her concentration remained on the blackjack dealer to her right.

She played the steep minimum bet as the flow of pitiable gamblers changed as frequently as her drinks. The stacks in front of her grew and shrank in a literal display of her fluctuating fortune.

She was down to her last stack of chips when Carla tapped her shoulder excitedly. "Trish is at a craps table and is about to roll the dice."

"Cash out," Melanie said to the dealer.

Trish was at a high-stakes table, decked out in micro-mini skirt, a sequined blouse and squealing. Everyone but she and Carla had changed into showy Las Vegas eveningwear. People had stopped, curious about the commotion.

"I don't know how to play!" Trish exclaimed in the flirty dumb-blonde voice Melanie had heard a million times.

"It's easy," said the middle-aged sports jacket with salt-and-pepper hair. "I'll teach you."

"Are you flirting with me?" Trish scolded. "I'm getting married in a few days." She lifted her ring finger on her left hand. "See."

"I don't want to own you, I just want to borrow you for the night."

"You're terrible," she slapped his arm. "Look, I've got one, two, three single friends. If you're nice, maybe one of them will give you the time."

Melanie squeezed out a spot against the congested table. Her hips to the polished wood, she checked out the placement of the bets and wagered in favor of Trish's good luck.

"Mel," Trish whispered. "What do I want to do?"

"Come-out with a seven or an eleven."

"Is that all?" she asked, the right side of her face scrunched up in a knot.

There wasn't enough time to distinguish if it was sarcasm. "Just roll, make sure you toss the die hard enough to hit the other end."

"Here goes, ya'll!" Trish hollered and the crowd hollered back.

Melanie held her breath, nervous. Though she doubted anyone would turn on Trish, not with her cleavage pouring out of her blouse. She could crap out a dozen times and these men would still throw their money down.

First roll out she hit a seven. A virgin shooter was always fun.

"That's good, right?"

A short man with an open collar beside Trish was the first to respond. "It's exactly how I like it. Do it again, Baby."

"Mel," Trish called, "is the porn star right?"

"He is." Melanie smiled and tilted to get a better view of the man. He had a cute face, hairy chest beneath an unbuttoned collar. His sultry presence screamed sex.

Trish was on a streak, shooting a nine series before missing her point and rolling a seven out. Pass Line betters made money off of her beginners luck. Melanie was one of them.

"That was super fun!" Lori said, collecting her chips.

"It's only the beginning, my friend," Trish said, moving the party to the nightclub and taking a few male tagalongs with her.

The strobe lighting bounced off the walls and flashed over the cages that were suspended from the ceiling above the dance floor. It was advertised as the most spectacular club in Las Vegas.

"Isn't this great?" Trish asked, grinning. "But you look like a hobo. Can't you go upstairs and change?"

"No," Melanie shook her head, uncompromisingly. She knew her cream-colored lace tank top and blue jeans were too casual but, "I've already had to threaten two drunks and I'm not even dressed like a professional."

"It's part of the experience. And it's a compliment."

"No, it's really not. They weren't quality drunks," Melanie said, grabbing Carla's hand. Trish would never scold Carla into changing. She wore her sour, 'stay the hell away' expression like a favorite sweater.

"Let's get something tropical to drink," Carla said happily.

The frozen daiquiris went down like liquid candy and by the fourth Melanie was feeling loose. The bridal party was sweating it up on the dance floor, partnered with unknown men while Melanie led a reluctant Carla onto the mix.

"Sexy," Trish said, making it a threesome and wiggling down to a squat before slowly rubbing her body as she rose.

"No, I refuse." Carla stood with her arms at her sides and her eyes darting. "Someone could be taking pictures."

Trish laughed, bent low and kissed Carla on the cheek. "You're funny."

"Mel, do something," Carla growled when Trish didn't stop.

"What am I supposed to do?" she laughed.

"Kiss me back," Trish teased, pushing her butt into Carla's side.

"Trish!"

"Maybe it's time we get back to the room," Melanie tried, but was drowned out by Kara and Lori joining the circle of female dancers. "Car, if you play along Trish will get bored."

"I can't."

"Try," Melanie encouraged. "Come on. Dance."

"Trish makes everything sexual." She grunted.

Melanie bit down on her cheek to stop from bursting out, the moisture from her eyes leaked out as Carla bent her knees, completely uncomfortable.

The die-hard gamblers were still glued to their seats as the girls staggered to the elevators. Melanie collapsed on the bed, squished the pillow into a fluffy mass and passed out.

An hour later, Carla and Jenny were breathing rhythmically in the darkness. The slim line between the curtains was already showing signs of the rising sun. Melanie sealed the curtains and gulped down a glass of tap water. It'd been a long time since she'd indulged, and the spinning room was a bad sign.

I've got to build up my tolerance, she thought as her head hit the pillow.

"Melanie, wake up." *I just fell asleep.*

Fingers were pressing into Melanie's shoulder and shaking her out of unconsciousness.

"Mel! It's ten."

"A.m. or p.m.?"

"A.m. Trish had an appointment with the wedding planner at nine. Do you think she made it?"

Melanie smiled and squinted gazing with blurry eyes at Carla.

"You didn't wake up. What are the chances Trish did? Let's get some breakfast and see if we can reschedule for her."

CHAPTER TEN

"Did you see that cabana boy?" Jenny asked, spreading out her towel on the lounge. "He looks just like Ryan did in high school."

Melanie lowered her sunglasses to get a better look at the tan body builder with biceps that stretched the elastic on the armbands of his logoed polo shirt.

"I know Ryan doesn't look like that now."

"Not even in college," Melanie answered, resuming her position on the lounge.

"He did, too."

Melanie took another look, "If you say so." She flipped her sunglasses over her eyes. "Can you believe Trish rented this tent and she's not even here to enjoy it?"

The cabana was a peaceful indulgence. Situated on the lawn beside one of the three large pools on the hotel property. Snaking between the pools was a river that carried inner tubers on a lazy journey. The poolside chairs had minimal shade and the glaring sun had bleached the world of color. But inside the yellow and brown striped tent was a ceiling fan, cushioned chaises, a table and chairs and a muscled cabana boy to bring food, drinks and smoothies.

"Car, you and I need to stay out of the sun," Melanie said. "Our gowns are strapless – well, mine has one strap, but tan lines would drive Trish over the edge."

"I really hope she's up by three. Should we have made the appointment for later?" Carla asked.

"It's noon and when I spoke with Kara, she said they were starting to stir." Melanie yawned. "Besides if she bails this time, we'll pick what we want and tell her there was no other choice."

Of course Trish was late. But once she was there, she was unbearable. Melanie twirled a sterling silver serving knife as Trish debated every minute detail. Time was ticking closer to five and each wavering uncertainty was zapping Melanie of her patience.

"Car," Melanie whispered, "I gotta go."

"You can't." Her glare harsher than the desert sun.

"I have to."

"What are you guys whispering about?" Trish asked. "I'm sorry if my wedding plans are boring you."

"Trish," Melanie said, taking a breath, "you're spending a half hour agreeing to a decision that has no alternative. There's only one band, nothing to decide. Roses and lilies, perfect. Stop asking everyone what they think and make a damn decision. There's only one choice of cake. You can't rethink what flavor, filling, icing and how many tiers. There's only one! Photographer? There's no choice. The meal. Chicken or salmon? Rice or pasta? You are making me crazy." She stared for a heartbeat as she realized she'd angered Bridezilla. An apology was forming but Trish's response came first.

"Fine," Trish said to the hostess, who miraculously still had a full head of hair. "Just give me whatever you have left."

Shit! Melanie breathed. "You know I don't mean that."

"It's exactly what you meant." Trish was up and out the door. "Jace and the others are arriving soon and my garden party starts in an hour. I hope it isn't too boring for you."

Everyone ran out of the room, chasing to comfort Trish. Melanie inhaled while staring at the ceiling, alone in the room but for the hostess. She covered her mouth, pulled down her skin and sighed.

"Thank you." The woman smiled and picked up her portfolio. "I'll get her the best we've got at no additional charge. It's worth not having to waste another hour of my life," she added before walking out and leaving Melanie completely alone and feeling bad. But only for a minute – it was ten to five.

In the basement she and four other new employees were given their uniforms, lockers, badges and handed over to a trainer.

"My name is Boyd and I'm supposed to make sure you know the ropes," he said, taking her through basement hallways to a secure door. Where a mini-replica had been set up like on the casino floor.

"Okay, let's see what you've got," Boyd said, taking a seat on the gambler side of a blackjack table.

Melanie dealt out the deck. She'd watched the dealers the night before and had learned their order of things.

"Pretty good but, here, let me show you," Boyd said. They exchanged spots and he showed her the secrets of the trade and where the cameras and pit bosses had the best angle. "And check this out." He was smooth with the cards. "It's not necessary but it's fun."

"Show me again," Melanie said, practicing through another deck.

By the time she made it back to the room, everything had changed.

"Oh God, I'm sorry," Melanie apologized, walking into her room and nearly bumping into Ryan wearing only a towel. Thoughts of the cabana boy filtered through her imagination … *nope,* she thought, *no resemblance to the man by the pool.*

"It's okay," Jenny and Ryan both said. The tension was high and it wasn't sexual.

"I'm just going to grab … you know, never mind. What I'm wearing is fine." She said, backing out.

"Mel, wait." Jenny ran to catch Melanie in the hall. "Do you think you can find somewhere else to sleep tonight? Ted's here, too, and he and Carla have a room. It would be awkward with you here."

"Oh, yeah." Her bag was still packed and littering the closet floor.

"You don't mind, do you?" Jenny asked.

Hell, yeah, I mind. "It's fine," Melanie said, taking an unnecessary step back into the room as her duffle bag was placed into her arms. "Okay. I'll see you down there … maybe." The door closed. "Or not." She stopped at the Bella Suite to drop off her things, deciding to check into a new room after an appearance at the party. She was already running late.

Trish had rented the south lawn. The yellow and brown striped tents they'd used during the day were included in the festivities. The lounges were replaced with tables and chairs and there was a buffet with hors d'oeuvres, fresh fruit and sandwiches. The setting sun cooled the arid weather by a few degrees and the bar serving icy beverages was popular.

Lighted paths guided the way to the far corner from the pools to a fire pit. Big round logs surrounded the sand and set up as benches. Silver pails, filled with all the necessities for s'mores, were placed beside each log bench.

More than seventy people had arrived and she was grateful for the turnout. But the number of people she knew was limited. She'd been bear hugged by Jason and taken around to meet his parents and younger brother, Ian. Trish and Carla were nowhere to be seen and the conversation with Jason ran out quickly.

With icy fingertips she looked at the groups of people, deciding where she and her beer should go next. The fire pit, for some inexplicable reason, was empty. She chose solitude and hoped it was cooler than it looked.

"Mind if I join you?"

"Not at all," she said, just having sat. "Are you going to play me a song?" She asked checking out the Taylor guitar strapped across his back.

"I get that a lot. I was hoping you weren't going to ask. It's just that I don't know how to play."

"You carry it around to confuse women?" Melanie asked, checking out the calluses on the tips of his fingers.

"Look at how well it works." His smile was nice as he opened his arms to show how many women were attracted to a guy with a guitar. Melanie looked at the empty spaces. "At least I got you."

"I was here first. And I'm here for the chocolate," Melanie said, "Sorry."

"That's it! I'm getting rid of this thing! I've been rejected for the last time." He tugged the strap over his head. "Do you want it?"

"No," she laughed. "I know you can play."

"A little. How about you?"

"I wish, I started to learn about a year and a half ago but life sort of got in the way."

"Show me," he said, handing her the instrument.

"Seriously?" she frowned. "I really only know one warm up."

"Seriously." He nodded.

Melanie wiped her palms off on her jeans and took the guitar. Drawing in a breath, Melanie played a simple tune she'd found somewhere online.

"That's about it," she said, looking up. He'd actually been watching her. She blushed, embarrassed.

"That's nice. What is it?"

"Not sure. But it doesn't require my disobedient fingers to play a cord," she said, showing him how contorted her left hand looked as she strummed a C chord.

"Sort of looks like you've got a disability. Let me see if I can help." He shifted to the edge of his log and angled his guitar so she was holding it only with her right hand. His fingers were warm as he took her left hand and gave it a light massage, flexing her fingers back and rubbing the pad of her thumb. "You've got small hands. Good hands. Flexible, long fingers."

"Thanks," she replied. If she'd felt any sense that he was enjoying himself too much, she'd have taken her long, flexible fingers and headed for higher ground.

"I'm Nate, by-the-way." He tuned her hand around and gave her a left-handed shake.

"Melanie."

"Anyone ever told you that you're gorgeous?"

"Not in a long time," she said, surprised by her smile that came with the compliment.

"That's really kind of you," Nate said, his grin reaching his brown eyes.

"What is?" she asked, confused.

"That you spend so much time with the blind – or is it the clinically insane? Because you should be hearing that every day." Neither had blinked or looked away as he spoke. "Do you know the bride or the groom?" he asked, still holding her hand. "Or better yet, are you crashing the party?"

"I went to college with Trish. How about you?"

"No I went to USC, but I am Jace's accountant."

She swallowed a gulp of beer down the wrong pipe and coughed. "An accountant? That, I would not have guessed." She eyed his faded T-shirt, torn at the shoulder, the red Vans on his sockless feet and the tattoo of a dolphin above his ankle.

"You haven't even seen me in my hat," he said, placing a straw Panama Jack hat over his thick, dark hair.

"Now you look like an electrician," she laughed.

"You're kind of cocky for a girl who can't hold a C chord," he said, placing her fingers carefully over the right strings on the correct frets. "Now try it."

She did.

"No. You've got to lift up on the tips of your fingers or you'll mess the whole thing up." He readjusted. "You really do have obstinate fingers. How about we try your right hand?" He said, flipping the guitar over so that the whole thing was backwards.

"Can you really play like this?"

"I don't know. I've never tried. Because," he looked up at her with laughing brown eyes, "it's ridiculous."

"Melanie," Trish scolded, suddenly hovering over Nate's side. "Stop fooling around and let the professionals do the playing."

"Professional?" She squinted at Nate.

"Didn't he tell you? He's in a band, has a CD and how many instruments can you play?"

"Two."

"Wow," Melanie grinned, "two whole instruments? Which two? Because you have me holding this guitar upside down."

"Well, now my reputation is shot. I guess I'm down to just playing a mean ukulele."

"Don't believe a word he's saying, Mel. Nate is talented."

"I thought he was Jace's accountant," she said, reevaluating the man who convincingly presented himself as a potential beach bum.

"Oh, he is. But his heart belongs to music. Right?"

"It used to, but I just fell in love with Melanie."

"Be careful, she's a heartbreaker." Obviously forgiveness hadn't entered Trish's heart, her tone was chafing and abrasive.

"Really?" he asked. Melanie felt her appeal-o-meter skyrocket as the mood in his dark brown eyes change.

"Really." Trish nodded gravely, missing the exchange. "Mel, can I steal you away for a second?"

"Promise to bring her back," Nate replied to Trish's curt request.

"Are you on the market?" Trish zoned-in on Nate, puzzled. "I thought you were a permanent bachelor. If not, I've got a couple of really super prospects for you."

"Jokes, Trish, all jokes. Besides, my heart belongs to only one." He shifted to look at Melanie. "So, why aren't you a super prospect?"

"I've got issues. Been locked up with the clinically insane, remember?"

Trish sighed. "Mel?"

"Someone's in trouble and for once it isn't me," Nate whispered as Trish walked away, expecting Melanie to follow.

"I screwed up earlier. But, trust me, if I'm around you've lost your top spot as troublemaker," Melanie said, standing to retreat to the sidelines with Trish.

Melanie tracked the trail of Trish's stilettos aerating the lawn. Her stomach tightened as she reached Trish with her arms crossed and her weight placed squarely on one very angry, long leg.

Best to get this over with, she thought. "Trish, I'm really sorry about today."

"You were incredibly rude."

"I know." *That's why I'm apologizing.* "I was totally out of line and I'm sorry." Melanie was prepared to grovel but Trish cut her off before she had a chance.

"I was worried about telling you this but now," Trish's strapless maxi dress lowered an inch with her shrug, "now I don't care."

"Okay," Melanie sucked in a restraining breath and looked up at Trish who, with her heels vs. Melanie's bare feet, dramatized the differences in height. Trish's gleeful expression was one Melanie hadn't seen before.

"It's about Jace's best man."

"Ian. I met him earlier." *This is about the wedding, about the bridesmaids' line-up.* Melanie already knew Trish was favoring Courtney for maid of honor. "I'm okay that you're choosing Courtney."

"Yeah, well, Ian isn't exactly the best man."

"No?" she said, taking a moment to readjust her thinking. The chill of something on the horizon broke through the sizzling heat.

"You promised not to get mad," Trish said, her stance and tone shifting to something less aggressive.

"I didn't." Melanie's body went rigid.

"Adam is Jace's best man." Trish took a physical step back after the punch that left Melanie breathless.

"Adam is here?" Melanie's stomach clenched. Adam. The flood of emotion was dizzying at the thought of him. He'd saved her life, she'd fallen completely in love and then he'd left. The nervous pounding in her skull was the beginning of a monster headache.

"I'm sort of surprised you didn't figure it out."

"I," she looked up dazed at Trish's smug expression, "I was concentrating on you."

"Right." Trish snorted. "Like you were so on my side this afternoon?"

"I'm always on your side," Melanie said, through a tight jaw. "At least you didn't spring this on me while walking down the aisle."

"Nope, I waited until this very moment." Losing her smile, her expression turned defiant. Her gaze lifted to the space over Melanie's shoulder. Trish's whisper reached her as Melanie felt a presence by her side. "You really shouldn't have been so rude to me."

She held Trish's gaze, the words filtering in through one ear, as she turned her head to see who had approached.

"Hi, Mel."

His shadow was tall and lean. Melanie didn't have to see Adam's face to know the look of guilt. His voice was filled with it and sent her body on high alert, confusing her instincts. Not knowing where the danger was coming from, adrenaline flowed in her veins, spiking her blood pressure.

"Damn it, Trish!" Her voice was low and threatening. "This is what you do?" She ignored Adam. "You ambush me? Why? Because I was rude?" She sounded calm but was on the brink of screams or tears, she wasn't sure which.

"Ambush?" Trish asked hotly. "Are you serious? Jace and Adam are like best buds. Why wouldn't he be in our wedding?"

"I didn't think about it."

"This was a bad idea, I'm sorry." Adam stepped between them.

His deep voice was difficult to hear beneath the roar of blood rushing in her ears. She hadn't seen him in months and now she couldn't even look in his direction.

"Forget it, Adam. Jenny is right, she's too selfish to think of anyone else!" Trish turned to Melanie. "You make everything about you. Hello. This is my wedding. My. Wedding. I'm sorry if I want it to be perfect!"

"Where'd all this come from?" She felt the pressure building as she fought to drown out Trish's words. Her body and mind were trapped in a storm of confusion.

"You purposely ruined my wedding because you are jealous. No one will ever love you enough and you will never get married. You think you're so special that no one is good enough for you."

The force of Melanie's voice, even through gritted teeth, drowned out Adam's.

"Shut up, Trish. Just shut up. Don't you say one more word or I swear," she couldn't breathe or look at Trish. She turned to Adam. "And you," she said, fire filling her eyes as she turned up at him, heart pounding.

"Shut up? Did you really just tell me to shut up?" Trish's voice was high-pitched.

"I was going to tell you to shut the fuck up, but I thought that would be rude."

"It's no wonder no one likes you."

Melanie clamped her jaw to prevent the hurt from breaking through.

"That's not true," Adam jumped in, "Trish, tell her you don't mean that."

Trish crossed her arms and glared.

"Mel," Adam started.

"Don't." Melanie shouldered past the two of them.

"You know what?" Trish shouted and Melanie spun around.

"Tell me? Tell me, what."

"Trish," Adam said in a low, cautioning voice. "Stop."

"Don't worry anymore about my wedding, because you are no longer in it." Trish's stare was cold and unblinking. "In fact, you're no longer invited."

"No." Adam's sound gargled from the back of his throat. He tightened his grip on Trish's arm. "This is my fault."

"You're kicking me out of your wedding?" Melanie sucked in the sting. "Fine." The muscles in her face flexed as she turned, walking past the gaping, curious eyes of the few people who'd congregated at the raised voices. She held in an angry breath and followed the pool decking to the steps through the lawn.

"Melanie."

She kept walking.

"I've got your shoes."

Melanie stopped to look over her shoulder. The guy with the guitar.

"You left them by the fire pit." He held up her flip-flops.

She nodded, her teeth too clenched to speak and the strain on her tear ducts pulsing.

"You okay?"

Melanie studied the rip in the T-shirt, barely holding it together. She loosened her neck muscles and shook her head.

"Want some company? My left side has a great shoulder and a sympathetic ear. The right side, not so much."

"No." The swallow went down hard. "Thank you, though. See you around, Nate."

CHAPTER ELEVEN

At the point where the hotel turned into a casino, Melanie stopped, remembering she had no room and her things were in Trish's.

I'm going home, she decided, feeling like shit, lost and unwelcome. "I need a drink."

Melanie stood in the threshold of the crowded bar, the idea of beating some prick off the neighboring stool sounded like a dangerous way to let off steam. Remembering she was on an assignment hit her at full speed. *I can't escape*, she looked at the people, each trying to make a connection … and turned.

She was standing beneath the rotunda, where there was nowhere to hide, when she saw Carla's little general stomp. Her every unpleasant emotion plastered on her scowling face. Adam was beside her. His stride was determined even as Carla's little feet cut in front of his path.

She saw them approach, and worse, they saw her see them. Her exits were few and none were smooth. But she pressed her imagination, hoping for a gateway into another life to open up and swallow her whole.

"Melanie!" Carla demanded.

There was nowhere to go. Melanie gave up. She was caught. Letting them reach her, studying Carla's warped expression. Not looking at Adam wasn't difficult, she was afraid of what she'd see and how bad the rip in her heart would feel.

"What happened?" Carla asked, her fists pressed into her hips.

"Mel," Adam started, his voice reaching deep into the numb part of her chest.

It was hard to breath when every muscle in her body was rolled into a tight coil ready to spring. "There is nothing to say," She told him, not daring to look beyond the seam of his shirt that was hanging loose over a pair of jeans.

"There's a lot to say." His words rumbled out like distant thunder.

"Mel, you don't have to listen to him," Carla added, her small, loyal face clamped, her eyes narrowed at Adam.

"You don't. But I'm asking you to."

Melanie shook her head. "How could you do that to me? Show up and expect me … to what? Forget? Forgive?"

"I just wanted to talk with you." His voice faltered. "I didn't know how," he stopped. "I didn't know if you would see me."

Melanie raised her hand, she couldn't hear any more. She looked over at Carla. "I've been tossed from the wedding."

"I know. I'm assuming the craziness started with him." She gritted her teeth.

"No, it started with," Melanie fought to keep the pain from her expression, "me."

Carla's stance softened. "What did she say to you?"

Melanie pulled in a breath that hurt, "that I was…" She looked away. "True stuff."

"No, none of it is true." Adam said, reaching for her and then changing his mind. "Mel you can't possibly believe she meant any of those things."

Melanie's lips formed a false grin. "She was pretty convincing." She sighed and raised her eyes to his shirt pocket. It was all she could manage. "You should've called me. I would've taken your call."

"Can't you look at me? Melanie?"

"No," she said, biting the inside of her cheek. "I don't know why, I just can't." She could look at Carla. "Car, I don't know what I'm going to do. I'll call you when I figure things out."

"I could talk to her, make her change her mind. You know whatever she said was in the heat of the moment." Carla's face strained with concern. "She didn't mean those things."

"Somewhere inside, she did," she shrugged, not knowing what else to say. "It's all right, I've been called much worse things."

Carla failed at checking her phone stealthily. "I'm going to let her cool down but don't give up just yet. Okay?" Her eyes flittered from Melanie to Adam and back. "I'm sorry, but I have to go. Ted is at the room and he doesn't have a key. You won't go, right?"

"I might."

Carla sighed. "I wish one of you wasn't so darn stubborn. Are you okay?"

"Why wouldn't I be?"

Carla sighed, giving Adam one last evil glare.

Neither Melanie nor Adam moved as the world swept past. It wasn't an uncomfortable silence. After a time, she felt her courage emerge. She allowed her eyes to drift, slowly up his blue pinstripe shirt. His shoulders were squared and broad. Melanie's heart faltered, throwing in a couple of extra beats.

Her nerves shook as she lifted her gaze. Adam didn't move, but beneath the tan skin of his neck his pulse quickened. Her eyes traveled along his sharp jaw to his ear. His dark hair was short and she had to catch her breath before looking into his eyes.

"Hi," he said, his brow arched.

His eyes were so green. Captivating and lit from within, she'd forgotten how intense he could be. The rage she'd felt by the pool was gone and the bad memories she thought seeing him would bring – weren't there. Other than the initial panic, she felt nothing.

"You look good," she said, remembering how seeing him used to create such havoc from within.

"You, too." His gaze that moved up to her hair was soft and gentle. "Just wanted a change?"

Melanie almost smiled. "Not exactly. I couldn't handle the lice anymore."

"Where were you?"

"Africa."

Adam nodded, his thoughts somewhere in the past, unfazed by her statement. But his eyes drilled, making her fidget uncomfortably.

"Listen, I don't know what happened back there – I sort of lost it." She was trying to explain something she didn't understand. "But I'm not interested in this, either."

"What do you think this is?"

She shook her head and sighed. *You belong to a time in my life that I don't want to remember.* As her thoughts washed over her, she cast her eyes down to the marble flooring. "*This* is pretending."

"I'm not pretending."

"What is it you want?" she asked, emboldened and daring to stare straight at him. The nerves from earlier had hardened. The way his emerald eyes used to send her blood into a fury was just a memory.

"I want a future with you." There was anguish in his statement. "I don't expect you to trust me right away, I plan on earning that back." His expression was determined, but instead of butterflies she felt cramps.

"Good night, Adam."

"Thanks for listening." He swallowed, the apple in his throat bobbed. He took one last look at her before getting lost in the crowd.

Standing alone in the foyer of the busy hotel, she watched him walk away. "It's over," she whispered, "and I can no longer be hurt." There was a sense of solitude and peace that came with a numb heart. *Get a grip, Mel.* She thought taking her place in front of a woman at the reception desk.

"I'm sorry, but we're completely booked," she apologized.

"There has to be something," Melanie pleaded, having lost the will to fight. "I'll take a storage unit."

"I'm really sorry, but we're hosting an Alzheimer's convention." The woman paused and blew out a tired breath. "And, no, it doesn't matter if they forget which room they're in … it's still booked."

"I wasn't going to ask," Melanie drooped, thinking about her next move. "Thanks."

Mike was her solution.

"I seem to have misplaced my room." She smiled at the sound of his voice. "Think you can work your magic and find me something?"

"I'm sure you aren't going to tell me how that happened, right?"

"And ruin the mystery? Not a chance."

"Hold on," he said, his tone tipping to pleasure, "something's up with their security system. Weird. This is going to take me a minute."

"Then since you're not busy could you unlock a room for me?"

"Any particular room?"

Minutes later she approached the green light on the electronic keypad of the Bella Suite. The room was dark but for the flickering lights and voices coming from the television in the bedroom. It smelled stale and clothes were thrown everywhere. Passing her duffle bag on the dining table, she headed directly for the alcohol station.

Most of the bottles had been drained, and she was checking the level of an open whiskey when the sense of not being alone crept up her spine.

"I guess we had the same idea," Adam said, his hands in the 'don't shoot' position. "You carry a gun to a booze raid?"

"Jesus!" She lowered her weapon. "I always carry my gun. Why didn't you turn on a light?"

"Why didn't you?"

Melanie looked at Adam's dark figure and flipped the switch. The florescent lights above the bar caused her to squint. "Happy?"

"Not really." He stepped up beside her and shuffled through the leftovers. "What're you going for?"

"Doesn't really matter."

"The Cuervo is mostly full."

"Sold." She pocketed a saltshaker and bundled slices of lime inside a napkin.

"Need a glass?"

"Nope."

Adam slipped a bottle of rum under his arm and grabbed a six-pack of Coke. "Want a bag of chips?" he asked, a playful grin on his face.

"Tortilla?"

"Um," he shuffled the bags around, "BBQ."

"No thanks." She clicked off the light, sending them back to uninvited guest mode. Adam held the door open for her as she stuffed the contraband in her bag. "No mask?" she almost teased, thinking about the cameras in the hall.

"No need." He smiled guiltily. "Old habits, and all that."

She nodded and stood shoulder to bicep with him, silently waiting for the elevator.

"Going back to your room?" he asked, staring straight ahead.

"No." *I'm currently roomless*, she thought, feeling for the familiar vibration of her cell in her back pocket. Nothing. She wondered if Mike had forgotten her.

"Not coming?" Adam asked, holding the doors open.

"Pass," she glanced at the couple making out in the corner of the elevator and shook her head.

"Bye, Mel." Adam's gaze dropped as the doors closed.

Melanie stood dazed, fixed to her spot. Elevator cars came and went, people flowed in and out, but she remained with nowhere to go.

You can't stand here all night, the voice in her head reminded her.

The elevator light above her head dinged and for a second Melanie thought she heard Trish's giggle – the door to the stairwell was latching before she could find out for sure.

Her flip-flops slapped the bottom of her feet as she hit the first step up to the rooftop. She'd climbed three flights when the door to the floor above opened. Melanie was still running up as Adam leaped over the guardrail, into her.

"Hey," he said, out of breath and catching her shoulders to prevent her fall.

"What are you doing?" she asked, breathing hard and grabbing hold of the railing as he dragged her down a couple of steps.

"Hoping to find you. Where are you headed?"

"Roof."

"It's going to be hot up there," Adam said, pausing before continuing. "It's cool in my room and I have a balcony if it's fresh air you want."

She thought of melting roof tar and abrasively loud air conditioning units. Alone and stewing. "I'm not interested in a discussion."

"Then we won't talk." He smiled, lifting the duffle off her shoulder. "We'll drink."

"Okay," she agreed, wondering how long it would take before regret overtook her. *Jesus, Melanie,* she chewed herself out, *what the hell?*

"Is this a bad idea?" she asked, as he opened the door to his room.

"I don't think so." It was the first real grin he'd given. "We're having a drink so neither of us have to be alone. Nothing more."

Adam was over six feet, dark hair that when allowed to grow curled at the ends and green eyes that could change to cold steel in an instant. He was strong, ambiguous with a mysterious past. When he left her, her begging hadn't reached groveling status but it was too close for comfort. She wasn't embarrassed but his rejection had been devastating.

"Nothing more," she repeated, passing over the line from hallway to private quarters. His cologne lingered in the air as she entered. "Has Trish been to your room?"

"No, why?"

"No reason." Melanie caressed the back of the leather couch in the sunken living area and looked at the bright lights of the strip from the huge glass windows. She slid open the doors and the pulse from the electrical glow penetrated her skin. Her lungs wilted in the heat but the summer sizzle didn't stop the party. Eight floors below hundreds of people walked the sidewalk or were stuck in traffic.

Laughter and conversation billowed its way up and Melanie leaned over to see the source. It was a group of women hailing a cab. Possibly drunk. Melanie blinked away the tears. Trish had told her she was not likable and a small piece of her knew that was true.

"They aren't having as much fun as you think," Adam said, placing a drink in front of her on the wide cement balustrade.

"They're still having more fun than I am," Melanie exhaled, picking up the glass filled with two inches of golden liquid. "Is this straight tequila?" she asked, her nose at the rim as she looked up at him.

Adam placed a dish of limes between them. "I didn't know what you wanted," he said, sliding another glass toward her. "Rum and Coke."

Melanie sighed and tipped the tequila down her throat. "I'm having a rough day." She coughed, her eyes watering.

"I know."

"Trade?" She slid the empty tequila glass toward him and picked up the rum and Coke. Without bothering to count, she filled her glass one after another and sucked the polluted air into her lungs. It was exactly what she needed.

"You going to be okay?" Adam asked, facing the palm trees.

"I just want to forget," she said, her vision unclear from the flashing neon bulbs. Melanie's eyes cut to the tequila, gauging how much she'd consumed. The line was blurry. "I don't like that I lost control tonight. I felt broadsided by Trish and you were totally unexpected." The words that hit her ears were pretty close to what she heard in her mind. She was slurring.

"What Trish said," he started, turning to face her, "it's not true. You're the most generous person I know."

Melanie's shook her dizzy head, dismissing his comment. "I am selfish. It's why I'm alone."

"Mel, you always put your friends and family first. They don't know what you go through or how difficult it is."

"But that's just it, to them I'm a crappy friend." She closed one eye, peering into her emptied glass. "So, that makes it true … at least to them." She bit into a lime, took the tequila out of his hand and swallowed. "I thought we agreed against a therapy session." Her head swam and she blinked his face into focus.

"Melanie." His voice was as soft as his gaze.

"No talking, remember?" His fingers were inches from caressing her cheek. "Don't." She was already on the verge of tears.

"I can't help it." He ran his thumb up over her forehead, relaxing her tension. "I've missed you."

"Don't." She breathed with no conviction.

"You are so beautiful." The words rode in on a wave of 80-proof gold. He seemed not to notice her rejection. "Melanie." His lips curved up at the corners and his fingers slipped beneath her chin, lifting it upward.

She didn't pull away, the part that wanted to resist had drank too much. He read her willingness. His lips on hers were soft, giving her time to refuse. She'd forgotten how strong his hands were, how his mouth caused her to relinquish all reason.

He held her face in the palm of his hands, studying her. "I love you, Melanie."

"Shhh," that wasn't what this was about. Her heart pounded

irregularly at his touch. *I'm not dead, yet*, she cheered, rising on her tiptoes, her fingers winding their way into his hair.

His cheek was by her ear, then at her neck. Tight against her ribs, his lungs expanded as he pulled in the scent of her hair. His mouth fell below her lobe and down the side of her neck to her collarbone.

She reached under his shirt; his skin was burning as she rapidly unbuttoned. Stopping his kisses for the moment, his hands splayed on her back pressing her against his chest and like a dance, guided them into the room.

It was her flip-flop that got caught on the metal channels for the sliding doors. He caught her easily. She felt the carpeting on her back as he laid her down.

෴

Time suspended. The night traveled in slow motion and she hadn't slept, but lay with her cheek on Adam's shoulder.

"Melanie," he whispered, his breath fluttering the hair at her forehead.

She twisted inside the hold of his arms, tilted her head back and gently placed her lips at the corner of his jaw. The length of his body against her hardened and she slid her mouth over his. The spark caught and his hands were as fierce as his kiss. In one swift movement she was on her back and he was on top. Weighing her down, he'd secured her wrists above her head with his hands.

"You've been diverting me all night," he said, grinning. "Haven't you?"

"Diverting? You didn't seem to mind." Melanie relaxed under the pressure.

"There are things to say, Mel."

"Why? Can't we just have this night without thinking too much, without consequences? We can ruin things later." She looked into the shadows of his face. "Please?" She lifted her head off the pillow.

Without hesitation or argument, she'd won. "Anything you want." His voice smooth in its surrender but his hold of her wrists didn't budge.

❦

Drifting in and out of consciousness, she opened her eyes; the room had lost its saturating darkness. Adam's arm was curled around her waist. His chest was rising and falling in a gentle rhythm.

The night was over and reality reared its ugly head.

This is how you lose control? You sleep with Adam? Could be worse, right? "You didn't just sleep with him," the voice in her head answered. Melanie shied away from thinking about how far they'd gone. Suddenly, life seemed to hinge on getting very far from this situation and the urge to run flipped on like a light.

Slipping off the bed as lightly as possible, she snuck to the outer room. The balcony doors were still wide open, the curtains blowing. Dressing as she collected her scattered clothing – her bra on the lamp, underwear under the couch, jeans on the coffee table, shirt … outside and her flip flop still stuck in the metal track.

It's wrong to flee, she told herself. *However, everyone is allowed to be chicken sometimes, right?* She was going to use her freebie pass this morning. Melanie had her hand on her bag, ready … *Shit! Damn it, Mel.* She groaned and went back to the desk to search for hotel stationary.

I'll leave a note, she thought equalizing the damage. *What the fuck am I supposed to say?* She stared at the blank page.

"Good morning."

Melanie sucked in a breath and faced the bedroom. "Hey." She said, lamely as she bit down on her bottom lip.

Adam stood sleepily in the doorway, running his fingers through his roughed-up hair and completely naked. She'd been with him all night but Adam, completely naked in daylight, was distracting. She swallowed down the lump in her throat and tried not to let him notice her excessive, admiring stare.

"You going someplace?" His smile was tender, kind and all too knowing.

"Just," she cocked her head over her shoulder toward the door.

Picking his boxers up off the floor, he continued toward her. "Don't go." His gaze pleading as his hands settled on her waist. "I would give everything I own to have breakfast with you." He lifted her chin when she tried to look away. "I'm in love with you, Mel. Not like the love people talk about," his green eyes were flooded with passion. "I love you beyond anything I can understand or explain. There isn't anything I wouldn't do..." he stopped, his emotion on the edge of spilling over the high barricades. The muscles in his jaws flexing as he fought to gain control, his hands tightened their hold.

She'd stopped breathing.

"Don't shake your head, please," he said, though she hadn't realized she'd moved. "I know you still love me."

Melanie clamped down on her bottom lip. *How am I going to tell him I don't feel that anymore?* "I'm sorry."

"You cannot possibly think that last night happens without love." She searched her heart. There was definite attraction, but the overwhelming, heart-bursting emotion of the past wasn't there.

"You love me," he stated simply after her pause. "There's just other obstacles in the way. Because last night was more than sex."

Her lips clamped shut under the strain.

"You're not ready, okay, I can live with that." He said, gazing deeply, taking in her every feature. "If you could do one thing for me," he asked, closing his eyes for a brief moment, "don't regret spending the night with me. Don't say it was the alcohol or a reaction. I need to believe it meant more to you, too."

She nodded her agreement, feeling like she was no longer in her own life.

"Thank you," his tension eased and his smile was genuine. "You are going to love me again. I'd do anything for you, for your forgiveness. For you to love me the way I love you." His forehead creased and sorrow swept into his eyes.

"Adam," she choked out. She was on a rollercoaster of emotional trauma.

"We can take it slow," his voice was deep and serious.

"It's too late for slow. No," she said, logic worming its way into her consciousness, clearing her head. *I'm not good with relationships and I can't even consider putting myself back in that place.* "Not now."

"I can wait," Adam said. "I'll wait."

"To be honest, I've done a damn good job at limiting how much I think about you."

"And you're all I think about."

"I'm sorry." She wanted to be careful. "I didn't mean for last night to be anything more than … I know you think it was love but it was my weakness."

"You can deny it but I'm aware of what it was," he said, his hand moving to tuck a strand of hair behind her ear. "We both know it went deeper than that, those were true feelings."

"I don't want to argue about this." She sighed, at the end of her rope and ready to crumble. "My feelings detector has been on the blink." She smiled trying to lighten the mood. "Can I ask about the tattoo?"

"Yeah," he said, his tone shifting down a notch.

She tried to read if he was uncomfortable about the tattoo or if it had to do with her putting an end to the conversation. Useless. She let her eyes fall from his face to his shoulder. Adam was standing with only inches of space separating them.

"Why did you do it?" she asked, tracking the artwork with her eyes. Death's skeletal hand breaking through his rib cage to squeeze the blackened heart.

"I got drunk, woke up in the chair."

She had to touch, her fingertips lightly passing over the images of pain and suffering. She followed the tragic story over his shoulder blade and down his back around his abdomen and dropping down below his hipbone.

"It's beautiful, in a horribly sad way." She inhaled as she looked up into his face. "Does it bother you?"

His smile was easy. "No. Does it bother you?"

Holding her breath, her tear ducts stinging, "It makes me want to cry."

"I'm sorry." He pulled her in the extra inches, his arms encircling her.

"It reminds me of how I felt when I first saw it. You nearly died." The terror of that night still turned her blood to ice. Frightened that whatever poison he'd ingested was going to win. "You were so sick."

Her bottom lip was clamped between teeth.

"I didn't die because of you. You were quick."

"I was lucky." She nodded. "We were lucky." The words stuck in her throat, she didn't feel lucky, especially when it came to Adam.

The easiness of it was tempting, leaning into his chest, being held. But the rocket acceleration of her blood pressure couldn't be pacified.

Suddenly she needed fresh air. It was time to make a break. At the door she turned, there was something to say but whatever it was got lost when she looked at him. She nodded and didn't inhale again until she was down the hall.

CHAPTER TWELVE

Mike had left four messages and three texts. Her room was 1777 and the code to bypass the key card was his birthday. It was his way of testing her.

Riding up to the seventeenth floor, she dialed Jack. "What's the word?"

"How do you feel about dealing the midnight to five a.m. shift?"

"Love it."

"They're a group of Syrians and they're scouting disgruntled dealers."

"Oh, I can be disgruntled," Melanie laughed. "Right up my alley."

"That's what I thought, too." He laughed along. "This might not go down at all. Our informant is no longer part of the inner circle, so the details of the operation are sketchy."

"What does casino security say?"

"They're in the loop, but keeping their cards close to the vest."

"Cute. It might be nothing, but will you do me a favor and check out hotel security. Mike said something about it being weird," *and*

Adam was able to bypass floor cameras.

"You got it. I'll let you know if there's any information to get."

"Adios, Jack," Melanie said, the rush of a job pushing out the insanity of life.

She skipped all messages from Carla and Jenny, but the one from her brother she played – "Hey Mel, we're driving in and don't have a place to stay yet, Cheryl called the hotel and they said they're booked. We were wondering how you felt about guests. Call me back."

"Shoot," she growled, he'd left the message last night. "Hey little brother," Melanie apologized. "I'm sorry, I just got your message."

"It's okay. We pulled into a cheap motel outside of the city. It was late and Olivia was getting restless in her car seat."

"Well, I think I've got a room," she said, reaching the seventeenth floor. "You're more than welcome to stay with me." Her offer was genuine, but filled with hope that this room was bigger than the one she shared with Carla and Jenny.

"Great! We'll be there within the hour. Thanks, Mel."

The seventeenth floor corridor was laid out differently than the others. It was wider and fresh flowers were arranged on marble tables beside eight sets of double doors. Beside the doors of room 1777 there was a keyless security box. She typed in Mike's birthday, June 17th … "Aw, shit!" she mumbled, looking at her phone. It was the 18th. She pushed open the doors and the amazement of the suite was lost to her overwhelming guilt.

"Wow," she said, dropping her bag on the plush carpeting.

The suite was fit for royalty, 2000 square feet of luxury. She wandered out to the patio, skimmed her fingers along the green felt of the pool table and sank her teeth into a perfectly ripe pear from the gift basket.

Throwing open all the doors to let the noise of the city in. It helped relieve the loneliness. She pressed the power button on the remote and went to check out the liquor situation.

Fully stocked. She grabbed a fifth of Jack Daniels, plopped onto the couch, kicked her feet up and swigged straight from the bottle.

"Hi, Mike," she said, ready for the guilt trip. "I'm so sorry."

His laugh on the other end of the line was a relief. "Is the room nice?"

"No, it's unbelievable."

"Good. You have it for three nights. I wasn't sure when you were coming back."

"I'm not sure, either."

"Doesn't matter, it's comped," he said, pleased. "And no worries about my birthday, you can bring me back a surprise from Vegas."

"I hope you're not thinking about a showgirl. Because I'm already in hot water for my last human transport."

"Ha!" he laughed. "I was thinking more along the lines of a T-shirt."

"I'll see what I can do. Thanks, again. Hey, what happened with the hotel security?"

"They're having issues. Put a fifty on red for me, okay?"

"Will do. See you."

Bruce, Cheryl and Olivia arrived like pack mules. Within minutes of opening the door the giant suite shrank in a world of pink baby gear.

"You should take your show on the road," Melanie said, walking around a pop-up crib, an ice chest and the stroller with … she picked up an item, clueless to its purpose.

"You think you're so funny but it's a serious pain in the ass."

Bruce shook his head and let out a sigh. "This is a nice place. Are you rich or something?" His gaze on the mural above the dining room table.

"Or something. Hey, there's two rooms, take the suite with the bathroom."

"Thanks. Um, Mel?" Melanie knew that tone, the slightly guilt-ridden one he used right before... "Can I ask for another favor?" ... exactly! She answered him with a single look. "We haven't had any sleep since Mom and Dad went to Montana. Do you think you could watch Olivia for a couple of hours?"

"What? I don't have any experience." Her transition to fear was instantaneous. "All I know about babies is that one day they'll be adults."

"You'll be fine. She's really easy." He was too excited and each increased decibel of his energy caused a palpitation in Melanie's heart.

"You sure you trust me with your baby? Maybe we should start off slower like with supervised visitations."

"Mel, all you have to do is change her, feed her and she naps. That's it."

Really? Then why are you both in desperate need of a break? "Okay, if you're sure. But..."

"Positive." When Bruce grinned he looked exactly like he had when he was ten. Thanking her, he clutched her shoulders and pulled her into a rare embrace. "Thank you. Cheryl," he yelled to the patio, "she agreed!"

Through a nervous laugh Melanie watched their excitement. "Just tell me what I've got to do," she said, her eyes falling to Olivia. "I can't believe how big she's gotten." *And adorable and perfect,* Melanie thought with horror that she wouldn't be returned in the same pristine condition.

"I know. It's incredible," Cheryl said, beaming at the chunky baby.

"Hey, kiddo. I'm Aunt Mel. We are going to have a good time," she said, shaking Olivia's chubby fingers.

"So, we brought everything she'll need."

"And more?" Melanie nodded toward the living room.

"Hardy-har-har." Bruce slapped Melanie on the back. He was in a much better mood than the last time she'd made the comment. "Cheryl's got everything written down for you."

Written down? She had been suckered. Cheryl pulled from her bag a three-page manifesto.

"I think I'm going to need to take a seat for this," Melanie said. "Or call my attorney."

Feeding seemed to take the most words to explain. How to warm bottles – in capital letters DO NOT WARM BOTTLES IN MICROWAVE!!! – Topped the page followed by strict instructions on baby cereal, baby food and orders to avoid anything not on the approved list. Melanie turned the page to diaper changing and then a three-quarter-page lecture on safety. The first and last rule: never let her out of your sight.

Fine. "Go take your nap, I've got it from here." Melanie felt a surge of unsubstantiated confidence even as Olivia was placed in her arms.

"About that. Mel, it's hard for us to sleep if you stay in the room. Even in this huge space, we'll still hear every sound."

Melanie's anxiety rose. "So, what is it you're saying?"

Bruce shrugged. "Could you take her for a walk around the resort or something?"

"Walk around the hotel for two hours? You sure you want to leave her with me, alone?" Melanie asked again.

"You'll be great and we're right here," Cheryl, the author of the Baby Olivia Doctrine, said as if she hadn't just laid out a set of mammoth rules for her to follow.

"Right."

"Thank you," Bruce sighed, relieved.

"But don't let her breathe in any of the smoke. Bye-bye Sweetheart," Cheryl giggled to Olivia "Be good for Auntie Melanie."

"But..."

"I've got her things all ready," Cheryl said, placing the plastic diaper bag on Melanie's shoulder. "Have fun."

Bruce gave the baby a kiss on her head and Melanie stood in the center of her amazing suite, a chubby baby hooked on her hip and pink baby gear strapped to her shoulder. *How did this happen to me,* she wondered as her brother pushed the stroller and ushered her out to the hall.

"Bye, Sweetie," the parents cooed from the closing crack between the doors.

"Say bye-bye," Melanie said, lifting Olivia's hand to wave at where the two faces had just been. "I guess it's just you and me." It was all she said before Melanie felt the gurgle in the baby's chest and the little face turned fire-engine red and squished like she was about to wail.

"Oh, no," Melanie gasped; quickly she grabbed the stroller with her one free hand and ran. She reached the elevator with a purely surprised Olivia, blinking rapidly and wondering what the heck just happened. *I made it, without a single teardrop ... from either of us.* "I see you like to move. Good girl. How do you feel about shopping?" Melanie asked. "I think I saw a baby store. Not that you need anything."

The baby had Melanie sweating. Entertaining an eight-month old was exhausting. All she wanted was to be held while Melanie jogged up and down the escalator. It was hysterical baby theatrics.

"All right, did you read anywhere in the document about not taking you to the pool?" Melanie asked Olivia as she pulled the tabs on the dirty diaper and tossed the ecological nightmare into the trash. "No offense, Kid, but that was gross."

Olivia laughed.

"You know what I'm saying, don't you?" Melanie laughed with the baby. She purchased two swimsuits, one for each of them, and a giant bottle of organic baby sunscreen. This hotel, not wanting to promote a family-friendly environment, had a kids' pool the size of a thimble. A UV- shade stretched over the small wading pool and either it wasn't sensible to have a baby out in the extreme heat or there were no other babies in the entire resort. She and Olivia splashed about undisturbed.

"Well, you're going to have to promise not to tell your parents. They're a little anal about you and your routine." Melanie chatted, her hand never leaving the baby. "When you're older you can hang out with me and I'll show you how to climb trees, fire a slingshot and all sorts of fun stuff."

Olivia's big, toothless smile reached her grey-blue eyes as her hands slapped at the warm water.

"I'm feeling a little bad about the anal comment. I'm really not anyone who should be criticizing others." Melanie looked around at the vacant oasis. "Can we talk?" she asked, "You seem like a really good listener and I'm going to trust you not to repeat anything I say. If you do … I'll have to deny it all."

Olivia screeched.

Melanie sucked in a breath, made a second verification that she hadn't missed someone, leaned down to little Olivia's ear and confessed. "I work for the government. I'm a spy." She looked at the baby, who actually looked surprised for a second. "I've never told anyone that before. Feels weird." Melanie sort of grinned and waited for the Earth to fall in around them. "I really love my job. It can be dangerous and since no one else is going to tell you, I'm pretty good at what I do."

Olivia giggled, splashing as she clapped.

"Boy, you really like this water." Melanie laughed at the tiny human. Talking did seem to be helping. "I know you're not going to judge me," she said, her fondness for her niece growing. "If you've got a minute, I have a few problems I'd like to get off my chest. Are you up for listening?" Complaining about Trish felt good. "I bent over backwards for her and what do I get? Kicked out of the wedding! Can you believe that?" Melanie smiled at Olivia. "Of course you can't, because you're awesome. You and me, we're a team." With the baby's little hand in hers she raised it in a triumphant cheer.

"There's more," Melanie sighed. "It's Adam. I, we, he and I," she paused, "You know what? This is just too complicated. No offense, you've been great, but this thing with Adam – I'm going to have to figure out on my own. In my head I think I love him. Like," she thought of a way to explain, "it's like I know my name, just something that's there, but I don't feel any love. I don't feel anything. Blank. Between you and me … it's the scariest part, feeling partially dead." Olivia rubbed her eyes. "Too gruesome? I'm sorry."

Melanie wrapped her in a towel and held her tightly to her chest as she took a bottle out of the ice pack and shook it, as instructed. They headed back upstairs, hoping not to interrupt marital bliss.

"We were about to order room service," Bruce said when Melanie walked in with a sleeping Olivia in her arms. "Want something?"

"How'd it go?" Cheryl asked.

"Mel, you want something or not?" Bruce grumped with the phone in his hand. "I'm ordering."

She shook her head and gave her brother a dirty look before turning back to Cheryl. "She's great. Adorable. Really sweet." Melanie smiled, handing Olivia back to her mother. Letting go of the little girl, Melanie knew she'd fallen hard for the kid.

Watching the dealers from a seat at the slots, Melanie heard talking beside her but was preoccupied. Lights, dings, digital images and the lure of a mission drowned out thoughts of Trish and Adam.

"Honey?" It was the physical touch on her shoulder that caused Melanie to look up.

"Someone is trying to get a hold of you."

"Excuse me?" Melanie asked the older woman.

"Your phone has been ringing nonstop."

"Oh," she said, "sorry." Quickly reaching into her pocket to silence the offender.

The woman was thin, pushing eighty and dripping in gold. Her white hair was curled in loose waves and her fingernails freshly painted a shiny mauve. Behind her gold frames was a pair of bright sparkling blues eyes.

"Aren't you even interested in who was calling?" she asked as Melanie slid the phone back into her pocket.

"I already know."

"Man trouble."

Melanie grinned. "Only partly. Mostly it's an angry bride."

"I didn't know they allowed same-sex marriage in Nevada. But I guess Las Vegas is cutting edge. I'm May Bird." She said, extending her thin arm.

"Melanie Ward. And I'm not the one marrying the angry bride." She laughed, gently placing her hand in May's loose grasp.

"Did you have an affair with the groom?"

"No!" Melanie recoiled.

"Is he in love with you?"

"No," she answered with less aggression, taking another look at May Bird. She wasn't the kindly grandmother; she was a dirty old broad. "I'm sorry to report nothing scandalous."

"Too bad. It's been hours since I heard any really juicy gossip. And I just thought … since you are avoiding calls…"

Melanie didn't say anything and after a beat May turned back to her machine. "I'm here with friends. We come a couple of times a year. Leave the husbands at home – well, those us whose husbands aren't pushing up daisies. We have a ball."

"That's nice," Melanie's throat tightened with the surge of jealousy.

"Are you married?"

"No."

"Shame," the old woman said. "A lovely girl like you would make beautiful babies."

Melanie suddenly felt as if she were seated beside her mom. "You have no idea what a disaster that would be."

"I've seen terrible parents, I was a school teacher for years."

"Well, there's no worries, I'm not very good at the relationship part of things."

"So, you're an old-fashioned girl." May's calculating gaze sent a chill down Melanie's spine. "I have a very nice grandson about your age. He's our chauffeur for this trip. And he's hot."

Melanie laughed. "No thanks, May. Nothing against your grandson but I'm done with men."

"Then how will you ever have children?" she asked with a sincerity that could not be ignored.

"I don't think about that kind of stuff."

"You will. One day."

Melanie considered for half a millisecond. "Nope. Can't even imagine being ready for that. I've never even had a pet."

"Well," May smiled, "things are different in this day and age. Women have choices. My husband and I were married sixty-two years ago and," she tilted her head, leaning the inch that put her in Melanie's territory, "most of those were good years. I used to think I would've chosen a career over Richard but now that I'm old, I try not to play the what-if game. He's a good man. When I was a girl I wrote a column for my high school paper." Her voice was distant. "I would have liked to continue on as a journalist."

Melanie shrugged. "No rule against you writing now."

"Too old. Have you been to the other casino for the Beatles show?"

"No."

"It was wonderful." May pressed the flashing buttons on her machine. "At least tell me you're in love with the groom."

Melanie laughed. "Still searching for something sordid? Nice to see your imagination is intact."

"Getting worse each year, I'm afraid. I think it's because of all

Kate Mathis

those awful reality shows I can't seem to get enough of. My husband, Richard, pretends to hate them but you won't ever see me on the couch alone. Do you watch them?"

"Never."

"Maybe that's what you need … you know, to get your juices flowing. Make you want a man."

Melanie squinted at the woman. *I'm sitting next to an 83 year-old Trish.*

"I'm teasing you. But you're much too serious for such a young woman. You need some fun."

"I won't argue with that."

"Charlie!" May yelled and waved. "There's my grandson. Over here!"

Melanie scanned the five men caught by May's call, settling her bet on a twenty-something with thinning hair and a fanny pack. The wave hello came from the mammoth man with dark blonde hair that could use a full three inches of trimming. His narrow blue eyes were deep and lighted up as they fell on Mrs. Bird.

"I told you he was hot," May whispered.

"You didn't say your grandson was Thor."

"He's a gem. Charlie, this is Melanie. She's single."

"Thanks, Gram. Hi, Melanie." Thor was clearly uncomfortable with the blatant hint.

"Well," Melanie said, standing and thinking about the missed phone calls, "I suppose I've got a few calls to return. Good luck, May." Melanie said, cashing out. "It was nice to meet you." She nodded to the comic book hero.

"You too, Dear. Charlie, get her number. Where are you from?"

Charlie's groan made him feel like a kindred spirit. His dark eyes

172

full of apology as he glanced at her nervously. "If I don't ask for your number the drive home will be hell."

"Don't worry, I have a mom just like her," Melanie said, stopping a waitress with a pen. "I grew up in La Jolla. My parents still live there."

"Oh! Charlie, did you hear that?" May asked eagerly. "We live in Solana Beach. How wonderful. We'll have to get together sometime."

"Sure." Melanie leaned down and gave the old woman a swift hug before looking at Charlie. "Bye."

"Good luck, Melanie."

She stepped away to endure the wrath of Carla. Her hello was lost beneath Carla's rant.

"Are you listening to me?" Carla grouched.

"Not really," Melanie answered with an unhappy smirk.

"You haven't been answering any of our calls. You promised me you'd stay in Vegas and now…" she continued and Melanie who had had enough – ended the call.

"Is it too early for a shot?" she asked the muscles behind the bar.

"It's Vegas." He grinned and gave a long pour.

"Thanks," she sucked in a solid breath and too quickly swallowed the alcohol. It went straight to her head. Suffering through a moment of dizziness, "What the hell was that?" Her hands pressed against the sides of her face trying to keep her head in one piece.

"Straight Zombie, my own creation. Did you like it?"

"I'll let you know when I can feel my tongue." Melanie paid the man, rubbed her forehead and held onto the mahogany for a moment to collect her senses.

Five minutes later she gave Carla another chance. "Are you ready to be rational?" she asked in the dead space between Carla's pants.

"Because I'm done with being scolded."

"Why didn't you answer my calls?" Her voice restrained.

"I was busy and I didn't want to hear you yelling at me."

"Trish is really upset that you checked out of the hotel."

"I was squeezed out of the room. Ryan showed up and there wasn't anything else available. The reservation for my own room wasn't until tonight."

Silence hung heavily in the space between them.

"Well?" Carla spat.

"Are you expecting me to say something else?"

"Where are you?"

"Look, Car, I'll be at the wedding, lurking in the background behind the potted ficus. Trish won't see me but I will be there."

"What is the matter with both of you? You're behaving like willful children, Melanie," she huffed, "would you consider rejoining the wedding party?"

"Will she say she's sorry?" Melanie felt the corners of her mouth lift, "or admit she was wrong?"

"I wouldn't bet on it. But…" the note of gossip was in the air, "she ticked off Jen and I think even Kara is ready to bail."

"What happened?"

"She put Jen on a crash diet. She wants her to lose ten pounds by tomorrow."

Melanie sucked in a breath. If there were a hundred things Jenny was too sensitive about, her weight was at the top of the list.

"Have I expressed how happy I am to be missing all that crap?"

"Great. You left me here alone."

Melanie thought it was called karma. Carla had gone bonkers when Ted nearly lost the election last year and Trish was there to pick up the pieces.

"Courtney is Maid of Honor because she matched better with the Best Man. Kara cried and locked herself in the bathroom." She cleared her throat. "I think Adam dropped out of the ceremony because Ian is the best man." Carla sighed, "It's a mess. Courtney arrived and Trish is completely infatuated with her. Oh, Mel, I'm not sure I should tell you this but that witch of a woman has set her sights on Adam. You know how handsome he is."

Melanie waited for the rush of emotion, a carnal need to defend her territory.

"He wasn't at the rehearsal breakfast this morning. The woman is a pure goddess, until she opens her mouth."

"Adam is a free man." Melanie said, contemplating her lack of feelings. She felt sad and disappointed, yes, but even those were muted. "If Trish wants me there, she'll have to ask me herself."

"I seriously hate you both."

Her grin spread to a full smile. "She's got my number. Otherwise you know where to find me during the vows."

"Oh, that's another thing! The damn vows. She wants me to write them. I'm supposed to remember how I *used* to feel about Ted and if that doesn't work I'm to watch that movie where the old people die."

"Tough spot. But I've got to go."

"Just so that you know, you are no longer my favorite friend."

"Bye, Car."

"Bye." Melanie dropped her head onto the bar.

"Would you like another?" The bartender asked, his grin dividing his face.

"Never." Melanie snorted and checked her caller ID.

"Hi Mel. I know you know it's me." Melanie let the pause hold, as if she didn't recognize Bridezilla's voice. "Fine. I'm calling to ask if you would let bygones be bygones and be a bridesmaid?"

"I don't know." It wasn't exactly an apology.

"Fine. I'm sorry. Okay, I'm sorry," Trish sulked.

Melanie knew even that effort, though terrible and lacking in sincerity, was difficult for Trish. "How about I come as a guest?"

"You're really that mad? I swear I didn't mean a word I said. Can I blame it on hormones?"

"I'm tired and the drama that's surrounding you is consuming."

"I am really sorry, Mel. I'll postpone my wedding if you don't agree to truly forgive me."

"No, you won't," Melanie said, having a difficult time judging Trish's tone.

"I will. I'm sick of me, too. Everyone is mad at me, and I'm thinking I should've just eloped." Melanie could hear the crumple of tissues and knew Trish was crying. "Please forgive me, Mel. I honestly didn't know how much Adam bothers you."

"Okay, I'm sorry, too."

"Yay! I knew you wouldn't stay angry. I'll see you tonight, the bachelorette party starts at 8 sharp. Love you."

CHAPTER THIRTEEN

At 8 sharp Melanie entered the chaos of the Bella Suite. Loud music was playing and women she didn't recognize were holding piles of bright clothing. Kara, wearing only a bodysuit of sheer lace, was pouring herself a drink.

"Jen?"

"Hey, Mel, I heard you left for D.C."

"I'm not a hologram." Melanie snipped. "What's going on here?"

"We're getting ready to go out," she said casually, as if she weren't wearing purple pants and a floral blouse tied in a knot below her bra, leaving her midriff exposed. "Didn't Trish tell you?" the confusion on her face should've been obvious. "She wanted a 70's theme so she rented costumes for everyone." Jen lifted her polyester bell-bottom pant leg to show off her glittery heels. "Aren't they groovy?"

"Far out," Melanie said, looking over Jen's head, around the room.

"You'd better get dressed. The clothes are in the bedroom." She lowered her voice. "Courtney is a diva. She called in a make-up artist and a hair stylist." Jen rolled her eyes. "She and Trish are having their faces done professionally."

"Where's Car?"

"Hiding." Jenny laughed. "You'll see."

Melanie nodded hello to Lori, who was in a striped tube top with hot pants and fishnet stockings.

"Trish is crazy," Melanie said, picking up the sole outfit in the back room, a magenta jumpsuit with a neckline that plunged to the rhinestone-studded silver belt. Knowing she was going to end up in the ridiculous getup ... she decided not to fight it.

Stripping out of her clothes she shoved a foot into the giving fabric and sighed. "Dear God, please let it stretch ... enough."

She squeezed into the jumpsuit, it was tight past her hips then the pants ballooned out like a skirt. She adjusted the collar and her breasts – it wasn't as hideous as she'd imagined. The 3" white patent leather platform sandals gave her enough height to pull the outfit together.

"Not bad," she nodded, seeing a shelf of wigs in the reflection. The Farrah Fawcett feathered blonde locks caught her eye and the beautician had left her cosmetics on the table. Quickly, Melanie rummaged through the suitcase, and using fresh cotton balls, added stick-on sparkles to the blue eye shadow. With a heavy hand she lined the outside of her eyes and swiped mascara through her lashes.

"Mel, you in there?" Jenny knocked.

"I'll be right out," she called.

"Most of us are heading downstairs."

"Okay," Melanie said, applying the final touches and adding a beauty mark with the eyeliner.

Her phone in hand, ID and cash tucked between her skin and the man-made fabric she rushed out into the disaster of a suite. She was alone. Melanie jogged the deserted hallway to catch the elevator down.

"Hi," she smiled and winked at the man who whistled as she crossed the slick tile of the hotel lobby.

Both sides of the wedding party had merged by the entrance of the elaborate resort/casino. The women in their psychedelic costumes outshone the men who were in jeans and button-down shirts.

Melanie scanned the crowd for the shortest member. Carla had positioned herself in the center, fidgeting in a long-sleeved, swirl-patterned shirtwaist dress that was barely long enough to cover the bottom crease of her ass. Melanie especially liked the knee-high, glossy, pink go-go boots and gold bangles that jingled from her wrist to her elbow.

"Hey," Melanie smiled at Bruce, happy to see he'd been invited out with the boys.

"Married," he said, nervously holding up his left ring finger.

"My mistake." She hid the amusement that her own brother hadn't recognized her.

"Oh, my…" Carla said, gaping at Melanie.

What? Melanie asked silently, turning to see who was behind her.

"Melanie?" Jenny asked with the same blank expression as Carla. "Is that you?"

Lori and Kara turned.

"What?"

"Hell!" Lori said. "You look damn good, girl."

"Thanks?" Melanie said, realizing she may have gone a bit overboard. "Are we ready? Where's Trish and…"

"Courtney," Carla said, still trying not to gape at Melanie but not taking her eyes off her face. "They're supposed to be on their way down." She rolled her eyes.

Jenny nodded. "You didn't see them in the room?"

"I thought everyone had left."

"Great. That's another hour." Kara snorted.

"We'd better go," Ian said, leading the men out. "See you ladies later."

"I hate being called a lady," Melanie whispered to Carla as they separated from the group.

"In that outfit I'm sure it won't be too much of a problem."

"Those are strong words from a woman whose ass is hanging out of her skirt." Melanie snickered.

"Is it?" she asked appalled and twisting to catch a glimpse of her backside and bumping into Adam.

He was hurrying to join the bachelor party. "Excuse me," he said, pausing to make sure Carla hadn't fallen. Adam was nearly to the door when he stopped and turned. Melanie smiled and waved as his expression changed. "Jesus. What are you doing?" His steps toward her were slow and deliberate and his eyes raked over every detail of her face, hair and down to her platforms.

"Going to a party. Is it too much?"

"I didn't recognize you," he said, still soaking her in.

"Where are you going?"

"Strip club." He answered distracted.

"Well, don't catch anything."

"Mel," he scolded her with her name, just like her mom would do.

"It's the costume talking," she lifted a shoulder indifferently.

"I can't concentrate on what I'm saying when you look like that." He rubbed his forehead and covered his mouth with his hand. "Can we talk later?"

Trish and Courtney burst out of the nightclub like a champagne cork. "The limo is here! The limo is here!"

"Sounds like I've got to go." Her hands up in surrender to Trish's will.

"Mel. Be careful." His eyes examined her from top to bottom, stopping at the strip of bare skin between her breasts. "Looking like that could attract trouble."

"It's okay, I've got my birthday present." She winked.

"Holy … where?" he asked, a cloudy expression filling his eyes.

Shh, she lifted her index finger across her mouth. *Being a 70's girl was fun*, she thought, feeling the weight of her .380 strapped to her calf. *Who knew bell-bottoms were so useful?*

Outside, the honking was for Adam. With a rush of relief and appreciation Melanie watched him climb into the Hummer. *He really is handsome*, her thoughts interrupted.

"Oh, Mel!" Trish squealed as Melanie stumbled into the back of the limo. "You look bitchin'! Isn't this fun?"

"So much."

At arms length, Trish stopped to admire Melanie's chest. "You'd better not get cold, those headlights could blind."

"I'll stay away from the air vent," Melanie replied hiding her blush.

"Headlights?" Carla looked around for an explanation.

"Her nipples." Jenny giggled.

"Oh," Carla breathed, her eyes on Melanie.

"I love the make-up! Court, doesn't Mel's look better than ours? Ooh, do you two even know each other?"

They nodded their hellos as each sized up the competition.

Courtney sat on the side bench inside the limo, her long legs spanning the narrow aisle. She was in a stylish navy blue, high-wasted satin mini skirt with a sequin halter-top beneath a fitted blazer. Her dark hair was short, cut in a blunt line at her jaw and pin straight.

As Trish chattered about Courtney's modeling career, Courtney didn't even pretend to be modest. "Don't forget the music videos."

"Sounds like you live an exciting life," Melanie said cheerfully.

"It's a lot of travel," Courtney complained. "I'm always on the road. I flew in from Peru for this girl's night out. Which is *exactly* what my agent said I needed, some relaxation. Are we going to Tryst or Hyde?"

"This isn't a girl's night out, it's a bachelorette party. And both of those places are too new to get into," Lori said, defending her arrangements.

"I didn't mean to offend," Courtney said, giggling and flipping her eyes to Trish.

"Is there any booze in this heap?" Kara asked, diverting potential disaster.

Jenny pressed buttons to open the moon roof, then the mini bar. "Bingo!"

Chris Brown blasted through the speakers and Trish sprung half out of the roof to finish out the song. Courtney and Kara bounced through the hole in the top vying for the spot beside Trish.

"How's Adam?" Carla asked in a low voice that cut through the noise.

"Fine."

"You okay?"

"Surprisingly, better than that." Melanie slid a look to her friend. "I don't feel anything. Do you think that's a bad sign?"

"No. You got over him," Carla said, pulling down the hem of her dress. "That was what Dan was about."

"I guess. I haven't considered that," Melanie sat back to think it over. "Hey, Lori, anything to drink over there?"

"Hell, yeah. I'll mix you up something that'll give you an orgasm right where you sit."

Melanie looked over at Carla.

"How about something a little less vigorous?" Melanie smirked.

"Have it your way," she scoffed. "I can still mix a drink that'll knock your socks off." Lori looked up with a smile. "Better?"

"An expression that doesn't involve soiled clothing is always better," Carla said, primly.

"Quit squirming," Melanie said, giving Carla a light shove. "Everyone has some body part hanging out, stop trying to cover them up. Thanks," she said, taking the pink drink from Lori.

"I really hope this strip club is nice," Lori said, biting her fingernails. "They have a great website. Wait until you see what I ordered."

Melanie polished off the drink as the limo slowed to a stop in front of a blinking tower of streaming day-glow lights.

They stared at the glaring promises: "GIRLS!" "NUDE!" "DANCERS!" "CHIPPENDALE!" The words lost their meaning as they blazed across the electric marquee.

"They've got everything here!" Lori said, ready to fling open the door.

"Do we want everything?" Kara asked. "We're not going bisexual, are we?"

"Why the hell not, we're in Vegas?" Courtney retorted, pushing her way out the door. "Don't knock it until you've tried it."

"I have to tell you," Carla whispered, "I've never been to one of these places. I'm kind of excited."

"You're going to have a good time."

"Yeah? You think it's okay to be curious, right?"

"Car, forget about all your rules. Just let loose, have fun. You're in Vegas with Trish, nothing you could do or even think of doing will ever match her."

Carla's grin put a glint in her eyes. "I am going to have fun. I'm not going to worry about anything. It's been so long since I've been able to act wild."

"Go for it."

Carla squeezed Melanie's knee before flying out of the car. Melanie looked out at all the flashing lights and felt drained. Strip clubs weren't her favorite places. They were filthy. She thought of a case she'd worked, the black light they'd used had illuminated all kinds of nasty bacteria and bodily fluids on the walls, the seats, the carpeting.

Straightening her top, she slammed the car door and followed the red carpet into a germ-a-phobia's nightmare.

This strip club was two stories of red velvet walls, brothel furniture, chandeliers and a gift shop. Like a movie theater, the entrance was roped off and if you weren't part of a party you had to pay your cover at the booth. Little men with big sticks hooked to their belts guarded their terrain with a look of ferocity.

"Look, Trish, there we are," Lori said, pointing to a chalkboard at the hostess stand welcoming eight events.

Melanie read the next four names and stopped. Catching Jenny's gaze she lifted her chin to the board. Number seven on the guest list was Johnson.

"There's a Johnson," Kara pointed out, "do you think it's Jace?"

"There must be a hundred clubs in this town, what are the chances that it's him?" Carla asked.

It took three seconds for Lori to ante-up, "Um, Ian and I did go to the wedding planner together and she gave us the same recommendations. And," she scrunched her face with guilt, "this was number two on the page."

"So, what if he's having his party here?" Trish shrugged. "If either of us was going to cheat it'd be me and I'm not. Besides how many girls do you think throw themselves at the ball players after every game?" She looked around. "Lori, tell them."

"A lot," she said, artfully.

Trish used her Bridezilla tone with the hostess. "We're waiting to have a good time."

"Follow me." The woman wore leather shorts and carried a whip as she led them through the velvet curtain. "This is our barbarian-themed retreat. We usually have cavemen in here – you know, the rough and tumble type. Not too bright, but big." Beyond the door were black walls, a penis-shaped stage and folding chairs arranged around the shaft and balls. "Conan will be your bartender. Appetizers have been set up on the back table."

Conan was wearing a fur thong. *Only* a fur thong. He looked like he'd spent his time bouncing from the weight bench to the tanning bed.

"If you need anything," the hostess pointed to an intercom by the door, "I'm just a button away. Have a terrific time. By the way, I love the getups." She gave two thumbs up before leaving them in the safety of Conan.

"Barbarians?" Melanie asked Lori.

"It was supposed to be icons of the seventies." Her face drooped. "I should go speak with the hostess lady, huh?"

"This is good, too," Melanie said, the waft of hot food reminding her that she was hungry. The other women gravitated toward the bar, either for drinks or flirts. She didn't care. Her eyes were set on the mini chimichangas, chips, guacamole and salsa.

"Better not eat too many. That fabric doesn't look like it can stretch too much farther and besides, then you'll have a paunch," Courtney kindly pointed out.

Melanie licked the salsa off her fingers. "Haven't you heard? Paunches are the new sexy."

"Not in my world."

"Thanks for coming." Trish smiled, handing Melanie a Corona.

"I wouldn't have missed your wedding for anything. No matter what you say." Melanie clinked her bottle to Trish's. "You're getting married tomorrow."

"Can you believe it? Crazy. Now you're the only free one left."

"I hold that title with pride."

"I'm going to send cute guys your way so you can bone them and then tell me all about it. Okay?"

"No."

"What's the point of being single if you're not going to take advantage of it?" Trish shook her head. "I don't care what you say, just know that when hot men flock to you, it's because I've sent them. Put some elastic in your morals and you'll be fine."

"I can't."

"You can. Just make sure they wear a slicker."

She sighed. "I'll think about it. What about Courtney?" Melanie asked, looking up at the woman who'd stood, quietly uninterested. "Why don't you send them her way?"

"She's picky."

Melanie blinked and held her tongue at the insult. "Well, then, send all those studs directly to me."

"I didn't mean it like that."

"Besides, I've got my eye on someone and I always get what I want," Courtney chimed in, engaging in the conversation.

"Good luck with that," Melanie said, thinking about Adam.

Trish cleared her throat nervously, swigged her beer and tried to brush the topic away.

"I don't need luck," Courtney added, bored. "Trish, I'm going to find a seat."

"She seems like a lot of fun," Melanie said after Courtney had strutted away.

"I wish you lived in San Diego," Trish said, looking out into the room. "I miss you. I like all these other women but sometimes I feel alone when I'm with them. You know?" She shifted her gaze back to Melanie.

"I know."

"We should've been gay. At least once."

"Shut up."

"No." Trish giggled, swinging her arm around Melanie's shoulder and cupping her breast. "Nope, you're too tiny. You do know they've got doctors for that."

"Stop it!" Melanie laughed, ducking out of the intrusive embrace. "I dare you to try that stunt with Car."

"Are you kidding, she'd clobber me. And then I'd be forced to sing American Pie in my head while she gives an eight-minute lecture about life in the public eye and that Ted's opponents have cameras. Too much work for a joke." Trish snorted and sipped her drink. "But I'll tell you what, Mel, you look like a bad ass in that jumpsuit."

"It's the hair." Melanie flipped it over her shoulder.

"It's fun, huh? Thanks for not moaning about the costume and giving me grief." She bumped her arm against Melanie's shoulder.

"Truth is, I kind of like it."

"That's 'cause you're hot. What you need is a superhero sidekick. Like Shaft."

"He's hardly a superhero." She thought for a moment. "I did meet Thor."

"Did you do him?"

Melanie rolled her eyes. "Yeah, he was out of this world."

"Really?" Trish's question was still on her tongue when she caught on. "You are such a liar."

"Why don't you bug Jenny?" She tried again to redirect Trish's overwhelming attention.

Trish squished her face, her puckered lips touching the tip of her nose. "Too much drama. You think you got pissed with Adam, triple the reaction and that's Jen."

"Ever think you butt into people's business too much?"

"Never. I help. Just like you helped me with Jason. I'm paying it forward."

Melanie was about to reject the blame when the lights flickered.

"Hello all you foxy mamas! You are looking fine. But I'm interested in the kitty named Trish." The man on the stage was in a tux and top hat and a little beyond his prime.

"Over here!" Trish yelled, swinging her bottle in the air.

"Get over here, momma! We've got a party to start."

Melanie hollered with the rest and migrated away from the food and drink to the empty seats.

"In line with your rad style we've got something special for you."

Four muscular men in chains carried a cheap, spray-painted throne out to center stage. Trish sat in the chair, a crown was placed on her head, the lights dimmed and the music began.

The Hustle. The screaming started as ten men danced their way out of the darkness and into the strobe light. These were the impersonators, ranging from Elvis to Art Garfunkel. The bridesmaids went wild, rushing the catwalk, sliding their hands over the sequin pants of the dancers.

In about five seconds the costumes were snapped off and tossed off stage. Opting for the more liberating banana sling, they gyrated and rubbed their hands over their bodies. The girls screamed for men that wouldn't merit a second glance on the street.

Melanie couldn't resist looking at the male bulge. The song changed to That's The Way Uh-Huh Uh-Huh I Like It ... Uh-Huh, Uh-Huh. It was less the song and more the fact that some of the underwear didn't hold in the entire hairy package that prompted her departure.

None of the women were in their seats, Melanie was alone in the shadows of the reflection of the disco ball. She slid her glance from Trish – who was surrounded by oiled-down dancers pivoting their parts along her body – to the exit sign above the door.

CHAPTER FOURTEEN

Closing the door on the flashing bulbs and overt stimulation she was able to breathe again. She lifted her chin to the red velvet ceiling, relaxed and let her eyes adjust to the light.

"I wondered how long you'd last in there," said Adam, sitting on a boudoir-esque love seat.

"I sort of got trapped. It was like watching a circus performer swallow knives, disturbing and yet fascinating." She shook off the prickly feeling and looked at him. "Why are you out here? Shouldn't you be slipping dollars into G-strings?"

"Not my thing. A couple of Jace's friends are a little too rambunctious and I'd rather miss the fireworks." He stood close and she tilted her face to meet his eyes.

Shifting her feet as the club's open area was a steady stream of traffic, mostly men but some women making their way into the general venue.

"This is quite a place. Something for everyone."

"I wanted to say I'm sorry for this morning." Adam said and

Melanie strained to understand. "We weren't supposed to talk, remember?"

"I knew you weren't apologizing for the sex." She smiled.

"Do I have to?" his expression turning to alarm.

"No! It was, you were…" she stumbled over her words before she shut her mouth to restart.

"It was, I was what?" his amusement extending across his face.

"I'm not going to say it." Melanie decided.

"I will." Adam said, standing he maintained eye contact. "Making love to you was incredible. The…"

"Stop," her shout rough and panicked. "I don't want to talk about this."

"I do," he said, his voice low as a whisper, his hands caressing her neck.

"I think that's been established." She said, taking a step back. "Besides, Adam, everything that needed to be said has been."

Adam's lips curved up. "Not even close. Please, Mel, ten minutes."

She felt tension surge in her forehead. "There's nothing I can say that you want to hear," she swallowed.

"I've waited months to hear anything you have to say." The pulse in his neck quickened. "I've missed you," he said, his green eyes warming and filling in that familiar way that used to clamp her heart. "You have no idea how much."

She studied his face. He was handsome, beyond handsome. Masculine, strong and there was that broken part of him, the unknown part that was so alluring. She knew his face, his hands, and felt as if he were someone from ages past. Someone she used to love. Melanie listened as he spoke and heard nothing. None of it mattered anymore.

"I'm sorry, Adam, but I can't do this." She hadn't intended to leave him staring after her but her emptiness was frightening. She was outside before she realized, breathing in exhaust, sweating not from the heat but from something else.

"Melanie."

Her vision was speckled. She hadn't had a migraine in years.

"We can get through this," he said approaching, she retreated. Melanie backed up until she was in the shade of the overhang and out of the glare of running lights.

"It's not that easy." She bit her lip.

"It can be." He leaned in toward her. "It can be that easy, Mel." The longing in his voice was almost tangible. "I love you," Adam said, the words choking him up.

She looked at him. His emotions were too intense, too forthright. She felt sick and angry.

"I love you," he repeated.

"No, you don't." Her voice was stronger than she'd expected.

"You know I do." He smiled as if she were playing a game.

Melanie held his gaze, communicating the legitimacy of her thoughts. "You love the idea of me. You love the chase. But you don't love me. You don't love me." She tightened her jaw, blocking the passage to her windpipe. She could read the exact moment that he understood.

"That. Isn't. True." He gritted his teeth, as his hands constricted into fists.

"It is true." Her soft tone was in contrast to his. "We don't even know each other, really. You don't love me because you don't know me." Her insides gripped knowing that even if he did know her, the outcome would be the same. *Nobody loves me because I'm just a shell of a person.*

He turned his back to her and she thought he was going to storm off. He took two steps, stopped and cocked his head so his profile was visible. His forehead was creased and the tendon in his jaw twitched as he looked over his shoulder at her.

In one forceful move, he gathered his height, faced her and with his brows pulled in tight he moved toward her. Her blood pressure spiked as she felt the anger in his eyes. "I can't talk to you like this." His breaths came out hard as he pulled at his shirt, untucking it and using the corner to wipe the make-up from around her eyes.

His hand shook as he held her chin and cleared off the blue eye shadow. Her face was damp with sweat and the cosmetics stained his shirt.

She stared at him as he worked, gently removing the 70's girl and bringing her back. The storm behind his eyes was easing and Melanie unclipped the wig, dragging her fingers through soaked hair.

"Adam," she started again more calmly. "We were together all of a few weeks and you couldn't wait to run. If we got back together, it'd be the same. You've forgotten why you left in the first place."

"No. I made mistakes." He stared with his jaw clenched. "I wouldn't ever leave you again."

She held his gaze, not believing a word, though he looked convinced.

"Is there someone else?" he asked. "Have you found another man?"

"Nobody." She replied quickly to relieve his fear.

"Is it Ashe? Are you still in love with him?" He did his best to hide his pain, but his eyes were wide and he wasn't breathing.

"It's not anyone. I've changed."

"I'll show you every day how much I love you. You'll trust me.

We'll fix this." He said cupping her face in his hands. "I know you love me, Melanie, I know you do. I felt it." He breathed through clenched teeth, the muscles in his neck knotted. "You have to."

"I do," she whispered. "I just don't feel it anymore."

"Don't say that," he tightened his lips until they lost all color and dread filled his eyes. "Don't say that."

Melanie tore her eyes from his.

"Please." His hands slid her arms to hold her wrists.

"Please what, Adam?" she asked, looking up. "Please don't leave me in this hotel. Please answer my calls. Please come back. I tried all of those. Remember? You left me. Even after you knew I wasn't with Danny, even after you knew I only wanted you ... you left. You shattered my heart. So, your 'please' doesn't carry much weight."

"I thought…"

"Yeah, I know. You've told me what you thought." She spat out the words. The rush of rejection polluted the air as she looked into his face. "Don't tell me you're sorry," she said, when it looked as if he were going to speak. "I don't care."

"Melanie," he started. The desperation poured out of him as he clenched her by her shoulders. "I was wrong." His body was rigid but his grip on her was gentle. "I know there isn't any reason for you to forgive me, but I need you to."

"I'm over it."

"Melanie," he tried again. The look in his eyes darkened as he shortened the distance between them. His leg was between hers when he took her in his arms, his hands on her back and at the base of her neck.

Brushing his lips to hers, she felt his pulse quicken. She breathed in his breath as his lips parted and he kissed her. The voice in her head told her to try, reminding her that somewhere inside she loved him.

Melanie folded her arms around his neck and leaned into his body.

Adam broke off the kiss and stepped back to look at her.

She blinked away the stinging of tears.

"I'm never going to give up on us."

"I don't want you to waste your time. There's someone out there for you and she'll make you happy. I'm just not that person." *I'm not loveable.*

"Stop. Stop talking," he said, closing his eyes. She didn't move, speak or think as she waited. When he opened his eyes they were glassy. "You're over me enough to tell me to move on … and mean it?"

She nodded. *I think so.* "I don't know if I'll ever come back from this. Will I cry at your wedding? Probably. But I want you to be happy. I want you to meet a woman who'll have a regular career and you can have a normal life. You'll open a restaurant and have a family." That part was tough to say.

"We could have those things."

"We've got too much baggage."

"I can't let you go."

"You already did. Months ago."

"Never. Even when you were with Ashe, I still thought of you as mine."

She wanted to tell him she had been his then and in some ways would always be his. But she stayed quiet in the knowledge that Adam and Melanie were officially over.

He shook his head. "I can't accept this."

Melanie's phone, stuck in her belt, buzzed. She ignored it.

"Answer your phone, Mel."

"Yeah," she swallowed, trying to sound casual and expecting Mike.

"Yeah? Is that what this world is coming to? Yeah?"

"Ben?" Melanie asked pulling the phone from her ear to check the ID she'd overlooked. "Something happen?"

"I'm sorry to bother you on your time off, but five minutes ago," Melanie held her breath, terrified, "Christopher Bell was found hanging in his cell."

She looked up at Adam, her body on the verge of exploding into action.

"Agent?"

Melanie nodded, feeling sick. "I'm here."

"And the ITC decided to allow your team a ranking, you came in fifth. Agent Williams is going to captain the team."

She was clenching the phone. Shifting hands, she stretched the muscles in her palm. "I thought something cataclysmic had happened." Her breath was shaky. "Though the Bell news is regrettable."

"You need to stop expecting the worse. There are still good things out there in the world."

"Where?" she asked looking up at Adam.

"I'm right here, for one." Ben said, sounding very far away.

"Thanks, I'll be home … at some point." Her soul wasn't in the conversation, she felt bruised and broken.

"The CIA gave your report to the administration and they passed it along to the UN. Your exploits snowballed and even the president had a hand in placing Ina in an appropriate home."

"That is great news." She said her isolation filling the holes in her heart.

"Both Krueger and I got a phone call of congratulations."

"Did the other teams hear about that?"

"I made sure of it." He smiled across the miles.

"I bet that went over well," Melanie added, already feeling the resentment from the other teams. And glad Williams was going to have to deal with them. Jason emerged from the club while she was on the phone and Adam was leaving her for him. "I've got to go, Ben. Thanks for the news."

"Angel!" Jason called out. He'd been drinking – a lot. "Come here! Whoa, look at that outfit. Man, did you see that?" Jason said, smacking Adam's chest with the back of his hand. "You do know you're making him crazy, right?"

Adam glared at Jason.

"Oh, stuff happening between you two? Angel, cut my boy loose." His breath tarnishing the air between them as he draped his heavy arm across her shoulder.

"Jace, shut the fuck up!" Adam growled.

Jason's light brows inched together, ignoring Adam. "What are you doing here, Angel? You strippin'?"

"Trish had her party here, too," Adam answered for her.

"What!? My bride is here, now, peeking at another man's Johnson?" He yelled, laughing. "I'm going back in there."

Melanie's phone rang in her hand. Three of his equally drunk friends struggled to hold Jason back. But he was really trying to break across the line.

"Where are you? The show's over and we're heading out." Carla's voice was barely audible.

"I'll meet you guys out front."

"Do you want me to grab some of this food for you? It's going fast."

"I'm good. FYI, Jace and his crew are out here, he's inebriated and waiting for Trish." Melanie watched the rowdy men tackling each other to the ground. Adam was off to the side. His broad shoulders were slumped and his shirttail was hanging loose. He looked down on Jason and his friends with disgust.

He's going to have to feel bad for a while, she decided. If she could survive, so could he.

Unable to tear her gaze from him, she watched as he ran his hands over his face and through his hair before joining up with the guys. "Is this a party or not?"

"Melanie?"

"Yeah?" she answered, tearing her attention away from Adam. "Nate. The player with the guitar." Her smile came out crooked. "Or was it the guitar player?"

They stood in a moment of awkward silence. She was keenly aware Adam was watching her every movement.

"You okay?" Nate asked, casting a glance in the direction she'd been looking, over at Adam. "Is he bothering you?"

Shaking her head, she focused on Nate. "So, did you go broke on the naked dancers?"

"There was some real talent in there. How about you? Did you visit the ATM?"

"Twice." She winked.

"There you are!" Carla laughed. "Oh my, that was the most bizarre thing I've ever witnessed. Where did you go? I know it was sort of gross but you should've stayed for the show."

Melanie looked at Nate and shrugged.

"You lied to me?" Nate asked hurt, his hand covering his heart.

"Carla this is Nate. Nate, Carla."

"This is my first time to one of these places," Carla informed.

"And now you're hooked?" Nate laughed.

"No! I think it broadened my horizon a few inches too far."

"A dirty joke from Carla?" Melanie was surprised.

"Drink! I need a drink over here!" Nate yelled to people on the street.

"Bathroom break," Melanie said, grasping Carla by the arm, "See you later, Nate."

The bathroom was crowded with women drying off their sweaty cleavage, powdering and spritzing for the after party. Melanie looked in the mirror. Adam had done a good job removing most of her make-up. She expected to feel bad but when she looked into herself, searching for a trace of guilt, there wasn't any.

"You're going to Hell," she told herself. She'd made amends about the carnage that came with the job. But this was her real life.

"Oh. My. God. Wasn't that awesome?" Lori exclaimed, jumping out of the bathroom stall and slapping her hands on Melanie's shoulders. "When those guys brought out the pyrotechnics, I thought I was going to die!"

"Me, too!" Melanie picked up her voice to match Lori's.

"What was with Trish's wand?" Jenny was at the sink, rubbing a wet paper towel over her chest. "How did she do it?"

"I didn't even think something like that was possible." Carla said, wide-eyed.

Kara pushed her way to the mirrors. "I want one of those wands. I could've used one for my last boyfriend. So frustrating."

"Everybody was Kung-Fu Fighting," Trish sang, as she kicked and karate chopped her way out of the bathroom stall. "Da, da, da, da, fast as lightning. High-Ya!"

"Watch it, Tiger," Melanie said, stopping Trish's slicing hand.

"I am so glad you're here!" Trish slurred. "I love you. All right, ladies," she said, checking that she hadn't smeared lipstick on her teeth. Then she looked up and yelled, "Are we ready to party? Because it's ladies night and I'm feeling right, oh, what a night!"

"Nobody noticed I was gone?" Melanie asked Carla once the conga-line had disappeared behind the door.

"It was pretty spectacular in there. Crazy." She cringed. "I will be editing this evening when I retell it to Ted."

"I have to ask. What was with the wand?"

Carla blushed. "I can't say."

"Oh, Car, come on!" Melanie sagged.

"She…" Carla looked at the other women in the bathroom and covered her mouth at Melanie's ear. "She made them rise."

"Rise?"

"Shh!" she scolded, gleaming at Melanie. "Rise." She mouthed, her index finger straightening at each joint.

"Really? How?"

Carla giggled and raised both shoulders.

"Where did everyone go?" Courtney asked looking around. "You both are Trish's friends, right?"

Melanie looked down at her outfit and Car's butt cheeks peeking out from the hem of her dress. "Yeah, we're with the 70's party."

"The rest left a few minutes ago. We'd better step on it if we don't want to be left behind," Carla added, purposely not meeting Melanie's gaze.

"I don't know about either of you, but I'm ready to get out of this," Melanie said, adjusting the top.

"What is that made out of?" Courtney asked, feeling the fabric of

Melanie's jumpsuit between her fingers.

"Lycra. I think."

"Isn't that the stuff they make condoms out of?"

Melanie watched Courtney strut off. "Did she just call me a penis?"

"I'm sure she meant it as a compliment," Carla giggled.

The loud group out on the sidewalk was a combination of both parties. Hanging out with the noise looked like a lot of work. Jenny was standing alone at the corner of the crowd, waving them over.

"How were the Asian girls?" Melanie heard Trish ask Jason.

"Who told you?" he asked, lifting her off her feet.

"None of those boys can keep a secret." Her lipstick left a mark on his cheek. "Where are we going? Or do you want to just hit the hotel?"

"You know the hottest club in town is at the hotel," Courtney added, breaking into their conversation.

"She's right," Trish said, biting on Jason's earlobe. "Want to come with me in the limo?"

"Definitely."

"We're heading back to the hotel. Find a ride!" Trish yelled out.

"Does she mean we're not going in the limo?" Jenny asked, confused.

Melanie shrugged. "I think I'd rather take a cab."

"I'll even pay," Carla said.

"That's bound to be uncomfortable to watch," Jenny said, motioning to the valet and ordering a cab.

They were last out of the parking lot. Melanie had watched Adam climb into the back of the Hummer with Lori and Courtney. That the women were attracted to him wasn't where the tension came from, it was the look in his eyes as she told him to move on. And it was that Courtney was awful and it was the way he touched her hip as he disappeared into the back seat.

"I hate sitting directly on this vinyl," Carla said, pulling her skirt down,

"Who knows what human fluids have spilled over these seats?" Melanie gagged, sticking out her tongue.

"Gross. Let me sit on your lap." Carla landed on Melanie's thighs.

"Jeez, you have a bony ass."

"You aren't so comfortable yourself," Carla complained.

"Sit on Jen, then."

"Because I'm plump?"

"You're softer than Mel," Carla said, scooting to Jen. "And you can't be insulted by that."

"I can turn any comment into an insult," Jenny retorted, shifting beneath Carla's weight.

"Who was Nate?" Carla asked, once settled.

"I met him at the garden party."

"He's cute."

"You're a married woman."

"Not for me, for you."

"Good idea." Melanie smiled, masking the worry seeping in over Adam's self-destructive side. She'd seen it before and she'd seen a spark flicker in his eyes. *It doesn't matter. I'm not responsible for him.* "I feel sick," she said, feeling sorry for herself and wanting her heart to ache just to know it still worked. He'd looked destroyed.

"I miss my kids. I miss how Ryan used to touch me." Jenny whispered.

"I watched ugly men take their clothes off," Carla groaned.

"We all have our problems," Jenny huffed.

"I wish Adam and I had been real."

"I wish Ryan hadn't cheated."

"I wish I didn't know what a cock ring was."

"Me, too," Melanie agreed.

Cheryl and Olivia were sleeping on the couch when she entered her room. Melanie peeled off the jumpsuit that was beginning to melt into her skin and jumped in the shower. The cool water washed the salt and plastic smell off her skin and eased the nagging agitation that had been building.

Her loose jeans, tank top and flip-flops were a wonderful contrast and she even appreciated her short haircut that left her neck free.

Her phone buzzed.

"Hello, Boss." Logan sounded young. "Do you have a minute?"

"What's up?"

"We're all here on a conference call. We just wanted you to know how much we miss you. And to plead for you to use your muscle to get back into the games." They all agreed.

"Guys," Melanie said, as she sat on the corner of her bed, "I have no authority over the Board's decisions. Agent Williams cares about the ITC. I'm sure he'll do his best and you three are awesome. I'm not worried and none of you should be, either. How's Bob?"

"I'm right here."

"How's Mike been treating you?"

"I've learned a lot."

"But?"

"No, he's the bomb."

"Is that good?"

"Most of the time."

She grunted out a laugh. "I'm sure you're growing on him."

"Like a wart. Actually, he sort of handed me over to Ed."

"Ed is a great researcher. Listen to him. Anthony, Fred. I want all of you to show Williams the same respect you showed me."

"Okay, Boss," the goodbyes were apathetic.

Melanie smiled at the dead line. There was something to be said about having admirers.

She found Carla and Jenny at the restaurant, still in their polyester. No one besides them had made it back from the strip club.

"I thought we were changing." Melanie charged.

"We became mesmerized by the lounge singer." Jenny answered, a glass of red wine in her hand. "What do you think happened to the others?"

"Who knows," Carla sighed. "I'm going to find Ted and," she grinned, "who knows?" the words having a different connotation.

"I think I'm going to find a handsome stranger and do the same."

"What about Ryan?"

"I was joking." Jenny grimaced. "What about you?"

"Lady Luck has to be in my favor, since Cupid seems to be absent." She hugged them goodbye.

Checking her watch every five minutes, Melanie was anxious not to be late for her first day as a Las Vegas dealer.

The opulent casino smelled of money. It might have been the gold gilded walls as if the painter's spray bottle was filled with 14-karat yellow and he didn't discriminate on where he aimed. Gold-leafed frames surrounded paintings of cherubs with gold bows and arrows, gold-plated tables and chairs, chandeliers, handrails.

She strutted past the machines that clinked out artificial sound effects from slots that no longer dropped coins but printed tickets. In the basement she dressed in her dealer's uniform, pulled the Farrah wig into a ponytail and headed to check-in with the pit boss.

"You the new dealer?" he asked, scrutinizing her with his left eye. The right was hidden behind a saggy lid that was nearly shut. "I thought they said you were a brunette."

"I was, yesterday."

"Mook said you were pretty good, but this isn't some tribal casino. This is Vegas."

"Who's Mook?"

"Boyd, the guy who trained you. We like to give mobster nicknames around here. If you make it, you'll get one, too."

"Cool." Melanie grinned, slipping on the non-prescription glasses she'd bought from the sex shop at the strip club. "What's your mob name?" His tag read Peter.

"Not until you've proven yourself," Peter said, leading her to a closed table. "Ophelia called in at the last minute, it's always her kids. You'll take her rotation. Questions?"

"I thought I was going to watch," Melanie said, checking out the packed tables.

"Scared?" Peter laughed a deep mobster guttural. "Sink or swim. You got through security clearance pretty quick. I don't like women who sleep their way into a job."

"Sure you want to close that door?" Melanie asked, her meaning echoed through her gaze.

Peter shook his head. "If you get in trouble, give the signal. Mook showed you, right?"

"I got it," Melanie said. She could feel the sweat build up beneath the wig. The first hour was painful. So much to concentrate on and Peter had to come over twice. But after that her dealer gene kicked in, the gamblers were more drunk than not and her fingers had loosened.

Her mind finding the blackjack current, she was able to focus on the people in the seats. On her feet she followed the guidelines of smiling rarely and conversing never, unless it was to instruct a novice.

"Come on, Babe, I'll show you how to play."

Melanie froze, holding her breath as her friends stopped at her table: Trish, Jason, Adam and another one of Jason's groomsmen.

She dealt; Jason showed Trish how to hold the cards. He hadn't sobered up. Adam didn't sit but paced restlessly behind the seat.

"Hey, Man, you're making me nervous. Sit," Jace said. "No baby, like this." He was having two conversations. "Buddy, you need to get over her." Adam took the stool beside Jace.

"I can't, I don't want to get over her."

Melanie swallowed and was careful not to let her hands shake.

"Dude, Courtney is literally throwing herself at you. She's a fucking swimsuit model … just give her a little attention. What the hell is wrong with you?"

Melanie dealt the hand with her eyes cast down, not daring to look up from the blue felt.

"I love Melanie, too." Jace put his arm over Adam's shoulders. "But, Man, how many ways does she have to fuck you over? She's cute, don't get me wrong, but Courtney's smokin' hot." He was whispering, ignoring the fact that Trish had bet fifty bucks with the dealer showing an ace.

"I hear you," Adam's voice held insight, she could hear his resolve swaying. "You're right." He sat, dropping a C note in front of him.

She changed his bills for chips. Jason scolded Trish. And Courtney ran over, covered Adam's eyes with her fingers.

"Guess who," she sang with her breasts hanging over his ears like muffs.

The waitress brought rounds of whiskey shooters; Melanie laid down cards and dragged chips back into the House's stash. And did her best to act natural.

"I cannot believe we got tattoos!" Trish snickered, loving on Jason. "I swore I'd never mark-up my body again."

Melanie had noticed the matching bandages on the inside of their left wrists. Tattoos, probably their wedding date. Mentally she shook her head.

Trish was a terrible gambler, losing money as fast as Jace could exchange the bills. Distracted by Courtney's tongue, Adam lost repeatedly. His interest was tilting from his wagers to the woman.

"Color up," Adam said, pulling his face out of her cleavage and sliding his chips to the center of the table. "We're taking off," he nudged Jace's shoulder. "Are you staying with me tonight?"

"Depends on Trish."

"Give me a couple of hours."

"That's the spirit!" Jace smiled, his bloodshot eyes narrowing. "Have a good time, enough for me."

Melanie felt the gravitational pull from her core as she swapped his chips for larger denominations and left the stack in front of him. Adam's mouth was at Courtney's collarbone, pulling aside the blue blazer as his lips made their way up her neck. Courtney's hands had vanished inside his shirt. Melanie's eyes darted to the edge where her makeup still stained the corner.

Adam came up for air, slapped Jason's shoulder. "Night, Man. Here you go," he said, sliding a generous tip toward the dealer.

"Thank you," Melanie said, before calling out to the pit boss. Feeling his stare, she hesitated but the temptation was too much. The instant their eyes met, recognition, confusion and dread filled his expression.

She understood his shock. Her movements were minimal, a shrug – designed for him only. He tried to look elsewhere but was magnetized to Melanie – for what felt like eons.

"Go Man, what are you waiting for?" Jace asked, shoving Adam away from the table.

Adam lingered. Melanie had a job to do and ignored him well enough that she lost track when he and Courtney left.

Secretly, she watched the interaction between Trish and Jace. No one else would be able to put up with her friend's antics. By the time Jace ran out of cash, Melanie was sufficiently satisfied that these two belonged together. Her spirits dampened by thoughts of her own unworthiness.

The suite was quiet as she snuck to her bed and expected to pass out immediately. But feelings and thoughts she hadn't allowed surfaced.

"It's been over for a long time," she said, trying to console herself. "Then why is seeing him nuzzling Courtney's neck so unbelievable? Do I hate her for other reasons?" she mused. Securing the fact that she'd hate Courtney even if she hadn't sunk her claws into Adam.

Melanie covered her face with the extra pillow.

CHAPTER FIFTEEN

In the distance, through the goose down, she heard her phone, Carla's ring tone.

"Crap!" She was awake. "I'm late for the wedding. Shit." Melanie raced from the living area, out the door and answered the call on her way to the Bella Suite.

"Where are you?"

"On my way," she said, flying down the stairs.

"What happened to you?"

"Hangover."

"Seems to be a pandemic. I have your gown ready and waiting."

"Thanks, Car."

WWIII had erupted in Trish's room. Courtney and Lori were both unaccounted for and Kara was heaving into the toilet.

"No one will ever say my bachelorette party sucked," Trish said, adjusting her veil. "But we're only minutes from show time." She was in a good mood despite her late bedtime.

"Where were you last night?" Melanie asked.

"Sorry, we forgot to call. We drove by a tattoo parlor and it was an impulse decision. Jace and I got matching tats!"

"Let me guess, you both have your wedding date tattooed on your asses," Melanie laughed.

"What, do you have cameras on me?"

"Predictable."

Trish stuck her tongue out at Melanie. "It was our wrists and we also got something special just between the two of us."

"What is it?" Melanie asked.

"I'll have to show you later."

"What about Courtney and Lori?" Jenny asked. "Neither are here, yet."

"I guess they miss the wedding. I don't need them to be there." She smiled and looked at Melanie in the mirror. "You look like hell. Baxter, fix my friend's face, please." She winked as she sent the make-up artist over. "Tell me how gorgeous I look."

Melanie held back a rush of unexpected emotion. "You do look gorgeous." Her heart clenched and her tear ducts burned.

"I know." Trish beamed. "Mel, I'm so excited. I can't wait for this day to be over and then I'll be married to Jason."

Melanie nodded. "We should get down there."

The retractable walls of the chapel were opened to hold eighty-five guests. The yellow and white flowers Trish had chosen were on each end of the pews, at the altar and in the hands of each bridesmaid.

"Where's the maid of honor?" the planner asked, ushering all the girls around.

"Passed out somewhere," Kara said, having recovered from her puke and now fixed Trish's gown. "Lori went AWOL, too."

"There's always at least one," the planner said. "Let me check with the boys and see how many of them disappeared. Meantime, adjust those bows." She pointed to Jenny's butt and was gone.

"I like her." Melanie grinned.

"Do you think I could have more than one maid of honor?"

"Just pick Kara, she's the tallest." Carla snorted, still holding onto the offense.

Trish turned to face Carla and for an instant Melanie expected Bridezilla to reemerge.

"Carla," Melanie stared as Trish spoke, "will you be my maid of honor?"

Melanie looked to Carla as she was gaping at Trish. Speechless.

"Are you messing with me?"

"No. You have been here for me this entire week and always are. We may not always see eye-to-eye and not just because you're so short, but you're someone I know I can count on. Be my maid of honor."

Carla's tears smeared her mascara. "Thank you. But if Adam is best man, I would look silly beside him. Thank you," she covered her heart, "but I'm going to say no."

"My guess is that Adam is among the missing," Melanie added.

"I'm here! I made it!" Courtney shouted and waved as she ran into the room. "We can start, I'm here!"

Melanie liked that the model didn't wear her indulgence well the next morning. It was more than her hair that needed attention. She carried purple bags under her eyes and her skin had bright red splotches.

"Okay, all the men are accounted for," the planner said, reentering the room and stopping short to appraise Courtney. "Well, you had a rough night. Does anyone have a comb or a mask?"

"I'm fine!" Courtney said, plying her tangles with her fingers. "I just need a clip."

"Line up, people."

"Wait for me," Lori skidded, with her shoes in her hands, tipping over the vase of flowers on the side table. "Sorry. Sorry. I'm ready."

"Fabulous." The wedding planner snapped her fingers and the girls lined up shortest to tallest.

The dresses looked better than Melanie thought they would and the procession walked down the aisle without any of the earlier drama. She set her gaze firmly on the minister but curiosity got the better of her. Jason, whose eyes were glued to the spot Trish was about to enter. He was standing like a post and Melanie wondered if he'd taken a breath since the wedding song started. His strawberry blonde hair was slicked back and he was gleaming with sweat.

Adam in a tux was too much of a temptation. *Just a quick glance*, she thought, her heart speeding up. If there was ever going to be a moment of desire, it was him looking down at her with his emerald green eyes full of apology. He lifted his hand to cover his heart as he watched her.

Melanie took her place on the steps before the altar. A moment later, Carla tapped her shoulder and handed her a Kleenex.

She lifted her hand to her face – it was wet – a clear fluid beaded on her fingertips. "Thanks," she whispered. "It's the ceremony."

"Sure." Carla's smile was full of pity.

The minister gave the super-short version of the wedding ceremony and the newlyweds were making out seven minutes later. Trish, holding Jason's arm, pranced down the aisle and Melanie hooked arms with a balding groomsman she hadn't noticed before.

"I don't know any of these people," Melanie said, tilting her head to Carla as they were ushered to the receiving line. "Great job on the vows."

"She did most of it. I wrote the words down but they came from her. They're going to start the toasts. We're you asked to give one?"

"No. You?"

"No." They chuckled.

Adam gave the first speech, speaking of enduring love. If she could've covered her ears and hummed American Pie, as a tribute to Trish, she would have. But his voice was clear and his beautiful lies fooled everyone within earshot, except her.

Courtney made the moment about herself and by the time the cake was served Melanie was itching to escape. Jack's call was a welcome distraction. "Tell me," she whispered on her way to a quiet corner.

"Hope your heart isn't set on dealing."

"What happened?"

"The ring had expanded to recruit a member of security. Right now five suspects are being held. I need you to interrogate. We're going to lose these guys as soon as the Feds arrive. The concern is where the money went."

"There has to be a trail?"

"That's what you're there to find out."

"Shit," she sighed, looking down at her bright yellow gown. "Jack, I've got a reception to attend. I could search their rooms or something less visible."

"I had our local agents scour their rooms, vehicles, everything. The data is being sorted. Just get down to the basement and supervise, I don't know the agents in Vegas."

"I'm on my way."

"Mel, if you could interrogate…"

"Jack, I'm in a yellow dress. You know I would, if I could. I'll oversee."

"Do what you can and get back to me."

She broke away from the party and descended to the basement. The five suspects were seated at one table in a locked room. "Why are they in there together? Separate them," she ordered. After a conversation with the lead agent she collected the phones and key cards that had been confiscated.

Forty minutes later they had gotten nowhere with the Syrians, she'd synced the phones to Mike's system and the Feds had arrived to take over.

Rejoining the party, nobody had noticed her absence. The band was playing. Melanie wandered uncomfortably, snagging champagne from waiters.

"You are a difficult woman to catch," Nate said, blocking her drifting ramble. "I've been watching you make trails across this entire room."

"Have you ever been a single girl, of marrying age, alone at a wedding?" she asked.

"Let me think."

"It's not pretty," Melanie said, reaching for another bubbly.

"If it'll make you feel better, I'll make the sacrifice and dance with you." He held out his hand.

"Chivalry." She inhaled, taking his open hand.

"Keeping in your style, we can wander around the parquet," he said, taking her in his arms.

"Making fun of me with flare," Melanie said. "Why aren't you here with a date?" His muscles felt solid beneath his tux jacket.

"I like to pick up on the single bridesmaids. They're easy targets."

He winked. "Lonely and desperate."

"FYI, Mr. Gentleman, you're wasting your time with me."

"You could never be a waste of time."

"I am if you're looking to get lucky."

"Get lucky?" he laughed. "Anyone ever tell you that you're cute?"

"Only the brave ones." She grinned, enjoying the uncomplicated task of flirting. "I hate to compliment you and run the risk that it'll go to your head. But you're sort of a good dancer."

"Musician. Ukulele, remember? Actually, my band is going to play the after party. You're welcome to be a groupie."

"I could scream out your name, if you'd like."

"I'd love that! I'd even be willing to pay." His brown eyes were bright and devilish.

"Excuse me," Adam was standing behind her. "Mel, could we go somewhere?"

Nate stopped dancing but tightened his grip on her hand. "Aren't you the asshole who caused her trouble the other night?"

Adam's back straightened.

"I really hate guys like you," Nate said.

"Nate, it's all right." Melanie pulled her fingers out of his hand.

"No, Melanie. This guy can't come in and take over."

She looked from Nate to Adam. "We've both made our positions clear," she said, hoping to remind Adam of his position with Courtney. "There's nothing left to say – nothing constructive, anyway."

"About Courtney..."

"Don't. I honestly don't care. You and I have no ties." Her grin was unrealistic and pinched. "You're a free man."

"Asshole, why don't you take a hike?" Nate said, putting himself between them.

"Stop." She squeezed Nate's bicep, weighing Adam's expression. And for a fraction she thought he was going to take a swing.

"Look, Man, I get that you want to strut in front of her but you have no idea what the fuck you're talking about. So just stay the hell out of this." He turned his chill to Melanie. "Somewhere else, please."

"How about we talk after the reception?" She relented, offering a compromise.

"When do you leave?"

The second I can escape without being noticed. "Depends," her gaze that met his was cold.

"Because of your extracurricular activities?" he asked, referring to her blackjack table.

"None of your business," she answered, cautioning him to back off.

"Are you talking about me? Because I could definitely be extra credit." Nate grinned mischievously.

"Next time." Melanie said to Nate.

"I think they're tossing the bouquet now." Over the loud speaker came the call for the single women. "That's you."

"I'm passing."

"No!" Nate's smile lifted his entire expression. "You have to. One of us should get lucky tonight. Over here! Trish, don't forget Melanie."

"I know what you're doing." Melanie pointed at Nate as she was pulled into the menagerie of frantic women and away from Adam.

"Then you can thank me later."

Dodging flying elbows, Melanie leaped out of the way as three women yanked and trashed the bouquet. By the time she got out of the fray Nate was standing alone, clapping for her.

"You almost had it," he said, as she brushed down her skirt.

"I almost had a black eye."

"So, are you heading out?" he asked, nodding toward the exit. Melanie caught the last bit of the white train as Trish and Jason raced away.

"Oh, thank God. I thought they'd never leave," she sighed and then sucked in a huge lungful of air. "You have no idea how much better I feel. Like I can breathe."

"Wedding anxiety. I hear it's a common ailment among single women of marrying age. Not pretty." Nate took the empty glass from her hand. "I can be booked for weddings or bar mitzvahs, any occasion you may need a date."

"Family dinners?"

"My specialty. Moms love me."

"You just climbed to the top of my list. Well," she said, looking around. She was safe for the moment. "Bye, Nate. Thanks for making things easier." About to place a small kiss on his cheek, he turned and their lips met for a brief instant. "I guess you did get lucky. See you around."

Saying quick goodbyes to Carla and Jenny, Melanie used the service elevator to sneak out, avoiding Adam, who was loitering by the exit, then out the door and up to her room to become Agent Ward.

❦

While the heat in Vegas had been searing and combustible, D.C. was muggy and oppressive. In the length of time it took her to pass through security at the Manor, Melanie racked her brain for the name of the guy who'd invented air conditioning. The green light on her retinal scan filled her senses with the feeling of being home.

Ben was in his office, the desk lamp bright and shining down on an open file while classical music played soothingly in the background.

"You look cozy," Melanie said, waving a hello to Ben's assistant, Judith.

"Hey, how was your trip?" He smiled, tilting his glasses so he could examine her face.

"Agony."

"Hmm." He settled the frames back to their usual spot on the bump of his nose. "Have a seat, I can see you have something to say. Want a drink?"

"I'll pass. Been doing too much of that lately." The chairs in front of Ben's desk were new and Melanie liked how she didn't fall into a sinkhole when she sat. "I'm here for my next assignment."

Ben didn't say anything, just looked through her with his pale blue eyes.

"I want to do damage. Tear down walls, fire off a few shots, go under cover and hide out as someone else for a few months. I want a vacation from being me."

Ben stood, went to his tray of decanters and poured her a glass of scotch. "No more time off for you," he said with the fatherly look that signaled his concern. "You come back in worse shape than you left."

"Exactly! So, do I get an assignment?"

"No."

Melanie groaned and her head fell back.

"Not when I've still got eighty million dollars unaccounted for and Syrians loose on casino floors."

"So I'm still on the case?" she asked happily. "The Feds arrived while I was overseeing the interrogation. I thought the case was theirs."

"We are no longer involved with the gambling ring. But from the cell phones you retrieved we have a few leads for the missing money. That, I'm not letting go." Ben pressed a button on his phone. "Judith could you locate Agent Scott and if he isn't busy bring him in for an impromptu meeting?"

"Yes, Sir."

"Tell me about Vegas." Ben said, his pale blue eyes concentrating.

Ugh, she thought taking a sip of scotch.

"I'm talking about the case, Agent." He clarified with an amused gaze.

"Oh," she chuckled before debriefing him. "Am I teaming up with Jack?"

"Not this time. But I had him arrange your cover story. What's your thoughts on Agent Sean Gibb?"

"I don't think anything about Gibb."

"What? Agent Ward without an opinion? Is it the end of days?" Jack entered the room laughing.

"All right," she grinned, "you want an opinion. I think he was a good agent, once. But over the past few years he's lost his grip."

"Six months ago, I would've agreed with you but he's pulled his shit together." Jack took the seat beside her. "Give him a chance."

"I don't even know what I'm up against," Melanie argued.

"Ever heard of Russell Everest?"

"Of course. He's the embedded war correspondent for national and cable television networks. Everest's been in the Middle East for a decade reporting on the wars. You're kidding me," she said looking from Jack to Ben.

"His was one of the numbers used by the casino hustlers."

"No shit!" she gasped. "This sucks." Melanie shook her head, "If he really is involved I'm going to be very disappointed. You invite a guy into your home every night and then to find out he's dealing with terrorists?"

"We don't know that," Ben reminded her. "The number we found in the Syrian contact list wasn't one Everest has listed, but on cross reference, we found that he made several calls to the newsroom using that number. It could be that he's working on a story, a perfectly plausible explanation. I have a call into the CEO of the network."

"How bright is that? He buys an untraceable phone and then uses it to call into work." Melanie's respect for the man plummeted even further. "What's the cover?"

"You're going in as a newswoman for a cable network, eager to catch a break. You're a fan of Everest."

"Everest is my target and I'm looking for…" she let the question hang for Jack to answer.

"His relationship to the gambling ring."

"Okay. When do I leave? And what about Gibb?"

"The plane is ready when you are and Gibb is your cameraman. He's been in Turkey, he'll meet you in Cairo."

"Give me twenty minutes to pack," Melanie said, standing.

CHAPTER SIXTEEN

Cairo. *Russell Everest couldn't cover the financial crisis in Iceland?* She was over being hot.

The hotel in Cairo was one used by the media; it had the basic amenities while maintaining cultural ambiance. Everest was a permanent resident. The network rented one of the condos on the property to serve as his base of operation while covering the Middle East.

Melanie met Sean in the parking lot.

"Hi," she said, barely recognizing him. "Good to see you, again." The Sean Gibb she remembered had been haggard, overweight and fizzled out. This man was the direct opposite.

"Veronica," his grin had been bleached and his brows plucked.

"Veronica Summer." Melanie laughed. "Someone was creative. I checked us in and I guess Everest can be found at the bar – every night picking up women."

"I heard on the news that the likelihood of a civil war in Syria has increased," Sean said, locking up the van he'd rented.

"We're on a mass media transport tomorrow. Everest has a personal plane but he's scheduled to be there as well." They sweltered across the grounds, which were designed to portray an oasis. Palm trees and murky ponds invited guest to different buildings of the extensive hotel.

The rest of the afternoon she and Sean prepped their stories and by evening she was ready to meet Russell Everest.

The gathering place was the hotel dining room where she met up with Sean. Russell was exactly where he was supposed to be, surrounded by women buying him drinks.

"Can you believe that guy? He's so cocky," Sean said after they'd spent their dinner studying the newscaster. "He doesn't give that impression on the news."

"No one would like him if he did." Melanie added, disgusted that she'd been one of the fools to buy into his shtick. "I think it's time to make my move."

"Really? Shouldn't you wait until he's free?"

"Do you forecast that happening anytime soon? Nope." Melanie stood, thinking about how all she wanted was to get into Russell Everest's room and fondle his … paperwork. "As much as I'd like to lay low, take my time with this assignment, there is an element of rush. We don't know what the hell Everest is doing and that makes me nervous. So," she stood facing Sean, "how do I look?"

"Hot."

"Good."

Squeezing herself between the other women and Everest she leaned against the bar and whistled to the bartender. "Give me a deep throat." Melanie said, smiling and turning toward her target.

"Excuse me," the woman she'd elbowed complained.

"No need, you're fine." Her eyes capturing Everest's. "Hi, I'm Veronica Summer." Her hand found its way into his.

"Russell Everest." He smelled of cigarettes and a heavy-handed layer of cologne.

"I know who you are, but I'm not like these fortune hunters or celebrity groupies."

"Are you positive?" he said, as slick as an oil well. "Because," he leaned back to take a long view of her, "you look exactly like the others."

"Well, I'm not." Melanie grinned. "I just came over to say hello and to pump up your ego. I love your work." She smiled at the bartender and took her drink back to Sean.

"What happened?"

"Not sure," she sat, sipped her drink and over-engaged in their conversation about current events. "Is he looking?"

Sean said yes between ventriloquist lips. "He's staring straight at me." He cocked his head toward Melanie. "He's coming this way."

The legend, Russell Everest, made himself comfortable at their table. He leaned back in the seat and flipped a toothpick between his fingers.

"I've met Veronica Summer. I'm Russell Everest," he said stretching out a hand to Sean.

"Sean Porter."

"Is she," he nodded toward Melanie, "always like that?"

"Brazen? I'm assuming but we just started working together," Sean shrugged.

Russell's famous grin shot forward and Melanie felt like she was watching him on television.

"Are you going to offer to buy me a drink?" Melanie asked.

"I'm usually the recipient."

"Sean, you buying?"

"Sure, I'll be right back, but you're drinking whatever I chose," Sean agreed.

Flirting with Everest was difficult. The banter was flat and the innuendoes flopped. There was no interest and the more she tried, the more he recoiled. Ready to give up and pull back, he became receptive, laughing louder, making eye contact and remaining at their table.

It was a game she couldn't figure out. He walked her to the stairwell and slouched in for a kiss that she averted, she was confused.

The next morning twenty broadcasters from stations around the globe loaded onto a military plane and were transported to Damascus. They were given an informational piece with the latest reportable news and lined up at a pre-designated photo op. It was on the roof of a government building, where they could report the news from a safe, yet, demonstrative locale.

"Holy shit," Sean gaped, "This is for fucking real."

On the street below the protesters' march had stopped, the movement had gotten too big and people moved in a directionless mob.

"Come on," Sean moved them to a far corner of their roped-off assigned spot and redirected the camera from a high angle. Trying to get a shot of the street. "We can do better from over here."

"Hi this is Veronica Summer, reporting from Damascus, where a civil war is looking inevitable." She'd written her bit on the flight. She was a fake reporter but the news was real and her clip would play on a cable network that no one watched but was in alliance with the Agency. Sean's camera rolled as she conveyed the information she'd received. "How was that?"

"Really good."

"I want to try again." Five times she presented the news, and on the sixth she spoke in French. Then Italian, German and Spanish. "Is that a wrap?"

"There was some interference on that last take. One more time," Sean said, looking over his shoulder as the press corps was being herded back to the plane.

"Bon jour, je m'appelle Veronica Summer."

The explosion was deafening and strong enough for Melanie to lose her balance. Grabbing the wall, she pulled herself to her feet and reported. "A bomb of some type was just detonated on the street of Damascus where thousands of people are protesting. The dust and smoke is so thick I can't see the extent of the devastation." She walked her hands up the wall and leaned over the top.

Sean filmed for a minute before the officials blocked his lens, forcing him to stop. The group of media, who was covered in dust and ash, was rushed under guarded protection back to the airport.

The first half of the return flight to Cairo was quiet, but the volume increased slowly and by the time they landed Sean was replaying the footage. He'd been the only one still rolling.

She communicated with one look – *this cannot go national*. His response, I know! The swarm of news crews surrounded them with questions.

"Veronica, you just hit the big time."

"Turn up the sound," one reporter ordered. "Are you speaking French?"

"Was I?" She'd forgotten. "I'd been practicing, but I think I reverted back to English after the bomb went off."

The palatable jealousy that had echoed in the fuselage faded and shrank in an instant.

"What network is going to want that?"

"Bummer for you."

Dinner at the hotel restaurant was the norm for the close-knit group of reporters and support staff. They clustered at three tables while Russell kept his post at the bar. Melanie and Sean sat alone.

"I have to admit, that was freaking scary," Sean said, sipping water. "You jumped right back in as if you knew it was coming. Fucking incredible."

"You were the one who knew where to set the shot." They laughed as they praised each other's brilliance. "What a boon that I'd been speaking French," she said, her phone ringing. "Ben."

"I hear you got some footage." His accusatory tone sent her into defense mode.

"It was Sean's fault." Her smiling eyes glided over to him.

"Apparently, there's going to be a bidding war. Ward?"

"Summer. Veronica Summer." She bit her bottom lip, knowing that her scolding was over but she'd left him in a bind.

"Has Porter sent the file?"

"He uploaded it to Mike as soon as we landed."

"Fine. I'll see if he can edit you out."

She was front and center in the frame. "If anyone can do it…"

"We'll handle it like we always do."

The call ended without a goodbye or a be careful or a good job.

"I think you're in trouble," Melanie said, looking at Sean and deciding it really was his fault.

"Well, well, little Miss Summer has sold a story," Russell said, dropping into his seat. That damn toothpick flickered around his mouth. "Congratulations. You might just make it after all."

A smart rebuff was on the tip of her tongue, but, she sighed, the game was getting her nowhere. She'd screwed up her approach to Everest and now Mike was going to be working around the clock to edit her out of the clip.

"Do you think I could take a look at the footage?"

"I don't see why not. Oh," she said, swallowing an awkward moment. Realizing he'd been asking Sean. "Sorry."

"I was going to check that the van was locked. You can come with, if you want." They stood at the same moment.

"Well, I've got a headache." Melanie picked up the check, "I'm going to bed."

"You're not coming with us?" Everest asked, as much emotion as he'd ever shown.

Reading him hadn't worked so far, Melanie gave it a quick effort before giving up. "You boys will survive without me. Sean, I'll meet you here bright and early tomorrow. We're back in Damascus."

"I'll come by your room later, you know," Everest sneered, "to check on you."

The table filled with media turned their faces to snicker. She received a few villainous looks from a couple of the women and a bottom-to-top body scans from a few of the men.

They think I'm sleeping with him. Melanie gritted her teeth, she hated losing her credibility – even for a fake job. But for the good of the case … Everest wanted these people to think they were having a relationship.

Melanie turned on her flirtatious smile and gave him an accepting nod. Watching Sean and Russell walk out she wondered about his secrets? And the comment about visiting her … he didn't even know which room she was in.

"Veronica?"

Melanie turned. "Hi." It was Scooter Sullivan, the Everest equivalent for the opposing network, signaling for Melanie to join her at the elusive table.

"I wanted to give you a little advice about Russell," she said, her silver bob and black-framed glasses were her trademark.

Melanie had seen Scooter hiding out in a private booth, keeping her distance from the common folk.

"I overheard his remark. I know he's successful and handsome, and those two attributes are a powerful combination, but Russell uses young, ambitious women. Whatever it is that he's telling you," She raised one dark brow, "he won't keep one promise. Somehow the women he's involved with are transferred to Dubuque or somewhere as influential. I've seen it a hundred times. I typically don't care but I was watching you today and you've got talent. I'd hate to see that thrown away on a man like Russell."

"Wow," Melanie breathed, it was a lot of information to take in. "Thank you. This is all very surreal, being here with my idols. It's like I'm dreaming."

"Don't be so star stuck and stay away from vipers like Russell. It reminds me of a tip that was given to me years ago by one of my favorite professors. I don't share this with just anyone," she winked, "the key to being a great newscaster is to report the news, don't be part of it. Okay?"

❦

"How'd it go last night?" Melanie asked Sean as they stood in line for the breakfast buffet.

"That's what I was going to ask you. What happened when Russell showed up at your room?"

"He didn't, doesn't know which room I'm in."

"Yeah, he does. He walked me back to my room and I told him you were down the hall." Sean and Russell had grabbed a couple of beers after reviewing the video. "He's a nice guy."

She told him about her encounter with Scooter Sullivan and the only thing she uncovered during her raid on Russell's condo was the cell phone used by the Syrians.

The journalists were delivered to a different part of the city – no bombs or explosions to get excited about. She reported the news she'd been given. The key correspondents had their own informants and were given extra tidbits of information. Veronica didn't qualify for preferential treatment.

That night at dinner she was going to discuss options with Sean, the case had hit a dead end. About to have that conversation when she looked up and intruded on a glance. Russell was looking at Sean.

It was in that one full admiring and yearning moment that Melanie had a revelation. Russell Everest is gay? It was a possibility she hadn't considered. For an hour she watched him and repositioned the pieces with the theory that he was in the closet.

"Okay," she thought, her role suddenly diminishing. "Hey, Sean, we need to regroup."

In the van they scrambled the airwaves, cranked the radio and Melanie whispered. "I'm not getting anywhere with Everest. I'm thinking that I'm just not his type."

"That's my opinion, too. So, do we call for a replacement?"

She shook her head and stared into Sean's brown eyes. "I'm not his type – but I think you are." She paused, allowing time for her meaning to sink in.

"But Russell is all over every woman."

She waited as Sean worked through his emotions.

"You really think so?"

"I do."

"What is it you want me to do? I'm not gay." The look of bewilderment flashed across his face.

"I want to know what Everest is doing and I want you to get that information, however you need to get it."

"Can't we do something else?"

"What? I'm open for your suggestion. I searched his room, his bank accounts, I've been over every broadcast he's delivered for the past year. What else am I supposed to do? His private number was found in the cell of criminals who'd ripped off casinos in excess of eighty million dollars. Where is that money?"

"Can't we just give him the shot of truth juice and be done?"

"Haven't you noticed that he never drinks alcohol? It's all a ruse. What happens when he wakes up with a hangover and zero recall of the previous evening? No, too suspicious. You said the two of you went out for a couple of beers … that's the most alcohol he's consumed. He's comfortable with you … that's all I'm asking. Get him drunk, preferably in his apartment, and then we can do what we have to without raising alarms. Sean, I'm not asking you to change your sexual orientation but you have a connection with him. Use it."

Sean stormed out of the van, slamming the doors and grumbling about it being too much to ask.

She didn't see Sean for the rest of the night but she didn't see Russell either. Instead she hung out with Scooter in the sacred back corner booth of the restaurant.

"I'm glad to see you took my advice. This is a tough business. You have to make choices and sacrifices." It was how the lengthy conversation started. Melanie knew all too well about forfeiting a personal life for her job.

"How did you know it was the right choice for you – to give up on the idea of having a family?" Melanie asked, hoping for insight.

"I never wanted a family. Thoughts of babies send me running. I can't figure out the benefit of kids." Her face serious and without a trace of perplexity. "Perhaps in old age when facing the black hole of death one feels the desire of a living legend. Leaving a piece of you in the world that will live on – but I think I've done that. Years of covering the world's news. Every significant event in the last twenty years has my stamp on it. My name will be in history books, on the Internet, young journalists will study my career. I'm at peace with my life."

"And love?"

"I've had lovers but my work fulfills me in ways no other human has. What about you? Will this sacrifice be too great for you?"

"I don't consider my life as a sacrifice. I've been doing this job for so long that I don't know what else I'd do," she said, keeping the rest of her thoughts private. *My mark on the world has been silent. I've created some of the news you've reported.* "I'm okay without notoriety."

Scooter barked out a laugh, "Then you're in the wrong profession. We're all dying for our faces to be projected nightly through four billion televisions. For world leaders to be listening, and governing by our voices. It is a magnificent power."

"What about regret? Do you have any for how you got here?" Melanie asked, thinking about what Russell was doing with his casino partners.

"Regret is an ugly word. I don't regret a thing. To get to this level of success there is a price. Tomorrow I will be back at the weekend anchor desk waiting for the suit to be pressured out because either he's too old and America is looking for a new perspective or the ratings have slipped. It's quite a game; there are no friends in this business. You must inspire trust, likeability, you need to be quick on your feet, tough and have a vast wealth of knowledge at your disposal. And be able to plunge a knife."

"Wow, brutal." Melanie said, surprised by the ferocity of the statement.

"It is. But, oh, so, rewarding. Look at who I've met, interviewed, had dinner with, the list is incredible. I'm next in line for the evening news anchor spot. And no one is going to stop me."

CHAPTER SEVENTEEN

The next morning a barrage of attacks between Israel and Palestine had the squad of media packing. Hustling to catch a break. Melanie stood in the lobby waiting for Sean.

He approached, dropped his bag between his feet and made bloodshot eye contact with her. "If we're going with the others, we better hurry," she said.

"No, we have to talk."

"You all right?" she asked, noticing that he looked unwell; pale and drawn. "Where are we going?" she said, nudging his suitcase with her toe.

"I'm going home."

Melanie stared. "You can't go home. We've got a job to do. Get your shit and let's catch the transport to the West Bank."

"Melanie," he sighed.

"Veronica Summer," she corrected, hotly.

"We don't need to follow Russell anymore." He said, Melanie waited for Sean to focus. "I'll tell you later."

"No, Sean, you're telling me now." In five minutes they'd be alone in Cairo and she wasn't missing out on an opportunity because he was having a break down.

"He kissed me," Sean said, so low that Melanie almost had to ask him to repeat himself.

"That's good," Melanie cheered, happy for a break in the case. She watched the media head out single file. "We can talk privately in the van."

Sean shuffled through the small lot, dragging his bag over the hot asphalt. "I don't want to talk about this."

"So he kissed you. Big deal. If that's the worse thing you've done for the job then I don't know where you've been working."

"You don't understand." He looked up at her with glassy eyes. "I liked it. Okay?" He dropped his face into his hands. "I liked it."

The three words hung in the air-conditioned van. "Well," she scratched her forehead. "He's a good looking, charming man. That can be persuasive. I think I have a crush on Scooter." She smiled.

"This isn't a joke, it's my life." Sean was distraught. "What if I'm gay?"

Is he expecting me to answer that? she wondered.

"I know you know about my breakdown. For the past year I've been seeing a shrink and she has me doing exercises." He rolled his eyes. "I'm supposed to meet the real me, the one I've been suppressing all my life. What if the real me likes men?"

"Look, Sean, I'm sorry you're confused but truthfully all I care about is figuring out this case. Do you know why Russell is involved with Syrian gamblers?"

"He doesn't know anything. Russell is being blackmailed. He told me last night. There are photos of him with another man and they got into the wrong hands."

"Blackmailed to do what?"

"He gets an anonymous call and told what to say over his broadcast, words to use and subtle changes in phonetics or terms. That's all he knows."

"And you believe him?"

"Yeah," he said, adding a slow nod to his gloom.

"How often does he get these calls?"

"No schedule, but a couple of times a week. We talked for a long time last night," he added as an explanation. "We have to help him, Mel."

"I'm more concerned about where the money is going. Okay," she let out a breath to start her strategizing. "We need to know who's blackmailing Everest. Who is getting the hidden messages and what are they doing with them? We need to intercept his next instructions and trace the call."

The hotel Cairo was deserted by the time she and Sean exited the van.

"Mike, I need to know who's using Everest's disposable cell."

"I already checked, Mel. The numbers are routed to bogus lines; pizza parlors and bagel shops. They're using sophisticated technology."

"Okay, then, I need to listen in on his calls. Any ideas?"

"Can you lift his phone?"

"Of course."

"Good. I'll need some information so I can link your phone to his. Whenever he receives an incoming or outgoing call your number will be part of the loop. It'll be a blind piggyback."

"Sean, I need Everest's phone."

"He's doing a late night shoot, he wants to set himself apart from the rest. He's probably rehearsing in his room … he and Scooter are engaged in an explosive ratings war."

"She is an ambitious woman. What are you waiting for? I need his phone. When you're done getting the information, come by my room. And Sean, don't take forever, or I'll come looking for you."

Melanie watched the news from her laptop, thinking about the multiple levels of inconsistency in this case. Russell was gay, okay. He's being blackmailed to deliver the news in a certain way, okay. How does the Syrians gambling ring, stealing millions from U.S. casinos come into play?

No one here seems to suspect Everest's sexuality. The hush-hush rumors were that he was sleeping with correspondents and none of them were men.

"I've got it," Sean said, sweating as he entered her room.

Within minutes she was set to intercept Russell's calls. Geared up for the waiting game she got comfortable on the couch and kicked up her feet on the wicker coffee table.

"Melanie," Sean started, redirecting the tabletop fan to blast his face. "Thanks."

She nodded. "If what he says is true, we'll trace the call and stop the blackmailing. Does he have any ideas who's behind it all?"

"No idea. He swears he was extremely careful and the photos were taken while he was in Beijing."

"Why doesn't he just come out?" Melanie said, weighing the pros and cons. "Then he'd be liberated from the burden of such a secret."

"He can't," Sean said. "He's afraid of what his fans will think. About losing their support, their trust and not being liked anymore. He's a public figure and if he comes out it'd be like all this time he'd been lying to them. He could lose his job and his reputation. No, too risky."

"You really like him," Melanie said, with a poor attempt at hiding her confusion. "You just met."

"It's weird."

"Does he feel the same?"

Sean nodded. "He's got more to lose than I do. He's cautious."

While they waited Melanie watched the broadcasts from the West Bank with a new appreciation for the task of reporting.

The press returned in the early evening and brought their energy with them. Scooter was in her corner of the restaurant and Russell was on the air, live from the top of the West Bank, reporting while explosions echoed over his head. The televisions in the bar area showed the dramatic scene.

"Guess we'll have another day of this assignment," Melanie groaned, scraping her plate, not hungry. This part of a case was torture, to be so close and yet completely out of control. Her phone rang. "Or not," she said, making quick eye contact with Sean and glancing at the television. The station was on a commercial break.

Listening in, Melanie thought Russell sounded shaky as he answered the call.

"I want you to say activity three times in the next segment," were his instructions, Melanie labored to recognize any attribute of the voice, trying to hear past the voice alteration to gain any clues.

"How long are you planning to keep this up?"

"Pictures last forever." The voice laughed. "Remember it's your business to report the news, not be the news."

Melanie's heart surged and her blood ran cold. Goose bumps prickled along her spine as she lifted her eyes to the private corner table. Scooter was ending a call.

"Did we get it?" Sean pestered.

"Let me think," she pressed her fingers to her temples attempting to understand what she just heard.

"What happened?"

What did happen? Melanie followed the line from Russell to Scooter to the…

"Melanie." Sean disturbed her in mid-thought.

Looking directly at him, one thing cleared. "I need you to go home. You're no longer part of this mission. Pack your things." Her tone was harsh but Sean's loyalties weren't where they should be and she couldn't think with him breathing down her neck.

"What? Why?"

"Because I don't trust you." Melanie's sharp tone wasn't meant to hurt him.

"You can't do that! You get your orders just like I do. You don't have the authority to send me home." His rant was as quiet as a rant she'd ever experienced.

"I do. You're out of here."

"Don't."

"Your involvement is way beyond personal and I can't justify allowing you to continue. If I let you stay, you'll fuck up my case."

"You don't like it that I'm…" Sean searched for a word.

"I don't care about what you do or who you are. I care about preventing deaths. How many fucking times do I have to tell you that? Damn it, Sean. This isn't about you!" She was louder than she'd expected.

He wiped his mouth with the white linen napkin, dropped it on his half eaten plate and shoved back the chair. Not about to chase him, she sat back and called Mike.

"Something got screwed up," he said, frustration surrounding each syllable.

"Let me guess, you're tracing the call to my exact location." Her disappointment settled in, she'd been hoping for a mistake.

"Yeah," he said, she felt his entire attention as the sound of him pounding on the keyboard stopped. "Why?"

"Because the person who's making the calls is Scooter Sullivan. She's blackmailing her competition. Now all we need to know is why and what the hell happened to the money."

"Sounds like that's all you."

"Not quite. I need you to retrieve her call history, cross reference the data and get me the name and location of who she's been talking to."

"Really, Melanie, and who'll do my job while I'm doing yours?"

"This is your job, helping me do mine." Her body twitched, shaking out the creeps. "Aren't you even a little astonished about Sullivan?"

"Nope. Why not her?"

"I feel gross," Melanie offered.

"It'll pass."

"Well, cross-reference her calls, please. I'll be expecting the list within the hour. One more thing," she said, "I need for you to distract Sullivan while I search her room. Oh, and I'm going to need to know which room to search."

"That I can do, but don't you have a partner? How do you expect me to buy time from here?"

"You're clever. Just do it," Melanie said, ending the call before he could complain or ask about Sean.

❧

Scooter's things were packed when Melanie broke into her room. She felt confident in her five-minute exploratory review of the small apartment. And was back in her room talking with Jack when Mike's list came in ahead of schedule. Leaving out the details, Melanie let Jack know Sean had been cut from the mission.

"It might have been too soon to fold him into an assignment. I think he's better off with the lite version of espionage." She didn't want to hurt his career so she added a positive. "I like the guy and he did fine but maybe a few more months behind a desk would be beneficial." She looked over the list of names and numbers as she spoke. "Hey, I gotta go. Real work to do."

The length of the list was outrageous. Did the woman do nothing but talk on the phone? Melanie wondered about the possibility of a cell-phone-induced brain tumor. "I think I just came up with her defense strategy."

Melanie was in the process of crossing out colleagues from the station when she ran across ... "Holy shit, she talked with the President twice last month."

Her conversation with Scooter came to mind, about the power to influence world policy. She had the ear of the President while her fingers were in the purse of terrorists?

The President wasn't the only interesting name on Scooter's list. Hollywood, royalty, athletes, politicians there were private numbers.

Jesus Christ, she ran her fingers through her hair.

Standing, Melanie opted for the direct approach. At Scooter's door, she knocked twice.

"Can I come in?" She asked Scooter, who was in a robe with face cream clotting in the corners of her features.

"Can't it wait?" She huffed, irritated by the interruption.

"No," Melanie said, bypassing the older woman and stepping into the room. She made herself comfortable on the plush chair beside the side table. "Have a seat."

"You." Indignation prevented Scooter from finishing her thought.

"I know you're blackmailing Russell." Melanie said, "Do you want to sit now?"

Scooter rubbed in the clumpy moisturizer as she walked stiffly to the couch, then sat at the edge with her back perfectly vertical. The two women stared at each other.

"Did Russell tell you it was me?" she asked.

"He doesn't know it's you. He thinks you're having an above-average competitive squabble." Melanie sat patiently. Face-to-face confrontation was her forte. "I didn't want to do this," she confessed. "Ask me what I want."

Scooter looked different without her make-up – older and her glare was hard and cold. "What is it you want?"

"I want in. Partners."

"Ha!" She hooted. "You think you can walk into my home and threaten me? As if I were an amateur? You've got a set of balls on you."

"I want thirty percent of your take."

"Fine. You'll get thirty percent of nothing." She eyed Melanie, her face distorted. "I don't do this," pausing, she sighed, "I don't do this for money. You wouldn't understand because you have no ambition."

"Humor me."

Scooter's presence shifted and she became more like the confident woman she'd been. Her tone was cold and calculating. "I hate Russell Everest. He's plastic. But he's popular and I wanted him to fall a few notches. Okay, if we're being truthful, I want him to plummet into a hungry lion's den." Her grin was crooked. "I don't care that he's gay but I've rattled his cage and he's making mistakes, he's slipping."

"That's a good story."

"Honestly, I don't benefit financially from tormenting Russell."

"If that were true why wouldn't you simply leak the photos?"

"Because I don't think it would do any long-term damage. Sure there'd be backlash but after a few weeks people wouldn't care. He'd get the LGBT in his corner and God knows he could become even more popular and it'd backfire in my face."

"Where's the eighty million the Syrians stole from the casinos?"

This time Scooter turned green. "I, I … don't know what you're talking about." She stood and went to the dresser. "I'm pouring myself a drink, would you like one?" The top drawer squeaked as Scooter pulled on the handles.

"No, thanks." Melanie transferred her weapon to her lap.

"You really should not have underestimated me."

"I didn't." Melanie sat still in her chair.

"I have to say, you are really starting to piss me off," Scooter said, turning red as she faced Melanie.

"You were a pioneer for women in broadcasting and now you're nothing. What do you think the history books will print about you now?"

"A puny cable station peon like you could never bring me down.

My legacy isn't in any jeopardy." Scooter aimed the gun she'd been concealing at Melanie's head and pulled the trigger.

"Do you have any idea how messy that would be?" Melanie asked, incredulously. "There are no bullets in your gun. I checked out your room earlier," she informed, standing and holding on to Scooter's glare. "Besides shooting me would not be your best option. Now. Tell. Me. What. You. Did. With. The. Fucking. Money."

"I want my lawyer."

"You are under the false impression that I'm with law enforcement. I'm not the police. You're going to tell me what I want to know and it can go easy or…"

"Or you'll shoot me?" she said, sounding a little more confident than the fear behind her wide eyes translated.

"Nope. You remember how you said you enjoyed tormenting Russell – this is my fun. My only decision is which of your crimes will be the one the world hears first. Which one will you be remembered for?"

"You have nothing on me," Scooter spat. "I'll sue you. You'll be sorry."

"Blackmailing, gambling ring … if an unambitious reporter like me, linked it to you," she shrugged. "You aren't as clever as I'd once thought," Melanie said, evenly. "But truthfully, I don't care about any of that – I want the money."

"It's gone. I spent it."

"On what?"

Scooters' shoulders sagged and she looked every part of the unscrupulous fiend that she was. "I paid for events." Her sigh came from a deeper place than her sorrow. "Starting an uprising is more expensive than you'd think. For hijackings, for bombs, technology, for whatever I could. I never meant for anyone to get hurt. I just wanted the scoop." She sat on the edge of the little apartment table. "I haven't heard from the casino crew in days. They probably realized they don't need me. So, too bad for you, you came in after it was too late." Scooter put the gun down beside her. "See, there is no money."

"I'm shocked." Melanie said. She hadn't blinked in minutes. "I have to tell you, I wasn't expecting this and I've seen a lot of things in my life … but this? Holy shit, Scooter. What would possess you to get so out of control?"

"Power. Fear. Talent." She grinned. "I'm getting older. One day you'll be in my Louboutins."

"No wonder you needed to create events, you're terrible at predicting the future." Melanie had zero sympathy for Scooter. "I'll see you around, Sullivan." Outside, she called Ben, she needed backup. "I've got to find out who her sources are," Melanie said, her mind racing to the next obstacle.

"Hold it, Ward." Ben's statement hardly fazed her. Mentally she was off chasing down terrorists and designing a plan. "You're on the next flight to Brazil."

"If we have the … wait, what did you say?"

"I need you in Brazil tomorrow."

"Brazil? But," she pressed her memories, "why? I've got a lot to do here."

"You don't. I'm sending a team to replace you and, well, I heard you sent Sean home. He's AWOL, by the way."

"Yeah, tread lightly with Sean. But I don't understand, what's in Brazil?"

"It's Williams. He was bitten by a spider yesterday and has swollen to the size of a Sumo Wrestler. You're going to Brazil to take over as

ITC captain."

The whistle of blowing air rang in her ears. "But I don't want to be captain. I want to investigate terrorists."

Before she could finish, Ben spoke. "Jack and Amy are your replacements. They're already en route, send them what you've got and bring them up to speed. Questions?"

"It's arranged?" She felt heartbroken. "But I want to see this through, I want to find out what happens."

"Your team is in the Amazon jungle without leadership. And the dangers aren't only in the wild."

Right. "Damn stupid Roland," she mumbled. "I assume you have a jet waiting for me."

"Do you think tabs need to be kept on Ms. Sullivan until Jack and Amy arrive?"

"Where is she going to go? She can't hide. Ben, just so we're clear, I'm doing the ITC under extreme protest."

"I appreciate your compliance. I know you have loftier goals but changing the ITC is important. It will impact every young agent that walks through these doors and it's because of you."

Accepting compliments weren't her strong suit. She changed the subject. "Any word on Bell?"

"Still dead."

"Autopsy?"

"The results aren't in yet."

"Why do I have the sinking feeling that we'll never know the truth about him?"

"Because you're a skeptic and live under the guise that there are sinister motives behind everything."

Melanie waited for the part she could disagree with.

CHAPTER EIGHTEEN

Sitting alone in the small fuselage, she pulled the shade on the endless blue sky and leaned her head back.

"Hello, Ms. Ward."

She squinted her eyes at the television mounted to the wall and met Jane's smiling face.

"Isn't this cool?" her assistant asked excitedly. "Why haven't we done this before?"

Because it's intrusive, Melanie thought but shook her head. "I don't know, but I have a feeling it's our new favorite."

"You're teasing me but that's fine because," she held up slips of paper with a wide grin. "I have your messages."

Melanie had to laugh. Jane went through her messages, emails, that her jungle wear would meet her at the airport in Manaus, and news at the Manor.

"Thanks," Melanie said, feeling better after the conversation. "Do you have a dossier on the ITC? What am I walking into?"

"Sorry. I tried but the Board is so tight-lipped that I had to ask Mr.

Jackson for help. He said he would communicate with you directly. I'm not sure if he meant directly as in immediately or directly to you. And Trish is eager for you to return her call. She sounds happy."

"Anything else?"

"Um," she said, flipping through the messages. "No, that's it. Good luck with the games. You're a long shot, but my money is on you."

"I seriously hope you mean that figuratively," she said, feeling queasy. "Bye, Jane." Her stomach rolled, the expectations were too high. Actual assignments, she could sink her teeth into but the ITC and their pettiness sucked. Melanie sighed and called Trish.

"God! There you are!" Trish bellowed. "I was beginning to think you were going to lord my mistake over me forever."

"You called yesterday."

"Still. I don't like being put off. Especially when I'm doing favors." The lilt in her voice was a happy Trish.

"I don't trust your favors."

"Why are we friends? You are such a pessimist and getting worse with age."

"What's the favor you're doing for me? Giving me concert tickets after the lead singer overdosed and the promotion company denied refunds? Or letting me borrow your car only when you were on empty and out of cash?"

"Jeez," she sighed, "Don't you ever forget anything? What about the good stuff I've done? Like when I offered to give you my kidney."

"I don't need a kidney and you only did that to enter a contest to win scuba lessons."

"True. But not this time. This time I'm completely legit. What are you doing this week?"

"Busy."

"Fine, what are you doing over the week*end*?"

Melanie went blank. "What's today?"

"The 12th."

"No, the day of the week."

"Sunday. Whatever you're smoking, it isn't good for you."

"Yeah, that doesn't help. My days are merging and about this weekend, you may as well be asking about next March. I have no idea."

"You've got the most whacked schedule. Well, you've got plans now. Mark your calendar we're having a girl's weekend in Mexico. My treat! And by that I mean I've booked the timeshare."

"Mexico?" It sounded like a hassle. "I need to go home, I haven't been in," she counted backwards, "forever. Can't we make it in San Diego or on a different date?"

"It's a done deal. Besides, you'd whine no matter what I plan. Suck it up and get your bony ass on a flight to Cabo on Friday."

"Let me see what I can arrange."

"You don't want me to dwell over the possibility that you're still pissed. I'll sulk all week and spoil the vacation for everyone. And then I'll be mad at you. And unlike you, I can hold a grudge."

"You are a pain. Send me the details."

"A high-tower condo right on the Sea Of Cortez. Drinks, parties, music, friends, the smell of coconut oil. Most of us leave tomorrow."

It was appealing. "Those weren't exactly the details I was looking for but all of it sounds good."

"I'll forward you the itinerary. We are going to have a blast!"

CHAPTER NINETEEN

When Melanie stepped off the plane in Manaus, Brazil, a vehicle and driver were waiting in heat so damp the air felt heavy. Three hours, two vans and two speedboats later, she reached the ITC hut.

Racing along the gigantic river had been refreshing, the wind and spray a welcome reprieve. As the boat docked at the main control center her lungs worked to pull in the pure oxygen.

The ITC hub was twenty feet above the ground; Melanie climbed the ladder that led to the floor access door. Soaking with sweat, she looked around the room filled with electronics and eight assholes – plus Bob.

"Boss!" Bob said, waving her toward him from the corner shadows and glancing at the rest of the teams.

"Good to see you all again," Melanie said, to the backs of her competition who were doing a magnificent job of ignoring her. "How's the game going?"

"Our station." Bob motioned to a table and chairs with a computer and a monitor. "God, it's good to see you. How's Agent Williams?"

"A dumb ass. All I know is that he's swollen," she whispered. "Tell me what's going on here. What's with the silent treatment?"

"Believe me, silence is the best option. If they aren't pissed and hate you, then they're the best actors ever. They've been spouting shit about kicking your ass."

"Really?" Melanie said, looking at the eight men. "Well, we'll just have to see about that." She grinned at Bob. "What have I walked into?"

"There have been some problems," Bob started cautiously as he led her to an electronic map of the ITC's section of the jungle. "Each team was given a color." He pointed to the five clusters. "See how they light up?"

The course was a twelve-mile trail with side corridors, inlets and dangers to avoid or overcome.

"Let me guess, we're green." The green team was less than eight miles from the start. The closest team was at the three-quarter point.

"We've fallen back almost a mile since Williams was rushed out of here. And that's not the worst part. Our GPS devices aren't working – Williams was fighting for new ones but it's against the rules to swap out."

"How many days have they been out there?"

"Six. And they need water." He put his finger on their lights and dragged it a quarter mile to a clean water source. "You get fifteen minutes a day of communication time. The Board wouldn't give me permission because I'm tech support and not a captain."

"Is there a specific time I can radio them?"

"No, but there's a timer."

"So, it doesn't have to be fifteen consecutive minutes." Melanie took a minute to study the map. "Do we have a smaller one of these?"

"Not electronic," he said, leading the way to their station. "Here. These x's are challenges that must be completed in order to win a flag. They need all twenty flags to finish."

"How many do we have?" she asked, dreading the low number.

"Nine. The other teams are at fourteen or fifteen."

"Any more bad news?"

"Did I mention we should be out of here in three days?"

"Let's start our fifteen minutes." The walkie-talkie felt heavy in her palm.

"Oh My God," Logan gasped. "Agent Williams."

"Sorry, guys." Melanie lowered her voice, doing her best not to be overheard by the rest of the captains.

"No way, Boss?" Fred's voice came through the clearest. "No one has told us anything! What happened to Williams?"

"He's being treated for a spider bite. We don't have much time." The air went dead. "Are you listening?"

"Yeah, Boss."

Melanie grinned at her young team. "I've got a plan. Please tell me at least one of you know Morse Code."

"I do." It was Anthony.

"Great. Since you have no GPS I'm going to lead you through the challenge by quick dashes and dots. We can't waste radio time. Anthony, teach the others the basics. Left, right, stop. What you can. You're a quarter of a mile from water. I can watch your progress on the lighted board. Let's do a test."

Melanie clicked the code for ahead and to the right. She and Bob waited, holding their breaths for the green glowing dots to move.

"Yes!" Bob said, throwing his fist in the air as he leaped, punching the low ceiling.

"Stop." Her voice was powerful and her glance told him to shut the fuck up! She didn't have to see that all eyes had snapped in their direction to know that was exactly what had happened.

"I found my contact lens!" Bob joked, bending to the floor, pretending to pick up the tiny piece of plastic.

"Hello, Melanie."

She turned. All eyes were set on her but it was the captain of the Los Angeles team who'd spoken.

"Hello, Batista."

"I guess your buddy couldn't handle the jungle." He swiveled his chair, laughing with his colleagues. "Didn't know enough to check his shoes before sticking his feet inside."

"Yeah, that's funny." Melanie said, considering the possibility that the spider had help inside Roland's shoe. "I wonder what the percentage is that it could occur twice in our little group."

The sound from his laughter was cut to silence, though his mouth remained open for a moment. "What's that supposed to mean?"

"Nothing. Look, I was pulled off a real assignment to deal with this shit. So I resent the hell out of this petty crap you've got going on. Excuse me, but I've got a fucking lame job to do." She turned her back to them and grinded her teeth at the green lights.

"Boss," Bob warned, his voice carrying a low under current of astonishment.

"You act like you're superior." Batista said.

"That's because I am," she answered, tapping in the code for her team – leading them toward water.

"Bullshit."

"It's not bullshit," she faced the room, "and you know it. That's why you don't want me here. But on a real mission, with danger and purpose, you'd want me on your team."

"Never."

"You would." She looked at a few faces. "Because I'm obligated to save your sorry, pathetic asses." Though she was pretty sure it was a bad idea and that she'd already gone too far, she continued. "When you look at me, don't you see the agent you could've been? Instead you copped out, softened, weakened and got fat. Comfortable in your training bubble, where triviality is overblown and your little minds shrink smaller than your limp dicks."

"You bitch."

"Maybe. But whatever stunts you pulled on Roland – think twice before you try that with me." She clenched her jaw and made an agreement with herself. *It's okay to take out any one of these bastards, no second thoughts.*

The vibration from the radio took her attention. They'd reached the water source.

"I don't want trouble. My job is to get those three agents to the finish line in one piece with some experience and knowledge. That's it."

The Denver captain and tech chuckled under their breath. "Good luck. They're miles behind. They'll have to be evac'd out."

That's right, Melanie thought, *go ahead and underestimate us.* A ringing bell got the grumbling men to their feet. She looked at Bob, ready to spring.

"Dinner bell. It's served in the lodge," Bob said, standing. "Aren't you coming?"

His question stopped the stampede.

"You can't stay here." Batista said.

"I just got here and my agents have already been without a captain for two days."

"I don't care, you aren't going to stay in here alone." The men were all in agreement.

"Your problem, not mine. I'm not leaving."

"Didn't she just say she didn't want trouble?"

Not only did they not trust her, they didn't trust each other. One half of each team stayed behind. The timer on her radio said she still had over eleven minutes of communication time.

"How are you feeling?" she asked, worried about dehydration.

"Anthony drank too much water, too quickly. He's barfing," Logan spoke quickly.

"Radio me when he's better or if you think he's not going to recover," Melanie said, her blood pressure spiking. She had no idea what the procedure was to get medical help to the contestants. Assessing his total health, she hoped he'd be fine. Focusing on the map, she charted the most direct route to the food challenge.

Her team took ten minutes to call back.

"Sorry, Boss." Anthony coughed. "I'm fine."

"I want you to set up camp," Melanie said, worried about their health.

"But we just started moving again," Logan complained.

"It'll be dark soon and I want you to hydrate for tomorrow. Do you have any food?"

"Some."

"There's a food challenge a tenth of a mile from where you are. I want you there by sunrise. Get rest, you've got a lot of distance to make up if we're going to place in this game."

They talked, keeping two emergency minutes on the day's calculator. Bob brought her a plate of local chow and Melanie fell asleep at their workspace.

"The team isn't going anywhere for the night," Bob whispered, tugging her shoulder. "Our bunks are all in one room but it's more comfortable and you should get some real sleep."

Melanie stretched out her stiff neck and shoulders, yawned and rubbed her face. "I'm not leaving."

"Boss," Bob's plea was in his voice.

Nuh-huh, she blinked her watery eyes.

"They are not going to like this," he said, nervously. "You're making a lot of enemies."

She exhaled. "Are they giving you problems? Because, if they are … I'll give them something to think about."

"They're afraid of you. Jesus, Boss, I'm a little afraid of you," Bob said, his throat bobbing in his pudgy neck.

Melanie stared for a beat. Her laughter was a surprise, but Bob really looked frightened. "I'm sorry," she said, catching her breath. "Am I too intense?"

"Jesus Christ." Bob swallowed down another lump.

"I'll take that as a yes." She was still laughing. "All right, I'll lighten up a little, but I'm not leaving."

The food challenge was a combination of endurance and teamwork. It was less than a day's ration for three starving agents. With clicks and dashes she guided them through the jungle.

Combining the ITC-provided map, a topography map and a trail guide she found on the Internet, Melanie charted the best possible route for her recruits. Taking danger and the distance between water and challenges into consideration, she paid attention to every twist and turn.

Midway through the second day there was a major choice, over the saddle of two shallow ridges or across a decent-sized gully. From their positions she could tell both Denver and Chicago had chosen the hillside. Both teams had lost traction.

"Boss, we've got a problem," Anthony said. "The bridge has been blown out."

"The map doesn't show a bridge, it shows a natural formation," Melanie said, feeling the rise of humidity under her thin T-shirt.

"Sorry."

Without an extra moment of hesitation she reevaluated. *Shit, it's too late to change course.* She looked at the location of the other teams. Her recruits had made excellent progress – Denver and Chicago were less than a mile ahead and they'd captured three more flags.

"If you follow the ravine north it narrows." She sighed. How am I going to get them across? "It diverges to the left and you'll have to backtrack."

"We'll check it out."

"I need you to double time it."

"We already thought we were." Logan groaned.

Melanie hunkered down over the cluttered levels of maps, tools, pencils, scratch paper, compass and rulers. The single bulb above her head swayed with the movement of the others in the hut.

"Boss, we're here. The gap is about twelve feet wide and Logan thinks she can traverse it."

"How? Never mind – 45 minutes and then we have to change course. Be careful," she said, saving precious seconds of communication time.

Forty-seven minutes later they signaled; they were across. If she'd been paying attention she'd have noticed the whispers and glares from the other team captains.

By nightfall the distance between them and the nearest team had closed to a half-mile and the finish line was less than three miles from the D.C. team's campsite. They needed four flags to be eligible to cross.

At the control hut, the other team captains and techs had taken up 24-hour residency.

Melanie gave her team four hours of sleep. The rainforest, predawn, was teeming with life and she was nervous. Her three green lights began their move in the dark while the rest of the board was still. The L.A. and Houston teams were neck-in-neck. The possibility of overtaking them was slight. But – she clicked their direction change and thought … *maybe.*

The sun hadn't yet risen above the lacey treetops as her agents stealthily passed first Denver and then Chicago. She was the only one awake in the control center and let the thrill of the best moment she'd spent in Brazil roll down her spine.

There will be hell to pay when these lazy bastards regain consciousness, she thought, settling in for a battle.

She let her team know their accomplishment, giving them motivation for the final push. An hour later the stirring began and it was downhill from there.

"What the fuck!?" was the call heard around the jungle.

"It's not possible," Batista raged. "You cheated!"

"If I were you," Melanie pointed to the board where her team was about to take the lead. "I'd be more concerned about coming in second or third. It's what happens when you sleep in."

Batista swore at his tech and the Houston captain was already on the radio. Denver and Chicago were dumbfounded for the moment before shooting into panic.

"I would love to watch them scramble," she whispered to Bob.

"But we're not done yet."

Five hours later the L.A. team crossed the finish line and twenty minutes after them was Houston. Melanie and Bob were there when Logan, Fred and Anthony dragged their filthy, listless selves to the end.

"You guys did awesome," Melanie said, embracing her tired, sweaty teammates.

"Can we please go home now?" Logan asked, dropping to the ground.

"Fred," Melanie said, her toes curling in her boots. She tried to sound calm. "Hold still." Using the radio still in her hand, she knocked an enormous brown spider off his shoulder.

Anthony stomped the thing to juice and the five of them stood staring at each other.

"Let's get out of here."

CHAPTER TWENTY

Gritty and dreaming of a shower, Melanie propped open her eyelids for the Manor's retina scan.

"Agent Ward." Melanie looked up at the two men she knew as the lackeys for the Agency's Executive Board. "Your presence is requested at Headquarters."

"You've got to be kidding me," she said, still holding her suitcase, the earthy scent of the rainforest still clinging to her clothing. "I haven't even taken two steps inside."

"Orders." They said without judgment.

"Boss?" The four worried faces stared back at her.

"It's fine." She pulled in a breath and checked her watch. *But I'm going to miss my flight to Mexico.* "Take my luggage to my office and try to mask your emotion. Lead the way," she told the two guards. From the back seat of the sedan she called Ben.

"I'm already here, been here for two hours." He sounded annoyed.

"What did I do?"

"There's been an accusation of cheating."

"What?! How!?" Her moment of outrage faded to annoyance. "God damn it, Ben. I thought this was over when," she paused, "when Finn died."

"We'll talk when you get here."

Neither of the goons was smoking but the stench of cigarettes was infused into the fiber of the car. She watched the familiar setting out the window. Finn was constantly throwing out false allegations, and each time she had been hauled before the Board to defend whatever action Finn felt was offensive.

Ben was in the corridor waiting for her. *Glum*, Melanie thought analyzing his expression.

"I didn't cheat, though to be truthful, I was never given parameters," Melanie declared with an arrogant grin before Ben could get a word out.

"Ward." Her name came out as a sigh – a tired, irritated sigh.

"Who says I cheated and what are they saying I did?" she was asking as the panel doors to the review room opened and one of the PA's poked out his head.

"The Board will see you now."

Melanie glared. "Ben?"

"I'm right behind you."

"Hello, Agent Ward."

Melanie took her usual seat at the center of the long table before the arched desk of the Board members. Hugh's empty chair did not go unnoticed. She cut a glance to Ben, who only gave her a curt nod to face forward.

"It's been a few months," said the balding old man on the far right.

"Missed me?"

"We knew we'd see you soon enough." The eldest Board member

was in his late eighties and still pulling in a fat government check.

She listened intently as he outlined the charge. Cheating on the second challenge of the ITC. Using a coded language to conspire with the recruits, directing them to the finish line.

"Seriously?" She looked into each of the squinty sets of eyes to weigh what she was missing. "I'm an agent, trained to use whatever is at my disposal. Hell, yeah, I used Morse Code. The GPS assigned to my team was faulty, probably on purpose. I cannot believe I have to defend this…" she looked over at Ben.

"It's a serious matter."

"Is it?" Melanie returned the charge without hesitation. "This is a waste of time. You and I," she looked at the line up of elderly Board members. "We've been through a lot over the years and," she stood, "when there's a matter of real importance, you know where to find me."

"Agent," Ben cautioned.

Her shoulders broadened. "What is it that you want from me? I used Morse Code and in three days I got my recruits through the course. Agent Williams was in the hospital being treated for a spider bite and my team was left to dehydrate and starve for two days." Melanie looked at her watch. "I've got a plane to catch. Let me know what you decide."

There was no one stopping her exit. She took in a breath and walked out with the sickening realization that this time she might have gone too far.

The on-flight drinks helped ease her anxiety but beneath the surface her teeth chattered. Had she really done the unthinkable, had she walked out during a meeting with the Board?

By the time the plane landed in Cabo she felt sick. Her stomach in knots and there was a strange tic behind her left eye. Caving from her self-torture, she decided to face the firing squad. Melanie stared at her cell, inhaled and frowned as she powered up the device. The shaking and buzzing in her hand was immediate.

I'm being scolded by technology, she thought, flipping through her texts and voicemails. Jane's message was that Mr. Jackson had called and wanted Ms. Ward to contact him as soon as she was back in D.C.

That there was no actual lecture from Ben, added a shiver to her already chilly bones. She dialed and counted the rings. On the fourth he answered.

"Hello, Agent Ward." Ben puffed out her name on a high wind of anxiety.

"Hi," her teeth pinching the inside of her cheek.

"How's Mexico?"

"We just landed, I'm still in the airport. I'm sorry, Ben."

"Don't be."

"Really? Because," she paused all of her voluntary internal movements, "I walked out on the Board."

"I was there." He reminded. "I wouldn't think memory issues should be a problem for a woman so young."

"Me? I was worried about you," she said cautiously. "So, that's it?"

"No. You were insubordinate."

"Punishment?"

"I'm verbally reprimanding you."

"You've been acting really strange for the past month. You don't have an incurable medical condition, do you?"

"Thank you for worrying." She could hear the suppressed pleasure beneath his tone. "I'm healthy. Busy. Have a relaxing weekend. We'll talk when you get back."

A weight lifted from her shoulders. Melanie perspired in line for a shuttle in a cloud of exhaust.

"Is the planet on fire?" she asked the lady behind her. "I swear, if my next destination is Hell I won't be surprised."

But the resort was pure luxury. Dozens of salmon-colored buildings topped with a heavy layer of red clay tile roofing were just a pristine hop, skip and jump from the deep, dark blue ocean. A mariachi band greeted her as the cab pulled in between palm trees.

Inside the foyer employees served mini glasses of margaritas, piña coladas and strawberry daiquiris while Melanie phoned Trish.

"Oh my God, tell me you're here!" Trish yelped.

"I'm in the lobby," Melanie said, the first smile in days reaching her lips.

"I'll be right there!"

Three minutes later Trish jogged up the concrete path, her breasts bouncing inside a knit string bikini. She looked completely different, her hair dyed jet-black and cut in an asymmetrical bob. But her big, happy grin was true Trish as she ran in like a hurricane, capturing Melanie in her arms and spinning.

"You're energetic," Melanie said, caught in the eye of the storm and feeling the effects of a multitude of tiny bottles of alcohol sloshing in her stomach.

The hard and fast kisses over her face were unexpected.

"Jace does this to me when I'm in a bad mood," She said. "He calls it speedy smooching." Her kisses lost their softness as her pucker stretched out into a grin. "It usually ends with us making out and naked but I can give you the PG-13 version. Aren't they fun?"

"Like a parade," Melanie laughed, smacking her own kisses on Trish's face.

"We're like the French," Trish added, stepping away and tugging on Melanie's elbow. "Let's get you out of these clothes … and into a swimsuit. Got you there for a second, didn't I?"

"No, because your delivery was terrible. Your pause wasn't long enough for me to figure out what you were implying," she answered as Trish dragged her out to the scorching sunshine. The air was thick with the scent of a flower Melanie couldn't name and the lawn between buildings was in par with any national golf course.

"We have the best cabana on the property," Trish said, walking along the trimmed path beside the large main building. "Right on the sand – which, by the way, is like golden sugar and the water is so soft it's like swimming in melting Jell-O."

"Who's smoking something now?" Melanie asked, unable to imagine a gelatin bath.

"You'll see. God, I'm glad you're here." Her smile was genuine. "I put you in the room next to mine, the one with a door directly onto the beach. Jenny and Mari have the rooms in back and the boys are on the second floor."

"Boys? What boys?"

"The boys needed for a girl's weekend. Can't have a proper girl's weekend without boys. Duh, Mel." Trish shook her head. "You haven't commented on my hair or my tan."

"I like it. Makes you look mysterious."

"Really? I like mysterious." Trish led them down the line of cabanas to the very last one and pushed open the door.

Melanie dropped her bag in her bedroom and shut the door. "You never answered my question, which boys?" she called, trading her clothes for a bikini that looked matronly compared with Trish's strings.

"Some you know and some you don't. Don't worry if you're thinking Adam. He's not here," Trish called from the kitchen. "I'm ordering drinks, poolside. Hope you like piña's."

She shivered, feeling as if she'd dodge a handsome, 6'3" bullet. Trish hadn't stopped talking and though Melanie missed a section, she caught up by the time they were out the door.

"Mari is a wet noodle. She lets men trample all over her and then says 'thank you'." Trish groaned. "She's really sweet and used to be unhappy because she was fat. But she lost like fifty pounds and now she's unhappy because she's saggy."

"You're all heart," Melanie said, already seeing Jenny in her typical fun-loving position, arms crossed and expression sour. "How'd you get Jenny out here?"

"This is my retreat for the downtrodden. Tell her you love the swimsuit, took me over an hour to get her out of the bathroom."

"How long did you take to add me to the downtrodden list?" Melanie asked, not wanting to be included with the loveless.

"You were first, the saddest sap of them all."

"I am not. Wait," she shaded her eyes. "Is that," his name was on the tip of her tongue, "Nate?" The Vegas beach bum, who'd been easy on the eyes and just interesting enough to be unsafe, was pushing himself out of the pool. Flexed, tan muscles with water droplets cascading down his chest, was a lip-biting site.

"Yeah," her grin was in her tone. "He actually forced his way in. He likes you."

Melanie wiped away the trace of the danger from her face and waved as his eyes met hers.

"He's nice and cute so I'm sure you'll break his heart," Trish said. "I told him you were a class A bitch, but he insisted on coming."

She wanted to argue the statement but her defense was weak. "Where are those drinks?" Melanie asked instead.

"Melanie, right?" he smiled, toweling off the excess water off his tan, toned chest.

"Be kind, Bitch," Trish whispered, hunching over to breathe in Melanie's ear. "Hi Nate!" Trish waggled her fingers and her ass to a lounge chair.

"Hi," Melanie said, an unreasonable blush coloring her cheeks. "It's good to see you."

"You too," Nate was in a pair of lifeguard-red longboard trunks and the sunlight highlighted the hints of gold and red in his brown hair. "Didn't you notice there's a party going on? Why are both your hands empty?"

"That's a good question," she said, squirming under Trish's penetrating gaze. "I thought you were my Boy Scout during weddings and family dinners."

"I did save you," Nate said, his eyes out on the horizon. "Trish had you set up with Gus Gomez."

Her forehead crinkled as she flipped through the names and faces that were connected with Trish and Jace. "Gus Gomez?" As the name swept off her tongue, she knew. "The guy who spits when he speaks?"

Nate nodded.

"No way. She wouldn't do that to me," Melanie said, knowing

Trish was likely to do anything. "Gus Gomez. You need a raincoat just to say hello. Thanks for putting yourself in the line of fire."

"I was hoping you wouldn't be disappointed. Interested in hitting the beach?" He asked, flicking his eyes toward Trish who was staring.

"Love to."

Connected to the hotel was a beachfront cantina. The loudspeaker announced drinking games and specials. The beach was crowded and messy, but the beer flowed and the seats were free. Melanie and Nate dropped down on a pair of empty lounges beneath a blue and yellow umbrella. Jutting out along the incredibly blue sea was a line of stark golden mountains. Without a hint of life the rocky cliffs glowed in the sunlight, the contrast was incredibly gorgeous.

"I didn't know this was a set-up weekend." She said, her gaze leaving the landscape to look at his expression, innocent and grinning. "Why are you laughing at me?"

"Would you have come if you'd known? This is Trish's way of paying it forward, that's what she calls it, not me." The corners of his eyes pinched with a half-dozen crows feet. "She wants everyone to experience love like she and Jace. Again, her words."

"She means well," Melanie rethought, "maybe she means well, but she over steps."

"Are you always so complicated?" He was laughing at her behind a pair of reflective sunglasses.

"I'm a complicated girl." Melanie answered. "I'm not entirely sure what Trish has said about me but…" she hesitated.

"Say whatever you mean straight out. I'm a big boy, I can handle it."

"Okay. If you're planning on getting laid this weekend, you'd better search elsewhere," she said, the sea breeze a relief from the blazing sun.

"I had my eye on the housekeeper, she's hot but only fifteen." He laughed. "Melanie," he said, in the most serious tone she'd heard him use. "Stop taking yourself so damn seriously. Two days. Let's have a good time."

He ordered two beers from the guy with an ice bucket. Dozens of vendors walked the beach selling everything from ceramic bowls to pipes.

"Melanie," Nate started. "I'm just wondering who you're still hung up on."

She tilted her head for a better view to appraise him; he wasn't going away and she supposed he deserved some explanation.

"It's him, isn't it? The prick from the wedding. I knew he was into you but, you, I couldn't tell."

She sighed. "It's not him. It's that I'm a mess." She said, "I'm bad with relationships, really bad, and to top it off, I screwed up at work."

"Are you going to get the pink slip, the boot, the old heave-ho?"

She snorted. "No, I'll get the scolding, the reprimand and the shameful finger wag."

Nate laughed. "When my dad was sick, do you know what he used to call the finger wave?" Melanie shook her head. "Prostate exam," Nate said, his eyes leaking with humor. He bent his index finger and gave her the wave again.

"That's gross." She couldn't say if the joke was funny or if Nate was. But she was laughing along, doing her best not to imagine a finger wave or wonder if the exam actually required two fingers. "Thanks, I needed a laugh," she said, sitting back in the chair and extending her legs.

"Can I be straight with you?" His eyes pierced into her for a second. "I like you, Mel, but if I just wanted to get laid I wouldn't have to travel to Mexico."

"I realize that. I don't want to turn you down, but..." she was looking into his brown eyes.

"Then don't," Nate said, moving his hand to her thigh.

"You're a glutton for punishment. Trust me, I'm not worth the effort."

"Melanie. Shut up." His eyes twinkled.

In one swift move she pinched his puckered lips an inch from hers. Pushing his face back she felt the muscles in his cheeks tighten as he tried to grin.

"No," she said, stopping short of smiling. *He really is sort of cute.*

"Sometimes women need a little nudge to make up their mind," he said as she released her grip. "I guess you're not one of them." Nate rubbed his jaw from side to side.

"And, Nate, I'm letting you off easy," she said, making eye contact. "Don't try it again." Melanie held off on the grin until she was certain she'd made an impact. "I don't want to break your arm."

"You know you're only becoming more sexy to me."

"This is where you two ran off to," Trish hollered from the sidewalk. "I thought you were off humping somewhere. Come on, it's happy hour."

"Doesn't she live in 'happy hour'?" Nate said, loud enough for only Melanie and sent her a finger wave.

Trish had everyone dress for happy hour, which stretched into dinner, followed by dancing.

During dinner Melanie traded spots with a stranger. "Hi," she said wanting to question Trish about being tricked.

"It's assigned seating. You know you're not really mad." Trish's giggle was cut short as her attention briefly flickered to Jenny.

"What's with Mari and Jenny?" The two had been inseparable.

"I don't know, but they're pissing me off. I invited Curtis and," she paused, "what's his name to entertain them but they've been ignoring the men."

"Maybe they thought a girls' weekend meant girls only," Melanie added snidely.

"What fun would it be without boys? Anyway, you like Nate," Trish sang softly. "I made a love connection."

"I thought Gus the spitting Gomez was my love connection," Melanie said, watching Nate with Curtis and What's His Name.

"I will never trust Nate with a secret! There's nothing wrong with Gus except overactive salivary glands. He can't help it."

"Can you imagine kissing that juicy mouth?" Both women squirmed at the thought. "I cannot believe you'd set me up with him."

"Nate is better, but Jace would murder me if he knew I brought him. He's not happy with you after you ruined his best friend."

Ignoring her, Melanie asked, "So, Jenny and Ryan are over again?"

"No, but I'm sick of hearing her bitch about him, so I made her come out this week. To give them a break," Trish shrugged. "It's too bad we leave tomorrow I wish you'd gotten here sooner. Kind of a quick trip for you."

"I needed to get away from work. It was perfect timing."

"The band is starting … want to dance?" Nate was crouching beside her chair. "They're really good."

"Have fun, Mel, or you'll turn into a cat lady." Trish's face scrunched, thinking about the similarities.

"I want to have fun!" Melanie said.

"You don't have to marry him," Trish added. "Just lighten up."

She looked at Nate. "Let's dance."

The band had a permanent stage under a tarp by the big pool.

"Trish says I don't have to marry you," Melanie laughed, shouting over the music.

"She told me the exact opposite!"

They danced to every song. The slow ones Nate sang gently into her ear, holding her against his body and moving them in unison.

They were still on the floor when the band announced their last song. Melanie turned to catch her breath but the air seemed to be taken up by everyone else.

"Air." Melanie gasped, reaching for Nate's hand and pulling him to the sand. She inhaled the salty atmosphere until her head swayed.

She was laughing when he wrapped his arms around her waist, keeping her upright. She felt the kiss coming and this time didn't resist. Their bodies were hot and sticky and the cool breeze breathed life back into her. Following his lead, she slackened her jaw and moved into him. The first try was clumsy and dull, he tasted of salt and there was sand. Whatever spark they had on the dance floor didn't reach their lips. Melanie leaned back, her eyes searching the sky for the moon as her lungs filled within the pressure of his embrace.

She straightened and smiled at Nate. His brown eyes were clouded with confusion.

"Let's try that again," he said. "I've got a reputation to uphold."

"Prove it."

"God, you're sexy," he slid his finger from her throat down the center of her chest to where her blouse gave resistance.

There it is, she thought, reading his emotions. *Come on, Mel, you can do this ... want him.* In the split second it took him to recalibrate she'd come up with a dozen reasons to fall for him.

Closing her eyes, she felt his breath on her cheek and turned to meet his lips. The kiss was more forceful than she'd expected, distracting for the first instant until she found the rhythm.

Her arms over his shoulders, the muscles under his light Hawaiian shirt rippled beneath her touch. The kiss changed and Melanie was pulled in, forgetting the sand under her feet and the thunder of waves in the background. Her mind was blank, dark and absorbed.

Melanie breathed in and slowly opened her eyes. For the briefest of moments she didn't recognize Nate. Swallowing, her brain instructed her mouth to stay shut. Afraid she would say the wrong name. "Hi," she said, and plastered a smile on her face to mask her delusional moment.

"Better," he grinned, oblivious. "I'll walk you back to the house."

It didn't sound like a proposition but his fingers entwined in hers and there was the slightest bounce to his step. She held her breath and tucked her lips together, trying to figure out what had happened – and not daring to wonder who she'd been expecting to see when she'd opened her eyes.

"I'd take you into your room," he said, mildly, "but I think I'd better quit while I'm ahead." As he spoke his fingers played with hers then a note of doubt filled his posture.

"That's because you know you're one step away from rejection." She felt her grin reach her eyes. "Thanks. I had a good time."

His kiss on her forehead was soft and Melanie entered her room not knowing what to think.

Great, I'm going to be up all night, she thought while foam from the toothpaste collected at the corners of her mouth. *You are such a fool*, she said to her reflection. *Do you even like him?*

Melanie settled in above the covers, snuggled up to an overstuffed pillow and passed out.

CHAPTER TWENTY-ONE

The muffled ring of her phone woke her. Teetering across the room, still half asleep, she shoved her bag off her cell and squinted at the unknown number. *615 area code?*

"Hello?" Melanie said, trying to sound as if she'd been awake for hours.

"Hi, I'm looking for Melanie Ward."

The voice was female with a Southern accent.

"This is Melanie," she frowned, rubbing her eyes.

"Oh, good." The woman sighed. "My name is Rebecca Evans. I'm Adam Chase's aunt."

"Yes, Becca." She was wide-awake and instantly worried. Adam's aunt Becca had been kind and sympathetic when Melanie had gone to the Evans' family farm in Tennessee to gain answers. It was the lowest of moments in her craze to understand him.

"That's right," the woman's smile passed through the phone line. "How have you been?"

Melanie blinked, her forehead knotted in confusion. "Fine. How about you?" *What?*

"Oh, we're well here, thank you."

"Becca, was there a reason for your call?" She bit her tongue at her abruptness and looked at the clock – 5 a.m. "What I mean is, is there something I can do for you?" The question was choking.

"Honey, I've been worried sick." The smile was gone and Melanie could imagine the woman hugging a mixing bowl in anxious fear. "It's Adam. I haven't heard from him in weeks and I'm about to pull my hair out! I've called and left messages. He's not answering and yesterday a computer voice informed me that his number had been disconnected." Becca sighed. "I don't know what to do."

It didn't sound like an emergency. Melanie refrained from allowing her apathy to echo through the receiver.

"Honey, do you think you could check in on him for me?"

"I," she pressed her fingertips to her knitted brows. "He's got friends…"

"Please."

"… that live in San Diego."

"But I don't know any of them. And when you were here, you gave me your business card and you said if I ever needed anything I could call."

Fuck!

"Becca, I don't think I'm the right person to check in on him."

"You are just the person. He listens to you. Please, Melanie, I'm at the end of my rope. Adam is so secretive but I know he cares deeply for you."

"The last time he and I parted … it didn't go so well." She'd ditched him. "I'm pretty sure he's seeing someone else now."

"What am I supposed to do?"

Melanie closed her eyes and tried to come up with an alternative. "This is such a bad idea." She couldn't help but voice her thoughts.

"But you'll do it?" Her hopefulness was immediate.

"Tell me what you know and why you're worried."

At six a.m. Melanie was knocking on Trish's door, quickly thanking her for the invite and rushing not to miss her flight. She was one of a dozen early risers and had her choice of seat on the small aircraft. The seats were like cardboard as she leaned back, stressing a little about Nate, but feeling more relieved to be avoiding him.

"In and out," she said, driving the I-5. "I'm going to tell him to pay his bill, call his aunt and I'll be back in D.C. tonight." Melanie thumped nervously on the wheel as she drove, it was to the beat on the radio but mostly it was the fast-paced rhythm of her heart. Adam lived in a khaki green, white-trimmed corner house. The many windows along the front were fitted with closed drapes. An expensive car was parked sideways on the driveway and her initial drive-by was of a quiet house.

"This isn't one of your cases, Mel. Just walk up to the door." She breathed, deeply, picked up the three newspapers on the brick walkway and rang the bell twice before doing her best not to look like a Peeping Tom to his neighborhood watch.

The backyard had citrus trees, a lawn and a patio set that looked like it should still have the tags. The screen was unlatched and each of the three locks on the back door was for mental security. She picked them in seconds. *Some assassin you are.* Grinning, she stepped into the laundry room.

It was that lock, the one into the house, that caused a string of curse words, a broken snake-rake-pick and twenty minutes of her time.

Melanie huffed out a sweaty breath she'd been holding as she turned the knob and entered the dark, cool, fermenting house. The smell made her eyes water and reminded her of when she'd return from a mission and opened her fridge for the first time.

Flipping the light switch, her hand twitched, wanting to cover the mess back in darkness. *It's no use, you can't unsee something,* she thought, trekking over fallen chairs, scattered magazines, ash trays and bowls that had been on the coffee table before it was overturned.

The den blended into the kitchen to create one open room and she stepped up to the stainless steel counter. The stench was choking as she made her way to the sink.

Covering her nose and mouth with her T-shirt Melanie turned on the water full blast and looked around to power up the garbage disposal.

"Who are *you*?"

Melanie turned toward the hall and had a straight shot view to Adam's bedroom. He was either passed out, or dead, lying on his stomach with his boots hanging off the bed. For a fraction of an instant, she held her breath. Until his chest raised and lowered in a rhythmic motion. The next question was about the girl sitting up beside him in bed.

"Melanie. Who are you?"

"God, not before I get some coffee," the girl answered, weaving her way to a standing position and colliding with a dresser, rebounding into the master bathroom.

Melanie blew out a heavy sigh. *What am I doing here? He's got a girl, a young girl, in his bed and I'm doing the damn dishes.*

Becca's weary plea was the only thing keeping her from high-tailing it home. She looked around the kitchen and in less than a minute gave up on the idea of making coffee.

Instead she pulled out the garbage, took note of the empty liquor bottles and took the first load outside to the recycle bin.

"I thought I imagined you," the girl, dressed only in lacy bra and underwear and knee-high socks said as she opened the fridge. "How'd you get in?"

"Front door was open."

The girl snorted. "It was a rough night." That kind of smoker's voice should've been reserved for a much older person.

"Who are you?" Melanie asked again.

"Crystal." The girl turned her eyeliner-stained face toward Melanie. "What do you want?"

"If you tell me you're under eighteen I'm hauling your ass out of here."

Crystal barked out a raspy laugh. "I'm old enough." She leaned forward on the counter, not shy about her dagger gaze. "I know you. I've seen your face. Does it bother you that I'm here?"

"I haven't decided," Melanie said. "What are you to him?" It was a less hostile way of asking if she'd been paid.

She tilted her head side-to-side. "A comrade. What about you? Did he ever strap you to the bedposts? Or wrap a belt around your neck until you almost suffocated?"

"Nope," Melanie said casually, but her heart began to race and her limbs felt shaky. Not blinking was the game, she decided, *and I am not going to lose.*

"He likes that, you know; to take me from behind. Did he ever do that to you?"

Melanie's mouth was filling with saliva as she tried to stop her imagination from creating the girl's fantasy.

"We fuck all night long."

"Yeah?" Melanie asked, not reacting. "Crystal, you are one hell of a liar."

Her smile was slow to stretch. "I do what I can," she said. Her gaze never wavered, though it lost the lustiness as she straightened her back. "He keeps your pictures in a drawer." The stare narrowed and intensified.

Melanie swallowed.

"In his bedside table," she said, matter-of-factly. "I thought you were a dead sister or something."

"Sorry to disappoint."

"I don't care one way or the other." She checked Melanie out from head to toe and back. "I'm getting dressed. You can watch if you'd like."

"I'll pass," Melanie said, piecing the puzzle together.

A few minutes later Crystal returned to the kitchen wearing a short, black pleated skirt and a shredded tank top. "Tell Adam I took the Audi."

"Not going to happen."

"He lets me take his car all the time."

"I don't care."

"How will I get home? I live in Hillcrest. That's pretty far away."

"I'll drive. I'm even willing to make a coffee stop."

Crystal grabbed her leather-studded jacket, zipped up her alligator skin Herman Munster boots and glowered. "Are you coming?"

Melanie drove, trying to make sense of who this girl was.

"Are you sure you're over eighteen?" Melanie asked, interrupting Crystal's chatter.

"Twenty-four."

"And your relationship with Adam is what?" She took her eyes off the road for a second to examine the girl. "Does he pay you?"

"I'm not a whore."

"What, then?"

"What do you care? You're not his girlfriend. I know because she's a tall bitch."

"Driver gets to ask the questions," Melanie said, *so he's still seeing Courtney.*

"We're friends."

"Friends?" Not a chance.

"Yeah, we hang out."

"At a bar?"

"I'm a bartender, but we're closer than that."

"Close enough that you sleep over?"

"Yeah, well, it's not what you may think," Crystal said, changing the song on the radio. "He doesn't tie me up or anything." She grinned. "That really bugged you, didn't it? Thinking about Adam getting sadistic with me. Did it make you jealous?"

Melanie looked over. "What's wrong with you?"

Crystal sighed and shifted her glare out the window. "Everything."

She was about to get off the freeway, about to run out of distance to get the truth out of Crystal.

"We're not fucking." When she looked back at Melanie her expression was defensive and her shoulders broadened. "Sometimes my boyfriend gets a little physical, only because he's under a lot of stress. When that happens Adam gives me a place to crash."

"The boyfriend hits you?"

Crystal didn't answer.

"Why'd you tell me?" Melanie asked, seeing that it was painful for the girl.

"Because I hate his bitch girlfriend and she hates you, so as I see it you might be all right."

"How do you know the bitch girlfriend?"

"She comes around to scream, sometimes."

"And why do you think she hates me?"

"He used to have a stack of photos of you." Her brown eyes, which drooped at the far corners, were still bloodshot. "One day I went over and there was just one. I found pieces of your face in the hedges and the rest had been tossed in the trash." She pointed to the top floor of a three-story building above a bakery. "I live there. But what about my coffee?"

"I have a better offer." Melanie parked, and shifted in the seat so they could have a full view of each other. "What will it take for you to drop out of Adam's life? Forever."

"No way. Are you crazy?"

"What's it worth? Name your price."

"You cannot be serious. He and I are friends, there's no dollar sign on friendship!"

"If you really believe you're friends," she mimicked Crystals tone of the word, "then you'll pick a number and take my offer. He's wasting his life and you aren't helping. Give me a dollar amount and walk away."

"This is wrong," Crystal said, squinting. "I won't go for less than a grand. He means too much to me."

Melanie put the car in drive, circled the block and stopped in front of a bank.

❧

His neck was warm on the tips of her fingers, his pulse steady but he hadn't moved since the first time she'd checked on him. Standing in the center of his mess, she collected the rumpled clothes off the floor, the back of the chair and on top of the dresser. The top drawer was open a couple of inches and as she passed it she saw a face she recognized.

Dropping the armful of clothes she peeked inside and pulled out a single photo. Her.

Right after she'd gotten back from Africa. She opened the drawer further and stashed in the far back were three more. Her chest ripped. They were of her and Danny.

I look happy, she thought, *and so young.* Melanie stared, running her fingers over her laughing face before placing her palm over the past. She turned toward the sleeping figure and replaced the photos where she had found them.

In the den she dropped the bundle of laundry on the couch and separated out the dress shirts and slacks from everything else. Shoving the 'everything else' pile into the washing machine she hoped he wasn't going to be stuck with pink shorts.

Even after she'd hosed down the counters and thrown out the trash, the place held on to the odor. Opening every window in the house, except for Adam's room, she let the light shine on the mess. She mopped the hardwood floors, righted the living area and dropped his dress clothes off at the cleaners on her way to the grocery store.

Having nearly dumped everything in his fridge and knowing nearly nothing about shopping, she roamed the aisles randomly picking food: a bag of oranges, apples, a dozen eggs, orange juice and a half pound of bacon.

"What are you doing?" Melanie asked out loud on the drive back. "You owe him." *That's it, when a guy saves your life you owe him,* she nodded to no one and drove. It couldn't be ignored that part of the blame for Adam's condition belonged to her.

The house smelled better. She put the groceries away, set the fresh flowers in a glass pitcher and stood back to admire her work. It'd been a long time since she'd had a place to clean, never putting much effort into her apartment. She was dusting when she heard him fall off the bed.

"Mel?" Adam swayed in the doorway.

"He's alive," she announced like a mad scientist.

"What are you doing?" he asked, his gaze falling to the dust cloth in her hand.

"Why don't you go take a shower, clean up and then we'll talk?" Melanie suggested.

"All right." The questions were etched in his forehead as he kept his eyes on hers. "You will still be here when I get out, right? You're not going to disappear?"

"I'll be here. I'll make coffee," she said, lifting her chin to guide him to the bathroom.

"Why did I say I'd make coffee? I suck at this," she sighed, nervously emptying a scoop of ground coffee into the filter. While that brewed, she turned to the stove and commanded the eggs and bacon to behave.

She couldn't help but turn her attention to his room as she heard the bathroom door open. Across the opened door he passed with just a towel around his waist.

The basketball shorts and grey T-shirt were about the last clean articles of clothing in the closet.

"I was half expecting that you had been a mirage," he said, his fingers leaving trails through his still-damp hair.

"That's what Crystal said, too."

Adam looked around as if having forgotten the girl existed. "I can explain."

"You don't have to. Sit. Eat." She pointed to the high stool at the counter.

He didn't take his eyes off her as she poured two cups of coffee. "You cleaned up?"

"It wasn't elves."

Adam looked around, nodding. "I'm embarrassed."

"Don't be," she said, feeling the same way about the plate of hard scrambled eggs and bacon with burnt edges. The up side was that the smoke from the bacon had absorbed the remnants of the earlier stench. And the smoke detector hadn't gone off.

"Thanks." He picked up his fork cautiously.

"I just bought the eggs, they probably won't kill you."

"It's not that." He looked up at her with open, emerald eyes that were full of regret. "What are you doing here?"

"I got a call," she said, rolling the coffee cup in her hand. "Becca's worried about you."

"My aunt called you?" Adam groaned. The mild embarrassment he'd spoke of inflamed. "That's so wrong." He laughed. "I'm not surprised. Actually, yes, I am. I'm also surprised you came."

"Why?"

"I didn't think you liked me anymore."

"That's childish."

"You said we'd talk and then you deserted me without a word or explanation."

There was that, she conceded. "Well, not wanting to talk doesn't lessen my obligations to you."

"Obligations?" He spat the word out bitterly. "You're not responsible for me, Mel, and neither is Becca."

"You can get righteous after you eat." She held his stare and his resistance sparked at her short fuse. "I just spent hours de-trashing your place. Tossing everything from your fridge, I dumped more empty gin bottles than I care to count and you've been passed out the entire time with a young girl in your bed. So do you really want to lecture me on your current lifestyle? Or are you going to eat your God-damned breakfast?"

For a moment, Melanie thought, *He's not going to give. A battle it is, then.*

He twisted the fork between his fingers before stabbing the eggs. "I'm not sleeping with Crystal."

"I know."

"You do?"

"Yeah, you're still with Courtney," Melanie said, picking up a strip of bacon. "You need to choose better confidants if you want your personal life to stay private."

"I've been in a rut," he said, tapping the tines on the plate.

"Drugs?"

He looked her in the eye before answering, "Only alcohol."

"And smoking too much," she added. "I cleared out twenty pounds of ash and butts from trays around the den."

"That too."

His wet hair shined under the pendant lights and his head drooped into his shoulder blades. For the first time in years Melanie was at a loss for words. She added a few drops of coffee in her already-full mug.

"That you're here, it means a lot. Even if it's only out of obligation."

She stayed quiet. It was easier to deal with him while he was passed out and silent. Now, she felt the embers igniting and she was starting to get pissed off by everything he said.

"Amazing that people care about you."

"You care about the 'obligation'."

Her eyeballs felt hot as her stare beamed into him. "I can leave."

"Go ahead."

"Okay," she said, feeling her keys in her pocket. "Remember to call your aunt and pay your damn phone bill." She gritted as she walked down the hall, feelings of rejection and anger building. *Your own fault, Mel, you knew better than to come here.*

"Damn it, Melanie. Don't go." He got to the door at the same time she did and blocked her path. "Don't go."

"I'll see ya," she said, the fabric of their clothing touching. She reached for the door handle.

"Why can't you just admit that you're still in love with me?" he asked, peering down at her, his jaw clenched and his open hands holding the door shut.

"Because I'm not."

"The hell you aren't. How long are you planning on continuing to torture me?"

"Torturing you? I don't love you anymore. Get over it." Her anger had taken control and she knew that part of her was liable to say and do anything.

"You do love me."

"I don't."

She blistered under his condescending stare and arched brow that spoke the two words. *You do*. Her rage detonated.

"I don't love you! I hate you! I hate you! You broke my heart and treated me like trash. I hate you." Melanie stopped herself, she'd been yelling. Startled, she stared up at his face and tried to understand her outburst. "You hurt me." Every muscle in her face was taut, her throat clenched and she felt as if she were suffocating.

Their gazes were locked. He looked as if he'd been slapped and Melanie was trying to calm her madness.

"I'm so sorry. Melanie," he breathed softly. His body had slackened and he lifted his hand from the door.

"I know." She'd heard it before and didn't care if he drowned in regret or sorrow.

"Do not scoff at my apology." His tension hardened. "I am truly sorry for what I've done."

"Maybe. But so what? Does it change anything?"

"I guess not. How long do you want me to suffer for my mistakes?"

She shook her head. "That's not my intention."

"Then what?"

"I will never give you the chance to hurt me again."

Adam's mouth tightened into a ball and the tendons on his jaw flexed. "You blame me, Mel, but you need to take your share of the responsibility for what happened."

"Yeah, I trusted you."

"That's all you're willing to concede?" he asked, stepping back.

She felt his confusion. "You left me."

"And you jumped into Ashe's arms the second you had the chance."

She gasped, unable to believe her ears. "You're kidding me." Melanie felt stunned. "I wanted you. I pushed Danny away until," she bit her cheek, "you made it clear."

Adam's hard expression didn't flinch. "I watched you. Maybe you kept him out of your bedroom but you didn't push him away." The anger she'd never seen before flared. "You held hands like lovers walking down the street. His arm around you like you were property and you weren't balking. I'm done taking all the fucking blame."

"That isn't fair," she replied, her body shocked. "You never gave me a chance. I," her throat went dry in mid-statement. "How was I supposed to know you'd be watching? You were never around."

"It shouldn't have mattered. You didn't wait for me. You don't remember being even a little in love with him?"

"I remember you tossing your phone over the edge of the cliff after you said you loved me!"

"You never thought about how great it'd be to have the picket fence dream with a simpleton?"

"Danny isn't simple."

"Not once did it cross your mind that he was a better choice?"

Adam stole her breath. "You weren't here ... I never got a choice."

"Admit it, I did you a favor. If I hadn't walked away you'd have cheated!"

The pain on her palm and the shock of what she'd done came simultaneously. Adam rocked back on his heels from the slap to his face.

The red handprint on his cheek began to glow as they stared at each other. Melanie's heart was racing and she realized it was anger surging through her veins.

He was coming out of the anger, they both were. The shouting match was over and neither won.

"I am so sorry," he said, his fingers pressing into his chest. "I didn't mean that."

"Yes, you did." She nodded, grinding her teeth and thinking about the photos in his top dresser drawer.

"I should've had more faith in you."

She choked down a lump of guilt. "I wouldn't have cheated."

"I know. I was so jealous I couldn't think straight." His forehead was creased. "I'm still jealous."

"I should've sent him away." Her voice cracked. "You're right, I shouldn't have let him stay."

"You couldn't turn anyone away." His gaze softened. "You're a good person, and I don't have much experience with your kind of generosity."

"No," she said, unable to accept the compliment. "I did, sometimes, think Danny was a safer bet." Her gut wrenched, but it was the truth. "I'm sorry. I knew you probably wouldn't like Danny hanging around but I couldn't," she paused, "I didn't want to let him go." She covered her face with her hands. "But, I was so in love with you. I don't know," she looked up, "I assumed you and I were too close to ever be broken apart." Melanie stared up into his eyes and felt sick. Time ticked before she could summon courage to continue. "I haven't forgiven you for betraying me. I thought I had but clearly I'm still holding onto the past."

They stood in silence.

"I wish things had worked out differently," she said. "That I had never run into Danny, that you hadn't left, that just about everything could be changed."

"I wouldn't change a thing," Adam said, through longing eyes.

"You're alive and well, and for that I'd be willing to give up anything."

"It was a high price for something that might have had the same conclusion," she said, shifting her balance from one foot to the other.

"I guess we'll never know."

Melanie sucked in a heavy breath. "We can't change the past, but I want you to stop whatever it is that you're doing. This," she sighed, "sabotaging your life. Stop drinking and smoking and quit hanging out with people who bring you down." His grin was loving, it was the way he looked when they'd first met. "That's not asking too much, is it?" she returned his smile.

"If that is what you want, I'll do it."

"Not because I want you to, but because you want to," she added, the gloom weighing on her heart. "Find a purpose to get up every morning."

His gaze didn't waver. "Done."

"Adam," she said, caught in the middle of a stare-down. "I'm serious."

"Me, too."

"I can't come back to you. There's too much history and pain."

"I'm not asking you to."

"That psychology won't work, either."

"Never took that class. I need to stop drinking, smoking, lose the wrong crowd and find a purpose, all because I want to. I'm suddenly a very busy man. I don't have time for a girlfriend, you included." She knew his raised spirits were only for show.

"There is one more thing."

"Anything."

"Will you make dinner for us tonight?"

This time his smile felt genuine. "I'm going to need to make a trip to the grocery store. I don't know if you've noticed, but my cupboards are bare."

"Appalling."

They went back to the kitchen and Adam finished his breakfast before actually checking out the state of his fridge. Melanie transferred the clothes from the dryer to the couch, the washer to the dryer and from the floor to the washing machine.

"Mind if I take a pair of those?" He asked as she folded the stack of Levi's.

"Take your pick." Melanie smiled, the laundry smelling fresh.

Ten minutes later he was dressed, jeans and a T-shirt that pulled across his broad chest and loose at his waist. His dark hair tossed into perfect disruption and his heartwarming smile thanked her.

"We're walking?" she asked as he handed her recyclable bags and ignored the askewly parked, expensive silver car.

"Traffic is impossible this time of year. It's not far, you'll make it." He smiled.

The pressure had abated and something else had taken its place. Not peace but a sort of comfort, a safety net or an understanding. Melanie was silently considering the situation as they strolled through his neighborhood beside the bay. Nice, modest, well-maintained homes that gave the impression of average – very nice average with price tags upwards of a million.

"Have you gotten shorter?"

"No." She laughed and shoved him off the sidewalk. "You've gotten used to the lingerie model."

"Not really. She and I have an understanding." He grumbled.

"And what would that be?"

"We're company. No strings, nothing serious."

"Right." Melanie smirked and rolled her eyes.

"We talked and it's what we both want," he said, stronger.

"You cannot be this foolish," she said, stopping and grabbing his arm, turning him to get a better read of his face.

"You don't know everything, Mel."

"She's agreeing with whatever you say, hoping you'll fall in love and change your mind."

"I know that type – but that's not Courtney. She's independent."

"Okay." Her will power took her only a few steps. "You like her?" she asked, looking at the side of his face and not feeling the pain she should.

"I don't like this conversation," he said, looking sideways at her. "I'm not ready to treat you like a buddy. I'm not ready not to be painfully in love with you." The apple in his throat bobbed. "Are you okay with that?"

"Yes."

CHAPTER TWENTY-TWO

The grocery store was busy and Melanie followed Adam through the aisles with the shrunken cart. She stopped short to answer the call of the ruby red, fist-sized strawberries. Melanie picked a pint and then went back for another as Adam scrutinized the bell peppers.

"Are you in charge of dessert?" he asked, adding a package of fresh spaghetti and hand-trimmed chicken breast to the cart.

"Depends on how you're feeling after eating breakfast."

"Best breakfast I've ever had."

"Then dessert it is. I can do that." Melanie agreed, thinking about an Angel Food Cake and a can of whipped cream.

Their fight had changed the mood between them. Shopping had been a distraction, and on the walk home they detoured by the bay.

"That I'm seeing Courtney really doesn't bother you?"

"Um," she smiled, "it does, but I think it has to do more with who you chose. Courtney is shallow and self-absorbed and I think she called me a penis."

"I don't know anything about the penis, but the rest of your description is spot on."

"Then why?"

"She loves herself way too much to fall for me. I don't see her that much, she's away a lot and it gets Trish off my back. Courtney must have told her we're dating." He shrugged unlocking his door. "Whatever."

"With all the crap you gave me about my apartment I thought your house would've been immaculate."

"I told you I was in a rut and I never said your apartment was crap." Adam set the bags on the counter. "What are your plans for the berries?"

"I don't know if I can find it in my heart to destroy them, they're so perfect. I say we eat them whole, or at the extreme, sliced."

"Your call." He paused, setting out the goods on the counter in an organized way – Melanie watched, fascinated at the care he was taking.

"You're going to throw all of that in a pot anyway, aren't you?" She leaned her hip against the counter.

"Mel, can I ask one favor?" his hands still holding the pasta. She nodded, hoping it was something basic, like pressing start on the microwave. "When you start falling for someone will you call me, warn me, so I don't have to hear it from Trish?"

He was serious. "You really don't have to worry about that," Melanie said, the pressure in her chest building. She knew he needed answers. "Adam, I am a decade away from dating," she admitted. "But if it'll make you feel better knowing that I'll be interrupting your kid's birthday party … consider it done."

He turned away so she couldn't tell what he was thinking. She held out longer than she'd thought she could, waiting for him to say something.

"Did I say something wrong?"

He was stirring the pasta. "You think you're the only one who gets to retreat from life. You want me to move on while you get to sulk. I don't want to go out with Courtney. I want to be miserable and alone."

"I'm not sulking. I didn't want a man around before you came along and I don't want one now. A choice."

"Must be nice to be able to make up the rules." The tendon in his jaw twitched as he clenched his teeth. "Forget it," he said, and as if all his bad habits had suddenly caught up with him, he looked worn out. "I don't want you seeing anyone else, anyway," his gaze grabbed a hold of hers, "everything I do is because I want you back. Everything. So, if you don't want me seeing Courtney, say the word and she's out."

"You cannot do that." Melanie fought down the rumble that was boiling in her core. "I can't have that much control over your life."

"Okay, then you don't."

"You are frustrating." Melanie closed her eyes.

"Only because you give me mixed signals."

"I am not. I think I've been pretty clear." Melanie's stated ardently, looking him straight in his cunning emerald eyes.

"We made love."

Taking a breath to defend her actions, she sucked in the air and stopped.

"Mixed signals."

"Moment of weakness." She defended, washing the berries again.

Adam shrugged, "I think it was a moment of insight but call it what you like." He kept chopping as he spoke, "How was Gus?"

Melanie stopped and looked at him. "You knew about this

weekend? About Gus?"

"Guilty."

"Well," she moved to a counter stool. "Gus was traded out for Nate."

Adam's hands stopped. "Did you have a nice time?" He asked through a clenched jaw.

"I did."

"He likes you."

"I know."

"Do you like him?" He asked, still not facing her.

"He's got qualities."

"Mel," he finally turned, "that's not what I asked. I don't care if it's none of my business, I have to know." His knuckles whitened as his fingers clutched the handle of the sharp knife.

"Don't worry no man in my life ever takes up permanent residence."

"I don't feel better."

"I've already told you I'm not interested in a relationship."

"You weren't looking for one when we met, either." His solemn voice caught in his throat.

About to clarify the difference when the stove timer and the doorbell rang at the same moment.

"Expecting someone?" she asked as he was enveloped in mist, leaning over the steaming pot with an orange noodle at the end of his fork.

"No, but this is done." He held out the banana squash pasta for her to try.

Tasted perfect to her. The doorbell clanged again.

"Could you get that?" Adam asked, up to his elbows in boiling water.

She left him with the strainer, grabbed her glass of lemon water and answered the door.

Melanie stood in the arch of the doorway and faced the lengthy stature of, "Courtney." She said, surprised. "Hi."

The happiness on the woman's face instantly vanished. "I know you," she said, pointing the index finger of the hand that was holding a bottle. "You're one of Trish's friends."

Melanie nodded slowly. "Yeah. I'm Melanie." *You might remember me from the stack of photos you destroyed.*

"Right. Well, where's Adam?" She lengthened her neck to peek down the hall.

"So, how've you been?" Melanie asked.

"What?" Courtney's thin brows pulled in and her eyes turned to slits. "I'm here to see Adam."

"He's in the kitchen." Melanie opened the door and stepped aside.

"Don't you live somewhere far away?" Courtney asked, looking down her nose at Melanie as she passed. "You do know that Adam and I are seeing each other."

"Congratulations."

"Who," Adam rounded the corner, "Courtney." He blinked over at Melanie, surprise and apology in his gaze.

Courtney wrapped her arms around his neck, her mouth suction cupped to his. Finally letting up for a breath, Melanie watched with an acid stomach.

"Court, what are you doing here?" he asked, his hands on her hips as he tried to keep her at arms length.

"Don't be silly. I don't need an invitation to come over." She held up a bottle of vodka. "I just got in from Russia and I brought the good stuff for us." She ran her finger down his chest, stopping at the button fly of his Levi's. Glancing over at Melanie with a smug expression. "Sorry, but this is really expensive."

"About that," Adam shot Melanie a look, his arm around Courtney's waist. "I'm on the wagon."

"Since when?" She kissed his neck and waved his words away. Pulling back, her wide smile aimed at Adam. "Seriously, this is the best. You can stop drinking tomorrow."

"Court."

"Were you making dinner?" she asked, letting him release her, her eyes on the table set with two plates and candlesticks. "Adam, what is going on here? Can we please speak in private?" Courtney asked, with a tone that said there was no choice.

"You know what," Melanie took her cue. "You guys have dinner, I'm going to catch a flight." Melanie said, wracking her brain to recall what she'd come in with … keys, sunglasses. "Adam, we'll catch up some other time." She smiled. "Don't forget to call Becca."

"Melanie, don't." Adam's voice was between commanding and begging. "Dinner was part of the agreement."

"Let her go," Courtney sighed. "I'm only in town for a couple of days, Baby." She turned to pull him into an embrace, her body pressed tightly against his.

"Court, let's talk in my room. Mel," he said, between breaks in the kissing, "take the sauce off the heat and turn the oven to broil but don't you dare leave."

His order had been powerful enough that she did as instructed. Melanie strained to listen but if they were talking it was too low to be overheard. At the seven-minute mark, the force of his authority had lost its persuasion. Instead, she yelled at herself for being stupid, again and tiptoed out the front door.

"Awkward," Melanie whispered in the summer night, climbing into her rental car. She sat behind the wheel and growled at the realization that she'd forgotten her phone. Whimpering, she reached around to pat her pockets. Thoughts of ditching the device were playing at the edge of her mind when the knock on her window made her jump.

"You wouldn't leave without this," Adam said, tapping her phone on the glass.

"Pickpocket? Isn't that stooping a bit low, even for you?" she asked, the heated feeling returning.

He didn't understand, stepping back and cocking his head to the side. "I didn't know she was coming. I swear."

"That's not what I'm pissed about," she said, her voice shaking. "I don't know what I'm upset about." But she did know, a small idea that they'd been fooling around in his bedroom had taken hold in her brain. It was stupid, she knew but … "Did you have sex with her right now? I don't care, it's just rude."

"What!? No, Mel. Are you crazy?" His chest rose and fell sharply as he spoke. "Get out of the car. Now. You cannot believe I'd do that." Their eyes met. "Please get out of the car." He stepped back so she could open the door.

She watched the artery in his neck. His hands trembled as they raked through his hair.

"We were only in the room five minutes. You know me better than that," he said, trying for humor.

"That's not helpful." It was. A little. She opened the door.

"Come inside. Dinner's ready. Mel," he took her hand in his, "we weren't having sex." He chuckled and there was a look she didn't like in his eyes. Like he'd won something and worse than that – it was like she'd lost. "I was *trying* to end things with her."

"I'm guessing it didn't work." Courtney was full of piss and vinegar as she leaned against the Audi.

"Don't bother calling, I have a shoot. I'll be in Fiji for a week. You could come. It's gorgeous." Her voice softened for Adam.

"No, Court," he said, the model's scowl fell on Melanie.

"For what it's worth," Melanie said, "there isn't anything going on between Adam and me."

"Right. That's why you ran out of the house and he chased you … because of nothing. Whatever. I don't even care," Courtney straightened. "Do you know how many men want me?"

"Millions?"

"That's right."

"There's enough pasta for three," Melanie offered, flinching from the pain in her left hand.

"Are you getting back together?" Courtney asked.

"No."

"Eventually," Adam answered.

"No, Adam, I don't see that happening," Melanie corrected.

"Mixed signals, Mel."

Courtney smiled a wicked grimace. "Don't worry, I won't slash your tires." She waved lightly, dragging her finger alongside the car as she went to her own.

"Wow," Melanie said. "I suggest you never fall asleep."

"Forget about her," Adam said, pulling Melanie into the house.

"I feel dirty, like I'm the other woman." Melanie thought about the rejection Courtney must be feeling.

"You aren't going to let her go, are you?"

She did call me a penis. Melanie considered an extra moment and decided that a dose of rejection may not be a bad thing for egomaniacal super model. "Just did."

Dinner with Adam was a complete experience. He'd set the dining table and arranged the plates like pieces of art. She'd forgotten how she could be seduced by his meals. How he was able to create food that melted in her mouth and raise his level of attraction to rock star heartthrob.

"What are you doing about opening that restaurant?" she asked shaking off the emotions.

"I'm thinking about it."

"You are insanely good at this," she said, sliding her plate away.

Adam smiled. "Thank you. But what about dessert?"

"I can't. I gotta go." She said, checking out her watch.

"The last flight out?"

She nodded. "The next time you're in D.C. give me a call."

"Maybe I'll try that."

"I'm really glad Becca called me. I wasn't sure about coming here but I'm happy I did. We're good, aren't we?" she asked him.

"We're getting there."

Melanie inhaled. "Don't waste your life waiting for me. The right person is out there for you. I just don't think it's Courtney."

"The right woman is closer than you think," he answered, his gaze not leaving hers. "You're going to wake up one morning realizing you're still in love with me. And, Mel, I'll be waiting for you."

"I do love you, Adam. I'm just *never* going to be in love."

"Have a safe flight."

CHAPTER TWENTY-THREE

Late the next morning she woke up in her bed at the Manor and considered how bizarre life was. The weekend was a distant blur, someone else's life, a movie or a dream.

Thinking, she searched for something to stress about and … came up empty. "Wow," she felt the strange lull, "everything is good."

She stayed in bed the extra minute, reveling in the feeling of satisfaction – knowing that it was fleeting.

From the gym, Jack was waiting for her at her office.

"I wanted to give you the Scooter update," Jack said, sitting in the crook of the couch.

"Unbelievable, right?"

"That woman is a wildcat. I swear, claws, fangs and her scruff were all crazed when we took her into custody."

Melanie sat in the chair across from him and leaned forward. "Did she really spend all of the money?"

"Hiring terrorists is expensive. She had overhead as well as salaries to consider. The CIA is going over her financials." His eyes glinted playfully. "And she wanted me to give you a message. "I'm coming after you." That's a quote. I told her to stand in line."

"Great."

"The network executives were told she had a breakdown and for the past few nights they announced her taking time off. Last night, she wasn't mentioned, it was business as usual. I suspect over time most will forget she ever weekend anchored. She'll just disappear."

"She must be dying. Her sole purpose in life was to make a mark. And Russell?"

"Everest is still on the air and from what I've heard Sean is taking a leave of absence from the Agency."

"I wish I could've been there. Follow a case to the end or at least hand her over to the CIA."

"I thought you'd been kicked out of the ITC."

"I wish," Melanie complained to Jack, putting her feet up on the coffee table. Her office was void of personality and though the couch was lumpy, it was good enough. "Can you believe they want to discipline me for doing well in that competition? You can bet Hugh is behind it."

"No way." Jack shook his head. "His assistant says the Senator can't even brush his teeth on his own."

"Really, Jack? Don't tell me you're buying that crap. We're not talking about just anybody. We're talking Senator Hugh Parker. The devil incarnate."

"You're too harsh."

She didn't bother with a reply.

"Jane says you've been grumpy."

"Really?" Melanie cocked an eyebrow at him. She didn't like them sharing information about her. "I'd rather not be the topic of a pillow conversation."

"Don't flatter yourself. I asked Jane if it was a good time to ask you for a favor."

She hadn't noticed, but he had been laying on the charm. She should've realized it the second that dimple on the left side of his face appeared.

"Ask away, Playboy. I've got nothing but time."

"Hasn't Ben spoken to you about the next ITC?"

"Not funny." She chuckled. "Ben would never send me back, Jesus, Jack! Where's Williams?"

"Recovering. That spider fucked up his nervous system. He's got to learn to walk again."

"No shit?" She thought about the flashing message alert Ben had left and she'd skipped. "Are you serious about the ITC?" Jack gave her an apologetic glance. "I knew it. I felt it in my bones, you know." It was why she'd been avoiding Ben.

"It's not for another week." Jack paused and Melanie couldn't bear to hear more. "Good thing is that it's being held in Paris."

"You have to leave my office now," she said. "I don't want you to see me cry."

"You need to work," Jack smirked. "That helps."

She remembered he had a favor to ask. "What do you want from me?"

"You need to take your old job back. Ben's great, don't misunderstand, but what is wrong with him?"

"He's part genius." She groaned, understanding the irritation.

"And the other part?"

Melanie laughed. "No clue."

"There's a case on his desk. I want it." She felt his eyes evaluating her. "There's a spy at NASA."

"Who's buying thirty-year-old technology?"

"It's not like that, they do a lot more than the old shuttle missions. Really cool, innovative types of spacecraft."

"That sounds impressive."

"Espionage, cutting-edge technology and space drones. I'm practically drooling. But Ben wants me at a desk."

"Ugh." She leaned back. "You are such a good soldier, Jack. That's why Ben likes you."

"Not everyone can get away with the crap you pull," he said. "How do you do it?"

"You make it sound like I intend on breaking rules. I don't. It just happens. I'm in the moment and I react."

"It can't be that random, Mel."

She shrugged. "I listen to my instincts. There's no conspiracy, no inside knowledge. We've worked together, you know."

"You've got a secret and I want it." The wistfulness in his voice caught Melanie off guard.

"Be careful what you wish for," Melanie said, shuffling her feet off the coffee table. "All I'm saying is that everything comes with a price."

"Maybe I'm willing to pay it." He looked at her as if she were going to deliver an actual dollar amount.

"I don't mean monetarily." She frowned at his naiveté. "I have no distractions" She opened her arms to her office. "No complications." *Liar!* "I've got nothing more than what you see here."

"You have friends." He smiled. "I'm your friend."

"We work together."

"We're sort of friends. But you never want to go out."

She smirked and nodded, letting him acknowledge there wasn't anything more to her life than work.

"Hey," he clapped his hands and pointed, "last month you were in a wedding."

"I used to have friends and they still have lives."

"So, you're saying to be a great agent I have to cut everything else out and focus only on the job."

"I would never recommend that," she clarified, catching herself about to reveal too much, that she was lonely. "I'm telling you my cost of being an agent. Maybe I would've been this way whatever my job."

They stared at each other for a beat. Jack's blue eyes alert. "If you're interested," he hummed, "A couple of my tennis buddies are single."

"See, even you have extra-curricular activities." Melanie sighed. "I do need to meet people. Not a boyfriend. I want friends. Where do I go to find those?"

"What do you like to do?"

"Work."

"What about some of the female agents?"

Melanie gave him a dirty look. "Name one female agent in this building who likes me."

"That's because you walk around sullen and angry. Try smiling more."

"Never mind," she said, giving up. "You want me to talk to Ben for you?" Melanie stood.

"Now?" he asked.

"What else are we doing?"

"Being friends. Sharing." He teased.

"I've got to talk with him anyway." Melanie said.

❦

She found Ben exactly where she'd imagined, behind his desk, wire-rimmed glasses perched on the tip of his nose as he pored over documents.

"Busy?" she asked, entering. "I could come back later."

"Have a seat," he said, looking at her from above the lenses. "How was Mexico? I'm surprised you didn't run into any cartels." His grin broadened into a smirk. "I was half expecting to get a call from the Federales."

"I'm not that bad."

"Drink?"

"I don't know, yet. What are we going to talk about?"

"The ITC."

"Drink." She sunk into her chair. "Stop. Please stop with the ITC."

"Oh, it hasn't been that bad."

Melanie looked at him. "You're right, it's been worse."

"I don't recall it that way."

Stunned, she examined the old man for possible signs of stroke.

"The final challenge starts in…" his eyes went to the calendar, "nine days. You cannot shake your head before you know what I have planned."

"Oh, yes I can. I'm not doing it, Ben. I'm not."

"Melanie," Ben started, his pale blue eyes fixed on her. "I need you to do this."

"Can't another agent do it? What about Jack?"

Ben shook his head. "No one is like you."

"That's not a compliment." She sucked in a breath and stared at her mentor. He handed her a glass and Melanie nodded her consent. "One condition."

"Name it."

"Jack. You have a case regarding NASA." Melanie looked at Ben for acknowledgement. "Let him have the assignment."

"But," he started.

"He needs a mission. He's a good agent."

"I know," Ben scratched the back of his ear. "Who will help me?"

Her shoulders raised and her palms went up. "I'd be here for you but, sadly, I've got to prep for the ITC. Unless?"

His mood lightened, "Nice play, Ward. However, I'll come up with an alternative."

"Jack?"

"Consider it done."

"All right." She slumped into the back of the chair. "Tell me about this third and final game. This is the final one, right?"

The next day she sent Logan, Fred and Anthony on a flight for a seven-day stint with Tony the Butcher. Tony was in his forties, 5'4" with hair plugs and the charisma of a cobra. Melanie had been part of the first wave of agents sent to him to hone their life saving skills. At the time, she and her fellow classmates hated Tony. Tony was nicknamed The Butcher because he chopped down anything in his path, including a trainee's self-respect.

It was an indoctrination into the Agency and her three recruits were about to experience his wrath.

"So, Boss, what have you got planned for us while they're gone?"

Bob asked, wide-eyed with expectation. "I could really use some R & R."

"Are you kidding me?" Melanie asked on her way down to the command center. "Did you see your piss-poor performance in the jungle?"

"I'm a hacker. The only outdoor experience I have is walking to the game store. How did you expect I'd do?"

Melanie looked at Bob. He was flabby, needed a haircut and he slouched. "We're going to work on your exterior presentation."

"What does that mean?"

It was the wrong question. Melanie strapped a body monitor to his arm, linked it to her cell phone and sent him to the gym with a goal.

"I'll be watching you," she said, leaving him without a doubt.

"But…"

"You can't be an out-of-shape agent."

"I'm a consultant."

Melanie shook her head slowly, pushed the basement button on the elevator and stepped off. Bob looked hurt, scared and hungry as the doors closed.

"That was fun," she laughed and headed for the kitchen, feeling hungry herself.

⸙

"Ms. Ward," Jane's voice filled her ear. "Judith has a stack of work for you to pick up."

The Post-it on top of the file folders, in Ben's swirly penmanship, reminded her that it was her suggestion to give Jack an assignment.

"Can I work here with you?" she asked Mike having dragged

the files from Ben's office to her own isolated one. But the solitude proved to be too quiet.

Relentless turned to restless by day three. When she finished Ben's case files, she began assisting Mike with his investigation. Scanning miles of electronic data, searching for variations. A blip could signal possible terrorist activities but – after hours of aching eyeballs – the results just looped around, giving her nothing for her efforts but a stiff neck.

"It's a good thing I'm helping you out," Melanie said chomping on a handful of peanut M&M's.

"Yeah, how's that?" He glanced over at her and popped a piece of blue candy between his teeth. "Don't you have your own work to do?"

"Finished. It's taking both of us to get through this brain-numbing crap you do."

"If you'd stop pelting me with chocolate I'd be more efficient."

Melanie laughed. "You were right, this is boring. Can't we let Ed do it? He plays video games all day."

Mike swiveled his chair to look at Ed, headphones on his ears and a controller in his hands.

"He's making sure there isn't any brainwashing technology embedded in the games our children are playing."

Melanie had been watching Ed for three days. "Have you considered the possibility that they've gotten to him?" Melanie stepped up to Ed's chair and leaned to stare into his face, inches from his grungy hair. "If he started drooling I wouldn't be surprised."

"You may be right." Mike snapped his fingers at Ed, who looked up with a glazed expression. "Take a break."

Ed nodded.

"Oh, I've got to take this call," Melanie said, reading the caller ID. "Hi, Car, what's happening?"

"Mel! I'm in D.C. with Ted, he's got a thing tomorrow night. We're here for a few days but the Triad has us booked solid. I put my foot down and made a big deal about my time and my needs. Please tell me you can meet us for dinner tonight."

The Triad was Ted's family, his mom, dad and sister, who guarded Ted more closely than the Secret Service.

"Name the place."

"Good." Carla sighed and said they had reservations at a steak house blocks from the White House. "The Bradleys are nothing if they aren't about image. They want Ted in showy places. Myself, I'd be happy with Outback."

"Do you think you could add one extra to that reservation?" Melanie asked, shaking her head at Mike who was telling her he was busy.

"Oh, really?"

"Get that gossipy note out of your voice. I'm bringing a…" What was Bob? A colleague? No. "A co-worker who has nowhere else to go." She tilted her phone away from her mouth, covered the receiver and scolded Mike, "Stop. I'm inviting Bob."

"Sorry."

"Don't pout." She rolled her eyes. "Do you want to go?"

"I can't."

"Fine. Don't be so delicate." She righted the phone. "8:30 is perfect. We'll be there." She groaned, "No, I don't mean we as in we are a couple. Bye, Car. See you tonight." She looked over at Mike. His spine was curved, hunched over the keyboard. "Your posture is terrible."

He straightened, then twisted into chair stretches. "It's not usually this dull around here," Mike said, his fingers back on the keyboard. "Where are you going?"

"Get some lunch and check on Bob."

"I'm hungry," Mike whined.

Melanie appraised him. "I'm going to trust you."

"Duh," he said, widening his bulbous brown eyes.

"I'm thinking we've been hanging out a little too much. You never would've disrespected me before."

"I'm sorry."

"You know the abandoned office on the top floor? Meet me there in twenty."

"What office?"

"Don't you ever go exploring? No? In the middle of the night when you can't sleep?"

"You're crazy. Do you know that?" Mike asked.

"Just be there if you want lunch."

According to her phone Bob had burned over 3,000 calories and it wasn't even noon. When she got to the gym she found him hard at work, laying on the sit-up bench with a bag of Cheetos and browsing the most recent People magazine.

"You're a damn hacker!"

Bob jumped, spilled orange powder puffs over the workout equipment and made a sad attempt at hiding the magazine behind the weights.

"I can explain."

"Yeah, you're a lazy bastard."

"That is part of it, yes, but also I can't help myself. I'm a victim of my own abilities."

"Are you spying on celebrities, again? Where'd you get access to a computer?"

"I just took this thing apart and made up some numbers. I did exercise for the first day, but it got boring."

"I was coming to invite you to lunch and dinner."

"Great. I'm starved."

"You are going to make this up to me," she said. "But in the end the only one you're hurting is yourself."

The southernmost room on the top floor had been vacant for years. Melanie couldn't remember who last occupied the space or why it was forgotten. But it had big windows that, when the curtains were opened, gave a splash of sunlight like no other space in the building.

The room had become a storage unit with scattered boxes, broken lamps and discarded paintings left to lean against the wall and a desk. The desk was old, made of solid wood, with brass, eagle handles on the drawers, the insert in the top was eighteen inches of cracked red leather and beautiful.

"Put the tray on the desk, but do not spill those drinks," she scolded Bob even before he'd done anything wrong. His mindless obedience brought her a wave of guilt. "Sorry, I just really like this old thing."

"Why don't you have it moved to your office? It doesn't look like it belongs to anyone."

"No, it fits here with the light and the masking-tape-colored walls."

"Boss, can you please assign me to do something other than working out?"

"I don't know what else to do with you. You complained about Mike."

"He doesn't like me."

"Hey, speak of the devil," Melanie said as Mike entered the room.

"This is a nice space," he said, pushing open the drapes on the western corner. "Fantastic view of the park and there's enough room to breathe. I like it. What?" he asked, shuffling backward a few steps. "I've been apartment hunting for a month."

"I swear, Mike, if you open your mouth about this place, to anyone, it's the last time I ever share a secret spot with you. Capiche?" He had blabbermouth tendencies.

"Can I use it sometimes?"

"Sure. If you can pick a lock." Melanie grinned.

"I want to learn that," Bob piped in.

Mike and Bob were still navigating the deadly sin of male territory protection. *I swear if they start pissing on the walls,* she thought not knowing what she'd do. But as Bob made a techie joke about salad dressing and terra bites vs. terabytes that Melanie didn't understand, Mike's laugh electrified the light bulb above her head. She wanted them to become friends. Friends that could bond over a common enemy. Her.

"Bob, the salad is for you," she said, taking her pastrami on rye and handing him the Cobb.

"Boss, I want meat."

"What happened to funny Bob?"

"You killed him," Bob moaned, sliding his bowl around to get an even perspective of the veggies. "I'm a man," he whimpered.

"What have you been doing to the kid?" Mike asked, the first note of concern for his competition.

"She called me flabby and stuck me on a treadmill. Did you see this?" Bob asked lifting the short sleeve of his T-shirt. "She monitors me like I'm a criminal."

"You are. You should be behind bars and you faked your numbers. Tell him."

As Bob detailed how he'd rigged the calorie counter Mike's expression turned.

"Isn't there somewhere else we could use him? I'd hate it if you treated me like a hamster. I never treated him like this. Did I?"

"Never. You were respectful of my feelings."

"You both complained about each other."

"Well, maybe we can find something else for him." Mike's gaze moved around the room. "He could clean this place up."

"Yeah, because he looks so tidy himself?" Melanie nodded. *Come on, Mike, you can do it.* "Bob we're having dinner tonight with friends of mine so I set an appointment for you with Maggie. She works in the kitchen but moonlights as the Agency's barber."

"She really is great," Mike added. "Hey! I've got it! Why don't we let Bob take over the video game threat and give Ed a reprieve?"

"I don't know," she held out. "Are you two going to get along?"

They looked at each other before jumping at the, "yeah!"

Melanie ate as Mike explained the job and fought to understand a deep sense of sadness. *Why can't I control my personal life as well?* She looked at the two men-children and wondered if they would become friends. She wondered if they would be considered *her* friends and if so, should she be able to manipulate friends? By the end of lunch the rift between Mike and Bob had softened.

Mike was howling as they rode the elevator down. Melanie wasn't clear what made Bob so funny. He didn't do faces or voices and he wasn't overzealous or the center of attention. What he did have was a keen sense of the absurd and a knack for twisting words.

"You done analyzing me?" Bob asked as she left him with Maggie.

"I'm just trying to understand you." She smiled. "You're all over the board, mixing traits that don't belong together."

"Ever think that maybe you think too much?"

"I think it all the time. I'll meet you in the garage at 8."

She was ten minutes early and Bob was waiting for her in a suit and tie. His lid, of dark curls had been shortened and styled, giving him a look that could pass for corporate.

"What do you think?" he asked, his boyish face the same under the façade.

"You're like a new man."

"Do I look like an adult?"

"You look like a guy ready to be taken seriously." Melanie hoped it was along the lines of a right answer.

"I look like my father," Bob said, dropping the corners of his lips to add sag to his jowls.

Melanie drove to the restaurant and let the valet park the car. She walked straight into Carla's arms.

"This must be your gentleman friend." Carla gave Bob the once over in the snooty way she'd been developing since birth.

"Hello, Ma'am," Bob replied nervously.

"Ha! You deserved that ma'am comment." Melanie laughed. "Carla and Ted, oh, and Mr. and Mrs. and Ms. Bradley," she added as the family stepped out of the shadows they'd been lingering in, "this is Bob."

"Nothing like being put on the spot to rev up the heart rate," he muttered to Melanie. "Wonderful to meet you," he said, shaking a round of hands.

"Congressman Bradley, your table is ready."

Melanie leaned her head down to Carla. "How are you holding up?"

"I won a battle," she grinned, "and it feels so good. Makes me want to win more."

"Order a beer, that'll get their motors running," Melanie suggested. "I'll get one, too."

"Maybe just a glass of white wine."

"Rebel."

During dinner Bob had made up an elaborate story about owning polo ponies and how he had to travel to Luxemburg twice a year for a match.

"Who is he?" Carla whispered after they both caught the tail end of one of his stories.

"He's new at work, a consultant. Doesn't know anyone in town, so I've been babysitting."

"Not your usual type, is he?" Carla peered at him with narrowed eyes and a lopsided head.

"No, he's not, which supports the fact that we're not dating."

"He's kind of cute," Carla lifted her head and opened her eyes real wide. "Could be that this is the kind of change you need. You know, forget about those pretty boys and go for someone … solid."

Melanie looked at Bob and wondered what part of him Carla considered solid.

"Have you spoken with Trish?" Carla asked.

"Does getting lured to Mexico count?"

"No! She didn't tell me. You were at the hook-up condo?" Carla tucked a strand of hair behind her ear.

"Why didn't you tell me?" Melanie laughed. *Hook-up condo?*

"I've been really busy and Trish's been preoccupied with setting up blind dates, which don't include me. She has weekly dinner parties for her single friends. I'm sure I'm not supposed to tell you this … but Nate asked her to leave you out of the rotation."

"Nate was the one who saved me from Gus Gomez."

"Isn't he the one that sprays when he speaks?"

"Overactive salivary glands," Melanie corrected.

"That's weird. Gus seems like an odd choice."

"Jace doesn't want me dating any of his friends. He's sort of mad at me."

Carla shook her head. "He's stressed. The Padres have been shaking up their roster. I think even Trish is worried about Jason's standing."

"He's their top player," Melanie said, wondering what would happen if he got traded.

Over a petit filet mignon and an array of steamed vegetables, she and Carla huddled, whispering, at the end of the table.

"I'm going to miss you," Melanie said, hugging Carla at the curb as the car was being brought around. "Any way you can get some free time while you're here?"

"Only if I feign a headache. But then I'd disappoint Ted, no I'd better not. Visit us at home, soon."

"I will."

Carla chuckled softly. "No, you won't. You're hiding out. You won't be back unless there's a gun to your head."

Melanie tried to hide her reaction to such a graphic statement.

"Please, Mel. You're up to something and I think it has to do with Adam."

"Adam and I are over."

"Maybe."

"Really, Car. He's with Courtney," she said with a grimace. "As unappealing as she is."

Carla's smile was disingenuous.

"I'm serious. After he dumped me and then the Danny thing…"

"If you say it's over then I'm sure it is." Carla placed a kiss on Melanie's cheek. "I didn't mean to upset you."

"I'm not upset," she said, feeling agitated. She rubbed her face, "I just don't like people assuming." She sighed.

"Honey, I'm sorry." Carla gave her a quick hug goodbye. "I'll call you tomorrow."

Forget it, Melanie waved as the taillights merged with the rest of the traffic.

"Can you believe those people? I'd hate to be their doctor, trying to work around those massive sticks up their ass," Bob said as she drove them back to the Manor.

"Stop," she reprimanded. "You going to be okay if I leave you with Mike for the rest of the week?"

"Are you kidding? Playing video games all day, sounds like what I used to do for free." Melanie parked in the lot below her office window. "Thanks for coming tonight."

"Thanks for inviting me. Your friends aren't the liveliest but I got to practice my agent skills. Did you hear me? I invented a whole other life and they bought it lock, stock and barrel."

"I heard."

"You cannot tell me you weren't impressed."

"You overdid it, beginner's mistake." Melanie said, discreetly inputting her pass code. Out in the open she felt exposed. "Let's get inside."

❦

"Ward."

She jumped at the sharp and unexpected company. "Guilty as charged." She accepted whatever blame was coming her way.

Ben's face cracked into a grin as he entered the office. "You automatically expect to be in hot water," he said, chuckling and leaning on the back of a chair.

"Can you blame me?"

"I came to find out what you did with all of my paperwork."

"Finished it," she said, beckoning to the various piles on her desk.

"You assigned cases?"

She nodded. "I returned some to the Feds, assigned the others and added to the report of the closed ones. Judith gave me the list of agents and where they were and..." She thought for a second. "You don't mind, do you? I thought I was helping."

"Where do you find the energy?"

"I don't have disciplinary meetings to go to for wayward agents." She smiled, knowing that part of his out of the office time was spent dealing with her. "And I felt bad about you losing Jack."

"You had ITC business to attend to."

"Satellite meetings. Mostly I worked on your stuff while they bitched and complained about me. It's going to take more than one year of challenges to transform that ideology."

"I wasn't expecting it to happen over night."

"Well, look for another sucker next year."

"We'll table that conversation for another time." His brows furrowed as he twisted and looked around searching the corners of her tiny office. "What have you done with Karlovitz?"

"Karwoski. He's with Mike, taking over Ed's job of playing video games. All day long."

Ben looked anxiously at her. "When you say it like that it sounds unimportant. It is an ideal medium for terrorists to reach our most vulnerable of citizens, our children."

"Couldn't the terrorists be corrupting our agents with these games as they search for brainwashing links?" Ben didn't blink. "Have you *seen* Ed lately?"

He pushed the button on his phone. "Judith, please schedule Ed from tech services for a psych exam."

CHAPTER TWENTY-FOUR

Paris was beautiful at night. Melanie and her team strolled the streets, window shopping and admiring the city lights. No one had much to say with their eyes too wide and their thoughts on the final challenge. Their nerves heightened with the calm before the storm.

The time for lectures was over. They knew it or they didn't, and no word had come down as to the nature of the task.

"We'd better get some sleep," Melanie suggested after stopping the three-hour what-if and worse-case-scenario conversation that just about had her to the brink of murder.

"How?" Logan asked. "I'm so hyped up I'm getting dizzy."

Melanie's tired eyes glazed over her crew. "Get your running shoes on." She shrugged off the groans. "If you can't sleep we work out."

"I can sleep," Bob chimed.

Melanie arched her brow and the four headed to their rooms to change.

In two hours they were dragging their sweaty bodies to bed without an ounce of energy left. She'd worked them hard and considered it payment for pushing her to her limit all day.

The six a.m. knock on the door brought an envelope and a service tray of breakfast.

Melanie held the thin folder between her fingers. "Doesn't feel like much." But the eager eyes of her recruits said so much more. "Ready?" she asked, sliding her index finger beneath the seal.

One sheet of paper with two sentences printed in bold type.

There Will Be No Captain Participation In The Third Challenge.

All recruits are to report to the Monet Conference Room in one hour.

"How will we do this without you?" Logan asked, panicked.

Melanie chuckled. "You don't even know what the task is about! You'll be fine and I get time off in Paris," she said, hoping they'd buy her cavalier attitude.

"Do you think this is because of us?" Fred asked, being polite not to point his finger at his over-involved captain.

Without a doubt. "Probably not. Remember to communicate, follow your instincts and everything else I've taught you over the last few months." Melanie laughed. "Above all, be safe and look out for each other."

"We'll make you proud, Boss."

"I already am. If the other teams start playing dirty, don't hold your punches. I'm not telling you to go looking for trouble but don't back down, either." It wasn't the most biblical advice, but she'd never claimed to be forgiving.

She walked them to the lobby, and shook off the jitters as she followed her team with her eyes. The four waved, entered the conference room and disappeared into the third challenge.

Melanie released a pent-up breath. She was alone in the foyer and found herself with nothing to do. Her first instinct was to stalk her contestants.

"This is one of those moments," Melanie said, her voice sounding mature. *God, I sound like my mom.* With her hands shoved deep into the pockets of her jeans she turned and hurried down the sidewalk.

The Parisian satellite branch of the Agency was only a few miles away. Melanie walked.

Her retina eye scan unlocked the outer door. Inside, she was greeted by a receptionist and after a background check, Melanie was allowed into the internal workings.

"Bonjour," Melanie said with kisses to two of the agents she'd worked with, Lorna and Sterling. She spoke to them in French and they returned their response in English.

"The ITC. How is that?" Lorna asked, looking down her nose and with a haughty tone. Had the roles been reversed Melanie would've had the same unpleasant expression.

"A pain in the ass," Melanie admitted. "Not my agents, but the rest is bullshit. This place looks the same."

Lorna nodded. "Always changing, so it's always the same."

"I understand."

"He's back." A young man rushed into the small quarters, speaking rapidly. The front line of his thinning hair gleamed with sweat. "What do we tell him?"

"Get the meeting point. And tell him this is the last time – he shows or we stop taking his calls."

"Yes, Ma'am."

Lorna lowered her voice and leaned into Melanie. "A man has called," she raised her brows. "I do not know how he got the number.

He thinks we're part of the French Intelligence, the DGSE. He says he was KGB in World War II and claims he has documentation that could change history. Supposed to reveal KGB in the Allied Forces."

Melanie whistled as she pushed out an impressed breath. "No kidding? Do we know anything about the caller?"

"He is always a no show, this is his third call."

"It's a hoax then?" Her face fell. What agent wouldn't love to have experienced life as an early-twentieth-century spy? It was the golden age of espionage, when the line of friends and enemies was so defined and yet so many in ranks had been converted.

"We ran the name he gave us and verified the information but, yes, it could be a farce."

The young agent was back at Lorna's ear. Melanie looked up, expectantly.

"A meeting at a café on the Champs Elysees in half an hour."

"Do you mind if I survey the nearby shops? I won't intrude on your agent's meeting," she said, hoping she'd get a chance to do just that.

"He said one agent," she said, cautiously.

"And what good has that done? I could be a tourist."

Lorna nodded. "Okay." She snapped her fingers. "Anton fetch Agent Ward a photo of Monsieur Barkov."

"Send it to my phone. I'm leaving now," Melanie said, scribbling her number on a piece of paper. Lorna called the number to verify it was Melanie's.

Melanie hailed a cab and was dropped off three cafés down and across the street from where Barkov was to meet Anton. She mixed with the other sightseers, reading menu boards and casually meandering toward the rendezvous. She wasn't alone on the tree-lined sidewalk but the level of traffic had slowed and somewhere in her heart, Melanie knew this was part of his plan.

Her phone buzzed and she was gazing at a black-and-white photo of Barkov. A proud youth in his sharp Russian military uniform and 77 years younger than the man she was watching for.

Her heart pumped madly as her eyes scanned the scene, taking in the wide view of the shops on the other side of the multi-lane road.

Maybe it was her strong desire for it to be true, but she walked the clean curb knowing the ninety-plus-year-old man was nearby. Anxiously she looked for that tiny something that was out of place, the hint that would lead her to her goal.

Careful not to be obvious, Melanie joined a conversation with a group of Japanese tourists waiting for their bus. All the while she let her instincts guide her movements.

She checked a giant clock on the side of a stone building; one minute and one café away. The energy within her body fever-pitched. If she hadn't been looking in the right direction she might have missed the flash. A blinding spark cutting through the green leaves – two floors above the meeting spot.

Upstairs? Third floor. Her eyes flew to the location, but the angle and tint on the window prevented her from seeing much. Melanie was jogging across the street before she'd known her gut decision had been made.

She dodged a bicyclist and shuffled around the outdoor tables to get inside the cramped café. She stood at the entrance where the rich smells of coffee and pastries were palatable. The waiters groused and gave her dirty looks. The small tables were covered in linen and topped with vases of fresh flowers.

In the far corner of the room was a set of stairs, obstructed by a thin metal chain and a Do Not Enter sign. An argument in the back distracted the staff: nobody was watching as she placed her palm on the turned banister, hopped the chain and skipped up the stairs. The place was musty as she headed away from the buzzing of staff activity.

She didn't want to walk directly in on Barkov. She hunted through the old building finding a forgotten restroom. Nestled in the dimly lit passage, behind an abandoned hostess pedestal was a door that had been feasted upon by active termites.

She turned the knob, breaking it off along with the bottom panel of the door. *Shit!* She stared at the damage, then gently leaned it against the wall. She peered into the hole. It opened to a very vertical stairwell that must have been directly above the aromatic kitchen. Quietly, she climbed.

Excitement prickled her skin as she cracked open the third-floor door.

There he was, sitting with his curved spine toward her and his nose to the window. The cheap suit at his side, a middle-aged man balding in two spots, was either his bodyguard or his son.

She stepped up behind them, her palms sweating with the thrill. "Monsieur Barkov?" she asked, anticipating others, friend or foe, to jump out of the woodwork.

The younger man whipped his head around at her voice, a surprised and vacant look in his dark eyes.

Barkov, with his snow-white hair and gleaming eyes, twisted as far as his arthritic back would allow. "Who are you?"

"I wish I could tell you," she said, barely hanging on to her angry, tough spy façade.

"Hmm." He rotated his body back to a comfortable position and gave an order. "Sit."

Melanie wanted to, the chairs were inviting but... "Can't." Her muscles were tense. "I would love to, though."

"American?" He turned his head to give her a view of his profile. "Interesting."

"Yes," Melanie answered.

"Sit, why not?" He chortled. "What am I going to do?" From her view Melanie could make out one proud brow rise. "Sit, please. I'm ninety-four and my joints aren't what they once were."

Melanie bit her lower lip, taking what seemed to be no risk at all, she rested on the edge of the chair.

"Much better." His blue eyes were not clouded, but alive and brilliant as he appraised her. "Average pretty. Not beautiful."

Melanie laughed. "I have to say I've been told otherwise."

"Men," he said, his laughter harmonizing with hers, "will say anything."

Through the insult she found herself drawn to the former spy. And wondering how former – he seemed quite active to her.

"I should be a sitting duck but no, no one finds me." He glanced out the window to the street below.

"I'm sorry. Have you considered that they're too busy with real matters to entertain your game?"

He sighed, "Yes. I'm an old spy who no longer matters."

Ouch, she hadn't meant to hurt the old guy. "Is that why you're doing this? For attention?"

He shrugged.

"For what it's worth, I wanted to meet you," she said.

The wrinkles around his mouth stretched as he gave her a grin. "Thank you."

"The papers, are they real or was this all a ploy?"

"I've got documents that mattered once. Not anymore. Now it's all about rush-rush. There's no art in espionage. It's planes and satellites and radar and sonar – all very advanced and impersonal – from behind a computer. Cowards."

She wasn't going to argue with an old man, who actually looked healthier than most people half his age. *And,* she mused, *he's got a point.*

"May I ask what picture you have of me?"

Melanie laughed. "You were seventeen."

"Yes?"

"It's on my phone."

As he snorted his discontent, she reached in her back pocket, entered the security code and handed him his picture.

Barkov croaked out a frog laugh that was followed by hacking, coughing and wheezing. Melanie rose to her feet, ready to perform CPR.

"Sit, I'm fine." He said, between gasps that were easing. "Look at me. I was handsome."

"I bet you still do okay with the ladies," Melanie said, sitting back down.

"You don't need the gun," he handed her phone back. "We're not armed."

Her weapon was still tucked into her waistband. "Tell me what it was like for you as a spy."

"Wonderful." Barkov took in a short breath. "Danger was all around. You couldn't spit without hitting a double agent and you could never be certain who you were dealing with. That included spouses. But," he smiled, "we all knew our places. We got along, when we weren't killing each other or setting the other up to be killed, there was camaraderie. Mutual respect."

"Sounds like good times."

"Best of times. Secret meetings, hidden files, film sewn into clothing, thallium pills, alliances. Is it still like that?" Barkov stopped and looked at Melanie, a youthful buzz of excitement in his eye.

"Not exactly. Different. I'm sort of a solo flyer."

"When it comes down to it, we all are." He sighed, pulling in short lungfuls of air through his nostrils. "They want to put me in a home."

Melanie nodded, not surprised. "Maybe it's the right thing."

"Perhaps. But I'm a man who braved the Cold War and now I can't take a bath without assistance. I still see myself as that seventeen-year-old. Growing old is difficult to comprehend – never thought I'd see thirty and here I am."

There was nothing to say. She sat watching Barkov with mixed emotions.

"I belong in a museum, not assisted living. Well," his chest expanded as he took in another short breath. "Thank you for finding me. It is not easy being unnecessary. Nobody loves an antiquated spy." He tapped on the handle of his walker and the younger man was by his side in an instant.

Melanie stood, keeping a distance between them as the old man leaned down to retrieve an envelope.

"You'll be wanting these." He left them on the seat of the couch and pushed the wheels of the metal support through the deep carpeting. "There are two files in there. One for your superiors and something for you."

"Do you have any regrets?" Melanie asked, his back toward her as she lifted the envelope.

She heard him gruff before shuffling his feet to face her. "Your side is not always right. It's not always wrong, but how can you tell which is which?"

"Trust?"

His smile was filled with gray teeth and he pointed a crooked finger at her. "You know better than that. Your government will be operating when you are my age, where will you be? Plan. For the unthinkable."

She nodded, not understanding but willing to consider. She watched the old man amble to the outer hallway. "You can lose the feeble act," Melanie said. "I know you don't need that thing."

"Sometimes I do." His grin widened, "sometimes I don't."

"Very convincing. What about the home, is that for pretend, too?"

His curved spine straightened slightly. "Sadly, that is the truth. If you get bored you can look me up. I'm in the book."

"You might hear from me."

"I'd like that." The old man's chest cough sounded real and full of fluid as Melanie ducked out of the room from the back way.

The hacking turned to a grinding laugh as his voice echoed loudly in the empty room above. "She vanished. I like you. I know you can hear me so I'll give you a warning. Better run. Sixty seconds before this place blows."

Melanie stopped short in the small stairwell. Her blood rushed through her ears and into her head. One minute. Flying down the remainder of the stairs to the main floor she used her shoulder to force open the unyielding door. The crash got attention. The shouts of the waiters scolding her for trespassing faded in her ears as she looked over the crowd. Too many people, too much furniture. No easy way to evacuate in 45 seconds.

There's no way he can get out in time, it would be suicide. The thought sent her nerves into overdrive. *He wants to go out with a bang!* She rushed through the maze, shouldering her way to the front of the café, where she could at least save a few lives.

Her mouth opened, ready to alert those seated by the exits, those with a chance to escape. Her chuckle rode on a gasp and her laugh solidified as her memory replayed his words: "… look me up. I'm in the book."

At the sidewalk Melanie headed left and kept walking. Her chest was filled with air, but she wasn't breathing. She was taking a calculated risk, and for the next fifteen seconds her heart pounded in her eardrums, petrified that she'd guessed wrong. Passing the minute mark, without an explosion or the familiar Parisian sirens, her grin widened and let out the pent up breath. Her feet barely touched the concrete. She traveled the length of the Champs and into the Tuileries Garden.

"Hi," she smiled, her phone pressed tightly to her cheek.

"Oh no, what happened?" Ben's experience surpassed his faith. "The ITC?"

"No," she sighed. "Captains have been excluded."

"Ward?" His voice tensed.

"I just had one of the most amazing days of my life." She started and with a few prompts from Ben she recounted the events. "He was so suave, Ben. I almost fell for his trick and when I snapped his picture as I handed him the phone, he had no idea."

"Ward! You met with a KGB agent! Do you have any idea how dangerous that was? What the ramifications are? You didn't try to apprehend him. He handed documents over to you!?" The list of rants went on longer than Melanie expected and though she tried not to let it, Ben's reaction had mildly dampened her spirits.

"Ben, he was in his nineties, what was I going to do? I think you're overreacting. The Paris team was going to meet with him anyway."

He sighed and the quiet remained until she asked if he was still there.

"What's in the envelope?"

"I don't know," she said, swiping her hand over the fibers. "It's going to be less than I hope, so I'm holding onto the moment of pure possibility."

"Ward?"

She laughed. "Ben, it was so incredible, I feel like I just met Elvis! Better than that, even."

"Ward you cannot befriend ex-KGB agents."

"A Christmas card, then."

"How is it that you have time to find trouble in the middle of the third challenge?"

"It's recruits only," she said, her fingers tracing the edge of the contents of the envelope, catching on a lump. "I'll catch you later."

Melanie adjusted her posture and took in her surroundings. Barkov could've sat at this very bench monitoring his mark. She doubted much had changed since the war – the buildings, the trees, the fountains.

She didn't like park benches; memories of Finn washed over her like a tidal wave. She was too exposed. Melanie clutched her package and headed back to the hotel, where she disarmed two listening devices, one video and sat on the couch. Her finger slid easily beneath the seal, cracking open the envelope.

The first file contained a menu for a dinner held at the Kremlin in May of 1940. The second page was the guest list along with the seating arrangements. Her eyes scanned the names, stumbling on a few of the familiar and stopping at the U.S. Secretary of War at the time.

Curious and interesting, she thought, holding the pages between her fingers and struggling with an internal debate. *But right now, it's too much to consider.* Setting the file down she tipped the envelope and into her open hand fell a large coin attached to a red and yellow ribbon.

Barkov received a Russian Medal of Honor. Melanie smiled, the weighty medallion covered most of her palm. "He gave me his Medal of Honor," she repeated out loud. His voice rang in her ears. "Camaraderie."

❧

Her team took three days to finish the challenge and Melanie paced the streets of Paris with the Barkov medal buried deep in her front pocket. She'd sent images of both Barkov's papers and his gift to Ben.

"I'd love to research that particular affair at the Kremlin," Melanie had stated, "but I can't. I'm mentally stretched as it is."

"Who was asking you to?" Ben's practical voice had cut through her tight nerves. "You aren't a historian, Ward. I'm getting this information to the Board and they'll most likely turn it over to the National Archives."

"I'm wearing out the soles of my shoes over here. But it is a beautiful city," she complained, checking the caller ID of an incoming call. "It's them. I've got to go."

"We just marked down our time," Anthony said. "We're catching a train and should be in Paris within the hour."

"How'd it go?"

"Grueling."

So many more questions to ask, but he sounded wasted. "I'm sure you did an excellent job."

"I think we came in second or third. Hard to tell. Fred wants to talk. See you in a bit, Boss."

"Okay." She waited for Fred.

"Boss, that was awesome!" he was full of residual energy, speed talking about tasks and artifacts and things that Melanie couldn't follow.

Relief eased into her subconscious. She'd been worried about them and now it was over. Just like that, done. The pressure that had been hanging over her slackened and her lungs expanded more easily.

Riding the Metro back to the hotel was comforting, with its color-coded mazes beneath the city. She traveled the trains, reading the advertisements and keeping her eye on her fellow passengers. There was a safety in the depth of the tracks; she could get lost in the mix of people and emerge anywhere in Paris.

On the street she positioned herself with the waitstaff and entered the luxury hotel through the back. An itinerary, which hadn't been there when she'd left that morning, had been set on the coffee table.

Private flights had been arranged. They were scheduled to depart out of Orly International the following morning.

Her team exploded through the door, talking all at once.

Chattering. It was Anthony who gave the breakdown of the challenge that had started in the hotel and led them through the catacombs. It was a glorified treasure hunt with clues and codes, using the skills of an agent to figure out who to approach. From Paris they went to Rouen, Normandy and, finally, Versailles.

"Hold on," Melanie said, receiving a notice on her cell. "It's a live feed from Krueger." She said, quickly running fingers through her hair and smiled politely. "Hello, Sir."

"Hello Agent Ward and the entire team." His eyes darted behind Melanie. "Congratulations on finishing this year's Intelligence Training Challenge."

"Thank you."

"I imagine the point calculation will take a few days and we'll meet again in D.C. to hand out awards and assignments to the third-year recruits." He nodded. "Get some rest and you'll be hearing from me soon. Good job, Headquarters, your contribution was outstanding, if not notorious."

⌘

Seventy-two hours later Melanie heard from the ITC.

"Good morning, Agent Ward," Krueger said, the bags under his eyes swooping down into his cheeks. Melanie took a moment to question, *why is he so set on video calls? He looks terrible.*

"Where is everyone?" she asked, having read the memo that said all captains were to join the conference call.

"The other teams have decided to boycott the ceremonies." He sighed. "Not a good start to this new career choice of mine, but," his shoulders went up. "I'm here to announce that your team came in third to L.A. and Houston."

"Third. Okay," Melanie wasn't displeased. She didn't care.

"But when the extra points are included you beat out Houston. Congratulations, Agent, you came in an overall second place."

"Second isn't first, and still the other teams are pissed?" She scoffed. "What a bunch of whiny bastards."

"Exactly. Well, your trophy and Agent Anthony Ma's assignment are with Agent Jackson."

"Thanks. Agent Krueger, I'm not upset for me but all of the recruits worked really hard and for the other captains to boycott the ceremonies seems to be setting a bad example. I take my share of the blame but in a few years these agents will be running the Agency. And we're teaching them it's all right to behave poorly, when we should be reinforcing camaraderie. It's not only unsportsmanlike, it's dangerous when we're working together out in the field."

Krueger was silent. "That was my reason for wanting the ITC to be changed. You're right, and I lost sight of that goal. Maybe banishing the games altogether is the best alternative."

"I didn't mean that, because that would be a shame, too."

"I will have many sleepless nights over this one. And Ward, no matter what is decided, I sincerely hope *not* to see you at next year's challenge."

"Deal." She stifled a laugh, ended the call and headed for Ben's office. She wanted her trophy, if not only to break it into pieces.

CHAPTER TWENTY-FIVE

"Ward," Ben said, clamping off any hint of what was happening and ushering her into the building. "You're almost late."

"Almost late to my own execution doesn't sound late enough," Melanie remarked, dragging her feet.

"There you go, jumping to conclusions."

"Who's jumping?" She snorted, "When was the last time I was called in front of the Board to be praised?" Ben paused and she answered for him. "Never. In all my years I have never sat in one of those chairs to be congratulated." Her shoes stuck, unwilling to move another inch. "Why am I here?"

"You'll see. Hurry, we don't want to be late."

"You are acting very strange," Melanie observed, allowing herself to be pressured to rush.

The doors to the boardroom were closed and the feeling of dread – that washed over her every time she stood in that spot – flooded her senses.

"I feel sick."

Eleven men, whose decisions controlled the fate of nearly every human, sat behind a semi-circular forum, stopped talking as she and Ben walked in. Usually when she was summoned she knew what she'd done, but not this time.

The man to the far right was the first to bring his palms together in a loud slap. Melanie looked up. *What the hell is wrong with him?* His motion continued. It took two more members to join him for her to realize they were clapping.

She looked around, her eyes finally falling on Ben, who was grinning and applauding *at* her.

Melanie stood rooted to her spot, stunned. Wondering if this was protocol before one's demise.

"Take a seat, Agent Ward." The senior board member instructed. "And let's get down to business."

Her eyes traveled the bench, feeling the hole left by Hugh Parker's absence. Ben rolled out a chair for her at the center of the rectangular table that faced the Board. The expectation that he'd be seated beside or behind her was a certainty and she waited to feel the movement.

Ben! She wanted to call out, her toes curling inside her shoes as her mentor walked up to the Board … *What's he doing?* She thought, her mind juggling with a plan to rescue him from himself.

Her hands tightened on the padded armrests as Ben placed his left foot on the steps to the rise where the Board sat. Then his right. Melanie stared, dumbfounded. Ben pulled the back of Hugh's old seat, wheeled it around and sat!

"Oh my God," she breathed without moving her lips.

Ben's devilish grin divided his face.

"I believe you know our newest Board member," said the most senior with the same gotcha expression as the rest of the old men.

"Wow, Ben, congratulations," she said, knowing that was expected but still staring. She let the image of him sitting up there sink in. "I'm going to need a minute."

"Senator Parker's recovery is going to take longer than expected and we, as a collective conscience, have decided it is not in the country's best interest to wait."

The men nodded in agreement. Ben looked completely out of place beside these … men. She'd lost respect for them and her descriptions were no longer constructive.

"Your activities during the ITC got the attention of the highest level. That's not what we're about – our agents are meant to blend in, conceal themselves from being noticed. You seem to be having trouble with that."

Here it comes, she thought, hanging on to the chair as her punishment was being decreed.

Jailed, fired, demoted … none the possibilities were pleasant.

"You also have a knack for getting the job done – sometimes using techniques I've never seen before."

Melanie felt her brows lower, considering this turn.

"You were exceptional during the challenges and not only impressed us with your skill, but also with your leadership ability."

"Thank you," she muttered.

"With the vacancy of Mr. Jackson from the Agency we find ourselves at a very interesting crossroads," the old man said, admiring her with the same eyes that had admonished her only months earlier when they accused her of having a hand in Finn's death. "Agent Melanie Ward, we are offering you the position of Executive Director."

She blinked each time her eyes shifted to a different person seated before her. "Are you kidding me?"

"No. So, what do you think, would you like Agent Jackson's old job?"

"Yeah, yes." She chuckled, nervously waiting for the guards to come and arrest her. The change in direction was unreal.

"Then welcome to the top tier of the Agency."

The applause resurged and the old men rose in their sensible footwear. Making her way up to their station, she felt like a fraud thanking them for the promotion, shaking frail hands and grinning like a fool.

A banquet of appetizers and beverages had been set up in an adjoining room and she was presented with gifts. A pen/pencil set and a badge. Melanie floated through the room, networking, as if in a dream.

She was still dreaming when Ben walked her to the car, giving her back a pat as she ducked into the back seat.

"Aren't you coming?"

"I've got work to do here," Ben said. Melanie felt lonely as her boss shut the door. She waved and Marcos pulled away from the curb.

Melanie knocked on the glass between her and the driver. "Hey, Marcos, I just got a promotion."

"Congratulations Ms. Ward." He smiled at her through the rear view mirror. "Shall I take you someplace special?"

"No. I just wanted to see what you thought about that."

"I'm sure it's well-deserved. What do you think about it?"

"Strange." She settled back into the seat and stared out the window. *Because of the stupid ITC, the Board had changed their opinion about me. I'm going to have to get that little statue out of the trash.* She grinned. *I have Ben's job. I'm the new Ben.*

She dialed her parents.

"That is wonderful, Darling," her mom said, oozing with pride. "It's unexpected."

"Well, you've worked so hard, it's about time those refs noticed you!" Her dad piped in.

"Thanks, Dad." Melanie laughed at his reference to the Board being blind by calling them refs. "I wanted you guys to be the first to know."

"We are so proud of you."

"Does this new job involve less traveling?" her mom asked.

"Um, yeah, I guess so." She hadn't had time to give any thought to what changes it caused to her life.

"A more stable job means more visits home, right?"

"I suppose I could arrange that, I am in charge."

"Don't get cocky, dear, remember where you're from."

"I promise." Melanie couldn't lose the grin and waved at Marcos before disappearing into the security of the Manor. "Well, I'm going to give Trish a call. Love you guys."

"Oh, wait, don't forget your father and I are going on that trip you bought us for Christmas."

Right, she remembered, forcing down the emotion that was building. "Finally." She said, cheerfully. This was the trip Danny had purchased for the two of them – before dumping her for his cheating ex, Lauren. He'd given the tickets to her and she'd regifted them to her parents.

"I know. This year has been one thing after another. But we're leaving for Rome in two days."

Melanie swallowed.

"We're there for only a couple of days and then we're staying in a villa on Lake Como. Well, you know all this, you made the arrangements."

"Tell me anyway."

"I've told all the women in my church group and they're so jealous. It's fantastic."

"Where do you go after the villa?"

"From there we take the train to Milan and catch a cruise and sail the Mediterranean to Greece."

Her mom talked of the ship, the gourmet meals and the passenger list limited to 25 – Melanie sighed and couldn't stop the film playing in her head. She and Danny together on that cruise, engaged … possibly married.

"The biggest mistake of my life," Rita said, jarring Melanie out of her daydream.

"What was?"

"Buying a two-piece swimsuit. I returned it immediately. Really, what was I thinking?"

"Well, have a great time, Mom, and tell Dad I love him."

"He's still on the other line. Roger?"

"He dropped off about ten minutes ago." Melanie's eyes watered as she said goodbye. Jane wasn't at her desk when Melanie returned to her office. Swiveling in her chair she thought about Ben's office – *my office*, she corrected – with the gnawing feeling that, in her mind, it would always be his.

She stuffed her phone in her back pocket – Trish would have to wait. She went to track down Jack. He wasn't difficult to find – at his desk, with *her* assistant.

Jane jumped when Melanie entered.

"Ms. Ward, I'm so sorry." She blushed behind her red-framed eyeglasses.

"It's fine, but I do need to talk with Jack."

"Of course," Jane said, running out of the room.

"You are so scary," Jack teased.

"I know." Melanie slipped into the chair, still warm from Jane.

"What's going on?" he asked, catching her mood.

Jack was her friend but there was also an unspoken competition between them and she didn't want to jeopardize their relationship. Bottom line, she didn't know how he was going to take the news of her promotion.

Dragging it out would only make it worse.

"I've just come from meeting with the Board." Their eyes locked. "They're replacing Hugh with Ben." She held the steady gaze. "And they're…"

"Replacing Ben with Melanie?"

She nodded. "You okay with that?"

"Why wouldn't I be? You totally deserve it."

"Jack." Melanie started, knowing him well enough to know when he was lying.

"Really, I'm happy for you." He swallowed and tapped on his keyboard, bringing his screen to life. "This does mean I get more assignments, right?"

"Whatever you want," she said, standing. "If you want to talk…"

"I'll find you."

She left him feeling uncomfortable and sad at losing the only person she could talk to.

"Jane, come in and have a seat," she said as she entered her office, not knowing if Jack had already delivered her the news. "You won't need to take notes."

Jane's nerves showed all over her face. "I'm sorry about not being here. I did have your calls forwarded to my phone but I shouldn't have been there."

"This isn't about that," Melanie said, sitting on the corner of her desk. "I don't want you there all the time but if we're squared away here I don't mind you taking a break." Jack hadn't told her. Melanie gave her the news and went through the list of changes.

"This is so exciting! Does it mean we get to move out of here?"

"Yeah, I'm not sure where but…"

Jane gave a woo-hoo. "I don't care. Anywhere has got to be better."

"I didn't realize you disliked this place so much."

"Aesthetics matter and this place hasn't got any."

"Well, you're welcome to decorate our new place any way you like … within reason."

"We're not taking Judith's office – I mean, Mr. Jackson's?"

"I kind of have my eye on another location, we'll see."

Her enthusiasm dropped. "May I ask how Jack took the news?"

"You'll have to ask him."

"Yeah," she sighed, tsking. "He values your friendship. Give him a day, he'll come around."

"Hope so." Melanie inhaled. "Better start packing."

"When will this take effect?"

"I think it already has," she answered, picturing Ben in Hugh's seat.

"Okay, packing it is." She shut the door between their offices on her way out.

Melanie sat with her thoughts and her excitement built. She called Carla who was *happy* for her.

Trish used the same lame expression. "I'm so *happy* for you, Mel."

She bristled. "No. You aren't understanding. This is big. It's what

I've been working toward. I got the promotion, I'm the executive director of the whole place."

"That's great. I'm over here doing cartwheels for you … what do you want?"

"Enthusiasm! I want fireworks and you're handing me a damn light bulb."

Trish's scream vibrated the tiny phone speaker. "Melanie got her promotion! You." She was yelling at someone, "did you hear me? She's amazing and now she has an amazing new job!" There was jostling on the line, in the distance Trish still cheered. "Cartwheels and handstands! Because Melanie is awesome!"

"All right." Melanie laughed, knowing Trish couldn't hear because she was talking to someone.

"Tell her," Trish said.

"Way to go, Melanie!"

"See, this guy is *happy* for you!"

"All right," Melanie repeated. "Where are you?"

"At the grocery store." In the background Melanie could hear talking. "You have many supporters at this little market."

"Great," she said.

"You kick ass, Melanie."

"Did you hear that?" Trish asked. "He's cute, too. Feel better?"

"Much. Thanks."

"I aim to squeeze."

Melanie rolled her eyes. "How's married life?"

"Capital A, awesome. Should I do cartwheels?"

"After we hang up."

"If you'd come home once in a while we could do them together."

"I'd like that. But right now I've got a new job!"

"Melanie got a promotion!"

"What did I unleash?"

"I don't know but it feels good to yell like that. Liberating. Try it."

"No."

"Chicken."

"Finish your shopping."

"Call me and let me know when you'll be here so we can really celebrate."

"Will do."

With no one left to tell, she set her phone down beside the Barkov medal. She'd never thought much about her office – walls, a window, a sturdy couch to sleep on and her desk – had always been enough.

"I'm moving up," she said, ready for whatever that meant. She'd set her goal on Ben's job years ago, the real prize was to be the first woman on the Board. Her mind drifted to the men on the bench. In their day they'd been heavy drinkers, smokers with high-stress lives. Now three walked around with oxygen tanks, others nodded off during meetings and none of them could hear worth a damn.

I'm going to have to come up with a bigger goal, she thought, *and soon. Once one Board member drops dead, the rest will go down like dominos.*

∽

"I thought I'd find you clearing out my desk," Ben said, from the doorway of her office.

"Actually," she started, "that's something I wanted to speak with you about. Do I have to take that particular one?"

"You don't want my office?" he asked, the left side of his grin higher than the right.

"No. That'll always be yours and it's just way too dark."

"Where were you thinking? Agent Parker's?"

"God no!" she shivered at the thought of taking over that expanse of a room. Finn would be over her shoulder every minute. "There's a vacant one on the fifth floor. Southwest corner?"

"Oh, yes." Ben nodded and the air of mystery swept through the room.

"Who did it belong to?"

"Agent Cooper. Do you remember him?" He searched her eyes. "He might have been a little before your time. He was a great agent."

"Was?"

"Captured." Nothing more needed to be said. For the moment they were silent. "But that is a nice space. How about we go take a look?"

"You sure?" She didn't want to impose on Agent Cooper's memory.

"Agent Ward, I'm handing over the keys to the Agency. The location of your office is the smallest decision you're going to have to make." He laughed like he was carrying a secret that could only be experienced.

"Your happiness is encouraging. It's great that you waited until now to become evil. What is it that they feed you Board members?"

"It's a secret sauce."

Melanie laughed and followed him out into the hall. "When are you going to make the announcement?" Melanie asked, pulling on the door to the stairwell.

"Tomorrow too soon?"

"This is happening fast, took eleven years."

"For you and me both. I never thought it'd be Hugh's seat I'd be taking." Ben shrugged.

"Ben, did you know this would happen when you pushed me into the ITC? Was it a plan?"

"You do have a high opinion of me. My goal with the ITC was to change the way we do business with our young recruits. I wanted the agents running the games to have their status quo ways shoved in their faces. Who better to do that than you?"

"Am I really that charming?"

"More than I could've hoped." He grinned. "You played it so well we both got bumped up a level."

The fifth floor was one above Ben's office and quiet.

"It's locked," Ben said. "I'll have Judith call maintenance."

Melanie cut her laugh short. "Are you serious?" she asked, taking a pin out of her pocket and twisting it in the keyhole.

"For some reason breaking into my own building has never occurred to me." Ben brushed off his surprise and led the way through the open door.

Melanie smiled when she entered the room.

"With some new carpeting, drapes, paint and an area for your assistant it'll be perfect." He walked around, going through the paintings leaning against the wall.

"There's an adjoining door to the small office," Melanie said, doing her trick with the lock. "And I don't particularly care about the rest of that stuff. Except maybe new drapes."

"While I'm handing my stuff to you, we'll have Judith train Jane and she can order whatever it is that you'll be needing." Ben's eyes filled with sadness as he scanned the room.

"What happened to Cooper?"

Ben inhaled deeply. "He made a mistake. Was on the wrong side of the fence at the wrong time. But you taking this space is a good move." He smiled. "You'll make it your own. I'm heading back, you coming?"

"I think I'm going to stick around here. I need busy work and moving dusty boxes will fit the bill."

"Tomorrow morning. Don't forget."

"I've already spoken with Jack. I think I'll wait a few hours before letting Mike in on the news."

"Any time before that and I might as well cancel the meeting."

CHAPTER TWENTY-SIX

"Good morning," Ben began, standing at the head of the table in the large conference room.

Melanie's nerves were knotted in the pit of her stomach as she stood behind him in the crowded, noisy room of her peers.

"I have a few announcements and position changes." At this, the group quieted; all eyes were on Ben. "Thought that might work." He laughed. "As you know, eight months ago Senator Parker suffered a stroke that has left him struggling to do everyday tasks. He decided that it was time to step down and focus on his recovery. We wish the Senator good health but with his leaving it opened a seat on the Board." He paused. Melanie never realized how unassuming Ben was – he was having difficulty stating that he'd been chosen to take Hugh's place. "I've accepted the position." The buzz began even before he'd finished the word accepted. "Okay," he used his hands to calm the rising speculations. "I know this comes as a surprise, but let me assure you that it's all under control. You all know Agent Ward." He reached back, motioning for her to step up. "I'd like to introduce her as the new Executive Director."

The room fell silent and Melanie thought her heartbeat could be heard to the farthest corner of the room.

Jack stood, raised his coffee cup and said, "To Agent Ward! You're going to do a wonderful job." He smiled and gave her an encouraging wink.

"Thank you," she mouthed the words with pure gratitude.

The whirlwind that erupted in the following hour gave her a headache. Agents lined up to congratulate and express their grievances over everything from the food in the kitchen to a particular assignment.

☙

"Mike," Melanie said, entering the control center. "Bob, Ed." She greeted the three most technical people working at the Agency. They were wearing matching, yellow, spandex shirts with some sort of emblem patch on the pocket. "Hey, I… What's going on?" she asked as a ship sailed across on the jumbo screen.

"Pirates," Bob murmured.

Melanie watched the boat bob along the royal blue waves. There was no sign of life on board and rocked as if it were anchored. "What do you mean pirates? A movie?"

Mike flicked the remote and CNN appeared in the corner. The brunette reporter spoke with an Italian accent from a beachside front.

"Real life," Bob said.

"Now?"

"Live."

Shit! She reached for her phone to call Ben – then realized that now she was Ben.

"What do we know?" Melanie asked, leaning forward to squint at the screen.

"Pirates hijacked a luxury liner in the middle of the Med less than an hour ago," Mike said. "I guess we should've called you … but we just saw it two minutes before you walked in."

"Pirates don't occupy the Mediterranean," she sighed, thinking about their contacts in Italy. "Mike, get me satellite feed." It was bad that the event had already gone out to the global media. It meant the Agency couldn't play a major role in the recovery mission. "Keep watching. I've got to make some calls."

Melanie rushed out the door, ran up a flight of stairs, stopped, speed dialed Mike as she reversed her direction.

"What's the name of that ship?" she asked through a rigid jaw.

"Um, the Seaward Osprey."

Her blood drained from her body and she forced herself to speak. "Get the manifest," she paused to push open the control room door, "without going through proper channels."

"Of course, one second," Mike said. He was tapping away on his keyboard as she looked over his shoulder. "Hey," he said, she dropped her face low enough to read the list.

"Ward. Roger and Rita Ward?"

"Dang!" Ed muttered and looked up at her with dread. "Your family is on that ship?"

"Anyone else?" she asked, throwing Ed a shut the fuck up glare. "Political, overtly wealthy, royalty anyone … anyone who's valuable enough to kidnap? Is there cargo? Weapons, drugs?" She pounded her fist on the desk. "Find me a reason that that ship," she pointed to the liner, "was chosen." The quarter of a second the techies had stalled was too long. "Now!" she yelled.

Two flights up, she stopped, leaned against the wall and closed her eyes. *Oh my God, my parents.* Her legs felt weak.

"It's got to be a mistake." Melanie heaved herself to a standing position. "No time to be pathetic," she whispered, feeling sick. In the stairwell she called Ben and informed him of the situation.

"Let me see what I can find out."

Out of comfort and habit she went to her old office. Small and confined, it was safe, she knew the corners and shadows. She sat in the dark and sank into her spine.

"I'm the executive director." The muscles in her forehead ached. "I cannot hide out." She needed the familiarity to calm her nerves, to think – to feel like her old self.

"Ms. Ward," Jane's voice came through the speaker of her phone. "Judith just called and Mr. Jackson wants you to hold the objective meeting in your new office. He's on his way and will be here in fifteen minutes."

"Okay," she exhaled. "I'll be there in a minute." Melanie ended the call, stared at her contact list and pressed the button. "Hi," she said, her voice low and raspy. "Do you have a minute? I need to talk."

❧

It was the first time she'd done anything official in her new office. Everything felt off. She didn't know where to sit, or direction to pace in the foreign environment. Breathing in short gusts of air, her tight chest constricted her airways and prevented her lungs from expanding.

"The ship was hijacked in the Ionian Sea about five hours ago. There hasn't been any demands made and all attempts at contact have been ignored or…" Ben left the *or* part hanging as he sat and followed

Kate Mathis

her with his eyes. "The Osprey opened fired on the ships patrolling those waters. Sit, Melanie," Ben said. "You're turning my gills green."

She pulled in a big, shaky breath and sat on the coffee table Jane had chosen. "This is so much more than a case. Ben, it's my parents. I have to go."

Pursing his lips, his head gave her the slightest of shakes. "I don't think that's a good idea. We've got the local authorities involved, the media is all over the place and you're too emotional."

"I know," Melanie said, the nerves ready to bust loose. "I have to pull it together and I will, but I have to be there. There's nothing more important to me than my family."

"That's the problem. You're not thinking rationally."

"You don't mind my irrational behavior when it's working on your behalf." Ben stopped the grinding of his teeth by biting down. "I'm sorry, but not even you can stop me from going." It wasn't the first time she'd disobeyed his order, but usually her defiance was done in a more covert approach.

"Can I give you something to consider?"

Melanie nodded with her eyes, her hands in prayer position at her chest.

"Don't go as an agent. Let Jack be emissary and you stay out of view. Do what he says and do not engage in this mission. Not even a little bit. Am I clear?"

She nodded. "I can do that." Her words were full of empty promises. Whether she admitted it or not, she needed his approval to take a step closer. "I can do that."

"Are you sure? Because I don't want you or anyone else to get killed because you did something stupid."

"I trust Jack." She did. "And if I'm there and he's keeping me informed I can live with that."

"And I trust you. Recklessness will not save your parents." His eyes were giving her the lecture that his tongue was holding back.

She sucked in a breath, nodding and tucking her fingertips between her knees. In this case, she decided, he might be right.

"The jet is fueled and the flight plan arranged."

"Thank you." Melanie stood and smelled the still-wet mocha colored paint. Ben was seated in her office when she hurried out and within ten minutes she was in the garage with Jack and Mike.

"Ms. Ward," Jane called, running down the hall. "I packed you a few things. Good luck, Ms. Ward."

"Thanks," Melanie said, taking hold of the small suitcase. She smiled as Jane waggled her fingers to Jack and his cocky grin softened. "Kiss her goodbye and let's get going." Marcos took her bag and dropped it into the trunk as Mike wrung his hands.

"I'm really sorry, Melanie. About your folks."

"I know."

<hr />

"What?" she growled looking up from her daze.

"Tea?" the flight attendant asked.

"No."

"She'd love a cup of tea."

"No, I really wouldn't." Melanie shifted her glare to Jack.

"It'll make you feel better." He gave a curt nod to the girl who looked conflicted, not knowing whose directions to follow.

"Tea will be fine," she said to ease the girl's discomfort. "Jack," Melanie sighed, "I'll give you the lead on this, but my digestive system is still mine."

"When was the last time you ate?"

"Grilled chicken sandwich for lunch."

"You are such a liar." He grinned.

"It's pronounced a-g-e-n-t." She returned his smile. "I've got a couple of things on my mind, in case you haven't noticed." She was still talking as the interior lights dimmed.

"Do you really think this is about your parents? The pirates are after the Ward family?"

"Seems a bit egotistical, doesn't it?"

"I've learned to respect your instincts." They shared a look.

She looked away from his guilty expression. "I don't have any concrete facts but I've been over the manifest and nothing else jumps out."

"Maybe they were hauling more than just passengers. Did you have the crew checked out?"

"Mike has been probing the backgrounds of every soul on that boat."

"Well, I won't let you down. I'll treat this as if my own parents were in danger, I know you'd do the same for me."

"I appreciate that," she said, her mind drifting back to the disquiet that was growing inside her stomach.

In Rome they boarded a small charter plane and flew to an island off the coast of Greece. The sea ranged from crystalline blue with sunlight gleaming off the shiny surface to a deep, menacing black.

Two local agents were on the runway waiting for them as the

plane rolled to a stop.

"Hello, Agent Ward. Hello, Agent Scott."

"Agents," she nodded. "What have we got?"

"The authorities have set up base on a neighboring island in a couple of wartime bunkers. The media is being kept away and a no fly zone has been issued."

"Unfortunately, there's nothing but a couple of broken buildings on the closest island. So, we arranged a place to stay on this island." The second agent added.

"Who has been taking lead on this?" Melanie asked.

"There's the Greek government, the Italians, NATO arrived a few hours ago and us."

"Let's go."

"Agent Ward," Jack warned.

"I just want to see," she said, reading the look he gave her, a look that only worked because they were *friends*. "I won't touch."

"I'm sorry Melanie, but you're not coming." He turned to the others. "Agents, show us to the hotel and then you can take me to the other island."

Both sets of eyes turned to Melanie.

"Agent Scott is taking point on this one."

The island fell short of the typical, tourist image of a Greek Island. There were none of the white-washed walls, picturesque paths that weaved between homes that were built up on a rock that jutted out over the sea. The low, brushy terrain could have been in Southern California. The rental house was a two-story home with balconies, a tiled roof, shrubs along the side and flowerpots giving color to the otherwise drab surroundings. *My prison*, Melanie thought.

"I'll be back as soon as I can," Jack said from the passenger seat.

"You going to stick around here?" he asked, looking up at the house behind her.

"I'm going to do my part from behind a computer." She lifted the shoulder that held the strap. "I want to find out who's behind this and why. Call me ten minutes after you get there with all the information." Her voice held authority.

"Will do."

As the car began to roll, she leaned down, "Thanks, Jack."

"They'll be all right."

She stepped away and under her breath she said, "They have to be."

The house was modern and open with high ceilings and exposed beams. Melanie wandered upstairs, left her bags on the low bed and unlocked the balcony to a rectangular pool. Beyond lounge chairs and a hammock were tall cypress trees.

Her sweep of the place turned up cameras and listening devices cast around each of the rooms and taped into the casings of the portable phones. Cheap, bulky boxes set into corners, poorly hidden within the decorations or taped to a beam on the high ceiling.

She gathered them in a basket and was about to slide them in a dark drawer when she found a camera in the curtain rod aimed toward the bed. "Sick bastards."

This wasn't just an owner concerned about his property. After a second clean sweep she crushed each of the bugs and dumped the pieces in the trash. At the kitchen table she opened her computer and called Mike.

"Anything?"

"I've got satellite images of the ship and Bob was able to hack into one of ... hold on, I'm sending it to you now, they're wearing masks and it looks like there's at least six."

"Thanks, Mike. Keep me updated," she said, eager to scrutinize the photo.

She thumped nervously on the wooden table. Pulling up the images Mike had sent and checking her watch … he'd said he'd call when he could.

Her gaze flickered to her cell as it rattled. "Hi," she said, conflicted.

"You okay to talk?" he asked, his deep voice slow and smooth.

"Yeah." She hadn't had a clear-cut plan when she called him in a moment of desperation. She hadn't wanted anything other than to vent her fear to someone she trusted, someone outside of the Agency. Adam hadn't hesitated, he'd grabbed a passport and was on his way to the airport before they'd ended the call.

"Are you in Greece?"

"I am. Adam…" Here's where the guilt plowed over her dread.

"Not now, Mel. I'm here and I've already made contact with an acquaintance."

"But," she stalled, not wanting to protest, "I didn't… I don't want to drag you into this. I'm sorry."

"You didn't drag me anywhere. And you won't be sorry when your parents are safely off that boat."

"Are you sure about this? I…" she wanted to roar out her meaning but the words were getting stuck.

"I'm sure." He said, firmly. "Where are you, exactly?"

She gave him the name and coordinates for the island, feeling an overwhelming sense of selfishness.

"There's at least six hijackers on the ship and it's still moored in the same location. Authorities have set up a base on the closest island and the media has been forced to remain on the mainland." She said, distracted by the schematic of the boat. The shadow of a plan was forming.

Adam was a couple of islands over and with slow transportation Melanie had time to clean out the cameras placed around the outside of the property, the pool, the driveway and the front door. The owner's perverse paranoia was a welcome distraction.

Finding a path hidden beneath vegetation that led to a decomposing boathouse. The painted hinges shrieked as Melanie used her shoulder, forcing the doors to budge. Behind her, the summer sun penetrated through the dust particles, leaving her shadow standing dead center of the room.

Waving the cobwebs out of her way, she checked the stability of a wobbly worktable. It held her weight and at that point the crooked old building became her personal command center. By the time she realized she needed a light bulb it was dark.

His footsteps were quiet and if she'd had electricity to distract her, she may not have heard him.

"Hi," she said to his silhouette that was darker than the darkness outside. "How'd you know I was in here?"

"I was making sure the house was clear when I heard a noise. How are you doing?" he asked, stepping inside and closing the squeaky door.

"Glad you're here," she said, feeling an ebbing of the pressure in her chest.

"Any news?"

She shook her head. "It's been oddly quiet. I don't want to appear unreasonably suspicious but I can't escape the feeling that this is happening because of me. That my parents are the targets."

"You can unclamp that bottom lip of yours. We're going to get them out." Melanie hadn't realized her old habit had reemerged and released the grip, leaving dents. "You can obsess about why another time."

She added a second breath to her already filled lungs and nodded. "I'll show you what I've got," she said, opening files. "The ship was overtaken yesterday in broad daylight. We've estimated the number of terrorists at six and there are thirty-three passengers and crewmembers. They're moored a couple of miles out and so far the only contact they've made is to fire on passing vessels."

Adam asked all the same questions she had and she answered him with the same lame responses she got.

"Hold on," Melanie said, reaching for her phone. "Hey, Jack. Where have you been? I'm going crazy over here. Waiting." She tore her eyes off Adam as she lied by omission and the feeling of betrayal settled in her gut.

"Sorry, I've been busy. I've got two organizations battling for supremacy and I'm doing the best I can."

"Okay. I know. Thanks for calling. But remember, I'm patiently dying over here, so even no news is news, okay?"

"I'll call when I can. I'm going to stay here overnight. Are you all right alone?"

"I'm fine. You do what you have to do to get my parents out of there safely. Okay?"

"I'm working on it."

"Thanks."

"Night. I'll keep you posted."

Melanie stared at her phone for a second, not liking the tone in Jack's voice. Tired and edgy. She looked up at Adam, the light from her cell reflecting harshly in her eyes.

"What I'm thinking is," she said, not skipping a beat, pulled out the schematic for the ship, "that there isn't any other option but to get on that boat and take those bastards down myself."

"How would you manage that?" Adam asked, his forehead creased.

"There's an island, more of a rock, really, not too far from where they're anchored. From there I could get on board and…" He was shaking his head. "What?"

"It seems complicated."

"It's not. Big rock, boat," she said, getting defensive. "I can pull it off. Look, Adam, I'm not asking for you to get involved or for your permission. I just need help acquiring the gear. I can manage the rest."

"I'm not letting you do it alone, Mel. What distance are we talking about? Have you considered a long-range shot?"

"It's over moving water and at a half mile. That's at least, what? 800, 900 yards," she said, converting the distance into land equivalent.

"Low wind, I can make that."

Melanie surveyed him for an instant. "The problem is that the hijackers aren't lined up on deck, waiting for their bullet."

"Tough crowd," Adam said, both sides of his lips rising in unison.

"But maybe," her mind whirling with how to use his skill to her advantage, "you could pick them off before I get aboard, leaving me less to deal with."

"I'm not doing that." He stood directly in front of her, getting her attention, his fingers curled around her biceps. "I'm here for you one hundred percent," the green eyes that zeroed in on her were shaded. "Understand? Do you trust me, Melanie?"

"Yes." Her answer came from a place that didn't need time to consider.

"Good, because I'd do anything for you." He tightened his squeeze. "I've never had a partner, never needed one, but I trust you and if we're going to get Rita and Roger back, we have to do it together. No shutting me out."

"Sharing isn't my strong suit." She paused. "And I'm afraid of you getting hurt, of my parents getting hurt. There's a lot at stake, I realize I'm too involved but I can't change."

"Let's go over our options."

It'd been a long time since she had a person to bounce ideas off of. Jack was great but during a mission with other agents she was always in charge. By dawn they'd whittled down their plan and Melanie crawled into bed satisfied that within 24 hours her life would be tilted back into balance.

Purple shadows tinted the skin beneath Jack's red eyes the following morning when he walked into the kitchen.

"Coffee?"

"I only have time for a cup, then I'm taking a shower and heading back to the barracks. Long night." He rubbed his eyes. "We're getting there. The hijackers tossed us a bone, they released fifteen passengers." He gave her a look. "Chosen at random. I couldn't very well ask for specific passengers." He put up his hands to stop her question.

"What did they say?" she asked, coffee pot in hand.

"That's the thing, not much. It feels like a shell game. Keeping us distracted here while the real job is being played to the side. Frustrating," he growled.

"God, I wish I could go in with you. It feels as if time is running out."

"It's not."

Jack was true to his word, back out within an hour. Melanie

hunkered down, going over her plan again and again.

The heat relaxed with the setting sun and the boats knocked gently against the wooden dock. Melanie dressed in jeans and a tank top. The calmness of agent work settled into her essence as she walked the shadows to the private dock.

"Hey," Adam said, holding his hand out for her.

"I can manage," she said, climbing into the small fishing boat.

"The wig threw me for a minute."

Jane had packed it along with a few other things. "Jack paid one of the local kids to keep watch on the house."

"He sounds thorough," Adam said with a tinge of bitterness. "Have you known him long?"

"Years."

Adam didn't ask anything else but she could feel his questions in the space between them.

"Jack's good at his job and he knows me too well. But he's a by-the-rules-guy, can't include him in anything like this."

"And you're not a by-the-rules-girl?"

Melanie felt the momentary confusion cloud her expression, forgetting that he only knew her in regular Melanie mode. "I try to obey the rules. It's just that sometimes this is easier."

His laugh was genuine and deep. "You ready?" he asked.

Through the dim light she could see the excitement burning in his eyes. *I wonder how much he misses his other profession?* Her thoughts caused a cramp in her chest.

"Ready." She said, reaching to release the line that kept them tethered to the dock. "Been ready for days. Why are you looking at me like that?"

"No reason," he said, emptying his expression and turning the ignition.

The boat had a step-up with a windshield and one seat behind the steering wheel. Melanie stood beside Adam as he smoothly motored across the black water.

"I did a drive by this afternoon. We're going to anchor between the media and the authorities – that rock island makes perfect cover. Your wet suit is in the back."

Melanie removed the wig and snapped the suit on over her clothes. On the bench he had laid out a line of equipment.

He drifted very close to the rock before dropping anchor and joining her with the supplies. "Face masks – we're going to need to keep these on so we're not recognized. High-voltage stun gun, as requested, inside the case," he said, giving it a shake before fastening it to her belt. He moved to the oxygen tank that was a bag made of lightweight plastic. "It'll deflate as the air is consumed. There's plenty for the round trip."

"Where'd you find these?" she asked, pressing gently on the package.

"I know a guy," he said with a wink. "But the best part." He tossed off a tarp that covered two rocket-shaped underwater propulsion scooters. A quick instruction was all that was needed before he lifted the first jet rocket and softly lowered it into the sea, holding on to a tether. "Lastly, suction cups. Press here," he said demonstrating as he held the round disc by a handle. "Attach it to the boat and attach the underwater propeller to it. The others are for climbing up the side to the first deck. The only way up. Questions?"

"No, but when we get to the ship," Melanie said. "I'll take the starboard bow and you take port stern. If for some reason the mission starts going south, I want you to abort. Get to this boat and then to the main island. Understood?" she ordered, pulling on her glove.

Adam rocked back on his heels.

"I'm not joking."

"I didn't think you were. What I do think is that you're a woman used to being in charge. But Mel, you aren't in charge of me and there's no way in hell I'm leaving that ship without you."

For an instant she was jarred. "But," she wanted to command him to listen.

Adam breathed quickly. "Since you brought it up, I wasn't going to do this." He swallowed as his concerned eyes locked on hers. "I don't want anything to happen to you. Jesus, Melanie I don't want to let you out of my sight. I know you're intense and it's all about the target but," he clamped his jaw and the muscles twitched. "These hijackers are real, their bullets are real and..."

"You're worried about me?" She smiled. "I'm worried about you. This is what I do, Adam. I jump into the black water, climb aboard and focus on getting the job done," she said calmly, merging her two selves. "I'm sorry about the harsh command a moment ago. I had a lapse." She eased the tension out of her face in an effort to reassure him. "We've already had the trust talk. I need you to concentrate on your part and not worry about me. In return I'll try not to waste time agonizing over your safety."

"So, you've got this? I'm not sure I like it."

"I've got it," she said looking up at the star lit sky. "We're losing darkness."

CHAPTER TWENTY-SEVEN

He lowered the second propeller into the sea without a splash. Off the side of the boat, Melanie drew in a sharp breath as her chest sunk below the surface. The water was colder than she expected as she tucked short strands of hair into her hood and lowered her facemask.

She dove down meters beneath the surface until she was undetectable. Working around the low visibility, they used the GPS to coordinate the location of the ship and held on as the underwater scooters raced them to their target.

In twenty minutes she was attaching the first suction cup to the hull as the boat rocked in the waves. Lightening her load, she clipped her oxygen bag to the propeller line and climbed to the lowest deck. The water dripping off her suit seemed to echo on the dark and quiet ship. Besides her, the only sound was an eerie wind whistling through an open door. She quietly jogged the deck toward the ship's bridge.

Stopping at the soft squeak of rubber soles on the moist decking, a man in a black mask exited the room with the noisy door. Melanie uncapped the stun gun case and didn't have to wait for a shot.

He never saw her. But his fingers reached for the dart-like electrodes an instant after they struck his neck and half a second before he collapsed.

She dragged the unconscious man a short distance to a supply closet and using the tie lines secured his limbs. Melanie felt her tension build as she yanked off his mask. Disappointment and shock filled her senses – she'd fully expected to recognize the hijacker.

Leaving him, her next quest was to eliminate the man in the captain's chair. She encountered no one as she headed toward the bow. The hijack-captain seated in front of the ship's control panel chewed on the butt of a cigar, humming and was completely unaware of her presence.

Hog-tied and sedated by 1-2 amps and like the hijacker before him … was a stranger to her.

Melanie maneuvered around the deck and through the narrow hallways, the feeling of being on a ghost ship was unnerving. Dead silence rang in her ears as she strained to make out any sound. She felt the vibration of footsteps resounding off the floorboards and ducked into a corner. She brought the stun gun up to her chest, her thumbs on the trigger and waited for a target to shoot.

Adam. He gestured with his chin, mouthed his meaning, "They're in there." He pointed to a door next to her and one next to him. She gave her nod of consent. "On three," he lifted his index finger. She took in a breath, pulling in the scent of lemon oil and on three, as she was ready to push on the panel door. The sound of footsteps rush from behind, right before she was slammed against the wall. Her head taking the brunt of the hit, sending a bolt of pain down her spine. Ramming her knee, nailing him between his legs was a reaction. While he was buckled over she kicked his kneecap and sent him in a rage to the ground.

It was good to get her aggression out, even if she got a little knocked around. She jammed the heel of her hand into his larynx to stop the screaming. Melanie staggered to her feet while he coughed and ripped the mask off his face.

"Tell me who you're working for!" She ground her teeth as he sealed his lips tight. Blood ran in torrents from his nostrils. "Fine." She pulled her gun, stood above him and aimed.

"Wait," blood spattered over the decking.

"Well?" *American*, she thought holding onto the small clue.

"Fuck you!" He groaned.

"Who hired you?"

Their eyes locked, Melanie swallowed down a lump as he flipped her off with his bloodied finger. His body shuddered from the jolt given by her stun gun. Feeling someone over her shoulder, she twisted. Adam was staring at her with a look of distressed amusement, handing her the mask that had been ripped off her face during the fight. "What are you doing out here?" she asked in Spanish. She couldn't risk her parents recognizing her voice.

"Watching you. I'll take care of him, you go to the passengers."

Her breath was soggy beneath the mask and the dark room was filled with tension. She reached out, slid her hand along the wall and pressed the toggle switch.

The passengers. Gagged and tied to their chairs. With her index finger vertical against her lips, she scanned the room, grateful that her expression was hidden. They all looked petrified ... her parents included.

Maintain control, she scolded, her heart leaping to her throat. She tore her gaze from her parents to approach the man closest to the door.

His gag had been tight and he wiggled his jaw as she cut him free.

"How many are there?" Melanie choked in a low whisper.

"Seven," the man answered in a heavy accent.

Three down, she thought, wondering how many Adam had gotten. Melanie sliced the ropes on his hands and moved to the woman next to him.

"They'll be back in another minute," the man said, answering more easily.

The entire room sucked in a breath as Adam stepped into the light. He was tall and fierce looking in his dark wetsuit covered from head to toe. Melanie realized how scary they must look to the hostages.

Her hands shook as she sliced the bonds that held her dad's hands behind his back. She placed her fingers on his shoulder and closed her eyes.

"Come," Adam said, pulling her away from her parents.

"There's seven, three are down."

"Five. I took out two on my way up."

"I'm going to look for the last two. Will you stay here to protect these guys?" She could see his dark eyes narrow, disapprovingly, under the mask.

"I'll be here. Yell if you run into trouble." He said, giving her her way.

On the floor above, she collided with a hulking blonde man. His eyes were odd, brown with a white ring around the iris. He was big, well over six-foot, thick as a tree trunk and smarter than the others. She kicked, he blocked, he punched, she blocked.

"You must be Melanie Ward," he said, reaching up and tearing off the mask, taking hair with it.

"Who are you?" she asked, her eyes watering from the scalping but aware enough for her fist to connect with his face.

He grabbed her wrists and twisted. She felt her bones shift and the burning sensation shoot up to her skull. He bent her arms behind her back to near breaking point and kicked open a cabin door. The small bed creaked beneath her weight, using the bounce she tried to get to her feet.

"Who are you?" she demanded as he snared her and used his size to fling her back onto the bed. "How do you know me?" Melanie asked, clenching her teeth as he climbed on top of her. She kicked and tried squirming out of his unrelenting hold.

"This is a perk." He leered, grinding down onto her pelvis. He'd pinned both of her wrists in his one bear claw.

"Have we met before? You don't look familiar but you're also completely forgettable." She groaned as he leaned forward and cut off her air.

"Never. But I promise, after tonight it won't matter."

"Who do you work for?" She strained, trying to force him off.

"You should know. You're the reason why we're all here." His sneer showed off his broken front teeth.

"Why is that?" she panted, trying to catch her breath under his pressure. She stopped struggling, it was useless and she was wasting energy.

"We're going to blow this Motherfucker up!" His grimace widened. "You and your parents are going to go bang."

"What about you? You coming to Hell with me?"

"Nice try, Bitch," he laughed, straightened his back to get a better view of her. "First we'll have some fun."

Tightening her every muscle she bolted up and rammed her head into his chest. He rocked back and she lashed out with her legs, upsetting his balance. Her calves encircled his neck and with all her strength gave one hard twisting jolt. She felt his vertebrae crack.

Melanie flattened out on the bed, his body becoming heavier as he crashed on top of her. With her last bit of strength she knocked him to the floor. Panting, she rolled off the bed and grasped the wall. *Holy shit.* She stood and gazed for a moment getting another look at his face.

In the distance she heard the sound of light, quick footsteps.

"Jesus," Adam said, his eyes first on her, then on the body at the foot of the bed. "They can't recognize you. Take my propeller, it's right there." He pointed. "I'll use yours. Go."

"There's a bomb on board." Melanie wheezed. "We have to get everyone off."

"Or disable the device. Can you do that?"

"I have to find it first." She said, rummaging through the dead man's pockets for his cell phone. "Jack I need you to get the bomb squad to the ship. Now!" She didn't stop to explain. "Just do it."

"I've got the passengers lined up and ready to be loaded onto the life boats. I'll hand them over to the crew and come back for you." Adam said. They were in sync as if they'd worked together for years.

"Good," their eye contact held for a beat, speaking volumes before she raced out the door and down the stairwell. The engine room stunk of chemicals. Melanie was at the door when the popping began and the first explosion knocked her to the ground. Crawling on her hands and knees she climbed up the stairs. She could hear the commotion of the passengers and the voices of the crew instructing them on procedures.

"Over here," Adam called from behind her. "They're lowering the first boat and loading the second. Your parents are already out."

A second blast rocked the ship and this time she could hear the ship taking on water. Melanie looked into Adam's eyes, "When that life boat safely hits the water, we're out of here."

"The one propeller is sinking with the ship." Adam said, waiting for her to make the decision. "I can go for it now."

"Too dangerous. Leave it. I already blew my cover … when I called Jack." She shrugged. They heard the splash of the second boat hit the sea. "I think they're safe." The deck was empty and peeking over the railing Melanie could see the speedboat of the rescue team approaching.

She took off at a run toward the end of the boat. Blocking her face from any long-range cameras she took a deep breath and dove over the side.

Together, she and Adam submerged, released the propeller from its leash and cranked the motor.

Melanie's heartbeat was out of sync with her breathing and she had difficulty holding her breath. Adam handed her the mouthpiece for the oxygen tank, she breathed in the air and handed it back to him. Sharing, there wasn't going to be enough for both to make it back to the getaway boat.

Her mind whirled as the black water rushed past her. She couldn't hold onto a single thought. The water had been icy on the way there, now she was sweating.

They rose to the surface, traveling slowly; her lungs ached as she ripped off her mask and took in a mouthful of salty water. The sloshing water prevented talking as they held onto the propeller and cut through the waves.

The moonlight glistening off the white vessel was a welcome sight. She climbed the ladder, leaving Adam to deal with the sea scooter.

As soon as she was safely on the boat, her panic ignited like a firecracker in her gut. She couldn't breath and the tight wetsuit was blocking her lungs. Her alarm caused her fingers to fumble as she reached behind her back, searching for the zipper.

She peeled off the rubber suit, shedding it like a second skin and filling her lungs in the clean air.

"Hey, you okay?" were his first words out of the water.

"Of course," she answered quickly, too quickly. It was instinct. She couldn't tell him she was having a panic attack. "We did it, huh?" Melanie exhaled.

"We did." His celebratory mood dropped. "What happened with that last guy?"

Her plan to tell him nothing had been decided before she'd hit the water off the luxury liner. "He attacked me. You saw how big he was." She sat on the wooden storage bench, slipping on her shoes.

"I saw."

"He clammed up. He was American, though," she said, her chest constricting.

"Okay, Mel. We'll play it that way. I'm here if you ever want to tell me."

"Can't," she said, slumping down.

"Then just say that. Don't make up a story." His tone was sharp as he changed out of the snappy fabric and into shorts and a T-shirt.

"Okay," Melanie chewed on her bottom lip.

"We'd better move." Adam took the driver's seat and, at a low speed, glided away from the shelter of the island's cover. The blackness of the night engulfed them as they traveled beneath a canopy of stars.

She leaned against his chair. "Adam." He grunted. "Thank you." She choked up as her fingers tightened on his shoulder.

"You're welcome."

His voice was soft and filled with kindness that she didn't know anywhere else. There was more to say but it was the best she could do. Standing with her hand on his shoulder until he berthed the boat on the rickety dock half a mile from her rental house.

"Take my hand," he said, reaching to help her.

"I can manage." She clipped on her blonde wig.

"I know, but this way we're lovers out for a midnight ride."

"Part of the ruse?"

"Yeah," he said, not letting go of her hand and leading her up the planks to a rusted, old motorcycle. "I'll take you home."

"In case we're being watched?" She buckled the helmet strap around her chin. "Do I have something on my face?"

"No. Are you the same girl I left here with?" he asked, climbing onto the bike.

"No." She let out a sigh. "I feel incredibly," she closed her eyes, "light. My burden," *for the moment*, "is lifted."

"You're beautiful."

Melanie snorted. "I've been told otherwise." She tossed her leg over and climbed in behind him, loosely wrapping her arms around his chest. "It's been a good day."

"Did you say something?" Adam asked over his shoulder as they sped down the narrow street.

She rested her chin in the crook of his neck. *My parents are safe,* "I don't know if I want to do cartwheels or cry. Maybe both!"

He couldn't hear her and it didn't matter.

Pulling off to the gravely shoulder, to the rental house, he cut the engine.

"Thanks for the lift," She said, removing the helmet, and using her fingers to fluff up her wig. Her back pocket buzzed. She looked away from Adam as she answered. The chaos of her emotions swarmed and kicked off another rush of adrenaline.

"Hello, Melanie." Jack said, accusingly.

"Hello." She answered, wincing.

"Is there something you want to get off your chest?" He asked.

"Nothing in particular, no."

"How'd you know about the bomb?"

"Satellite." She grimaced.

"You sure you want to stick with that?"

Her thoughts were all over the place. "Jack," she started, unsure where she was going.

"Forget it, Mel. I don't want to know." He sighed, loudly. "I'm just not sure how to feel or what to think about all of this."

"We'll talk when you get here."

"Let's just let it go. We're heading to your island with the rescued passengers and hijackers and we're being followed by a storm of media."

"Okay." Melanie felt overwhelming guilt. She slid her phone back in her pocket. Her gaze glued to Adam's troubled expression. "You all right?"

"Why wouldn't I be?"

"I don't know, you look funny."

"Just my face." His grin was off and his eyes held something she couldn't place. "I'll see you back home."

"Bye." She leaned forward to place a peck on his cheek. "Thank you."

"See ya round, Mel."

Melanie watched the red taillights and for that moment it felt as if they were linked. The tugging in her heart was an actual, physical strain.

"Adam!" She yelled, ran a few yards but the puttering of the diesel engine bike muffled her shout. *Adam.* "Oh my God," she breathed out the startling revelation and feeling wide-awake. "Adam."

On the sea breeze, olive and grass scents filled her lungs as she jogged under the strange celestial pattern to the rental house.

CHAPTER TWENTY-EIGHT

After 52 hours of pacing the blue carpeting at the local clinic, Melanie was ready to fasten her seatbelt. Across the aisle she beamed, through bloodshot eyes, at her parents.

They'd been questioned regarding the hijacking and had to take a psych exam before they were released from custody.

"We're fine, Honey. Stop worrying." Rita said, rubbing her back against the plush leather seats. "I've never been on a private jet before."

"Pretty swanky stuff," Roger said. "It's almost worth being tied up and starved, to fly home in style."

"Roger!" Rita reprimanded.

Melanie leaned back and closed her eyes. Everything was good. The corner of her mind that held the face of Hugh was pushed to the recesses. This moment was dedicated to gratitude.

Jack had been giving her the cold shoulder. Tossing her only bits of the information obtained during the interrogation of the six hijackers that were captured.

"Did they say anything interesting?" She'd probed.

"Why aren't you with your parents?"

"They're being questioned. Some shrink wants to keep them under surveillance for a few days, to evaluate their level of trauma."

"It's for their own good," Jack said, his rigid tone softening slightly. "But we can arrange for an expedited recovery in this case."

"What's going on in there?" she motioned to the interrogation room.

"They're hired help."

"Day laborer hijackers?" she questioned.

"Something like that, yeah. I think the one that was killed, he was the leader."

"Did you try fingerprints?"

"Not back yet."

"Nationality?"

"Nothing, Mel. They haven't uttered a word. I'm telling you." Melanie chewed on her lip, thinking. "Take the jet, I'm going to stick around here until we get answers."

"Honey!" Melanie opened one eye. "I cannot believe you flew all the way to Greece to pick us up," Rita said for the hundredth time.

"I know, Mom." Melanie smiled.

"There they are!" Rita shouted, jogging across the tarmac toward Bruce and Cheryl. "Oh, my baby." She cooed at Olivia and pressed into her son.

"I've never been happier, to be home." Roger said, clasping Bruce and patting his back.

Melanie stood back, watching from the sidelines as her family was reunited.

"What? Do you want a special invitation?" Bruce called out to Melanie.

"Yeah, you got one?" Melanie laughed and wrapped her arms around her brother. "Gained a little weight?" she asked, tapping his spare tire.

"You're crazy, I look good," Bruce said, tightening his squeeze. "Help me with the luggage."

With the van loaded, Cheryl climbed in back with the baby and the grandparents. Melanie took the front passenger seat and Bruce drove.

"The welcome home party sort of took on a life of its own." Bruce confessed from behind the wheel.

"What does that mean, exactly?"

"Mom's church group called yesterday." His shoulders lifted to his ears and his neck disappeared. "They may have notified the media."

"Bruce!"

"Don't scold me," Bruce said. "What was I supposed to do with the church ladies? I couldn't stop them," he whined. "I was okay with the tent, but then one of their grandsons plays in the high school marching band, and, well…"

"A marching band?"

"In uniform. Some of Mom's friends have been cooking non-stop. One said I'd been a chubby teenager but matured nicely."

They both eewed.

"You should tell mom about her party," Melanie said.

"No way. You know how she feels about surprises."

"Mom," Melanie twisted to view the middle seats. "Bruce has

something he wants to tell you."

"You suck," Bruce said out of the corner of his mouth as he cleared his throat. "Mom, your friends wanted to throw you a welcome home party."

"Aren't they sweet?" Rita grinned. "But, Melanie honey, if you knew about it earlier you should've told me sooner."

Melanie didn't have to see Bruce to feel his gleeful expression. They stopped along the way for Rita to freshen up.

When they drove up to the church, cars were parked along the side and all meters were taken.

"Is the president in town?" Roger asked.

Bruce parked in the one vacant space left specifically for them.

"Is that Whitney Barnes from the news?"

Melanie retreated in her seat, hiding into the shadows as the side door was slid open "Surprise!" the church group yelled.

Her parents were whisked away.

"Holy cow, Bruce. What is this?"

"A circus," Cheryl said, sticking her head between the front seats to admire the band's baton twirler. "I always wanted to be that girl."

Melanie laughed. "No offense, but you're clumsy. I'm surprised you don't have Olivia on a bungee cord."

"Leave her alone, she's cute," Bruce said, coming to Cheryl's rescue.

"That's why I *wanted* that gig but never got it."

"Look at all those balloons. Oh, there's Trish." Melanie hopped out of the van.

"There you are. Can you believe all this?"

"I don't know half these people," Melanie said, in Trish's embrace.

"You must have been going nuts. I've been thinking about you

… was it as terrible as it seemed? Buccaneers capturing ships in the Med? Jesus, what year is this?"

"I was terrified. More so than either of my parents." Melanie scanned the faces.

"Of course. It's way easier to be *in* danger than to watch someone you love in danger."

Melanie smiled. "When was the last time you were in danger?"

"Daily." Trish huffed.

"Yeah, that's right. I forgot how you drive."

"I cannot believe you just said that," Trish said with her plucked brows, angling down. "Dead. That's what you are."

"Does that mean I'm in danger?" Melanie laughed, "You're right, it *is* easier to be in danger than to watch someone else."

"All right." Trish stuck her long index finger into Melanie's chest. "I'm going to give you a pass because that was funny. Carla!"

Melanie searched but didn't see anyone familiar.

"You have to look low to the ground," Trish explained. "Jenny is here, too. But watch out because she and Ryan have broken it off again. I swear, that relationship is like a ping-pong match. It's pointless and gives me a headache."

"I thought you meant because … never mind."

Carla was carrying a plate of cookies with her. "Oh Sweetie, thank God you're all safe!" Her hug was limp and the pats to her back were gentle. "You know, Ted had already contacted the administration about stepping in and getting involved. These cookies are delicious," she sang.

"I really appreciate that. Thank you."

"The mob around your parents looks like it's never going to subside, I'm going to go say hello," Trish said, standing on her tiptoes.

"I'll come, too." Carla added.

Melanie looked around. She hadn't seen Adam. Her nerves fluttered as she dialed his home number. "Hi." Her smile was automatic when he answered.

"Hey, you sound close. Are you in town?"

Melanie laughed a second longer than his non-funny joke deserved. "There's a hoopla going on," she said.

"I just saw it on the news."

"Were," she started slowly, holding on to the sound in her throat, "you going to show up?"

"I thought about it, but…"

"You should be here," she interrupted. "I mean, you're part of this and should enjoy the celebration."

"Then we're on our way."

Melanie's heart skipped and this time she wasn't able to blame it on her parents. She was feeling all those things that had disappeared and thought were dead. Her stomach was in uncomfortable knots. Her smile stretched to say hello to strangers as she kept an ever-constant eye on her family.

Aunt Pauly and her daughters were in a circle, all speaking at the same time and using their arms to exaggerate their remarks. Melanie pulled her cousin Penny off to the side.

"God, it's good to see you." Penny said, "You look worn out."

"It's been a rough week."

"Excuse me." Martha, of the sponsoring church group, took hold of the microphone and banged on the speaker. "Thank you all for coming." Her voice shook as she started listing people that Melanie had never heard of, the media and the rest of the congregation. "It was a terrifying situation for my good friends. Because of their firm belief in our Lord everyone on the ship was released safely. Before we all give a big hand for Rita and Roger, the heroes, let's lower our heads for a prayer of thanks." Martha led the prayer before handing the microphone over to Rita.

Rita, overwhelmed, wiped away tears as she gratefully thanked everyone and proclaimed it had taken more than a pair of ruby slippers to get them home.

"Love your families," Roger said, his mouth in a thin line. He stood with the mic in his hand for seconds that stretched, uncomfortably into a minute. His emotions were raw as his eyes fell on Melanie, Bruce, Cheryl, Olivia and Rita. "Love your family."

Media or not, Melanie walked directly into her dad's arms. Bruce contained them in his embrace. Strangely, the speeches continued behind them. "I love you, Daddy."

The clapping erupted as the family wiped tears, laughed and were slow to part ways.

On her own, Melanie perused the food tables. Hours of church cooking had been reduced to crumbs, leaving one red potato left in the potato salad bowl.

"Jeez, a bunch of damn vultures," Trish called out to the crowd as she stood beside the empty platters.

"You can't say that!" Melanie scolded.

"Can too. I'm starving over here!"

A reprimand was on the tip of Melanie's tongue but coming over the grassy knoll, she first noticed his walk.

"Aww, shit. Look Mel, I didn't invite him," Trish claimed, her hands on her hips.

"It's fine. I did."

"You what?"

"You heard me," Melanie said, cutting the distance between her and Adam. "Hi," she grinned and raised her arms, open for an embrace. It wasn't until then that she realized he was holding onto someone's hand.

"Hey," he said, awkwardly disengaging his fingers and loosely hugging her. "How are you?"

"Fine." She backed off. "Really good. You?"

"Yeah, hey," he reached out for the girl who Melanie finally looked at. "This is Sonja. Sonja, Melanie."

"Hi." Melanie's smile was automatic and completely phony. The girl was young and pretty and in an inappropriate pair of very short cutoffs. Melanie had to admit, the girl had great legs.

"Hi," she said, smiling big to reveal two rows of shiny, white, perfectly straight teeth. "Thank God your parents are safe, right?"

"Right." Melanie nodded.

"Uh-um," Trish cleared her throat and poked Adam in the arm. "Hello, Adam."

"Hey, Trish," he said, his grin changing as he gave her a hug.

"Oh my God, Trish!" Sonja squealed, "we were just now watching the news and saw you on television. You look like a goddess."

Melanie mentally rolled her eyes. Feeling like the odd man out as Sonja lavished Trish with praise, and Trish preened with pleasure.

"A girlfriend?" Melanie whispered to Adam, who shrugged.

"Wow, seems so incredible," Sonja said, turning back to Melanie. "It's so horrible what happened. It's been all over the news. I want to meet them."

"They're right over there," Melanie pointed. "Trish'll introduce you."

"Sure. Come on, Sonja." Trish hooked her index finger around the girl's purse strap and tugged.

"Aren't you coming?" she asked, looking over her shoulder at Adam.

"In a minute." He smiled and Melanie felt her own smile. "Your parents look good," he said, his gaze shifting across the lawn. "Better than the last time I saw them."

They've had sleep, Melanie thought, catching her parents in an energetic conversation.

"I wanted to tell you about Sonja," he said, getting her attention.

"How long have you been seeing her?" She asked, keeping her eyes everywhere, except on him.

"Few weeks. She's pre-med at Scripps."

"I'm sure she's great." Melanie's sentiment was genuine. She stole a quick glance at Adam, "I'm happy for you." Her eyes immediately switching to study Sonja as the girl approached Rita. She was cute; in her early twenties, 5'7"-ish, tan with straight brown hair that touched her shoulders. "How'd you meet?"

"I started playing volleyball again and she's on the team." Melanie was still looking at Sonja but heard the humor in Adam's voice. "She's not very good."

Melanie nodded at him. "I just want to thank you for everything." Her emotions were rising, ready to cut off her air supply. "I don't know what I'd have done if the outcome had been different. I couldn't have done it without you."

"I'm glad I could help."

"Me too," she said, her vision blurring.

"I guess I should say hello to your parents." He placed a kiss on the side of her head and was gone.

Melanie's heart sunk as she looked at her surroundings. The

colorful welcome home banner lifted her mood, and she felt less like crying as she noticed Penny and Rachel were huddled and giggling.

Growing up, Penny and Melanie had been inseparable. Penny had creamy fair skin without one freckle, bright pumpkin-colored hair that either wanted to frizz or, on a good day, frizz less. Her blue eyes watered in bright sunlight and as a kid her rosy lips were always chapped.

The two had gotten in a lot of trouble, mostly because Penny's older sister Peggy, aka Rachel, lived to tattle. But they weren't limited to torturing her. Neighbor kids were their usual victims. Once they'd collected a month's worth of seaweed and teepeed a tree house. Melanie thought back on those summer days with a great fondness and a wish that she could be that kid again.

"Hi," Melanie grinned, being around her cousins gave her gut a twist of excitement. As if she were already doing something bad. "Congratulations," she hugged Rachel. "Where's the husband?"

"I can't wait for you to meet him! He's around here somewhere. Probably fixing the sprinkler system."

"Your mom and dad are so cool!" Penny said, draping her arm over Melanie's shoulder. "My mom would've finally had a real heart attack and keeled over."

Aunt Pauly was always suffering from some malady or incurable ailment that turned out to be nothing.

"Oh no," Bruce groaned as he walked up and stood by Rachel, who was his only childhood ally. "The sight of you two together makes my teeth hurt. I packed my bags to run away every summer until high school."

"You were such a baby. Remember that summer our goal was to make him cry twice a day?" Penny threw a sucker-punch toward

Bruce's broad belly.

Melanie felt the twinge of guilt that Penny was lacking. "We were pretty mean to him."

"Still a softy," Penny snorted at Melanie. "That was the summer you gave him all of your allowance and he bought a broken Go Kart."

"Yeah!" Bruce breathed. "Melanie went and kicked that kid's ass and made him give me my money back plus interest."

"See, I wasn't such a bad sister."

"The worst." He laughed and shoved her away. "Hey, I guess the party here is breaking up. Mom wants you to go to the Burrito Bus and bring home dinner for everyone. There's about twelve of us and I want red chili."

"Now? I don't even have a car. Do you?" Melanie asked Penny.

"Rachel and Ron drove."

She looked up. The crowd had decreased to a couple of dozen. "Trish is still here, I can ask her," Melanie decided. "I'll see you guys at home?"

"Mel," Trish started, "we're going to grab some dinner and then hit the clubs. Go home. Change. We'll pick you up."

"I can't. I've got family in town. But I need a ride."

"You can hold onto the bumper if you'd like." Trish's reply was snarky. "We're in the Porsche."

"Shoot." Even in the last few minutes her options had dwindled. "Maybe Bruce is still here. I better catch him."

She jogged to the corner and looked down the block. No one.

Pushing people away for years really does achieve its desired effect, she thought. *But you are Executive Director.* "Good thing you're also self-sufficient," she said, phoning in her mega-burrito order before dialing up a cab.

The owners of the Burrito Bus were brothers, Jose and Jesus. They'd seemed to be permitted for any vacant lot within a ten-mile radius. Roger was their biggest fan.

Along with the twenty burritos Melanie bought out their supply of rice, beans, salsa, guacamole and chips.

"We threw in some extra stuff and added desserts," Jesus said, exiting the mobile food truck and placing the box in the back seat of the cab. "We heard Roger didn't get fed well on that boat." He shook his head in disbelief. "Tell your dad his next ten lunches are on us."

"Will do. Thanks."

On the cab ride to the house, Melanie checked her phone twice. Nobody had called. No word from Jack or Ben. With her tip for the cabbie, she added a burrito and heaved out the box.

"Food's here!"

At least they're happy to see me, Melanie huffed, slightly put out that no one had missed her. Not even a little. The house was full and in the kitchen Rita had arranged plates of crackers.

"Thank God you're here. This is all I had in the house. Pitiful," Rita said. "Get a knife and start halving everything. Oh, good, you brought sides," she said, peering into the cardboard box.

"Mom, you should relax. Go enjoy your company," Cheryl said, taking the spoon out of Rita's hand. "Go. Melanie and I have this."

The mom thing still made the hairs on Melanie's neck rise in protest.

"Oh, Cheryl, I'm so worked up, I doubt I could stop." She said, wiping her hands on her apron.

Melanie stayed in the kitchen, cleaning and washing while the party gathered in the living room. Aunt Pauly, Penny, and Rachel and Ron were staying over.

"Rachel and Ron get your room," Penny said, leaning against the counter.

"My mom gets Bruce's room and I guess you and I are on the couch." Penny elbowed Melanie in the side. "What do you want to do? God, I feel like a kid. We could steal a bottle and get wasted on the beach," Penny suggested.

Melanie laughed. "Or, I overheard someone talking about a new bar over by the art college."

"We could ogle cute boys. It doesn't matter that they're most likely gay or a decade too young, we're only window-shopping. Do you know how long it's been since I've been on a date? Forever," Penny sighed.

"Me neither."

"Are you kidding? I saw you with the hot guy today."

"I'm not sure if you noticed, he arrived with a girlfriend." Melanie thinking about a well-deserved drink, paused and scrunched her face. "You know, we don't have a car."

"You could borrow your parents' – they'll never know."

Melanie and Penny sprayed out laughs.

"You are such a bad influence," Melanie said, wiping her hands and draping the dishtowel over the oven handle.

"I'm only bad with you. Let's wear our trashiest outfits," Penny said, pushing off from the cabinets.

"Are you guys going out?" Cheryl asked, entering the kitchen with a full garbage bag.

"To a bar. Want to come?" Penny asked. "We're going to dress up and pretend we're other people."

"Sounds like exactly what I need. But I don't have any other clothes."

All three sets of eyes dropped down to the elastic-waistband of her khaki's and frilly purple blouse.

"That's not going to fly. But Mel, I'm going to have to raid your closet, too."

"What makes you think I have so many trashy clothes?" Melanie laughed and shoved Penny.

"So being whor-istas is out?" Penny's back slumped.

"Afraid so," Melanie nodded.

"I need elastic, which Mel doesn't have, and I need a size 10, which she doesn't have," Cheryl complained.

"Leave it to me." Penny added a wink to her cryptic tone.

Upstairs, Melanie sifted through the leftover clothes from previous summers.

"I call the white jeans!" Penny said, entering Melanie's bedroom with a black dress on a hanger. "For you, Madam," she said, presenting it to Cheryl. "It's Rachel's and I think it'll fit."

"It's nice," Cheryl said, wide-eyed. "You sure she's okay lending it to me?"

"Oh, yeah. She's totally fine with it."

Melanie looked away and pitched the jeans at Penny's lying, thieving face.

It was after ten when they snuck Cheryl out of the house. Their getaway car was a cracker-infested minivan. Cheryl, not knowing she was wearing a pilfered outfit, backed out of the drive at an incredibly slow speed.

The bar was in an old strip mall that had been renovated, revamped, restored and refurbished over the years, leaving it a jumbled mess. Penny, Cheryl and Melanie rode the outside escalator to the second floor.

The drinking crowd hadn't arrived and Melanie stood at the entrance surveying the land. Leather booths on one wall, tall chrome tables at the center of the room. In the corner next to the dartboard and pinball machine was a two-person stage. On the balcony, looking over the trees in the parking lot, were couches and heat lamps.

"You can sit anywhere," said a woman in a black T-shirt and hip-hugging shorts. "What can I get you ladies?" she asked, following them to the table at the center of the room.

"We're on a tropical holiday," Penny said in well-practiced British accent. "We would like three piña coladas."

"No, I'm still nursing. I'll have a Sprite with a slice of pineapple and a cherry." Cheryl ordered in her boring American inflection.

The waitress tipped her imaginary hat and was off.

"Tell me," Penny said, leaning toward Cheryl. "What's it like being married? The longer I go without a boyfriend the more interested I am in marriage."

Melanie sighed and escaped into the music streaming from the jukebox. Springsteen. Marriage was not a welcome topic of conversation. But neither was thinking. She checked her phone. Missed a call from Trish. She sent a "What the hell is going on?" text to Jack and returned Trish's call.

"Where are you?" her friend grouched. "We stopped by your house but no one knew where you'd run off to."

"I'm at a bar with Penny and Cheryl."

"Where?"

"Damn, you're bossy."

"Just give me the address." And for her goodbye, "A bunch of us will be there in ten minutes. Make sure there are enough tables."

"I hope you meant it when you said the more the merrier. That was Trish," Melanie told Penny.

It wasn't long before the relatively quiet ambiance of the bar was disrupted. Trish and her posse walked in like they owned the joint. Jason, Adam and Sonja were part of the twelve along with Lori, the bridesmaid. And the only other person Melanie recognized was Nate.

Trish ran over to hug Melanie as she ordered tables rearranged. "Closer together!" She barked and pointed.

Melanie's eye flutter met Nate's grinning nod. She waved and he saluted. He looked casual in his loose, dark blue linen shirt and beach bum hat.

"He's cute." Penny's rum-scented breath filled the narrow gap between them. "Who is he?"

Melanie gave a brief description of the surfer accountant.

"Is he single?" she asked.

"I just said he was permanently on the prowl," Melanie answered, looking at Penny.

Penny's left shoulder shrugged. "Me, too. Can you get him to come over?"

"You and I have both been staring," she said, and was about to say more when Nate made his move.

"Come here often?" he asked, dragging a stool from another table.

"I practically own the place." Melanie smiled. "How are you?"

"My complaints are random and immaterial," he said, his eyes falling on Penny and then on Cheryl.

Melanie introduced him to her cousin and sister-in-law. And though Penny had been criticizing her flirting skills, she did a pretty good job with Nate. Melanie did give her a swift kick under the table when Penny's giggle got too over the top.

She hadn't let herself look at Adam. The conflict was between her mind and her heart. *I just want him to be happy,* was one argument. But since he seemed happy with Sonja, her heart wanted to be selfish.

The breaking glass behind Adam caught her attention, her face lifted and she found herself staring directly at him. He was talking with Jason and Melanie took in his chiseled features, strong jaw and a mouth that formed a perfect smile. She kept her eyes on him, even when his gaze fell on hers. He lifted his chin in greeting. Melanie nodded and without breathing she folded back into Nate and Penny's banter.

"They're fine," Melanie whispered as Cheryl checked her phone, again.

"I know. I texted Bruce and he wants to come and hang out with Jace." She shook her head. "I used to be jealous of Trish."

"Your asshole friend is here." Nate elbowed her in the arm.

Melanie laughed. "He's not an asshole. It'd be easier if that were true."

"Mel, what should I say to Bruce?"

"Will you have more fun with him here?" Melanie shrugged and Cheryl tilted her head side-to-side.

"I'll be right back," Melanie said, to anyone who cared to listen. Jason had finally drifted out of Trish's range. *Shoot*, she grumped as she followed him down the narrow path to the men's bathroom. "Jace," she called out softly before he pushed open the penis only, restricted area.

"Angel," he said, surprised, his hand on the brass plate. "You coming in?"

"Not unless I have to." She grinned. They hadn't exchanged more than a few words since Thanksgiving. "I was hoping for a minute."

"Sure, I can hold it." The smile was slow to spread, but to her relief his teasing was back.

"It's about Adam and Sonja."

"Oh." The humor vanished.

"I need to know if he's happy with her, if it's serious?" Melanie swallowed.

"Angel, I try to keep out of it and Adam's been pretty secretive about this one." Jason sighed, shifted his weight and sucked in a breath. "I think he's good. He's almost back to normal."

"Okay," she said. Releasing her cheek from its bite, she looked up at him. "I don't want to disrupt his life, but would you do me a favor? Will you call me when or if they break up? I don't want to ask Trish, she'll overreact."

In the tinted light Melanie could see his muscles tighten. He sighed, looked over her head, to the ceiling and back at her. "No, man, can't you leave him alone? Don't you see what you did to him last time? Jesus," his voice came out in a growl. "Melanie, he's finally recovering and you want me to toss him back? Hell, no, is my answer." He was angry, the flare growing in his eyes, the vein throbbing in his neck.

Melanie stalled for something to say, frozen by the venom in his words, his tone and the fire that blazed in his eyes.

"Look at him," Jason continued. "He's happy. When was the last time you've seen him smile like that? Don't take this the wrong way, but you're bad news."

Melanie blinked.

"I like you, really." Here she felt his tone soften. "But Adam's my boy. The farther away you are the better. If you care for him at all – and I'm not sure you do – then stay the fuck away. Got it?"

She nodded, dazed. "I got it." She whispered, feeling low like she wanted to crawl away, humiliated. "Just so you know, I do care. I care." Melanie felt pummeled as she backed away from Jason. "I'm sorry."

"No. Damn it, I'm sorry, Angel. Come back," he shouted to her back.

Coming out of the hall felt very strange. Her skin prickled as she realized the rest of the world had continued over that minute. People were drinking, laughing and everyone was in the same seats, except Cheryl. She tried to shake off the ugliness as she slipped in between Nate and the empty seat.

"I was just telling Penny about my car. It's parked out front," Nate said. "Want to see it?"

"Um, of course." Melanie was still stunned. "Where's Cheryl?"

"She's on the phone," Penny cocked her head to the back of the room.

Melanie followed Nate and Penny out to the parking lot. She was lost in the brutality of Jason's words. Nate led them to the end of the row to a long Cadillac. It was pristine and glistened even under the poor orangey light.

"A metallic gold 1973 El Camino," he said, his back straight as he placed a hand on the hood. "With pinstripes."

"It's beautiful," Melanie said, sticking her head into the driver's side window. "Did you fix it up?"

"Me? No. These babies," he held up his wiggling fingers, "are meant for strings. I bought it from a guy. Want to hear about engine size?"

"Only if we can have the rest of the conversation in a foreign language." She said, grateful for his knack of making her feel better.

"I love it. Will you take me for a ride?" Penny asked, running around to the driver's seat and settling in, pretending to drive.

"Is there something wrong with her?" Nate asked, in a low whisper.

"Yeah." Melanie nodded. "She likes you."

Hmm. Nate grunted. "And you don't?"

"I do." She looked into his brown eyes and was reminded how nicely all his features worked together. "I've been ruined. Go take my crazy cousin out for a spin."

"Okay," Nate said, looking at Penny waving like the Queen of England out the window. "She looks like fun."

"She is." Melanie smiled. "She's a blast."

"All right, Darling," Nate said opening the car door. "But let's get one thing straight, I'm king of the castle."

Penny gave Melanie a wink as she slid over to the other seat. "I can work with that."

On the boulevard, crossing the intersection a heavy sports vehicle ran the red light, Melanie looked up just in time to catch the impact. It was an earsplitting squeal of tires, impacting metal and then a thunderous explosion that shook the earth beneath her feet. It all ended, suddenly, with a dead thump.

Nate was yelling something as Melanie leaped over the small hedge that separated the parking lot from the sidewalk.

"Call 911!" She looked into the windows of the crushed car but the airbag blocked the view of the driver.

The SUV revved its engine, tearing away.

"That guy's leaving!" Penny's astonished voice was gasping, her fingers poised above her phone.

"Call!" Melanie yelled. Others had descended on the wreckage as her name boomed over the din of entranced voices.

"I'm here," she shouted, standing and pushing past the people who'd gathered.

"Melanie!" She followed Adam's frantic voice. As she reached the curb, he was jumping over the hedge, anguish clouding his expression.

"I'm all right. I wasn't in the accident." She stated the obvious. His face was drained of color.

He walked straight to her, an unreadable look in his eyes as he reached to hold her face with both hands.

"I'm not hurt."

His jaw muscles twitched and his emerald eyes had darkened to the color of cold steel. "I thought…" His inhale was shaky as he pulled her against his chest. Enveloped in his embrace Melanie closed her eyes and let him hold her. His face in her hair as she felt him exhale, a warm breath on her neck. They didn't move again until the ambulance sirens swirled to a fever pitch and stopped.

"I thought you'd been hurt," he said, his hands trembling as his fingers pressed through her hair and her jaw cradled in his palms. He stared into her eyes. "You're okay?" his gaze softened. He dipped down, his faced turned and the pressure on her lips was fleeting.

Leaving Melanie breathless and wanting. "Adam," she started, her heart ricocheting and not knowing how to tell him her feelings had changed. Not knowing if it was the right thing to do.

"I'm sorry." He said, misunderstanding her intentions. Shouldering his way past the onlookers, he rushed toward the escalators.

"Adam," she called out again. He halted turning his profile toward her. "I love you." Her heart leaped, saying the words but clogging in her throat as he gave her a nod and continued to Sonja.

He didn't understand. He thought you meant I love you like a friend. Her thoughts chaos in her mind, *he's still in love with you. You could get him back. Just go there and finish that kiss!*

Jason's torrent of words echoed in her ears. *Fuck Jace and his opinions! I want Adam and he wants me.*

Determination carried her for five paces, until her head spun. *There's no turning back from this. If you break up his relationship with Sonja and you aren't ready, then what?*

She stopped with one foot on the walkway. "Let him go." The voice in her head didn't sound like her. She sounded wise.

Melanie looked at her phone and read Jack's reply. "Heading to D.C."

She wrote back. See you there.

CHAPTER TWENTY-NINE

Three of the surviving hijackers were American and Ben was able to pull strings.

"How's it going?" she asked, standing shoulder to shoulder with Jack as he watched through the two-way mirror.

"Punks, that weren't trusted with any vital information. Their fingerprints have been filed off and the names they're giving us are bogus. This one," he pointed to the one singled out, "he's our best bet. Is there anything you know that would be helpful?" He asked, looking at her through the reflection of the glass.

"Wasn't like that." She said, facing him.

"What was it like?" Jack didn't budge, his stance remained rigid with his arms tightly crossed.

"Your hands were tied with bureaucratic bullshit. I went around that."

"You could've told me."

"No. That would've put you in an awkward situation. This way you're safe from scrutiny."

Jack rotated his neck to glare at her in the eye. "I wish you trusted me."

"I do." He turned his attention back to the hijacker. "Well," Melanie sighed, "let me know when you've broken him. You should get some sleep." She patted Jack's back. Instead, of heading to the Manor, she found a quiet spot to wait.

"I've turned off the audio and visual. We're not being recorded and there isn't anyone behind that plate glass," Melanie said, slipping into the seat opposite the guy with the shaved head. "We both know you aren't going to talk to anyone else."

"You think you're a bad ass."

"Sometimes. How about you? You a bad ass?"

"I'm a tool."

Melanie cocked her head to the side, surprised by his statement.

"Rich people use me to get their dirty work done." His voice was scarred from years of abuse and his eyes shone with the coolness of death.

"Don't let them. Tell me who sent you." His eyes remained fixed on hers but he shook his head. "Why not?" She pressed.

"It's not personal."

"It's very personal! Tell me what else is planned." She could feel the heat flowing up her neck and it took her years of restraint not to jump across the table and strangle him.

"I've got nothing." His slumped shoulders rested above the top of the chair. "I'm a hired hand."

"Am I supposed to buy that?"

The tool nodded. "Look, lady, all I know is we were to hang out on the yacht. Scare the shit out of people. There was supposed to be a speedboat for us after a few days. I didn't know anything about a bomb." His head tilted back, grinning conspiratorially. "All a big game, a mental game." Moving his head to check out her face, he whispered. "You like games?"

"Is it Parker?" she breathed, losing patience.

"Is that who you want it to be?" He grinned.

"You're going to be in here for a very long time."

He held her gaze while his head teetered centimeters from side to side. "Don't be surprised when the judge throws out the case."

She wanted to disagree, loudly shout the impossibility.

"My lawyers will be excellent. It will appear that the cards are stacked in my favor and they will be. The most I'm looking at is a slap on the wrist."

"You were pulled off the ship you hijacked. There's no question."

"I'm not saying I know how it'll be done … just that it will be."

Melanie felt the icy chill down her spine. "Unless they decide it's too much work and let you rot in prison."

"*They* won't."

"How do you know?"

"I'm valuable."

"A valuable tool?" Melanie started at him, his smile plastered to his face. "And what do you get out of this arrangement, money?"

"That, and I get to play out my fantasies. I get to release my inner demons without consequences. You're lucky I like red-heads."

"You're full of shit."

"Am I?" He leaned back in the metal chair, raised his brows. "We'll see."

The interview was over.

CHAPTER THIRTY

It was after eleven when the bar started to really get going. The music was loud behind the chorus of chatter and Adam felt pretty good about sinking the last ball into the corner pocket.

"Way to go, Baby!" Sonja cheered, always cheering. Her beer bottle raised in a barley and hops high-five.

Mercifully he clinked his bottle with hers. "I think that makes it six-to-two."

"Trish!" Jason's complaint was part whine and part frustration. "Seriously, Babe you're going to have to try harder."

"Whatever." Trish rolled her eyes, "I only like to play because it looks sexy."

"But I like to win, Babe."

Sonja placed herself at Adam's side and ducked beneath his arm. Standing into his embrace, "That was great!"

"How about I buy us another round," Adam offered.

"No, we lost, I'll pay." Jason said, sulking.

"Well, we're going to the ladies room," Trish said, linking arms with Sonja and strutting away.

"She can be maddening." Jason rubbed the sides of his buzz cut. "But," his mood energizing, "you and Sonja look damn happy."

"She's great." Adam added as much enthusiasm as he could muster. *Sonja is great*, he reminded himself.

"I knew it," he said, poking a sharp elbow into Adam's ribs. "I knew you'd get over Melanie with a little time and a hot chick."

"Yeah, well, you called it." He said, banging his knuckles on the bar and raising four fingers to order the beers.

Jason clapped Adam on the shoulder, "I saved you my friend. Saved you. There was a moment when I thought…"

"What are you talking about?" Adam asked, suddenly giving Jason his full attention.

"Oh," Jason's blue eyes sparkled, "remember when Melanie was here, we all went to that artsy club?"

"Yeah." Adam released a slow breath.

"She cornered me."

"Who?"

"Melanie." Jason said, dropping a couple of bills and taking two icy bottles. "She was asking me about you and Sonja, wanting me to call her if you ever broke up. Can you believe that? After all the shit she put you through."

"What did you tell her," Adam's voice was husky and restrained menace.

"I told her to fuck off." Jason grinned wide, proudly dividing his face in half.

The blow was thrown with full force, effectively knocking the smirk right off his face. One punch and Jason was on the ground sitting in a pool of imported beer, his fingers pressing the wound, as his tongue tasting the blood. "What the hell, Man?"

They were encircled by dozens of onlookers tracking the conversation. Looking eagerly at Adam for his response.

"I love her, Jace," he growled. "You know that. How could you? How could you send her away?" Adam tried to blink out the betrayal in his eyes as he stared at his best friend sprawled on the ground. "She's all I want," he added swallowing down his heart that had leapt to his throat.

"Adam?"

His gaze left Jason's to search the small crowd for Sonja. "I'm sorry."

CHAPTER THIRTY-ONE

At a quarter to one, Melanie found herself in a dark corner of an exclusive brothel. It was off the beaten path and away from surveillance cameras.

Years of monitoring the Parkers hadn't been a waste. This was Hugh's weekly weakness. Melanie had kept the place on her radar. But this was the first time she'd actually drugged one of the prostitutes into unconsciousness and invaded her space.

The bedroom reeked of aromatic stimulants. The perfume, powders and candles were strong in the private quarters. Fanning the air in front of her face, she checked the pulse of the woman she'd left in the closet on a pile of skimpy costumes.

She had envisioned the place differently. More like a luxury burlesque boudoir with sexual appliances hanging from the walls. Instead, it was more on the level of an upscale hotel. Clean, bright with only one rectangular table littered with gels, lubricants, condoms, feathers, straps, handcuffs and silver balls that Melanie didn't want to know about.

She'd swept the room for any devices, rummaged through drawers and broke into the wall safe.

"Ginger?" Hugh's raspy voice called out as the door shut and the bolt thrown. "Come on, Honey." The fumes of his cigar mixed with the dusting powder to create a sweet and sickening scent.

"Hello, Senator," Melanie said, stepping out of the shadows. He was in a wheelchair and an oxygen tank was hooked around the handle. Other than the props, he looked the same.

"Agent Ward. This is…," he paused, looked her up and down, "an interesting surprise. You're taking Ginger's position?" He undressed her with his leer. "I can't say I'm happy about the change."

"Don't be vile, old man." Repulsed, Melanie felt her skin crawl.

"Then why are you here? You already murdered my son."

"We both know it was you that killed him. Why pretend?"

The blood rushed to Hugh's face and for the moment Melanie thought he was going to lunge at her. Prickles of fear raced through her body.

"What is it you want?" He glowered, his fingers thumping on the arms rests.

"I want you to leave me and my family alone," she commanded, wavering for an instant as a cloud of puzzlement crossed his face.

"So," he leaned back, his mind working like a clock behind the fallen lids of his sharp eyes. "Someone kidnapped your parents and you automatically assume it was me. I'm flattered," he said, a warped grimace on his face. "I find it impossible to believe you haven't any other enemies."

"You're honestly telling me it wasn't you?" Melanie asked with a grunt.

"No, it might have been me." Hugh's evil eyes were reduced to slits. "Torture is so much more fun than immediate death. I enjoy making you suffer, daily, for what you did to my son. And if I need to include your family, I will."

"I'll kill you first." Melanie said, feeling the chill.

"My life's mission is for you to become on intimate terms with the definition of pain." He spat. "Death doesn't scare me, Agent Ward. Nothing scares me." The arms of his chair rattled as he rose to his feet, dropping his lit cigar. "I am immortal." His cackle was like that of a hyena.

He looked crazy. She was scared of him. Always had been. There was a power, a loathing in his soul that she did not understand. And that was frightening.

"Want to test that?" she aimed her gun at his chest, where a human heart should have been, though Hugh looked more devil than human.

"You've got a beautiful baby niece, don't you? What's her name?"

Her scalp singed with electricity.

"Wouldn't want anything to happen to her. Precious child."

Just kill him. Her breaths were coming hard and heavy and the nerves at the tip of her trigger finger were on overdrive. *You've killed for less.*

His stained grin twisted, contorting his face up to his narrowed eyes. "Try it and see what happens."

Do it, Mel!

"You're weak."

The pressure built in her skull and her rapid heartbeat echoed in her ears. Breathing in through her nose as her mouth was clamped in a grimace.

"Even if you kill my flesh, your terror won't stop. It will live with you constantly. I cannot die!"

"You're crazy." She lowered her weapon.

"Like a fox." He dropped back down on the plastic seat. "Put me out of my misery, I dare you."

She pulled up on her gun. Every muscle in her body was rigid as she inspected Hugh's eyes. She felt cold and empty as she turned her back on his laughter.

Melanie slipped out the way she'd gotten in, the bathroom window. A block away, one hand on the brick wall and the other on a dumpster, her stomach clenched and the acid burned as she vomited in the alley. *I've failed.*

Ben's job, like so many of her dreams, was not what she expected. She shuffled paperwork, assigned cases and monitored the overall health of the Agency. What bothered her the most was the sucking up. There weren't five minutes of peace before Jane announced one problem or another waiting to see her.

She'd never been so popular, and the constant attention contributed to her short temper. Jack had labeled her cranky. But it was so much more than that.

"I'm going for a run," she told Jane, who was keeping up with the change in better spirits.

"At the gym?"

"No. Yesterday I was barraged on the treadmill. I tried increasing my speed but there was no getting away. I'm hitting the streets and I'm turning off my cell." *I need to think.*

"I downloaded music to your phone, would you like a pair of headphones?"

"Thank you," Melanie said, feeling guilty for taking her mood out on Jane.

"I'm sorry it's been a difficult transition." She handed Melanie a brand new package of ear buds.

"When are they going to make these things wireless?"

"Would you like me to contact R&D? I bet they can do it now."

A grin emerged from her stern expression. "You know that's not a bad idea. Voice activated with a two-way conversation aspect with the cellular device built-in." She said, exiting her office.

Melanie took the lesser-known passages through the Manor out to street level. She surfaced in the woodsy part of the park. Running with the music in the background, she thought about Hugh. When she wasn't being pestered at work, she was strategizing.

There was only so much surveillance she could put on her family. And there wasn't enough technology in the world to keep them safe.

Mentally, she bumped into walls at every turn. One thing was clear: she had to get to the root of the problem, and Hugh was the root. There was never a question, never another consideration.

The idea of eliminating a U.S. Senator made her nauseous. And the core truth was she was incapable of doing it. That had been proven. She felt like her insides were bawling, recklessly miserable. If she began to feel normal, Olivia's chubby-cheeked grin, drool running down her chin, popped into Melanie's mind.

If he hurt her … and you sat back and waited … Christ! She was back, entertaining the idea of doing the unthinkable, picking off a U.S. Senator.

Melanie ran faster. She was panting when she stopped to read the caller ID. Adam.

"Hi," she gasped, taking in a gulp of air and holding it.

"Please tell me you're not being strangled."

Exhaling. "Pleasure run."

His laugh sounded carefree and for a brief instant she felt part of his easiness. The moment didn't last and life pressed in.

"I was wondering if you had plans for tonight?"

"You're in town," she said, gaining control over her lungs as she recalled Jason's scolding.

"I can pick you up."

"Um," her brain was working slowly.

"You're apartment, what time?"

"Oh. No, not there," she said, shaken. She hadn't been back there since the last time with Danny. "How about I meet you at your hotel after ten? Is that too late?"

"No, that's not too late, but…"

"Where are you staying?"

"Um," he hesitated before giving her the name.

"I'll be there a bit after ten," she said, already looking forward to that time. "Okay."

The euphoria of endorphins wore off ten minutes after returning to her office. She locked the door, kept her head down and cleared up paperwork, cursing life in general.

"It's ten. I'm going home. Do you need anything else?" Jane asked, standing in the doorway.

"Jeez," Melanie stretched, glimpsing the clock as she did. "Shit!" She jumped out of her seat. "Nothing else, and you shouldn't be staying so late."

Melanie was still in her yoga pants, sweat guard T-shirt and running shoes. She was late. She locked her office and ducked into the costume closet, grabbing a pair of pants, a blouse and a pair of ankle boots. Hoping it all matched, she rolled everything into a ball and shoved it in a bag, then took a set of underground tunnels to the touristy part of the city. Big clean hotels with shiny brass fixtures and employees running around in slacks, button down shirts and matching vests.

She was heading for the bathroom to change when to her left, she saw Adam. He was standing at the curb beside the motorcycle parking. Her body surged and she grinned stupidly.

"Hi." She felt the jumble of emotion grip her chest in a scary, elated way. "I'm sorry I'm late. Should I change?" she asked, glancing at his snug jeans and dress shirt.

"No, we have casual plans," he said his smile reaching up to his eyes and lighting his entire face. He released a breath that deflated his chest. "You're not late." He scanned her body, increasing the flutter of nerves in the pit of her stomach. But his brows pulled in and darkened his gaze "Everything all right?' he asked, lifting his hands so that his thumbs followed her cheekbones.

"Do I look that bad?"

"You're always beautiful," he said, the distress changing the color of his eyes.

"I'm okay," she shifted trying to wiggle out of his stare. "Is this yours?" she asked, looking at the Ducati beside him.

"Yeah. I thought we'd go someplace different." He handed her a helmet and then put on his own.

"This feels familiar." She smiled, thinking about their ride in Greece. Her arms wrapped around his chest, Melanie closed her eyes. Adam's heartbeat was strong; she felt it going haywire beneath his dress shirt. He held her hands in his, pressing them against his heart in a tight squeeze, then they were off.

She didn't pay attention to where he was taking her. She closed her eyes and tried to forget everything that didn't belong on that bike. He smelled wonderful.

"We're here," he said, patting her hands.

"Look at that," she said, pulling off the helmet. They were on a hill overlooking the lighted Lincoln Memorial. "I've never been here." Her mind traveled the possible options of arriving to this spot.

"Amazing, isn't it? I thought you'd like it," he said. "Are you hungry?"

"No, I'm okay." She was starving and though Jane had arrived with a plate of hot, oozing macaroni and cheese for lunch, Melanie couldn't remember if she'd eaten more than a few bites.

"Are you sure? Because," he grinned and unbuckled the saddlebag, "I packed us dinner. And you look hungry."

"You packed food?" Her smile was involuntary, her mouth watered and her stomach growled. "Now that you mention it, I'm starving." She watched him flip a blanket in the warm breeze and float it down to the grass. "Can I help?"

"Plates?" He handed her a box.

Inside were utensils, glasses, napkins and plates. "I've heard of these picnic basket things, I've just never seen anybody use one."

He flicked on a lighter and started the wick of a candle. Her heart did a rapid acceleration as the flame caught and the gold light reflected in his eyes. Melanie swallowed down hard.

"Where's Sonja?"

He shrugged.

She licked her lips, her blood flowing in torrents through her veins. She stared at him as he lit a second candle.

"What are you doing?"

"Feeding you." He answered with a calm smile.

"Adam."

He set the candles down and when he faced her, the smile was gone, the muscles around his lips taut. He moved toward her until they were inches apart. "I missed something the other night, in the parking lot of the bar. Didn't I?" his green eyes intense, steamy and overflowing with passion. "When you told me you loved me?"

Her nod was slow as she felt her heat rise to her cheeks.

"Why didn't you just tell me?" His gaze was pleading.

"I couldn't." She held the air in her lungs. "You looked happy with Sonja and that's all I want, for you to be happy. In a healthy relationship."

"Oh Mel," he sighed, his torn expression turned up toward the sky.

"I know you love me but," she stopped, thinking of a way to state what Jason had yelled at her but in a more civilized way. "We've caused each other a lot of pain and I thought..." the muscle in his jaw twitched as she spoke.

"Fucking Jace." His eyes bored into her memory, searching for the truth.

"No. He's looking out for you." She tried to defend him, but Adam's fierce gaze made her stop.

"Melanie. I went out with other women because you told me not to wait for you." He was close, his chest rising and falling quickly and his breath sweet and soft on her cheek. "I am religiously, devoutly in love with you. Whatever Jace said, forget it. Can you do that?"

"He made some really good points, things that I've wondered about."

"Do you love me?" he asked, cutting her off.

Melanie bit her lip. "Yes."

"Is it more than gratitude or obligation?"

She was grateful. For everything. "Yes. I'm grateful but," she blocked the tears, "yes, I love you."

"Can you forgive me, really forgive me, for the past?"

"I think I already have."

He stroked the side of her face with the back of his fingers and the overwhelming emotion flowed from his touch. His eyes washed over her face, taking in every inch and stopping at her mouth.

He leaned forward, his gaze lifting to lock onto her eyes. "I love you. Without question."

Her heart swelled and its pounding was the only thing she could feel or hear. Adam ran his fingers through her hair and slipped them down the contours of her neck. Her skin shivered and the fluttering ache took hold.

His lips brushed against the corner of hers. It was, painfully soft. She turned to meet his mouth with hers. He restrained, and with their lips pressed together, held the moment. Then he grasped hold of her back, pulling her to him, kissing her deeply.

His lips moved across her jaw to her ear where he lowered her face and tightened his grasp around her.

"Adam?"

"I need a second."

Melanie squeezed into him, filling any gap between their bodies and ran her hand up from his spine to the back of his head. He smelled delicious, like he'd spent time above a steamy trail of spices.

"I won't screw up, Mel."

"I might." She smiled, relaxing her hold on him.

He looked up at her, gliding the tips of his fingers across her face.

"It's so hard to believe."

"Feels oddly comfortable," Melanie said, leaning into his touch "We've got a lot to figure out. Pitfalls to avoid."

"Let's get the first thing straight, we're right for each other. There's no one better for me, no one safer or healthier. Okay?"

"Me, too." She felt the lump grow in her throat. The lump with Danny's face, the lump that stunk of guilt. Melanie sucked in the silence, afraid to say the wrong thing, and pushed Danny out of her mind.

He smiled and the vulnerability in his drooped shoulders and the aching questions in his expression caused Melanie's heart to throb. "I have to tell you something." He swallowed. "I lied to you."

"Okay," she said, her nerves mixing with fear.

"I'm not staying at that hotel." Her mind raced to find the fear in that. "I bought a place in Georgetown last year. When you asked where I was staying, I panicked. I didn't want to tell you over the phone and so I lied. I'm sorry." He reached for her arm and his palm was clammy on her skin.

"Okay," she was starting to understand that it was on his conscience. "You bought a place in Georgetown?"

"I did."

"Why?"

He swallowed before confessing. "It was a spur of the moment thing. I was coming to D.C.," he tilted his head, "often. I missed you." His eyes were dark and heavy on hers. "Sometimes it got to be too much and when I thought I was suffocating I would come to D.C. It made me feel closer to you and the house gave me hope. I thought maybe, one day, you'd stop hating me and we'd..." he stuttered his way through.

Melanie bit her lip. "You bought a house?" It was such an incredibly insane thing to do. She smiled. "A house."

"Yeah." He sighed.

"Wow." She looked at him as he waited for her signal. "I've never in my life considered buying a place." He was much more alive than she'd ever been. "I'm not scared anymore. Of us being together, of getting hurt. I'm not scared."

"I swear I will never take you for granted. I'll communicate, Mel. And I will not ever, ever cause your heart to break. If I ever make a mistake it will never be an unforgivable one." The hint of humor played on his face.

"The vows between a spy and an assassin? I can live with that." Her smiled relaxed under his kiss.

"Is it too early in our reuniting to make love?" he asked. The catch in his voice, caught under her skin.

"No," she said, her breath on his lips. "But we're still in the park."

"Good point. Let's pack up."

Nothing had been eaten. Her hunger forgotten.

He pulled to a stop in front of a three-story house that was attached on one side to a line of two-story homes.

"Jeez, Adam. It's gorgeous."

"Wasn't when I found it. It's the best house on the block but it was in need, seriously, the walls were crumbling and the roof was saggy. I've got nothing if not time and money." He drove around back and raised the garage door. Her hand in his, he led her into the kitchen. "I have about enough will power to give you a quick tour. This is the kitchen. Over there is a living room, dining room." He pointed, tugging her up the stairs. "Bathroom down the hall." He took her in the opposite direction at the landing. "Bedroom."

She didn't see much. He was stealing her breath as he took her in his arms, his hands on her waist, pushing up the bottom of her T-shirt. His mouth on her throat. Melanie felt dizzy; her head swayed but her fingers deftly handled the buttons of his shirt.

She pushed open his shirt, he was fit and strong and his skin rippled beneath her touch. *God he was sexy.* On her toes she reached around his neck pulling him down to her. Kissing, she ran her fingers through his hair as his hands were on her back, traveling along her sides.

Adam pulled off her shirt and unhooked her bra in one move. She was in his arms as he lifted and dropping her squarely on the bed. His mouth moving down her neck she could feel the deep groan from the back of his throat. Melanie reached for his button-down-fly and yanked it open.

❧

"Hey, Mel," his breath brushed over the hairs on her arm. "What just happened?"

"Nothing." She said, laying on her back with her forearm bent across her face to cover her eyes.

"Please, tell me," Adam's voice came out in gusts. He was winded from the exertion and now from anxiety. Resting above her, leaning on his elbow he gently swept her hair off her forehead.

Melanie wanted to dry her eyes, her emotions too raw to hold in. "I'm sorry." She swallowed down the lump that was clogging her throat.

"What for?" He asked, lifting her arm and using his other hand to wipe her cheeks.

"It's just," she looked up at him, "I just felt too much." She tried to laugh it off but it sounded more like sobbing.

"Like your heart is too big for your chest?" He asked placing a hand above her breast.

"Yes," she nodded.

"That's how I feel every time I'm with you." Adam said, caressing her face with the tips of his fingers. "I am so in love with you."

"Me, too, you." She bit down on her bottom lip to stop the tears.

Adam skimmed his nose along hers, gazing down into her eyes as he placed a kiss on her cheek. His smile caused the crinkles around his eyes to appear.

"Hi," she smiled back at him.

She felt the change in his breathing and the look in his eyes darkened. Her heart raced with the single, intense glance. Melanie leaned forward, her lips parting and connecting on his. She pulled him down, his weight comfortably pressing her into the mattress. Melanie gave herself the freedom to completely let go.

CHAPTER THIRTY-TWO

The light of dawn in the Eastern sky prompted Melanie to consider getting back to real life. She lay with her head on his shoulder. Adam had fallen asleep an hour earlier and she'd watched him breathe steadily. She'd studied his face and knew she'd always carry secrets, even from him.

Her fingers caressed the side of his jaw, where it led to his ear. She let her fingers slide along his hair before tracing over the light stubble to his chin. Her fingers grazing over his lips thinking about how little they knew about each other. Her mind searching for bits of information; his middle name, his birth date.

He loves me, she thought, her heart soaring on a wave of happiness. *We have time.*

"Hey." His voice was hoarse, his grin crooked and satisfied. "Did you sleep well?"

"Yeah." She closed her eyes as her lips met his and the light blush invaded her cheeks. *I cried during sex,* she thought reigniting the rush of blood. "You?"

He smiled, quirky and so unlike the tight-lipped man she'd gotten used to that the threat of tears was powerful and the feeling of connection strong. Forgetting to breathe, Melanie read the thoughts behind his tender emerald eyes. They're saying, "I told you so! I knew you loved me."

She sucked in a breath as he shifted, letting the sheet fall to his hips.

"I. Love. You. You know that, right?" He smiled, cradling her face with a serious expression.

"I know." Her eyes holding his, "I'm sorry it took so long for me to realize…"

His head was shaking before she'd finished her apology. "I'm just glad you came to your senses as soon as you did. I fully expected to wait much longer." Adam said, the laughter dying from his eyes as his finger skimming down from her neck and along the inside of her bicep. He sucked in the air between them before leaning over her, his mouth an inch from hers.

⌘

This time she didn't cry, but rolled onto her back to catch her breath. "It's like all my problems belong to some other unlucky bastard."

Moving onto his side, up on his elbow looking relaxed and completely pleased with himself – but for the concern between his eyes. "I won't ask. I want to, I want to fix everything for you."

"Thank you."

"I forgot to feed you last night."

"I'm starving." Melanie admitted.

"Can't have that, I'm here to protect you from everything, including starvation." He slipped his jeans over his boxers.

"Do you know what I did with the bag I had?" She looked around the clothes they'd been wearing, which were now covering the floor.

"Right here," he said, handing it to her. "If you want a shower, I'll have breakfast ready by the time you're out."

The bathroom connected to his room was small, with a walk-in shower, toilet and sink. She felt good under the hot stream, she sniffed his unscented carrot extract shampoo and closed her eyes.

The towels were thick and warm. She could definitely picture herself living here. The clothes she'd chosen at random didn't match but were clean and they fit.

"Leftovers," Adam said, fixing two plates. "I had to toss the containers from last night, forgot them in the saddlebags. Good thing I had made extra." He set the dishes on the counter as she hopped on the stool.

"Smells delicious." She said, cutting into a personal-size quiche. "Oh my God, Adam." Melanie's eyes rolled back in her head as she felt the impact of his cooking. When she opened her eyes he was staring and she instantly regretted the fact that she had to work.

As if reading her mind, the lustful look in his expression faded, he asked, "Do you have time for a stop? I want to show you something."

The grin wasn't one she could refuse. He drove fast through the muggy morning.

"I think you missed a turn," Melanie said into the microphone inside her helmet. They were cutting through the roughest part of the city on an expensive, desirable bike. A snort of laughter was his response.

Adam rolled to a stop at the side door of an old block warehouse.

Reinforced steel and two large keyed locks gave the impression of fortitude in a wild environment.

"What are we doing here?" Melanie asked once the helmet was removed and she could get a better look at the place. "A soup kitchen?"

"In a way, yeah," Adam said, finding the right key on his ring. "I want you to meet someone."

He grinned, the sunrise catching the glint in his emerald eyes. Melanie sighed and tucked the long-enough strands of hair behind her ears.

"Gordy?" Adam called out, entering the industrial kitchen.

From her vantage point Melanie spotted six or seven men in white coats and aprons.

"Mr. Chase," answered the big man with a scar that crossed the left side of his pocked face. "We weren't expecting you this morning." He shifted his gaze to Melanie. "Hello," he said, surprised, quickly drying his hands and offering one to her.

"Gordy, this is Melanie Ward."

"Nice to meet you, Ms. Ward."

"It's Melanie," she said, capturing the scent of breakfast on the big man. The young men at the fryers and stovetop gave the appearance of disinterest as they scrambled eggs.

"Gordy is amazing," Adam said, with his hand on Gordy's back. "He's teacher, counselor and friend to everyone in the neighborhood."

"Ah, that's nice. But I'm not alone. Look at this place. All state of the art and we're changing lives here," Gordy said.

"Really?" Melanie asked, looking around. "How many people do you feed?"

"Thousands. When I first opened The Place – that's what we call it, The Place – it was my wife and I feeding the hungry. Now it's much more than that." Gordy explained. "Mr. Chase came in and brought with him a bigger dream and a much-needed cash flow." His laugh was boisterous. "It was his idea to take in these young folks, train them in real life skills and get them off the streets. We give them a trade, educating these formally unemployable youths and getting them ready for a paying job. It's a miracle."

"How long have you been doing this?" Melanie asked Adam.

"Fifteen years," Gordy answered. "But it's been in the last year that we've sent three new chefs out into D.C. restaurants. I'm pretty damn proud of that."

"Me, too. What are you guys cooking up for breakfast?" Adam asked moving toward the men standing before the stoves.

"He's great with them," Gordy said in a low voice as they watched Adam. "Even during the days that I could tell he was struggling with his own demons, he was patient."

With his sleeves rolled up and that look of passion in Adam's eyes, he reminded her of the first time she'd laid eyes on him.

"Well, I've got to get Melanie to work," he said, their eyes meeting. Her emotions ramped up from that one simple grin.

"It was wonderful to meet you," Melanie said, feeling comfortable enough with Gordy to give him a hug.

The line to be fed was wrapping around the side of the building by the time Melanie and Adam pushed open the reinforced steel door.

"Pretty cool." She said.

"I invested." Adam held out her helmet as she considered the line of hungry people. "But really it was because of you," he said, catching her attention. "I wanted to be someone worthy of you. I wanted to change my fate. If there is an afterlife I wanted to get into the same place as you. I don't know if spending ill-gotten gains is the way to do t, but it's a start. And I'm not done yet." He winked.

"You're leaving me speechless," Melanie said, her mind whirling. "But somehow I think you've gotten the wrong impression of me. I'm hardly guaranteed a spot at the good table."

❧

Melanie had him drop her off in an alley with a backdoor to both a sausage deli and a secret entrance to one of the Agency's underground passages.

"Mel?" Adam said, casting an unsure glance of her choice of location. "Is there someone specific you're hiding from?"

"Now that I've got a desk job I'm doing what I can to keep life interesting. You'll pick me up here tonight?"

"You have my new number?" His tone didn't sound convinced of her safety.

Melanie lifted her phone and pressed the only number without a name attached. His pocket rang.

"I'm fine," she said, moving closer, his hands reaching for the small of her back. Putting her face in front of his, forcing him to look at her and not the shabby alley. "I'll see you tonight."

His smile held traces of worry. "Promise?"

A wave of grief passed through her, she wasn't a fan of promises. "I'll see you tonight." Melanie distracted him with a kiss and waved goodbye as she slipped into the rank deli.

She left him with a smile but the pressure in her heart was filled with sorrow. Ignoring the unfounded feelings, she raced through the dank tunnels entering the Manor having forgotten about the murkiness of the kiss.

The rumblings of an unsatisfied urge, gnawed at her unconscious mind. The image of Adam sleeping lingered in her memory, the revelry ending with sickening feeling in her gut.

"Ms. Ward?"

"Yeah?" she said, startled out of her daze. "Jane."

"You have a few messages." Jane was standing behind her desk holding out a stack of pink notes.

"Thanks."

"You're welcome," Jane said, scrutinizing the odd outfit. "Would you like me to get you a change of clothing?"

"Please. And don't let anyone know I'm here yet."

Melanie awakened her computer to check her email as she leafed through her phone messages. She clicked on the email without a sender address and double-clicked the link.

A video.

It was the silence that got her attention. Filming with night vision gave an eerie quality to the image and Melanie had to squint to make out the form. It was a crib with lambs and clouds on the bumpers.

She stopped breathing and her throat went dry as she realized she was watching Olivia. Olivia. Asleep in her bed, her chubby cheeks puffing out with each breath. *Did Bruce send this?* Was her first, hopeful thought, but then the cameraman redirected his lens down the hall. Bruce and Cheryl were sleeping soundly, snoring lightly as an intruder violated their home.

The fear held her captive for a long moment. She stared at the black screen while her whole body vibrated.

"I'm going to kill him." It was said in the dead space between fear and fury. More than wrath, it was an oath. She strode out of her office to the garage and, choosing the closest sedan, tore off toward he Hugh's mansion.

Her calmness gave her extra confidence that this wasn't a rash decision. It didn't matter that she had a death grip on the steering wheel and the gas pedal was pressed to the floorboard.

I'm going to walk in there and kill him. She imagined looking into those evil eyes through the sight of her gun. Her finger on the smooth trigger, her mind set to resolve and then, and then … *Do it!* she yelled at her vision. *He invaded Bruce's home! Do it!*

Over and over she repeated the event. Each time, stopping right as the pressure to her index finger was just enough to release a round.

"I can't." She blinked in the glaring sunlight. Experiencing an awakening, she realized she was already out of town. Alone on a two-lane road approaching the personal, tree-lined drive that led to the gates of the Parker Estate. Her foot shifted from the gas to the brake, leaving tire tracks, she skidded to a hard stop – dead center in the road. Her shoulders fell and she punched her forehead to the top of the steering wheel. Releasing her grip, she rubbed her face and breathed in gulps of air. Melanie glanced up at the ceiling of the sedan and exhaled. From the rearview mirror the movement caught her eye. A car, traveling at high speed, was approaching fast.

Making a U-turn, she stayed on her half of the road. But there was something about the black SUV that put her instincts on full alert.

"Fuck!" she growled, stepping on the gas. Her back forced against the seat, she aimed for the approaching car. Melanie focused on the shadow that was the other driver. *This isn't going to end well,* she realized, changing her mind at the last moment. Swerving an instant too late, the two cars screeched on impact as the two passenger sides scraped along the full length of the vehicles. The sound was deafening but she punched the gas with more vigor and drove. The SUV u-turned to catch her.

Steering with one hand, Melanie grabbed her phone. The last call she had made was to Mike. She hit redial.

"Hey!" The voice was familiar but wrong.

"Jack?"

"No Mel, Adam."

Oh, crap! Her mind too occupied to come up with a lie. She was speeding with a car on her tail. The two-lane road was ending and the other car was too close to choose caution.

"Hold on!" she dropped the phone to her lap and skidded onto the highway, fishtailing right at an oncoming semi. Startling the driver in a blink of the eye, he veered, lost control and sideswiped cars in two of the four lanes. Melanie slammed on the brakes, but she'd been flying.

She was bearing down on the carriage of the semi; with no options of escape she threw her body across the center panel. Curling her feet up onto the driver's seat, gearshift pressing into her abdomen, while her head and shoulders crossed into the passenger side.

The glass shattered, flying everywhere as the hood of the sedan crumbled. Fear flooded her senses and the images of her family and Adam flashed beneath her eyelids. The wind was knocked out of her lungs. Losing consciousness for what must have been only a moment, her eyes flung open, the airbags in her face were suffocating. She was coughing in a chemical powder. Melanie reached for her gun, pulled the trigger and sent a bullet into the air bag. The noise echoed in the car but releasing its bulge, she could breath. Melanie groaned in pain.

"Oh, God," She gasped, the dizziness returning. In the quiet she could hear a far-away voice. *Adam's on the phone,* she remembered, reaching under her thigh. "I'm okay."

"What the hell is going on?"

"I was in a car crash," she said, too unplugged to realize she'd hit his biggest fear.

"Where. Are. You?" His voice came through too calm.

The sawing of metal echoed inside the cab of her car. It's his men!

"Melanie!"

"Shhh," she whispered, adjusting her body to face the driver's door. "I'm going to have to call you back."

"No! Do not hang up this phone."

"I need you to contact Jack Scott. Call my work number and tell Jane to pinpoint the position of my cell."

"Where are you?"

"It's Parker. Adam, please let the Agency handle this. I gotta go. I love you. I'll be fine." She ended the call and slipped her phone into her boot.

The car jostled violently as the men removed the door. The guy with dark glasses and a suit caught the first bullet in his chest.

She got off two more rounds before a stinging pain struck her arm. She reached, pulled out a dart and looked at the shooter.

"I know you," She gargled, before the world went dark.

EPILOGUE

"Melanie!" He shouted into the dead phone until his throat felt raw. His fingers shaking he dialed Melanie's work number as he seized his keys off the table.

"Melanie Ward's office, may I help you?"

"Jane. My name is Adam Chase I'm a friend of Melanie's."

"Yes, I remember. She isn't here."

"I know." Adam swallowed as he climbed onto his bike. "I was on the phone with her when there was an accident."

"Oh my gosh, is she all right?"

"No. Jack, she asked for Jack. Please, you have to pinpoint her location. Use her cell phone. Send someone to find her, she's in trouble."

"Okay. But Mr. Chase I wouldn't worry. Ms. Ward is very capable and I'm sure she's fine. I'll have her contact you when she's returned." Jane said, suspiciously.

"Now! Just find her." Adam said, placing his phone in his front pocket and gunning out of the garage heading to the Parker Estate.

Agent Melanie Ward Returns June 2013 in...

CHASE Book 4 of the Agent Melanie Ward Novels

ACKNOWLEDGMENTS

Thank you readers for your support, for sharing the story with your friends and the kind words of encouragement. It is much appreciated.

As always, I'd like to thank Brent and the girls who put up with me. Brent who listens as I arrange and rearrange Melanie's life, adding insight as I think out loud during my occasional dips in a pool of quicksand. Sam and Syd for their above average sense of equality and unconditional, crazy love.

Special Gratitude and Love:

My Mom and Dad, for the introduction to a great childhood, which I am still enjoying.

My three very cool brothers who gave me the tools to fight back. Frank, Mercy, Ralph, Steve, Linda, Amy, Jack, Kelly, Ryan, Eric, David, Nicholas – thank you, guys.

Jill Jordan-Spitz. Thank you for all of your efforts, your patience and your keen knack for words, commas and everything else I don't understand.

An Extra Special thanks to Amy Anderson, Joyce Mathis, Steve Rosenberg, Sharon Schaum, Jessie Montano, Mike and Cynthia Duran.

PowWow Publishing. Thank you for the long hours, the awesome covers and tireless dedication.

In Loving Memory Fernando Gallardo

Kate Mathis

is the author of the Agent Melanie Ward Novels. She is also the author of a Young Adult series. Book 1: Moon Over Monsters, a modern day fantasy, about a girl, a dragon and an elfin prince. A graduate of the University of Arizona, Kate is a native Tucsonan, where she lives with her husband and twin daughters.

Kate Mathis on Facebook
http://www.facebook.com/pages/Living-Lies/228205853872791

Kate Mathis Blog
http://book-writing-tips.blogspot.com

Kate Mathis Website
http://www.KateMathis.net

CPSIA information can be obtained at www.ICGtesting.com
Printed in the USA
BVOW070105031212

307116BV00001B/4/P

9 780985 957711